THE RED HILL

THE RED HILL

DAVID PENNY

RIVERTREE PRINT

THE RED HILL

DAVID PENNY

ALSO BY DAVID PENNY

THE THOMAS BERRINGTON HISTORICAL MYSTERIES

The Red Hill

Breaker of Bones

The Sin Eater

The Incubus

The Inquisitor

The Fortunate Dead

The Promise of Pain

The Message of Blood

A Tear for the Dead

A Death of Innocence (prequel)

Unit-13

An Imperfect Future

The Luck of the Devil - coming 2022

For Megan
Who has shown great patience

SPAIN, 1482
GRANADA, ANDALUSIA

CHAPTER ONE

Three men lay tumbled in the bed of the cart, but Thomas Berrington knew only one would live. He had saved a score such as these today and knew more waited his judgement. He lifted the head of the first and stared into blank eyes. Gone. The next … possible. The last had acquired a wound to his stomach, another to his chest. Blood frothed at a gaping hole each time he exhaled.

The dying man's eyes searched the pale sky, flicking left, right, as if seeking something to latch on to, each laboured breath an agony. Eventually the man recognised the figure leaning over him and Thomas saw a slow resignation fill his eyes.

Thomas leaned close. "You fought bravely. You are a hero." He had no idea if he spoke the truth or not, and nothing in the man's eyes offered a clue. Instead he began to struggle. He might die within minutes, or draw

this torture out for hours. Thomas had seen men cling to hope long after they should have let it go.

He leaned closer, his left hand closing around the man's right arm in case he tried to resist. His right went to the weapons belt to withdraw the knife there. Without needing to look, without hesitation, Thomas slipped the blade between the man's ribs to pierce his heart.

For a moment the soldier's eyes widened, but already life was fleeing—then gone. Thomas closed the man's eyes and straightened to find the cart driver watching, his face expressionless.

"There's a place for the dead over there." Thomas turned away to the third man, the one who might be saved. He dragged him clear and caught the stained body as it rolled free.

Behind him the pale walls of the city of Gharnatah rose, the eastern gate thrown wide to welcome the returning victors. Thomas had been born in a land a thousand miles to the north, but considered this city his home now, and wanted for no other.

He carried the injured man to an infirmary tent set hard against the city wall. Screams and stench greeted him as he drew near. Hell enfolded him as he entered—hell in all aspects but one. Many of these men would return to fight another day.

No free table remained, but Thomas saw the occupant of one no longer had need of it. He tipped the body off and laid his patient down.

"You!" Thomas shouted at one of the boys providing help. "Drag that corpse out of my way and put it with the others. And fetch my instruments."

He leaned over and opened the man's leather jerkin. His shoulder had found a home for a musket round. Thomas dug his fingers in to search for the iron ball, causing the man to groan and rouse.

"Don't touch me!" The man swung a blow with his uninjured arm, but Thomas blocked him without effort.

The musket ball was too deep to reach without cutting. "Do you want to live, or shall I tip you onto the pile with the dead?"

"I want a real surgeon." The man's voice was slurred, his brains scrambled from loss of blood and pain.

"I am a real surgeon."

"You are *ajami*. I want a Moorish doctor."

"Want all you like, it's me you've got."

The boy returned with a box of instruments. Most seemed almost clean. Thomas picked out what he needed: a hooked blade and small forceps.

"Fetch me poppy liquor."

"I don't need—"

Thomas smiled at the wounded soldier. It was not a reassuring expression. "You will thank me when I start. Did we win?"

"It was a great victory."

"Aren't they all? Now lie still and shut up while I speak with a colleague." Thomas turned away. Stopped.

"And don't run off or I'll drag you back and start without the poppy."

Da'ud al-Baitar glanced up as Thomas approached.

"Help me here a moment." A pale-faced man lay on the table, a slash to his side only half repaired. "This one doesn't know how close to death he is."

Thomas put his hands on the man's shoulders and pinned him down while al-Baitar worked fast. The stitching wasn't pretty, but soldiers boasted of their scars, each a testament to their courage—or foolishness.

"I need you to assist when you are finished here," Thomas said.

"A few minutes. You can leave if you want, I can attend to your patient on my own. You have been here since before dawn. Go back to that pretty wife of yours."

"I will stay." Thomas was unwilling to face the barely understood reasons behind his reluctance to return home. Most men would be only too willing to rush back to Helena, more than content to have been made the gift of a concubine of the Sultan's harem.

Instead, Thomas watched his friend work. Al-Baitar's movements were sure, confident—but too gentle for this place. It was why Thomas stood outside deciding who to bring in for treatment, the one offering solace to those who would die in agony without his mercy. He knew why the man lying on his own table didn't want him. Not because he was a foreigner, *ajami,* but for his other name —*qassab.* So be it. Thomas had been called far worse, and this butcher saved lives as well as took them.

4

Thomas spat in an attempt to clear the bitter taste from his mouth and drew the long tail of his tagelmust across his face. Dust coated his skin and gathered in the three-day stubble on his cheeks. His wish for a quiet life had been thwarted once more. He had saved the man in the cart, but wondered why—in a month he would return to fight again. All Thomas had done was delay an inevitable fate.

Cart wheels raised more dust from the bone-dry earth. A gust of wind brought the scent and sound of water from the Hadarro which ran close by, its flow hidden behind trees, its water running through a grill embedded in the city wall. The sun touched the tops of the Elvira hills and soon Thomas would follow the returning soldiers' footsteps and pass through the western gate into the city. Once his work was complete.

He watched the passing soldiers with emotionless eyes. Those who caught his gaze looked away, uneasy at the coldness of his stare. Thomas was trying not to think of the time he had been like these men. A time richly coloured in his mind—that colour mostly blood-red.

He shifted his attention from the men as a feeble cheering came, followed by the rapid clatter of a horse in full gallop. Someone came fast alongside the slowly moving line. As they passed, men raised tired arms and hoarse voices to a figure they recognised. Thomas

narrowed his eyes, shook his head when he saw who it was.

Yusuf, the Sultan's younger son, reined his horse hard and jumped to the ground even before it came to a halt. A slack body lay draped across the beast, wedged between saddle and shoulder. Blood streaked the horse's flank.

"Save him, Thomas," said Yusuf. "I would have you save him. He is not dead yet, I think. You saved me, you can save him."

Thomas went to the figure and grabbed a handful of hair, lifted the head. He leaned close. The boy still breathed.

"Why this one?"

"Because you can." Yusuf's voice was stern and Thomas almost smiled.

He turned to the horse and tugged at the unconscious boy's belt, caught him as he fell. The movement aggravated the wound. The boy's eyes opened and he started to fight.

"I know you." The boy's voice barely rose above a whisper.

"Good for you."

"You are the Sultan's pet." The expression of distaste on his young face reflected his feelings.

Thomas was used to such judgement. He glanced at Yusuf to see if there was any reaction to the mention of his father, but the young prince, already skilled in diplomacy, gave no sign of having heard.

6

"Can you walk or do I have to carry you?" The boy swayed, but appeared to be getting stronger all the while.

"I am going nowhere."

"Then you can die where you stand." Thomas turned away.

"No," Yusuf said. "I promised you would save him."

"I save those who want to be saved, not fools."

"I order it!"

This time Thomas did smile, drawing his tagelmust across to hide the expression.

"Oh, I see. In that case..." Thomas grasped the boy's arm, but he pulled away and started shouting, calling on the passing soldiers to save him from the butcher.

Thomas grabbed him again, but already five men had stepped from the line and formed a barrier between him and the tent.

Yusuf moved to stand between Thomas and the men, believing his position as the Sultan's son protection enough.

"Let them pass."

"The boy doesn't want to go," said one.

"Let him loose," said another.

There was no leader here, Thomas saw, only soldiers protecting one of their own. All five were scarred, stone-faced, their tunics stained with blood and worse. Thomas had seen their kind many times over the years, grown up alongside them in a distant land he no longer called home. He was not afraid of them. They were only five in

7

number. He took a step forward, dragging the boy alongside.

Two of the soldiers blocked the way, jostling against him. One of them tried to loosen his grip on the boy, but failed. Thomas was stronger than he looked, and did not plan on releasing his prize. He knew where Yusuf stood. If any of the men drew their swords, he would step back and pull the young prince's weapon. Yusuf himself would be no use—Thomas had treated his shoulder a year earlier and knew his right arm remained weak. The prince pretended he could fight with his left, but it was a poor substitute. It was fortunate he was the younger son and had no need to rule.

Thomas pushed at the men.

Behind the two blocking him, someone drew a sword.

Thomas released his grip on the boy and stepped back. The man on his right grinned, seeing only weakness. Thomas stepped back again and his hand found the hilt of Yusuf's sword, drawing it fast before the prince knew what was happening.

Now they were all grinning, as if they hadn't seen enough fighting already today. These were hardened troops—killing was what they did, and a chance to kill this foreigner was too good an opportunity to pass over.

"Stop this now!" Yusuf stepped between them. Thomas grabbed the prince's robe and pushed him aside. The boy he had been trying to save swayed and his legs went. He sat hard on the ground, head hanging down.

Thomas decided to start with the man to his right. A fast thrust to the thigh, then a backswing to disable the other man before stepping past them to the last three. He expected them to run, but sometimes he was surprised. He didn't want to kill anyone who had no need to die. He was meant to be saving lives today.

Other soldiers stopped to watch the entertainment. They formed a barrier around which some passed and others stuck to the edges like flowing blood to a scab.

Thomas relaxed, his mind stilling. It was time.

"What the fuck is going on here?"

Or not time. Not today. Not here. But he knew these men would remember him.

Olaf Torvaldsson sat astride a small Arabian horse, his bulk making it look like a mule. The Sultan's general wore chain-mail, marking him as someone of importance, but unlike that of his master, his was workmanlike, unpolished, nicked here and there from a hundred battles.

"Our friend does not want to go with the *qassab*."

"This is Thomas Berrington. He will not harm the boy."

"I know who he is."

Olaf dismounted and bullied his way between Thomas and the soldiers.

"And you know who I am."

The speaker nodded. Of course he did.

"I order you to let them pass."

"He is—"

"Let. Them. Pass." Olaf spoke each word slowly, accented and thick against his tongue.

Thomas reached out and handed Yusuf his sword. There was no need of it now.

Already his thoughts had turned from the soldiers to the injured boy.

———

By the time Thomas returned from the infirmary tent, it was growing dark, not only from the setting sun, but also the clouds that gathered above the Sholayr, dark and threatening. Occasional flashes of lightning darted from their bellies, followed a long time later by soft thunder. The storm was distant, but coming. There would be rain later to dampen the spirits of the returning troops.

The line of soldiers moved more slowly now, the last gasp of returning victors. The knot of onlookers had dispersed, but Olaf remained, talking to a group of well-dressed men. Thomas knew he couldn't simply ignore the old soldier. They had a link of blood now.

"Where is your father?" Thomas asked Yusuf.

"He is coming. You know he always has to be last through the gate. And there is entertainment planned."

"In that case I may leave before he arrives." Thomas could guess the manner of entertainment and wanted nothing to do with it. "Stay with Olaf until he comes."

"I don't need protecting," said Yusuf with the confidence of his fourteen years.

10

"Of course not. Stay with him to please me, then." Thomas knew how the young prince felt about him even as he wished it were not so, but saving the boy's life could not be taken back.

"You are eager to return to your wife," said Yusuf, old enough to know of such things, even more so as a member of the royal household who had lived within the harem most of his life.

"Not my wife…" Thomas started to object, then gave up, knowing it was pointless. Let people believe what they wanted to.

"She has been with you half a year now," said Yusuf. "It is time you made her your wife."

"I don't need a wife."

"Then throw her out."

Thomas shook his head. He could not do that.

"She was beautiful before she was attacked," said Yusuf. "Besides, you cannot leave yet. Father says he wants to see you."

"Then I have definitely stayed too long."

A fresh wave of cheers sounded, some almost enthusiastic. Thomas raised his eyes as Yusuf's father approached, surrounded by the usual entourage of guards and hangers-on. It was a large group, swelled by several members of Gharnatah's elite. Yusuf's older brother Abu Abdullah rode beside his father.

11

"I see you are repairing the dead again, my friend." Abu al-Hasan Ali, Sultan of Gharnatah, ruler of the remaining territories of al-Andalus not yet taken by Castile, drew his stallion to a halt and dismounted.

"Malik." Thomas used the honorific as he bowed from the waist, making ornate gestures with his hands. "Congratulations on a magnificent victory. Allah has been kind."

"Stand straight, surgeon. You have no need to bend your knee in my presence."

Thomas straightened, but his gaze remained lowered.

The Sultan clapped Thomas on the shoulder. He was shorter than Thomas, who crouched a little to offer the man an advantage. Abu al-Hasan Ali tossed his reins aside, knowing someone would be there to lead his horse into the city.

"I want to talk with you, but first there is a matter of honour to attend to."

Thomas had noted the two men tied back to back on a single horse, but could not summon enough curiosity to wonder what crime they had committed.

"I have the injured to attend to, Malik." Thomas hoped he could leave before the punishment was carried out.

The Sultan put a hand on Thomas's shoulder. "Stay. We may have need of your skill here." He turned and raised a hand. "Untie them and form a circle."

Thomas knew any chance of escape had gone. Around him soldiers laughed and cheered, forming into a

circle to leave an open space. The Sultan stood at the front of the crowd as it gathered. Returning men slowed and stopped, the crowd growing, noise rising. Men began laying bets even before they saw who was fighting.

"What did they do?" Thomas asked, knowing there would be little logic behind whatever answer came.

"The short one accused the taller of cowardice. The tall one accused the shorter of killing men without need."

"It doesn't seem much."

"It is enough," said the Sultan.

The men were dragged to the middle of the circle and the ropes binding them cut.

"Give each a sword," said the Sultan, his voice commanding, carrying to all those gathered.

Two blades were tossed into the ring. The short man picked his up. The tall one remained where he was.

"See, a coward," said the Sultan to Thomas, then more loudly, "Someone, give him the sword."

A soldier darted in, picked up the weapon and pressed it into the hand of the tall man. The Sultan raised his arm, his voice rising with it. "These men accuse each other on the field of battle. Let Allah decide the truth through trial by combat." His arm came down. The crowd roared as the short man rushed in, his sword flashing.

The tall man turned at the last moment to deflect the blow. He stepped back, reluctant to fight, doing the minimum to protect himself as the attack came again. The noise ratcheted higher. Wagers were offered and

accepted. The crowd pressed forward, those at the front struggling to hold their position.

"I need to talk with you about something," said the Sultan, his voice conversational. "Come to find me in the bathhouse later."

Thomas wondered what it would be this time, still unsure of the value of the gift the Sultan had made him after his last request. He wished he had never been offered the friendship of this man, but knew it was not something that could be refused.

The clash of blades rang in his head, raising memories he didn't welcome. At least it looked as if the contest would be over soon. The tall man moved backwards, circling the arena, only using his sword to deflect the other's blows. The crowd began to hoot and chant, the noise rising to a crescendo as they grew restless. Thomas glanced at the Sultan, wondering if he would intervene before one of the audience took matters into their own hands, but the man's eyes were fixed on the combat, a tight smile on his face. The last rays of the setting sun painted the killing ground red, as though ushering in the inevitable gift of blood.

It ended quickly, but not as expected.

The short man came in fast, a dervish, his sword a crimson arc. The tall man fell back and suddenly went to one knee.

Sensing an advantage, his antagonist attacked, using both hands on his sword.

The tall man reached down to his boot and pulled a

dagger free. As the short one loomed over him, his hand darted out, the knife embedding itself in flesh.

The crowd hushed.

The short man swayed, staggered back, not yet aware he was dead. Thomas saw it before anyone else. The knife had pierced his liver. Blood ran down his side to pool at his feet. He swayed again, then went to his knees. For a moment he tried to raise his sword, then toppled sideways.

The silence held a moment longer, then uproar broke out. Soldiers argued over their bets, cursing the victor for losing them money.

The Sultan stepped forward and raised his arm, waiting for quiet to resume.

He moved to the centre of the ring, turned to survey the crowd. His eyes found Thomas and hesitated, a smile coming to his lips before he moved on.

"I declare this man the winner," he said, "but he remains a coward who won the contest by foul means. Behead him." Abu al-Hasan Ali didn't even watch as one of his soldiers drew a scimitar and stepped forward. The Sultan walked around the body of the losing man and returned to Thomas's side as thunder sounded, closer now.

"Does that mean Allah is pleased with the result, do you think?" he asked.

"It is a storm, nothing more." Thomas made no effort to disguise his lack of faith, or his disgust at the outcome of the contest.

"I hate a cheat," said the Sultan, his voice soft, reasonable, as though he hadn't deliberately caused the deaths of two men. And deliberate it had been.

The Sultan patted Thomas's shoulder. "Do not forget to come to the bathhouse. Come and enjoy yourself, for tonight we celebrate Allah's victory over the heathen Spanish."

CHAPTER TWO

As Thomas made his way through the streets of Gharnatah, he felt detached from the atmosphere of celebration. He was exhausted, feet stumbling, head swimming from too many hours of duty with yet one more remaining. One he could not avoid. He knew the Sultan would not forget his invitation, but the temptation to return home was almost too strong to resist. Being a friend to the most powerful man in al-Andalus was not the blessing many considered it to be.

Alongside the river, raised above all but the worst floods, the pathways were laid of stone, and the houses large and prosperous. Every small square—and there were many—held a fountain or pool, water a constant presence in this city. It was one Thomas welcomed. Unlike those in the lands beyond the borders of al-Andalus, where they prided themselves on a lack of even

basic hygiene, he had grown to love the act of bathing that had once been so alien to him. To the outsiders, cleanliness was an affectation only the heathen Moors lowered themselves to indulge in. At one time, Thomas had shared that view, but no longer.

A knot of hangers-on milled around the street doorway to Aamir's Hammam baths and Thomas almost allowed himself to be discouraged from entering. His small, neat house lay nearby and the climb through the alleyways of the Albayzin would prove a welcome distraction, as would the presence of Helena when he arrived. He was starting to turn away when a young voice called out.

"Thomas—I waited in case you got lost. Come inside, Father will want to reward you."

Thomas pushed through the crowd as Yusuf slipped an arm through his. Inside the bathhouse the usual hush and calm had been replaced by noise and confusion. Soldiers guarded the entrance to the main baths, but Yusuf was recognised and allowed through into a large room filled with steam, the scent of oils, and noise. In normal times, the aromas might have eased Thomas's mind, but not tonight. The usual attendants had been added to with many others. Young men and women, some barely clothed, strolled around the steaming pool or stood beside the elite group of bathers. Their presence no longer shocked Thomas as it once had, but it was one of the reasons he would have preferred to avoid the Sultan's summons.

"I don't see your father anywhere," he said to Yusuf.

"He will not be here, but someone will show us where."

"Not us. He will want to see me alone."

Yusuf ignored Thomas as he led the way along the edge of the main pool. The real cleansing took place against the walls where hot water streamed from pipes. The pool was for those who wanted to see and be seen.

"Ho, surgeon, come here."

Faris al-Rashid, one of the men Thomas had managed to avoid earlier outside the city walls, lounged at the edge of the pool surrounded by a dozen hangers on. Most were members of noble families, rich men who mined or farmed or traded—except not one of them undertook any real work. There were servants for that. Faris was a notional leader to these men, his wealth rumoured to exceed even that of the Sultan. He was also considered by some to possess more power. Thomas knew him, as he did many of the others lounging around, their arms draped over the shoulders of young women and men.

Once Abu al-Hasan Ali had picked him out as his surgeon, many of these men demanded his services. Thomas made sure he charged an extortionate fee, but knew his bill meant little to men such as these.

Aware he couldn't ignore Faris, he changed direction, Yusuf trailing along behind. The boy removed his clothes and slipped into the warm water while Thomas crouched on the edge of the bath.

Faris reclined against the tiled margin, arms stretched out, pressed on either side by two young women, their bodies wet and slippery with soaps.

"Here, surgeon, come into the water and have one of these girls. Are they not delightful?"

They were indeed both beautiful, both nubile, the skin of one the colour of ebony, the other a northerner as pale as her companion was dark, her blonde hair reminding Thomas he had a woman of his own waiting at home.

"I am too tired to do either justice, Lord."

Faris laughed. "You need do nothing, they will do all that is required."

"I thank you, but I must wash myself first."

"As you wish. Yusuf, take this Nubian, she is almost an age for you."

"I am looking for the Sultan," Thomas said as the girl wrapped her legs around Yusuf's waist. The prince might be young, but he knew how to deal with her perfectly well.

Faris waved a hand towards the rear of the bathhouse, his attention distracted by the blonde. "He is that way somewhere with Abu Abdullah. What do you want with him?"

"He wants to speak with me on some matter." Thomas began to move away, trying not to be distracted by the sights around him. He was no prude, but preferred his coupling to be done in a less public manner.

"What matter?" Faris's voice was casual, as though uninterested.

"I will know that when I see him."

Thomas drifted towards the far side of the pool, ignoring those who called out to him. He hoped he could slip away once he had spoken with the Sultan, but before his escape, he needed to cleanse the stink of surgery from his body. His bones ached with a deep weariness he doubted even expert hands could banish.

"Thomas!"

The raucous bathhouse lay behind as he wound his way through narrow passages off which lay private rooms. He stopped, knowing it was impossible to pretend he had not heard.

"My Prince." Thomas bowed. He called Yusuf by his given name, but knew not to attempt such an air of familiarity with Abu Abdullah. This one had ambitions to rule one day, despite rumours his father might be plotting otherwise.

"I wanted to thank you for your work today." Abu Abdullah lay on his belly as two women kneaded the knotted muscles along his back. The young man was broad, strong, with dark hair and a narrow beard. Thomas had witnessed him in battle and knew one day he would be as great a warrior as his father. The puckered skin of a scar ran across his shoulder. Thomas

21

remembered treating him after a battle at Malaka when Castilian galleys attacked from the sea.

"I was only doing my duty, Prince."

"A duty nobody else could do so well. Do not underestimate your skills."

"My skills are your father's to command. Yours too, of course."

"We should talk soon, Thomas. You are someone I can trust, as my father does, and there are few enough like you in this city. When are you visiting the palace next? You attend Safya, I hear. Is she due soon?"

"Weeks at most. The baby will arrive before the next full moon."

"Another son, I trust."

"It will be as Allah wishes." Thomas could spout religion if need be, and knew Abu Abdullah was devout.

"Allah be praised. But a boy will be good. Can you not tell, Thomas? The women of the harem say she is bigger on the right side so it must be a boy. Is it true you can tell from such signs?"

Thomas smiled. "There are a million ways women will determine such things, but it is all superstition. No one can tell the sex of a child until it slips from its mother's womb."

Abu Abdullah rolled on to his back and the women began to knead his thighs. Thomas had lost his Anglo-Saxon prudishness a long time ago, but he preferred not to witness what might come next, even as he knew he

had welcomed such attentions himself before Helena came to his house.

"Has someone offered you a girl?" Abu Abdullah stretched his arms above his head and arched his back.

"I have a woman of my own, Prince."

Abu Abdullah laughed. "Of course. One of my father's cast-offs. Such a shame—she was a great beauty once. Did Father speak to you on the matter he wished to discuss?"

"He speaks to me of many things, including how proud he is of his children."

"Yes—he says that all the time. Sometimes I think he even believes it. I meant this other matter, the killings."

"What killings?"

Abu Abdullah sat up and pushed the girls servicing him to one side. "He seeks your help, though I told him it would be better to ask the big northman. What use is a surgeon in such matters?"

"Without knowing more, Prince, I cannot say."

Abu Abdullah shook his head and lay back. He waved at the girls to continue their ministrations. "He seems to have faith in you. I have no idea why. As far as I can tell, you do your duty, as we all do."

Thomas agreed, but said nothing.

He found Abu al-Hasan Ali in a private chamber some distance from the main bath. Here no women pleasured

him. Instead a strong Berber worked on the wiry muscles along his back. The Sultan looked up as Thomas entered the room, squinting a little. His sight was not good. Thomas had offered to remove the cataracts plaguing him, but knew the man would not agree until he could no longer see his hand in front of his face.

"Did you have difficulty finding me?" There was no trace of reproach, but Thomas heard it anyway.

"Only in avoiding others." Thomas sat on a stone bench, cupped hot water from a running channel and sluiced it across his head.

"People know I confide in you. Everyone wants influence one way or another. You must be weary, shall I call for someone to massage you?"

"My day has been nothing compared to yours, Malik."

The Sultan smiled. "I do little fighting these days, I am not so stupid. But yes, it was a long day, and hard."

"If you are ready to tell me why you wanted to see me, then we can both ease our tired bones. Your son said something about killings."

"So he was one of these others, was he? Did he say anything more?"

"I didn't ask. I knew you wanted to talk to me directly. Though I am puzzled why you chose me to tell about such events. Abu Abdullah suggested you consult Olaf Torvaldsson."

"He was the first I thought of, but he is not a subtle man, and I believe these are subtle affairs. You are

24

someone I trust not to broadcast what he discovers throughout the city." The Sultan pulled a face as the Berber dug fingers in along his spine.

"What has happened?"

"There have been attacks inside the palace. On servants inside the harem. There are two dead I know of, but others have been attacked and lived. One of them I gifted to you."

"And you thought to seek my assistance in this matter?"

"You are someone who understands death, are you not?"

"Not this form of death."

"I have seen you on the battlefield, Thomas. You deal with this manner of death all the time. And I ask it of you. Demand it of you."

It always came to this. A polite request followed by an order. Such were the ways of power. Thomas bowed his head, accepting whatever the task might be, despite a deep reluctance.

"Exactly what is it you want me to do?"

"Investigate, of course. Find out who the killer is and bring him to me so I can take his head."

The Sultan was fond of taking heads, as Thomas had seen demonstrated less than an hour before. He stared at the Berber as he pummelled the Sultan's back and shoulders. At least he was being allowed a moment to consider the request, though they both knew only one answer could be given.

Thomas nodded. "As you wish, Malik. I will have to speak with people, and some will no doubt talk in turn. It will be impossible to keep the matter secret."

"The facts are known within the palace. Such barbarity cannot remain secret long."

"I have some concerns," Thomas said.

"Ask then. We are both only men here at this moment."

From a demand to a pretence of friendship within a minute. Thomas smiled. "Why me? I am a physician. I deal in healing bodies and, failing that, easing their passage from this world to the next. There are many you could choose before me."

The Sultan sat up, shooing the Berber away. When they were alone, he swung his legs over the side of the wooden bench and stared hard at Thomas.

"I considered Olaf first, of course. He is a good man, but not an intelligent one, and this matter needs a sharp mind. There are others close to me I might have entrusted with the task, but..." The Sultan hesitated, then dropped from the table and came to sit beside Thomas. "A man in my position has many enemies. A man in my position is not always sure who he can trust. There may be only one I can trust completely." He slapped his hand on Thomas's leg, leaving it there, an uncomfortably familiar gesture, particularly as one of them was naked.

"And when Olaf refused you thought of me?"

The Sultan put his head back and laughed, slapping Thomas's leg again. "This is why I love you, Thomas

26

Berrington. No one else dare speak to me as you do. I am surrounded on all sides by flattery and greed. Everyone wants something from me. Everyone except you. You will do this for me?" The Sultan stared into Thomas's eyes, his own clouded.

"With what little ability I possess. But this is not something I am familiar with. You must know I might fail."

"No one else would admit that to me, either. Do what you can."

"Who has been killed?"

"Serving girls. No one of importance, but that does not matter. I will not have murder done in my palace."

He doesn't even know what he says, Thomas thought, *and why would he? This man leads a life unrecognisable to the rest of us.*

"When?"

"The second a week ago. The first two months before."

"You believe the events connected?"

"Two servants killed in the same place? How could they not be?"

"The same place? Where?"

"A bathing chamber. And no, not the same place, but the same kind of place. Different chambers. Both killed in the same way, with a sword. A powerful blow, struck by someone who knew what he was doing."

"You saw the bodies?"

The Sultan turned to Thomas. "Of course not, but I

spoke with those who did. I went to Tahir al-Ifriqi first. When he failed to discover anything, I thought again of asking Olaf, but magnificent general that he is, he lacks imagination."

"And I do not?"

"No, you do not. Will you do as I ask and put me further in your debt?"

"A Sultan owes no debt to a man such as me, Malik."

The Sultan smiled. "Tell that to my treasurer, he will beg to differ. And you know I owe you a debt no man can ever repay."

"I was doing my duty."

"You saved Yusuf. You likely saved Abu Abdullah, too. No other man could have done what you did."

"Any competent surgeon would have saved them."

"Others have told me different. You are intelligent as well as imaginative. Too intelligent to underestimate yourself. We both know without your presence, Yusuf would have died that day on the battlefield. But you distract me from the answer I need. You will do this, Thomas?"

I have a choice?

"I can talk with anyone I want?"

"Agreed."

"Members of your family, those within the palace walls? Even within the harem?"

"You are no stranger to the palace, so yes, anyone you wish. When do you visit Safya? She is close, is she not?"

28

"I come within a week. She is not as close as that."

"Come tomorrow. This matter cannot wait a week. Do what you must to find this man before others are killed. Before he turns his attention to someone more important than serving girls."

come within a week. She isn't as close as that."

"Come tomorrow. This matter cannot wait a week."

Tomas, you must to find this man before them, as killed." N.... to turn his attention to someone more important than saving girls.

CHAPTER THREE

Thomas hoped Helena would be asleep as he returned to his house set among the steep, twisting alleys of the Albayzin. As he climbed, the sound of revellers faded. The night grew warmer, and occasional thunder sounded, closer now than when he had stood with the Sultan beyond the city wall.

It had taken the half year Helena had lived beneath his roof and shared his bed for Thomas to begin to feel comfortable at her presence there. He had been too long alone, grown too used to his own company to find it easy. Only slowly was he growing accustomed to the sharing of his life with someone else. There was guilt too at accepting the gift, as if she was some kind of slave, though he tried never to treat her as such. Then there was the ease with which he had accepted her into his bed, and how swiftly that had happened.

He hadn't wanted the gift even though it was

impossible to refuse. Helena had joined the Sultan's harem as a concubine at the age of fifteen, and left after seven pampered years when she was attacked and disfigured. The harem was no place for a scarred concubine. Thomas knew their new domestic arrangements must be harder on her than they were on him. As his feet mindlessly carried him towards home, he thought about the Sultan's claim that Helena's disfigurement might have been caused by the man he now sought. He wondered if she knew that? He suspected not, but it might be worth the asking.

The house was quiet when he entered, a single lamp burning in the hallway as it always did. Thomas hung his cloak on a peg, unwound the long folds of his tagelmust and put it next to the cloak, where it draped to the ground. He climbed the stairs as quietly as he could and removed his clothing with as little noise as possible.

The bedchamber was small, dim, a faint illumination coming from beyond the door. Helena's scent filled the air, her body curled away from him on her side of the bed.

We have our own sides of the bed now, Thomas thought, smiling. *How like a married couple we have become.* And then, because he didn't want to think of marriage, he pushed the thought aside. He slid beneath the cotton sheet and lay on his back, staring at the rough ceiling as Helena rolled over, not asleep after all.

"You are late. And you smell good." Her hand reached out to rest against his face. "And your chin is

smooth." She kissed him. "You know I like it when your face is not rough." She ran her fingertip across his features, from forehead to mouth, brushing his hair aside where it fell across his face. She traced dark eyebrows, the bones of his cheeks and chin, the fullness of his lips and the width of his mouth.

"I could hardly come straight from the battlefield. I visited Aamir's bathhouse." Thomas closed his eyes, enjoying Helena's touch, feeling himself stir. He spoke for the sake of it, his words without meaning. "The Sultan wanted to celebrate his victory."

"So it was a victory?" Her fingers moved to his chest, tracing old scars that crossed his skin. She seemed fascinated by them, perhaps seeing some reflection of her own mutilation. Despite only a faint illumination from the hallway, she had tilted her head to one side so her face lay in shadow.

"Victory of a sort, but a small one. Too many dead, even more injured."

"You did your duty, I am sure." Her fingers moved from his chest, searching for something of more interest. Thomas hated the way his body reacted to her, as if he was some youth instead of a man of almost forty years, but knew he couldn't resist her. "As I wish to do mine." She came across him, her mouth kissing his, then his neck. "Your skin is soft and you smell good."

"Aamir massaged me."

Her breasts pressed against his stomach, her body lissom across his. She kissed the scars on his chest,

moved lower. Thomas groaned, knowing what was to come, no longer shocked at her wantonness.

Afterwards—and it had taken hardly any time at all —she lay close, her fingers once more tracing the raised marks on his body, and said, "Have you given any more thought to what I asked?"

"You ask many things. Which was I meant to think on?"

"You know which one. Lubna. Have you made a decision?"

"I can't see how there is room in the house for another woman."

"Could you not make room? If you say no, I fear what will become of her. She is my sister, Thomas, and I do love her even if we do not share the same mother." It was so like Helena to qualify her words. "And she will be useful to me." Now they were getting closer to the truth.

"I need more time," Thomas said.

Helena kissed his earlobe, the side of his mouth, her breath sweet against his face as her hand moved once more beneath the covers.

"Do not take too long or she will be despatched somewhere awful." Her fingers found their target.

"I am tired," Thomas said.

"And I am not finished yet."

"I cannot get hard again so soon."

Helena laughed. "You underestimate me, Thomas Berrington."

33

And he had.

Thomas woke to the sound of rain, confused, unsure where he was. Heavy and persistent, the storm beyond the mountains had finally arrived. He sat on the edge of the bed as thunder shook the tiles above his head. Beside him Helena stirred, mumbled and drifted back into sleep. Despite his exhaustion, he knew further sleep would elude him until the storm passed. He rose and pulled on a robe, descended the stairs and opened the door into the courtyard.

Rain fell relentlessly. It bounced from the paving stones to cast a shimmering haze above the narrow rill which ran the width of the flagstones. Thomas stepped beyond the door to shelter beneath a balcony that ran from the kitchen to his workshop. Rain sheeted from the roof and fell vertically on to the slabs. It was as though Thomas was trapped behind a waterfall. A wooden bench stood hard against the wall and he sat, his bare feet speckled by splashes of water.

He was hungry, but for the moment remained content to sit and watch the rain as his mind slowly turned over the events of the day. He failed to understand why the Sultan had asked him to investigate the killings. It made no sense. Despite his doubts, Thomas knew he could provide more help than the Sultan suspected. He possessed skills which would be useful, abilities the

Sultan knew nothing about. Abilities Thomas made sure to keep secret from everyone—sometimes even from himself. His life before he had become a surgeon was one he would rather forget. His real life had not begun until he had almost died, and now he was being asked to resurrect what he had fought so long to suppress.

The sound of a door catching against stone made Thomas lift his gaze from the mesmerising fall of water to find Helena standing under the balcony. She had pulled on a white linen robe to cover her nakedness, but it did little to hide the shape of her beneath it.

"There you are." Her accent was coloured like his, but the colouring different. "I woke and you were gone."

"I couldn't sleep. I didn't want to wake you."

"I would not have minded. I am awake now anyway. I notice when you are not beside me." She dipped her head, pale hair falling across the scarred side of her face.

Thomas wished she wouldn't do that. The scar didn't bother him. He thought she was beautiful anyway.

"Are you not tired?"

Helena smiled, the movement misshapen, her mouth lifting more on the left, and once more she brushed hair to cover her face.

Thomas started to speak, stopped.

Helena turned from the rain to look at him. "What did you say?"

"Nothing."

She continued to stare at him, her gaze impossible to break. "Say it, Thomas." She straightened her shoulders,

as if defying both him and herself. She tossed her head back to reveal both the full beauty and terror of her face.

"You have no need to hide yourself from me, not here," he said. "You know I think you beautiful. I always have."

"Even this?" She lifted a hand and traced the line of red puckered skin with her finger.

"Even that. It is nothing to me."

"No. But to me ... to me it is everything. I am grateful to you, Thomas, but do not pretend this is nothing."

Thomas sighed. "I am sorry if life here is a disappointment to you."

Helena looked away, shook her head. "This is my life now. It is the life I lead and I am pleased to be here. You know I speak the truth, Thomas. I am happy you allow me to share your bed, to be with you, but I can never forget what I have lost."

Thomas wanted to tell her she had lived a lie, feted, protected, but knew his words would fall on ears that refused to hear. Helena's entire life had been one of unashamed luxury and indulgence.

He recalled the first time he saw her, face torn open by a madman—most likely the same madman he had been tasked with finding. Thomas had been called in the dead of night, another summons he couldn't refuse, as he couldn't refuse this one. And then, after he had repaired her face as well as he could, there had come a conversation with the Sultan. An offer. As though Helena

was nothing more than a trinket to be passed on now its beauty was tarnished. Thomas knew he should have refused. Dreaded what might become of her if he did. So he had said yes.

He glanced at her now, knowing what she was thinking.

"The scar is young," he said. "It will heal. It is already better than it was."

"But it will never heal completely, will it?"

"No, not completely." Thomas couldn't lie. Sometimes he considered it a weakness in his chosen profession. There were occasions when telling a man he was going to die might be handled better than with the truth, but he left such pretence to others. "One day, not too far in the future, you will barely notice it." This was the truth as well.

"I will always notice it."

"We will see. I will remind you of your words a year from now."

"A year? As long as a year?"

Thomas smiled. "Perhaps less."

"By summer?"

"Perhaps by summer, yes. I have a formula for a salve al-Baitar gave me. He claims it has great power for healing. I will make some up for you." He glanced at the falling torrent. The sound filled the courtyard, but Thomas knew the rain wouldn't last. In this land, it never did.

He was aware he had made a decision, but had no

idea how, why, or even when. Sometime as they spoke was all he knew.

"I have to visit the palace in the morning."

"Tomorrow? May I come with you?"

"If you want to, of course. Will you be made welcome?" He couldn't recall the last time Helena had accompanied him to the hill, and wondered why she wanted to do so now, but the thought didn't remain long after she left to return to bed. Thomas sat watching the rain as his mind searched for the reason the Sultan had asked him to investigate the deaths, and could come up with nothing. Tomorrow, perhaps, all would become clear.

CHAPTER FOUR

As they climbed to the palace, Helena slowed where the trees thinned to catch her breath. The overnight rain had scrubbed the air clean and the view spread out across the fertile plain to distant hills glittered with a rare clarity.

"Lubna will be no trouble, Thomas."

He walked on, knowing Helena would raise the matter again, and yet again, until she got her way. It was how she achieved her objectives, he knew. Except in this instance he was reluctant to agree to the request. There truly was no space. He was only now getting used to the presence of one woman in the house and didn't welcome the idea of a second.

"She is small," said Helena as she caught him up, "and there is that space above your workshop. Nobody needs a roof as high as you have in there. You could build a platform of some kind, a place for her to sleep.

And she will help me clean and cook. She is quiet. Very quiet."

Thomas plodded on. They had ascended two-thirds of the slope and still the Albayzin on the opposite hillside seemed almost close enough to touch.

"I have no time to build a platform."

"I did not mean for you to do it." A look of horror crossed Helena's face. "There are people. You have had them do other work to the house since I came."

"Your sister calls herself Lubna. Why a Moorish name?"

"She wants to be a Moor like her mother." As Helena shook her head at the strangeness of such an idea, sunlight caught at golden strands of hair fallen loose from her headscarf. "She believes she belongs in this land."

"And you don't? This land has been good to your father, good to you."

"This land gave me this." Helena drew the scarf aside to reveal the scar. "This is being good to me?"

"A madman gave you that. And you enjoyed a wonderful life before then. Do I treat you so badly?"

"Of course not. I am grateful for all you have done. If not for you, I fear what would have become of me."

"The Sultan would not have seen you destitute."

"Which is why he offered me to you."

Something in Helena's tone caused Thomas to slow. He knew the life she now led was nothing compared to the one she had experienced before, but a scarred

concubine had no place in the harem. Thomas might not agree with the sentiment, but he understood it. He barely noticed her scar anymore.

"I will always be grateful to him for sending you to me." Thomas wanted a change of subject. "Are you planning to visit anyone special?"

"No one in particular."

"I am sure you could visit without me if you wished."

"Perhaps. Although the harem may not want reminding of how fleeting their comforts are. Besides, with you I have an excuse. Everyone respects Thomas Berrington."

"The soldiers hate me. You know what they call me."

"Believe what you will." Helena raised a hand in greeting to a dark-skinned Berber guarding a little-used entrance to the palace. A narrow doorway was set deep into the thick wall on the side of the hill. Inside there were more steps to climb, but the ascent was almost done. Helena emerged first, as ever unable to follow protocol. Thomas followed into a shaded courtyard. Water ran silently along a rill from one side to the other. Flowering trees and palms shaded the flagstones. Swallows cried as they chased insects in and out of sunlight.

As they moved deeper, they passed more guards, servants, those who lived permanently within the walls. None showed the slightest interest in the new arrivals. Thomas was known, and whoever accompanied him was always welcome. The harem was situated at the far end

of the palace and Helena stepped ahead, eager to see old friends.

Thomas knew she missed this life, would still be enjoying it had someone not taken a blade to her face half a year before. As the months passed, the outward scar improved, but other secret scars darkened her soul, scars beyond his skill to heal. He knew he should have questioned her about the night she was attacked, but had not the heart to do it, not yet. Soon, he knew, he would have to.

Thomas found Jorge sitting in the courtyard of lions, as still as the statues guarding the area. Helena had gone to find whoever she was so keen to visit and Thomas entered slowly, enchanted as always at the beauty and opulence of the Sultan's palace. Tall trees in large earthenware pots decorated with passages from the Qur'an offered shade as well as refuge for small birds.

Jorge sat in a splash of sunlight, his smooth head uncovered, eyes closed, his face turned up to the warmth. Everyone loved Jorge, women especially, though whether because they believed him safe, or because he was simply too handsome not to love, Thomas was never sure. Jorge was unlike anyone he had ever known, and he wished they could be closer friends. Perhaps this task would do that—or destroy whatever little liking they had for each other.

Thomas stood in the entrance to the courtyard, unwilling to disturb the man he had known from the boy he had turned into what Jorge was now—a palace eunuch.

Only when he sat beside him did Jorge open his eyes.

"Is Safya well?" Thomas asked.

Jorge lifted a shoulder. "She is expecting a baby. How am I supposed to be able to tell? That is your job."

Thomas started to rise. "Is she ready for me?"

Jorge laid a hand on Thomas's wrist, drawing him back to the stone bench. "Not yet. A little more time is required. A Sultan's wife cannot be rushed." He smiled. A knowing smile. "I believe she wants to look her best for you."

"One day you will go too far and they will ask me to finish the job and take your cock as well as your balls."

Jorge sighed. "A man needs some amusement otherwise life becomes far too dull."

"I believe you get plenty of amusement. More amusement than is seemly."

"The Sultan loves me, as he loves you. Are we not among the blessed of this city?"

There was always cynicism beneath Jorge's words, and many times Thomas didn't know how seriously to take them. Often the cynicism masked a deeper truth.

Jorge was dressed in loose robes of fine silk, delicate slippers on his feet, his head shaved to the skin. It was either an affectation or a demand of his profession,

because Thomas knew the man could grow a full head of hair and beard if he wished.

"Yes, we are blessed, I suppose," Thomas said.

"How is that new wife of yours? Behaving herself?"

"I have not taken her as a wife…" Thomas left the end of the sentence hanging, knowing Jorge would find it impossible not to respond.

"Yet—but you will."

"I'm not sure I like sharing my house with someone else. And now she is asking if her sister can move in."

Jorge laughed, the sound soft, as if raucousness was out of place in this courtyard. From beyond a curtained doorway, Thomas heard female laughter mirroring that of the eunuch, but responding to some other secret amusement.

"You do share your bed with her, don't you? You have to—it is what she was made for."

"What we do in the privacy of my house is none of your business."

"You can be a prim bastard sometimes. She was born to give pleasure. As I was born to serve, and you to heal. Helena was made to give pleasure to others. I do not mean to denigrate her. We are the people we are given to be."

"Then perhaps she was made what she is just as much as you were." As always, Thomas felt a need to protect. He knew Jorge taunted on purpose, enjoying the reaction his words brought.

Jorge shook his head and smiled. "She threw herself

44

into the life of the harem body and soul. Helena was an enthusiastic concubine. You cannot make someone love their job as much as she did. That has to come from in here." Jorge patted his chest. "But perhaps people change."

"As have you?"

Jorge laughed, the sound still barely audible, years of training behind every mannerism he showed, every sound he uttered. "If you had not taken my balls, I would be dead by now, or living in some back street of Qurtuba thieving and selling my body for my next meal."

"You could have died when I changed you."

"Oh, of course, remind me of how much I owe the great Thomas Berrington."

"I didn't mean it that way." Which was the truth, but Thomas understood Jorge's reaction. He had been one of Thomas's first surgeries and he meant what he said, that Jorge would likely have died had someone else carried it out. The making of eunuchs was not a subtle art, not then, involving much blood, hot coals and searing agony. Before Thomas's time, fewer than one in nine survived. Since then he had lost only a few to his new procedure, using gentler techniques to unman each boy that was sent to him. It was not something he was proud of. He would have preferred not to perform the procedure at all, but knew the alternative was worse. Far worse.

"You may not have meant it," said Jorge, "but that is what I heard."

"Then listen more carefully." Thomas allowed his

45

irritation to show, as controlled in his own way as Jorge, but his irritation was not with him. "I seek no thanks, but I do need your help."

"Now there is a first. How can a humble creature such as myself give aid to an exalted servant of the Sultan?"

"Sarcasm does not become you."

Jorge smiled, waiting.

"I must attend Safya, and then I want you to take me to talk to some people." Thomas stood and walked to the edge of the rill. The water was almost perfectly still, moving only slowly, the better to reflect the beauty of heaven.

"Specific people, or will anyone do?"

"Have you heard anything of deaths within the palace?"

Jorge shrugged. "Many people live here. They come, they go. People die all the time. Because they are old, because they are ill."

"These were not natural deaths."

"You mean the girls in the bathing chambers, I suppose?"

"So you do know."

"Everyone knows."

"Are they afraid?"

"A little, but more puzzled than afraid, I think. They don't understand why those two were chosen."

"When I return, I want you to take me to anyone who has first-hand knowledge of—" Thomas broke off as a

slender woman entered through an archway, but she had not come for him. She walked across the courtyard, her steps elegant and slow. She nodded towards Jorge and Thomas, smiled and passed on. A moment later, her scent drifted to them on the breeze and Thomas inhaled it.

Jorge closed his eyes a moment. "Why would you want to do such a thing? You are a physician, not a law-keeper."

"I don't want to—I have been asked by the Sultan."

Jorge's face reflected his puzzlement, but before he could delve further, three young women emerged from behind a silk drape, and this time they had come for Thomas.

"She is ready for you, physician," said one, while a second giggled into her hand.

Thomas nodded and started towards the doorway. "I'll come and find you when I have finished."

Jorge nodded, his gaze distant, as though examining some memory.

CHAPTER FIVE

Safya was waiting for Thomas in a nook at the far end of the harem, making him walk the entire length of the chamber. He believed she had positioned herself deliberately to make him uncomfortable—in which case, she had failed. The Sultan's wives and concubines always liked to tease those few men allowed access to their chambers and he was well-used to it by now. Jorge lived here permanently and often passed on tales he hoped would shock, but Thomas had stories of his own, and those he never told. The lives of these women were pampered. They were more than mere playthings for the most powerful man in al-Andalus. They read widely, spoke of politics and history and culture, listened to and made music, created works of art through their weaving and needlework, and even greater works of art through attention to their bodies.

"How are you, Highness? Do you have any discomfort?"

"Call me by my name, Thomas, for you have seen me as only one other man has. And of course I have discomfort."

"If you would relax and allow me to examine you, Highness?" Thomas stepped back, waiting for Safya. She glanced at him, a teasing look which was wasted. Eventually recognising her body was no more than another task to the surgeon, she allowed her outer robe to fall away, her modesty maintained by a simple silk cover. Thomas indicated the waiting couch and she sat, reclining slowly.

Thomas touched Safya's neck. Her pulse was a little fast, but he put that down to her nervousness. Despite her casual air, Thomas knew this was difficult for her. Custom and society dictated no man who was not family could look on a member of the harem without the Sultan present. And a near naked wife reclining on a couch was certainly well beyond convention.

"I will listen, if I may?"

Safya assented with a tilt of her head, lay back and closed her eyes.

Thomas unfolded a paper cone from his leather satchel. He rested the wide end on her stomach, set his ear to the other until he found the soft murmur of a foetal heartbeat, almost too faint to detect. Thomas knew many physicians would be unable to find this sign of life, but he had always possessed acute hearing. At times it

seemed as if it was not his ears doing the hearing, but something else which sensed the presence of a second life nestled within the first. He registered the softness of the silk against Safya's skin, the scent of her body, the rise and fall of her belly beneath his touch, but it was all no more than a distraction from what he sought.

He lifted his head and laid a palm against her belly. His fingers moved, pressing, tracing the shape of the infant, building its contours in his mind. As if sensing his presence, the child moved, rolled, and he felt a leg, a foot.

Safya laughed. "I think he wants to play."

Thomas ran his fingers along her legs, testing her ankles, pleased to find no swelling.

"I will need to examine you more intimately now, Highness."

"Then you will *have* to call me Safya, won't you?"

Thomas removed a bottle of oil from his bag and poured a little on his hands. As he examined her, he felt nothing other than confirmation of the mother and child's health. When he was done, he rose and turned to the window, wiping his hands on a linen cloth.

"I am finished, Highness, you may dress now."

He heard Safya sigh. She had given up on him.

Thomas moved to the window to allow her privacy. He looked down on the pathway that led from the main palace to the Sultan's chambers. A deep ravine separated the two, and a narrow rope bridge had been constructed

so that travel between them did not require a long descent and climb.

A female figure emerged from a doorway on the far side and moved towards the bridge before stopping. She turned back as a second figure had called to her.

"How is my son, Thomas?" Safya came to join him at the window. "Is that Helena?"

"I think it is. Your child is well, Highness." Thomas could not clearly see who Helena was speaking to because the other person stood in the shadow of the doorway. A man, tall, broad shouldered. Possibly a guard. Their conversation ended and Helena walked back out across the bridge.

"Has she been visiting friends in the palace?" asked Safya. "Helena is still missed on the hill. You are a lucky man, Thomas. When will my son be born?"

"I know I am. Within a month, Highness, likely sooner."

"Allah be praised. Will there be pain?"

"Some. The gift of life does not come without a price, but I can help ease it if you wish."

"You will come when called?"

"Of course."

"I would rather you were closer. I know my husband has offered you a house in the Alkazaba. You should take it."

"He is most generous, but my place is across the river with my people."

Safya laughed. "Your people? Your people are many miles from here, are they not?"

"No longer. My people are all around me."

Thomas wished Safya would leave to bathe. She made him uneasy with her pretence at equality. Her presence, now he no longer looked on her as a patient, unsettled him. He didn't know how Jorge managed to live among these women and remain sane. Thomas knew he couldn't move away until Safya did, so he waited, staring across the valley of the Hadarro to the jumbled white and terracotta houses that climbed the far hillside. He tried to make out his own house, knowing he could see the palace from his courtyard, but from this direction, everything appeared different.

"Perhaps for me, when my time is near, you will weaken and move closer?"

"I will consider your request, Highness."

Thomas's answer appeared to be enough because Safya moved away. Once alone, he turned to retrieve his bag.

"Are you all done here?" Jorge's voice was close, and Thomas looked up from where he knelt. He had not heard him approach. For such a large man, Jorge could move with surprising silence. "I have found someone you can speak with."

"Yes, I am finished." Thomas rose to his feet and fell into step beside Jorge.

"Safya is healthy? The baby too?"

"Both are well, though she's convinced it's going to be a boy. What will she do if it turns out to be a girl?"

Jorge laughed. "She will try again, of course. And girls are loved, too. There are many girls here. Personally I prefer them to the boys."

"That is because, despite your protests, your heart is as soft as your head is hard. Where are you taking me?"

"To talk to someone who really knows what goes on within these walls."

CHAPTER SIX

Thomas remembered his surprise, almost twenty years earlier, when he'd visited al-Hamra for the first time. He had expected it to be similar to the large houses he had known in England, France, and other parts of Spain. In those places servants were kept at a distance, generally ignored so long as they stayed in their place. In al-Andalus—at least the part Thomas lived in—there was less differentiation. The palace was like nothing he had known before. It didn't house the Sultan, who preferred to spend his time in the surrounding hills, living like the nomad people his ancestors had left behind centuries before. The main purpose of the palace was to house the harem, and to impress with its beauty and grandeur.

Surrounding the enclosing walls was the Alkazaba, another town almost as large as the city of Gharnatah itself, and it was here most of the servants lived and

worked. It was to one part of this sprawl close by the rear palace walls that Jorge led them.

He was greeted in a way Thomas had not witnessed before. Within the harem, Jorge was treated with respect, even a little deference, as though it was he and not the Sultan's wives who possessed true power. Now as they entered a large kitchen rich with the smells of baking, cooked meats and the tang of oranges and limes, the mostly young women working stopped to greet him. Embraces were exchanged, with kisses to both cheeks. Jorge introduced Thomas, but made no explanation of who he was or why he was with him.

Jorge led the way through the kitchen, stealing a fresh roll, tossing another to Thomas, then on into a wide corridor. More servants moved here, carrying, talking, a constant motion—all with some purpose Thomas failed to discern.

A little way along the corridor, a wider doorway stood open, and it was here Jorge made for. A large woman sat behind a fittingly large table covered with papers and scrolls, small plates of food resting on some, carved boxes of cedar and pine hiding whatever lay within. Thomas was surprised to see the walls lined with shelves containing many books. He wanted to explore, but knew now was not the time.

"Jorge! You incorrigible rogue." The voice was as large as the woman's frame, rich with laughter. "Have you come to service me as you used to as a youth?"

"I fear I would only disappoint you now, my sweet.

55

You are far more of a woman than ever you were before."

"Are you calling me fat?"

"Of course not." Jorge went around the table as she rose and they embraced. Jorge held her face in his large hands, staring into her eyes, something close to love in his own, then he kissed her full on the mouth. "You are as beautiful as ever, Bazzu. Even more so."

"Of course I am." She glanced at Thomas. "Who is this handsome man? Not a Moor, but no Spaniard either."

"This is Thomas Berrington. Thomas, this is Bazzu. What she doesn't know isn't worth the knowing."

"At last—I get to meet the famous surgeon the Sultan favours." Bazzu came around the table, moving delicately for such a large woman. She took Thomas's hands in both of hers and stared into his eyes. "I was starting to believe you didn't exist. I am relieved to find you here before me."

"You are unwell?"

She laughed, the sound rotund and salacious. "I have never been ill a day in my life. I wanted to meet you because you intrigue me. I hear much about you in the palace. You are the Englishman, no?"

"I am."

"Such a long way from your homeland. Do you not miss it?"

Thomas smiled, enchanted by the woman. "There is nothing to be missed. England is cold and wet and grey. I

belong here, where the sun shines and a man can pick sweet oranges from the trees."

Bazzu glanced at Jorge and winked. "And such a sweet tongue on him. No wonder old Abu al-Hasan Ali puts his trust in this man. Is that why you are here to see me?"

"Why doesn't it surprise me you already know what we are seeking?" said Jorge.

"I am the spider in the middle of this web they call the palace. I know everything." Bazzu sighed and returned to her seat. "And so, if you are not here to ravish me to within an inch of my life, what is it I can do for you until that moment arrives?" She rested her elbows on the table, chin on her hands, and stared at them, dark eyes sparkling.

There were no other chairs in the room so they stood.

She glanced from one to the other. Thomas realised the silence was stretching uncomfortably and stepped forward when he saw Jorge was not about to speak.

"If you are the spider, as you claim, then you know about the girls who were killed."

"Of course. But they were servants. Why are important men like you asking me such questions?"

"Because I have been asked to. And because I care." Thomas glanced at Jorge, who had moved some papers so he could perch on the edge of the table, eating the warm bread roll he had stolen, tearing small morsels free and slipping them between his lips. "I want to speak with anyone who knew them, anyone they worked alongside,

and in particular anyone who was close by when they were killed."

Bazzu sat up and blew her cheeks out. "That is a lot of people. Practically the whole of the palace. Can you not come up with a shorter list?"

"We can start with those who were close when the first two died."

Bazzu rubbed a hand across her belly, a slow, sensuous movement she seemed completely unaware of.

"That would prove simpler, certainly."

"I have the dates when they were—"

She shook her head. "I remember each day like it was yesterday. These were my girls, physician—did you think I would not?"

"You cared for them?" Thomas said.

"I care for everyone here, but yes, those two perhaps a little more than some others." Bazzu offered no reason.

Thomas wished he could start over. "Tell me where the attacks took place."

"You don't know?" Bazzu appeared surprised and a little disappointed in him. "Both were killed in bathing chambers."

"Didn't you think it strange their deaths were not investigated at the time?"

"But they were. Surely Jorge told you?" She glanced at the eunuch, who shrugged. "At times he is less useful than he looks. The Vizier's men investigated the deaths. Fairly thoroughly, too, I believe. Isn't that right, Jorge?"

"So I understand."

"And these investigators," Thomas said, "did they come to any conclusion?"

"That wouldn't be for the likes of me to know of."

Thomas smiled and waited.

"I believe—and understand this is rumour only, and may bear no grain of truth—that it was decided their deaths were due to jealousy."

"Jealousy?" Thomas couldn't hide his astonishment.

"Their places were much sought after. The women of the bathing chambers are closer to the harem than others. Closer to the Sultan's wives, and hence to power and influence."

"And this is fought over? To the death?"

"Ask your friend." Bazzu nodded towards Jorge, who had listened to the exchange in silence, as though uninterested.

"Oh, I have several things to ask him."

Jorge glanced up, unconcerned. "We should speak with whoever carried out these investigations and find out what they already know."

"You know who they are?"

"Of course. They spoke with me too, but I was of no help to them. I knew nothing. They were Tahir al-Ifriqi's men. Scribes mostly, but clever men, and methodical."

A slip of a girl came to the door. "They need you to decide on the dinner menu, Bazzu."

She rose from behind her desk, trailing her hand across Jorge's shoulders as she passed. "You must excuse me, I have duties to attend to."

"A moment," Thomas said, and Bazzu stopped in the doorway. "If you think of anyone else we should talk to, anyone close to the two girls, will you let me know? Anyone who might shed some light on what happened."

Bazzu glanced down at the waif standing at her side. "Go ahead, Prea, tell them I'll be there in a moment." She turned to Thomas. "I thought this matter was settled. Why is it being dug over again now?"

Why indeed? Thomas thought, but when he made no reply, Bazzu shook her head and left.

CHAPTER SEVEN

"When were you going to tell me you already knew everything?" Thomas strode along the corridor beside Jorge.

"Not everything, and I would have told you when I found an opportunity. But you came to me less than an hour ago, and for most of that time you have been with Safya. When did I get a chance?" Jorge continued walking, turning and turning again. Thomas believed he knew his way around the palace, but Jorge was confusing him.

"Tell me now, then."

"We are almost at the bathing chambers. There will be women there who knew the dead girls. We can talk later when there is more time."

"We must speak with the scribes, too," Thomas said. "They'll have made a record of all the information they found. It is somewhere to start."

"They were sent to cover things up."

"You know this?"

"It was obvious from the start. They asked all the wrong questions. No one wanted the story to get out. Murders within the palace walls? People would start asking why—if the Sultan can't control his own palace, how can he control a city? The men were the Vizier's, and he will want palace secrets kept where they belong."

Thomas shook his head. The air in the corridor had changed, growing warmer, humid, scented. "So why did the Sultan ask me to look into this again? What does he gain?"

"That puzzles me, too. There—" Jorge pointed to the end of the corridor where a slight figure dressed in a flimsy dress crossed from one side to the other, carrying some kind of pot. "That's Alisha, she knew both girls." He raised his voice. "Hey, Alisha, I need you."

At first, Thomas thought the girl hadn't heard, but after a moment she re-appeared from around the corner.

"I am going to Safya," the girl said as they approached.

"How long will you be?"

"As long as I am needed. She is ready to bathe and will scold me if I am late."

"I need to ask you some questions."

"Then find me later. Much later." The girl sprinted away.

"Can we talk to Tahir al-Ifriqi now?" Thomas asked.

"There will be someone else, there is bound to be." Jorge turned left in the direction Alisha had come from.

"There will be other ladies bathing, Jorge, we shouldn't be here."

"I am invisible to them. And you are the famous physician Thomas Berrington. We can go wherever we wish."

"Everywhere except a lady's bathing chamber."

"I don't plan to spy on anyone, but this is where the girls work. There will be someone else around. We can talk to those cold fish of Tahir's tomorrow."

When the scream came, it cut through the warm air like a blast of ice water. The terror in the voice made Jorge turn sharply and start to run. Thomas followed, leather satchel slapping against his hip with each stride.

Ahead of him, Jorge skidded and careered against a wall, shouting a curse as his feet slid from under him, and he landed in an ungainly heap. Thomas leapt over him and kept going.

He reached a junction and hesitated, unsure which direction to take, then another cry came, this one a sob.

"Help us, please help us, she is dead!"

He turned right and ran on, looking into each of the chambers as he passed. The sight of blood brought him to a scrabbling halt and he grabbed at the doorway as he entered a bathing chamber.

The scene that greeted him was like some distorted battlefield. One girl knelt beside Safya on the floor, while another crouched against the wall, arms wrapped around her head. A third lay face down in the bath, her blood staining the water. Safya lay on the far side, half out of the water. Something was wrong with the left side of her body.

Jorge came into the chamber and ran past Thomas. He reached into the pool to drag the bleeding girl to one side. He lifted her clear with one strong movement and flipped her on to her back. He glanced at Thomas.

"I think she's gone."

Thomas was on his feet again, moving. They reached Safya together.

Thomas knelt, feeling again as he had so recently for any sign of life at her neck. This time he found nothing. He moved his hand. Was that something? A faint pulse? Perhaps, but surveying her wounds, he doubted it.

He turned his attention to her injuries. Her left arm was almost severed at the shoulder. Blood had arced high from the initial wound, splashing the walls and floor, but now it pulsed only slowly. Her left leg was also damaged. It looked as though someone had tried to hack through it, but failed. The wounds were clean, precise. It would have taken tremendous strength to inflict them.

Thomas sat on his heels, oblivious to his robe draping through the blood.

"Is she dead?" Jorge asked.

"Dying."

64

"Save her."

"I can't."

"You're a surgeon. Save her!" Jorge punched Thomas's shoulder, slapped his face.

"She is beyond saving." Thomas barely felt the blows, watching as tears filled Jorge's eyes and spilled across his cheeks. "You loved her, didn't you?"

"I love them all."

Thomas looked down, reaching once more for a pulse, and stopped. The distended skin on Safya's belly moved as the child within turned, the movement fast, as though the foetus was in distress.

"My bag! Fetch my bag."

Jorge scrambled away and ran to the entrance where Thomas had dropped his satchel.

Thomas tipped the contents out, unwilling to take the time to search inside. He saw what he was looking for, a sharp blade, but any blade would do.

"I recommend you look away," he said, even as he started to cut, his mind cold now, analytical. He felt a hard blow between his shoulder blades as Jorge hit him. "I'm saving her baby! Now turn away or watch, whatever you want, but don't blame me for what you're about to see."

There was no time for subtlety—and besides, she was a patient he had no need to piece together again afterwards. He cut along the base of her belly and blood pooled, not as much as there would have been if most hadn't already been emptied from her body, but enough.

A roll of intestine slipped free, the copper smell of slaughter filling the room. From somewhere in the distance came the sound of more feet on hard tile, of voices shouting, wailing.

Thomas extended the incision, cutting upwards. He pulled open a flap of skin and muscle, pushed his hand inside, searching blindly. He withdrew, judging, then slid the blade into the opened cavity and cut again, tossed the blade aside and used his hand once more. He closed his eyes, concentrating. He pictured his fingers moving through the layers of a body he knew so well.

He found a tiny leg, traced it upwards.

The commotion grew louder, and Thomas opened his eyes as he grasped the child cradled within Safya. He drew it clear, glancing back over his shoulder to see Jorge standing tall between him and three guards, each with swords drawn.

"Stand aside, eunuch!"

"He is saving her."

One guard approached, his sword raised. "He has his hand inside her belly. If that is saving her, then I will save you, too. Stand aside."

"What is this? Safya, no!" The Sultan had arrived. The small bathing chamber was growing crowded.

Thomas eased the tiny figure free, knotted the umbilical cord and cut it. He slid backwards, his passage made easier by the blood slicking the floor, and dipped the child into the bath. He held the infant in the water to

wash it clean. It would need repeating again in cleaner water, but was sufficient for now.

"Thomas, what have you done?" The Sultan shook with rage. "Guards, arrest this man!"

"Malik," Thomas lifted the baby, who at that moment decided to utter its first wail, protesting at the manner of its coming into the world, "you have a new son."

CHAPTER EIGHT

The Sultan barely glanced at the mewling infant.

"Take them away." He flung an arm out to encompass everyone in the room. Two guards came to stand on either side of Thomas. One of the young women took the baby. A third guard went to Jorge.

"My bag," Thomas said, as he was led from the room. "Someone fetch my bag."

One of his captors stopped and looked back, an expression of distaste on his face as though Thomas had asked for instruments of torture. *Perhaps that is how they see me*, Thomas thought, *for when I appear to men such as these, I always bring pain.*

More women arrived and one of them took the newborn child from the girl. The tiny head turned, its mouth seeking a breast.

The men were rougher than need be as they hustled the small group through the corridors and squares of the

palace. Thomas, Jorge and the two girls were deposited in a small room and the door locked behind them. A window offered a view down a sheer drop to the Hadarro hundreds of feet below.

The girls clung to each other, their thin shifts wet. They shivered, but more from fear than cold. Jorge unwound his outer robe and handed it to one. After a moment, Thomas did the same for the other. The girl reached for the robe, hesitated. The grey linen was stained with blood, but finally she took it, judging her near nakedness worse.

Thomas gripped the shoulders of the older girl, though neither could have been more than sixteen. "Tell me what happened."

The girl shook her head.

It was the other who said, "A djinn appeared in the chamber and killed Safya."

Thomas turned to her. "Whoever did this, it was no djinn."

The girl shook her head. "It was black, all black, but on fire, its head, its body. It had no legs. Only a long tail it sat upon. It carried a sword, an enormous sword, and it —" She stopped abruptly, the memory overwhelming her.

Jorge reached out and drew the silent girl to him, enveloping her within his arms. "And you? Can you tell me what you saw?"

She shook her head, burying her pretty face in the folds of stained cloth.

"This is not the work of a desert spirit," said Jorge. "It is the work of a man."

"No man can enter the harem," the girl muttered into her coverings.

"Thomas was there," said Jorge, glancing across the chamber. "And I live within its walls."

"You are not a man." There was no judgment in her voice, only a statement of fact. "And Thomas is different. He is a physician, he is allowed."

"Do you think they are going to question us, or simply behead us?" Thomas said, immediately realising his mistake as the girl shivering in Jorge's arms uttered a whimper.

"No one's going to do anything to us," said Jorge. "We are innocent. These girls saw everything." He came to stand in front of Thomas. The girl he had been comforting immediately embraced her companion.

"You saw the Sultan's face."

"What do you expect, walking into that? He'll calm down and realise Safya's death was not our doing." Jorge took Thomas's arm and drew him away towards the window. "Stop talking this way. Those girls are frightened enough already."

Thomas pulled free. "Now is the time to question them, while events are clear in their minds."

"No, Thomas."

He ignored Jorge and walked across the room to where the girls were huddled together for comfort.

He crouched in front of them. "Tell me again—and think carefully, I need to know exactly what happened."

The elder girl hid her face, but the younger showed anger. "Haven't we told you enough already? It was the djinn who killed the Sultana!"

Thomas washed a hand across his face. It wasn't only the girls who were afraid. "Assuming it was a djinn, then tell me how it appeared. Where did it come from?"

The girl offered a scathing look. "Djinns appear wherever they wish. How else would it get there? How else could it come from where it did?"

"Explain."

"It came from nowhere, from the alcove above the bath. There is no doorway there, no way in. Only a creature of the spirit world could appear as it did."

"You are sure of this?"

The girl nodded. "Of course I am sure. Alisha came in with a pot of oil and saw it first. We had our backs turned, helping the Sultana into the water. Alisha threw the pot and the djinn struck her first, then the Sultana. I have never—" She broke off.

"It is too soon." Jorge sat beside the girl and drew her against him, offering what comfort he could.

"Now is when they will remember best."

"Now is when the scars are fresh. Tomorrow, after they have slept, they will have time to consider their memories more rationally."

Thomas rose to his feet. "Tomorrow is no good. Girl, stand, come here."

She glanced at him, at Jorge, who drew her tighter against his side.

"You're doing her no favour." Anger mixed with fear made Thomas's voice harsh.

"And neither are you. Let her be."

"She'll forget."

"Then let her forget!"

Thomas shook his head and strode to the window. Couldn't Jorge see? If the man was this stubborn, Thomas was starting to believe he would be better off working alone.

Jorge spoke softly to the girls, too softly for Thomas to make out his words. He tried to calm himself.

"Tell me what he looked like."

Jorge gave him a sour look, but the girl was coming out of her shock and Thomas knew her interpretation of events was wrong. He wanted answers, but lacked the compassion required to tease information from her. Jorge overflowed with compassion, but had no sense of the urgency of the situation.

"Was he tall?" This time it was Jorge who asked the question, and Thomas wondered if he had judged him too soon.

"He was..." Her eyes turned inward, seeking some memory. She shook her head. "I couldn't tell. He was a column of black fire. He might have been ten feet tall. I don't remember."

Impatient, Thomas took over the questioning. "When he struck Safya—how much bigger was he than her?

How high did he raise his sword?" The pain his words caused showed clear on the girl's face, but Thomas had no intention of easing off.

"He was taller."

"How much taller?"

The girl shook her head. It was her companion, silent until now, who supplied the answer.

"I was further away. I ran when he killed Alisha. He was ... he was not much taller than the Sultana, but she is tall for a woman."

Thomas nodded. "She is. His sword—in which hand did he hold it?"

The girl frowned, closed her eyes. Thomas watched as her hands came up, moving as she replayed events.

"His right hand. He held his sword in his right hand."

"And his left—was there anything in his left hand?"

The girl thought a moment, shook her head. "Nothing."

"He knew he wouldn't need anything else, not against a woman," said Jorge, his face showing disgust.

Thomas returned and knelt before the girls once more. He reached for the hand of the elder, who had found her courage, but she pulled away.

"Did you see him enter the chamber?"

"I told you—it was a djinn, there is no entrance where it came from."

"Could he have slipped past while you were helping Safya?"

"We were facing the doorway. No one could have

entered without us seeing. Besides, he would have been seen by the guards when he approached."

"And going? When he fled, in which direction did he go?" Thomas reached out and took her hand, and this time she let him. It lay like a small bird, trembling within his own.

Once more she closed her eyes and Thomas was moved by her courage. But when she opened them, she shook her head. "I don't remember. I was weeping, on my knees. He stood over me and said he was the last thing I would ever see. I didn't want to look."

"He spoke?"

"I told you."

"What were his words? His exact words?"

She pulled her hand from his and turned away. "I don't want to remember them."

He reached for her again, resisting when she tried to pull free, gripping her tighter. "Tell me. Was he a Moor? His accent, what did it sound like?"

"I wasn't listening."

"Did he sound like the Sultan? Like Jorge? Like me?"

"He sounded like none of you."

"Then how did he sound? He spoke to you, you have to remember."

"I don't *want* to remember!" She tried to pull away, but Thomas held her fast. He knew he must be hurting her, but he didn't let go. This was too important.

"You have to." His voice was soft, but there was no

74

comfort there. He glanced at Jorge, who stared back with an expression of disgust.

The girl let her breath loose in a long exhalation and Thomas felt her hand relax within his grasp. He loosened his grip and stared into her eyes, trying to make his own sympathetic, but knew he likely only scared her more.

"He wasn't a Moor," she said. "Nor Spanish. And not at all like you." She half smiled and her gaze met Thomas's before skittering away. "I have heard how he sounded before, but—"

They all started as the door crashed open. Thomas spun around, an instinct to protect flooding through him. Two guards stood in the entrance.

"Come with us," said one.

Thomas started forward.

"Not you. Them." He pointed at the girls, who huddled even closer together.

"The Sultan will want to speak to me," Thomas said. "I should come with them."

"You haven't been asked for. You stay. The girls come." He moved forward.

Thomas blocked the way. He sensed Jorge come to stand beside him.

The guard stopped, a sneer on his face. "Do you want to die now? I am happy to send you to the next world if that is what you wish." He pushed Thomas aside and reached for the girls.

Jorge moved and Thomas grabbed him, pulling him aside. "No."

The girls cried, fought, but they were small and the guards large. Thomas and Jorge watched as they were dragged from the room and the door slammed shut.

Thomas saw Jorge's shoulders slump and felt the strength leave his own body. He knew they had both been putting on a front for the girls.

"I wonder if Helena knows where I am?"

"No doubt someone will delight in telling her."

"I wish those guards had come a little later. The girl was starting to remember."

"Kitma," said Jorge. "Her name is Kitma. And her companion is Mahja. They're good girls, both of them. They should never have had to see what they did."

"But they did, and that makes them our only witnesses."

"Then we can talk to them again." Jorge went to sit, leaned against the wall and pulled his knees to his chest.

"If we are given a chance. Did you notice they stopped referring to their djinn as *it* and started saying *he*?" A nervous energy thrummed through Thomas's body. He could barely believe they might be in danger, but he knew the Sultan made irrational decisions—had seen the evidence only the day before. Jorge had been right to stop him talking of their fate in front of the girls. "Now they're gone, perhaps we can talk about what's going to happen to us."

"That will be up to Abu al-Hasan Ali."

"He must know we were trying to help." Thomas's words sounded empty in his own ears.

"He saw you with your hands inside his wife's belly. How would you interpret such a sight?"

Thomas stared into space. "Why ask me to investigate the deaths and then accuse me of the same crime?"

"There were three men beheaded this morning, did you know?"

"And two more killed outside the city wall last night. Why were they executed?"

"Cowardice in battle. Abu al-Hasan Ali believes it encourages the others."

"Most men don't need encouraging."

"I can see why."

"Why did you tell me? Are you trying to frighten me?"

"I told you because in this city, men are executed on a whim. We both know it. All we can do is pray the Sultan comes to his senses before anger gets the better of him."

Thomas went to the door, pushed against it, pulled. He hammered his fist on the solid wood.

"Don't waste your energy," said Jorge.

Thomas abandoned the door and moved to the small unglazed window. "It's mine to waste. How can you be so calm?"

"Because I have no choice."

Thomas's anger flared. "You think yourself safe, don't you?"

Jorge shook his head. "Why would I be a suspect? There was no blood on my hands. And the Sultan has known me since I entered the harem."

"He claims he trusts me. He says it often enough."

Jorge smiled. "Trust is a fickle commodity to stake your life on."

Thomas strode across the room and grabbed Jorge's shirt, tried to drag him to his feet. He wanted to hit someone, anyone, but there was only one person he could vent his fear against and Jorge remained where he was, a solid weight on the floor. The silk of his shirt ripped, slipping through Thomas's fingers.

"Show some emotion, damn it. We could be dead by nightfall."

"Will panicking do us any good?" said Jorge. "If you think so I'll gladly curse and wail along with you, but I've never found it to be much help before."

Thomas punched the wall. He only succeeded in hurting his hand, but knew it was better than punching Jorge. He strode away, wanting to put distance between them. "We are innocent."

Jorge barked a laugh, cut it off almost at once. "The graveyards are full of the innocent. The Sultan is angry. We can only hope his anger wanes with the daylight."

Thomas stood at the window, clutching the sill. He breathed deeply, held the air in his lungs as long as he

could, exhaled. He repeated the exercise. It helped, but only a little.

"Why kill Safya? Who has she displeased? The Sultan? The Vizier? Another wife?"

"The Sultan was excited to be getting a new son." Now an imminent attack seemed to have passed, Jorge rose to his feet.

"It could as easily have been a daughter."

Jorge strolled across the room towards Thomas. "But it wasn't. Thanks to you he has a new son. I expect he'll see the foolishness of locking us up soon enough. He knows you wouldn't kill Safya and save the son."

Thomas rubbed his nail into the lime mortar between the stone making up one side of the window. It came away, powdering on to the sill. He believed if he worked long enough, he might loosen the stone and make a space large enough to crawl through. He looked down at the drop outside and stopped rubbing.

"Who would do this?" Thomas returned to the only thing worth considering, seeking to lose himself in questions. The danger they were in hovered on the edge of awareness, but he had ignored danger before, was merely out of practice.

"Who wants to hurt the Sultan?" said Jorge.

"A thousand people."

"Exactly. Are you going to interrogate the entire city? We both know he's not a popular man. He's too harsh and the people of Gharnatah have become pampered and

soft. The mountains protect us from Castile, but for how much longer?"

Thomas scowled at the hint of outrage in Jorge's voice. "The Spanish are your people."

"Not anymore. My life is here. I have a place in society and women to love."

"The Moors took your manhood."

Jorge looked at Thomas. "No—*you* took my manhood. Part of it, anyway. Or did a busy man such as you forget what he did to me?"

"I haven't forgotten." Though Thomas was uneasy at the reminder. "What I meant was the Moors took you captive, forced you into the life you have now. All I did was help you avoid most of the pain and a likely death."

Jorge bumped against Thomas's shoulder with his. "If that was avoiding pain, no wonder the soldiers call you butcher."

"Would you rather someone else had performed the procedure?"

Thomas thought back sixteen years to the skinny, shivering boy who spoke no Arabic. His only crime was to be tall, pretty, and captive. The boy was the first Thomas had operated on to turn into a eunuch. He had been only twenty-five years of age himself, and newly arrived in Gharnatah. His pale skin and strange accent had, for some reason, amused the Sultan. Thomas would deliver his eldest son Abu Abdullah, and later Yusuf too. Almost all the children in between and since. But it had been the way he treated men in battle that picked him

out. He had been fearless, unafraid of the clashing swords and barking cannon, throwing himself into the heart of the chaos as if he cared not whether he lived or died. Only a few years earlier, he had been like the men around him. Worse than them, because he had fought for no cause other than greed and lust and the rage of youth.

"What are you thinking about?" asked Jorge.

"Why do you ask?"

"I can tell by the look on your face. You were somewhere else."

"If only that were true." He glanced at Jorge. The man had turned from pretty boy to handsome man, and Thomas considered him a friend, even closer than a friend. Although he knew their relationship might appear less simple from Jorge's side. "I was thinking about what you said. How you came to be who you are."

"Don't expect my thanks."

"I wasn't looking for any. Can you still speak your language?" Thomas was uneasy at the memories their conversation evoked.

"Possibly. Can you still speak yours?"

Thomas wondered which language he could call his own anymore. His days of conversing in English were long gone, and in between he had learned and forgotten some French, Occitan, and Spanish. Now he spoke only Arabic like a native born to this place, as did Jorge.

"If I tried, I suspect I could, but why would I want to?"

"Don't you miss it?"

"England?"

"Is that what it's called?"

"Mercia is where I was born, on the western fringes of England."

"I was born in Qurtuba." Jorge used the Moorish pronunciation, disdaining any other he might once have known. "But I was born poor and grew poorer the longer I lived. If I hadn't been captured and turned into what I am, I would be long dead by now. I owe the Spanish nothing. Nothing at all."

Thomas heard the vehemence in Jorge's voice.

"It may be worth remembering some of your old language," Thomas said. "This land won't remain in Moorish hands much longer."

"They haven't succeeded yet, and they won't. Abu al-Hasan Ali is strong, he's fierce, and the land is on our side. This is our land, not theirs. They gave it up seven centuries ago and it's the Moors who made it great. Could make it greater still."

Thomas smiled. Jorge had distracted him from the worst of his fear. He patted his friend's shoulder. Jorge looked down as if Thomas's touch was tainted.

"I wonder what those girls really saw," Thomas said.

CHAPTER NINE

It was an hour before the guards returned. There were four of them this time, two each to flank Thomas and Jorge as they were led through the hallways. Thomas thought it some kind of compliment they were considered so dangerous.

But not as dangerous as he suspected, for when they reached their ultimate destination, the guards were dismissed. There was no sign of the two young women.

The Sultan sat in an ornate chair. To his right stood Tahir al-Ifriqi, the second most powerful man in al-Andalus. To the Sultan's left was Abd al-Wahid al-Mursi, the leading cleric of the city, a tall, painfully thin man with the face of an ascetic. Thomas knew him by reputation only as a man of firm beliefs. He had heard it said that Abd al-Wahid al-Mursi believed all the ills of al-Andalus could be blamed on its people shunning strict

religious practice. It seemed he and Jorge were not the only unbelievers in the city.

Beside him Jorge moved uneasily from foot to foot, his gaze directed downward. Thomas waited, knowing he couldn't speak first despite the thousand questions racing through his mind. Several hours had passed since the killing. The rage and grief that must have filled this room had tempered into a cold anger, displayed clearly on two of the faces.

The Sultan would want to strike out at someone for what had happened. Thomas only hoped his wrath would be directed at the guilty.

"Who did this thing?"

"I do not know, Malik."

"Then who does? Those silly girls claim it was a desert spirit. What do you say?"

"They are mistaken."

"There is more to heaven and earth than you know of, physician." Abd al-Wahid's voice was as cold and emotionless as his eyes.

"Indeed there is, Imam. But it was no djinn did this."

"You do not believe in the world of the spirit?"

"I believe in what I can see and touch."

"I have heard it said you do not follow the true faith, Thomas Berrington."

The Sultan interrupted before Thomas could answer, or the argument escalate. "Faith or not, I also do not believe a djinn killed Safya. And if it was no spirit, it must have been a man." He stared hard at Thomas. "You

and Jorge were the first there. Tell me, was it a man did this? Or could it be another woman?"

Thomas shook his head. "A woman wouldn't be capable of inflicting such wounds."

"Not even with a sharp blade?" It was the first time Tahir al-Ifriqi had spoken. He was a hard man in both body and voice, his eyes cold, calculating. Thomas knew him as a tough administrator of the city, backing up the Sultan's often irrational decisions.

"There was no time for subtlety, Your Honour. This was done fast and with great force."

"Could there have been more than one man?"

The Sultan waved an impatient hand. "I am tired of discussion. Now is the time for action, not words. Thomas, I would talk with you alone."

"Sultan." Tahir al-Ifriqi reached out, almost laying a hand on the Sultan's arm before realising his error and withdrawing. "We have not yet decided if either of these men are guilty of a crime."

The Sultan laughed, a harsh sound. "Thomas is no killer." It seemed there was no need to include Jorge.

"He has the skill."

"He is no killer," the Sultan repeated. "He saved my son on the field of battle. He has saved many men. And he saved my newborn son this day. I would trust him with my life. I would trust him above all others." The Sultan rose, looking old and tired as he turned aside.

Thomas hesitated, glancing into the faces of the Vizier and Imam. He saw no help there, so followed the

Sultan into a shaded courtyard where water shimmered in a wide pool along the centre of the space and birds sang in the tops of palm trees.

The Sultan took a seat on a marble bench where a tree cast shade. Late afternoon sunlight caught the far side of the courtyard, cut at an angle across the water to cast dancing reflections across the tiled walls.

The Sultan patted the bench beside him. "We have lost much time. I apologise, I should not have locked you away."

Thomas sat at a respectful distance, but the Sultan shuffled along so he was pressed almost shoulder to shoulder with him. There was a long silence while they stared at the water, the trees, the bushes. Thomas wondered if the Sultan was thinking of the loss of his wife. Did men such as him ever think in such a way? The man had a dozen wives, two dozen concubines; surely he must feel something for each of them? But when he spoke, it was as if he was more concerned for Thomas.

"Where is your robe? Shall I send for something for you to wear?"

"I am fine, Malik. I gave it to one of the girls." He hesitated. The questions bubbling inside could no longer be suppressed. The Sultan was right: too much time had been wasted. "You spoke with them—where are they now?"

The Sultan shook his head. "Silly girls. I sent them back to work. Too pretty to be clever, clever enough to

know not to lie. They know nothing other than what they imagined. This was no djinn."

"I agree. It was a man. This has to be connected to the task you gave me. I understand if you want to call on someone else now. Someone more suited."

"Are you refusing to help?"

"I am saying there are people who are better qualified."

"But none I can trust as much as you. I want you for this task, Thomas, not some flatterer who will tell me what they think I want to know."

"You want the truth, as do I, but there are men more capable than me."

The Sultan cast him a glance. "I do not want other men. I want someone who will speak with an honest heart. You have never treated me like a master. Sometimes that has annoyed me, but at this moment it is exactly what I need."

"I will have to examine Safya," Thomas said.

The Sultan rose abruptly and paced to the edge of the rill. He stared down into the still water. "She has already been prepared. She will be interred before sunset."

Thomas glanced at the sky. "It is important I see her, Malik. I would not ask otherwise."

The Sultan turned, his face grim. "I forbid it."

Thomas rose from the bench, but didn't move closer. "Then I would pay my respects."

"Come to the interment."

"I am not of your faith."

"Then don't come. Whatever you wish. We will talk no more of it. Find me the killer before he chooses another of my wives to slaughter."

Thomas was unsure how hard he could press, but said, "Other than the girls you told me of, and now Safya, have there been any other attacks?"

"Another girl disappeared. Some say she ran away, some that she was another victim."

"Why was nothing done sooner?" Thomas knew a commoner should not speak to a Sultan in such a way, but he grieved too.

"Of course we acted. Those men in there, together with myself, decided the matter was best kept within these walls. Tahir was asked to set his men to the task. But what do scribes know of life and death? I wanted to ask Olaf Torvaldsson, but was persuaded otherwise."

"He's a soldier. He knows how to deal in death, but this matter requires more subtlety."

"We wanted the matter kept private. Olaf is nothing if not loyal, but I did not ask him. I should have come to you at the start, Thomas."

"I told you last night, I know nothing of investigating such matters, Malik."

The Sultan cast a cold gaze on Thomas. "You are the cleverest man I know. And you are a survivor. You adapt. But most of all, you are honest, and there are scarce few honest men in this city."

"There must be others you trust." Thomas

experienced a shiver of unease at the thought he might be the only one.

"Trust? Who can a Sultan trust? My own son wants my crown, Tahir is worried I spend too much gold on this war, and as for that prissy Imam, he considers me ungodly."

"He considers everyone ungodly."

Abu al-Hasan Ali made a sound through his nose. "That is true. You will catch this man for me, Thomas?"

"Because I am the only man in al-Andalus you trust?"

The Sultan glanced at him. "And I am not entirely sure I should trust you—an *ajami*." He softened his words with a brief smile.

"Then ask Olaf Torvaldsson, as you meant to. He has skills I don't possess."

"He is *ajami,* too."

"He is your man."

"And you are not?"

"You know the answer to that, Malik."

The Sultan stepped across the rill and strode to the far side of the courtyard, pulled a fig from the tree growing there and sniffed it, tossed it aside as unripe. He reached into his robe and withdrew something, holding it inside his closed fist.

"Come here." He held his hand out, whatever lay within hidden.

Thomas walked to him. He knew he could not refuse.

"Do what you must. You act under my authority. Go

where you will." As Thomas held his hand out, the Sultan dropped something small and heavy into it. Thomas looked at the object. A seal. "Take it," the Sultan said. "There are only three such in existence. It will grant you access anywhere you wish to go. Do not let me down—whatever you do, do not let me down."

Thomas closed his fist around the seal and nodded.

The Sultan turned, leaving Thomas alone to wonder at the implied threat in the man's words.

"They told me I'm to work with you," said Jorge. "Not for you—*with* you." Jorge sat in the chair the Sultan had used, his long legs stretched out.

"You enjoy living close to the edge, don't you? Is that what was really said?"

"Perhaps not, but it is what I chose to hear." Jorge rose as Thomas turned away.

"You don't have to help me. I could be about to make matters worse, not better. You would be wiser not associating with me."

Jorge fell into step as they entered the corridor.

"Then it is fortunate I am known for my beauty rather than my wisdom."

"Where do they keep the dead before burial?"

"Safya?"

Thomas smiled, a mere thinning of the lips. And

Jorge claimed he lacked wisdom? "I must examine her while I still can. There was no time before."

"You asked the Sultan?"

"I tried. He must know nothing of what I am going to do."

"I don't know where Safya is, but Bazzu will."

"Then we will go to find Bazzu."

CHAPTER TEN

The chamber was cold and dim, lit only by guttering candles. Thomas despatched the women tending Safya and told them to fetch lamps. He knew they were unhappy, but Bazzu's presence added weight to his words. The women would no doubt tell someone of his presence, which meant speed was vital.

Jorge stood against the wall, as if trying to press himself through it, eyes locked on the woman now wrapped in a white linen sheet, her body and face obscured. The cloth was not yet tied with rope, which made Thomas's task easier. A second slighter figure lay on another stone bench. Thomas could no longer remember the girl's name.

"You don't need to stay," he said, moving around the body. He had no intention of starting with anyone else in the room.

"She doesn't look like Safya anymore," said Jorge.

"You can't see her, of course she doesn't look like her."

"She was always so full of life, so full of fun. She would tease me all the time." Jorge's voice broke.

"Yes, she liked to tease. I want you to return to the kitchens with Bazzu."

"I'll stay."

"No, you'll go. Seeing Safya before was bad enough. This will be worse."

"Have you no humanity?" Thomas knew Jorge was referring to what he was about to do.

"A surgeon learns to ignore what cannot be changed, to see beyond what lies in front of him. You cannot cure without witnessing suffering and horror."

"This is beyond horror," said Jorge as the women returned carrying two lamps. Behind them, a slight figure remained outside in the corridor.

The women placed the lamps on alcoves in the walls and retreated with Bazzu following them. Thomas stared at Jorge, waiting. Jorge returned the stare, but eventually his gaze darted aside. He took a shuddering breath, pushed himself from the wall and followed Bazzu out. Thomas closed the door before returning to Safya. He began to unwind the wrappings.

Someone had made an effort to tidy her body. Neat stitching closed the ragged wound to her belly where the baby had been torn out. More stitching drew tight the slash to her arm and leg. It took him long minutes before she lay revealed. Thomas stepped back, a moment of

93

grief rising sudden and sharp through him. Only a few hours before, this woman had taunted him, coy and sultry in turn, more full of life than anyone he had ever known. Now she lay on a cold stone slab, all her vibrancy eliminated. There was nothing of Safya left. He wiped an arm angrily across his face and set to work, losing himself in the routine of his profession.

It took almost an hour, and the whole time he listened for approaching footsteps, expecting to be found out, but none came. He suspected Bazzu had taken the women aside and impressed the need for secrecy. Whatever the reason, Thomas was grateful. This woman—once so vibrant—was now nothing more than a clue in the puzzle set before him.

The hour passed before he straightened, twisting from side to side. His body ached, weary from attending soldiers returning from battle, weary from the events of the day. He re-wrapped the sheets around Safya. As a mark of respect, he tied the wrappings with rope. He might not share her religion, but he knew its rituals. Only when he was finished did he turn his attention to the dead girl from the bathing chamber. He shook his head, still unable to recall her name. Alice kept coming to mind, but he knew that was wrong. This girl would have a Moorish name, not an English one. And why was he even thinking of English names? England was no more than a faint memory. Was it the thought of approaching defeat—a defeat that could no longer be denied? Thomas frowned and shook his head. He wasn't thinking of

returning, not after all these years, was he? This place was his home now, not some cold, distant land.

As he worked, he felt something shift inside him. Losing himself in the ritual stilled his mind, and through the stillness came certainty. He had agreed to help the Sultan because refusal wasn't an option. In this cold room, Thomas knew it wasn't the Sultan he would pursue the killer for, but these two women, and the others before them. To prevent more suffering the same fate. He was sure if the man wasn't stopped, there would be more. Would Abu Abdullah's mother Aixa be next? Or Zoraya, the Sultan's new wife?

With a sigh that emptied the air from his body, he turned to the second figure and began to re-wrap the coverings, so that she too could ascend to her heaven.

The bathing chamber had already been cleaned. Steam rose from the fresh water that now filled the sunken bath. Water dripped from closed faucets.

"When did this happen?" Thomas asked.

"They would have cleaned the room immediately," said Jorge. "It would not be seemly to leave the room tainted."

"Then they have destroyed any chance of us finding whatever spoor he left behind, do they not know that?"

"It is how things are done in the palace. No, they did not know."

"Someone should have. The Sultan or Vizier. Didn't they think?"

Jorge offered a look. He had been in a subdued mood when Thomas found him in Bazzu's room, and had stayed that way the entire time since.

"A woman they loved was murdered here. They wanted no reminder."

As they had walked from the kitchen to the bathing chambers, Thomas tried to tell him of the discovery he had made, but Jorge only waved him aside and walked faster.

"Too soon," Jorge had said, and the look he gave Thomas showed all the pain and anger he felt.

Now Thomas surveyed the room, moving on already. He went to the shallow steps leading into the water.

"How does this work? You belong in this place. Where would Safya be, the girls?"

Jorge had calmed a little, but his voice remained emotionless. "I may have many privileges, but witnessing a Sultana bathing is not among them."

"But you know, don't you?"

Jorge came to stand next to Thomas, pushing him aside.

"Safya would have stood here, a girl on each side helping her into the water in case she slipped. As we know, Alisha came in with a pot of oil."

Of course—not Alice but Alisha. Thomas looked around.

"From that doorway?"

Jorge nodded.

"It's the only doorway into the chamber?"

Jorge nodded again.

"And the girls—"

"Kitma and Mahja."

"I know their names." Thomas didn't, but his voice was sharp. "They said the man came at them from behind." Thomas went to the closed head of the chamber. "From here?" He turned to find Jorge staring at him, a rictus of pain across his face. "I know this is hard, but if we are to catch the killer, we have to put our own feelings aside."

"That is easy for you to say. I don't believe you have any."

Thomas didn't bother with a reply. He turned to the wall. A small alcove obscured the deepest corner of the chamber. He went to it and stood pressed against the stone.

"Can you see me from there?"

"I can see your cloak," said Jorge.

"But if you entered the chamber without expecting someone to be hiding here, would you look for them?"

"Why would I? Besides, it's not possible to be concealed there. Before Safya entered, a guard would have searched the room. They always do."

"Thoroughly?" Thomas emerged into full view. "The women of the harem bathe at least once a day, sometimes more. Guards grow careless. A man could have hidden here, and then stepped out to attack."

"To do that, the killer would have to get here, have to pass through the length of the palace. He would have been seen and stopped."

"Unless he was a familiar figure."

Jorge joined Thomas at the head of the chamber. "Such as?"

"Who has access to the palace? Guards and eunuchs. I can't think of anyone else. It would explain why the guard who was meant to search the chamber failed to find anyone."

"Sultans and princes," said Jorge. "And physicians."

"You suspect a member of the royal family?"

"I suspect no one, I'm only stating the options. So a guard, do you think?"

"What of the other eunuchs? Could any of them have done it?"

Jorge shook his head. "Two are too old, one too young, the last too delicate."

"What if the guard who was sent to search the room stayed behind, hidden in the alcove? Is there any way of finding out who that would have been?"

"There is a roster. One of Olaf's men will have it, but so will Bazzu."

"Is there anything that woman doesn't know?"

"Not much, no," said Jorge. "Are we finished here?"

"Not yet. Help me examine the walls."

"What do you expect to find, some secret entrance?"

Thomas glanced at Jorge. "You'll make a valuable assistant if you keep thinking that way."

Jorge scowled and appeared to be about to say something else, then shook his head and bent to the task. Between them they pushed and kicked at every stone in the alcove, but nothing sounded different, nothing moved.

Thomas straightened, back aching, but he felt progress had been made, a faint excitement welling within him.

"A guard, then?" he said. "Perhaps even the guard who was meant to protect Safya. We must find Bazzu and ask her."

"She'll think I'm stalking her."

Thomas allowed himself a smile. "Will she be displeased at the idea? I don't think so."

But when they reached the kitchens, Bazzu wasn't there. The girl Prea told them she had gone to attend Safya's interment.

CHAPTER ELEVEN

Thomas and Jorge descended a hillside painted blood red by the setting sun. From above came the sound of voices raised in prayer, the deep tones of the Imam rising above the others. Several times Jorge slowed and Thomas almost spoke, still wanting to raise what he had discovered during the examination. It had nothing to do with Safya. Her body, despite its injuries, offered little in the way of information he hadn't already known. It was the servant Alisha he wanted to talk of. He didn't believe he would ever forget her name again.

When he glanced at Jorge's face, it was grim, his mouth a compressed line, brows drawn together, and Thomas knew he couldn't raise the matter yet.

"She won't have suffered," he said, believing he could read the thoughts inside the man's head.

Jorge stopped and looked back up the hillside. Smoke from burning fires rose in lazy spirals, their bases grey in

the palace's shadow, tops catching a new flame in the dying rays of the sun.

"I don't believe you," said Jorge. "I saw her wounds."

"It would have been quick. Men take terrible injuries in battle and only later does the pain come."

Jorge shook his head. "Safya was no soldier. Hers was a life of ease and luxury."

Thomas put his hand on Jorge's shoulder. "She is beyond all suffering now."

Jorge shook him off and continued his descent. As they approached the point where Helena had stopped on the climb that morning, Jorge slowed and came to a halt once more. The city lay below them. Beyond its walls, cultivated land stretched to distant hills. The air had grown heavy with haze once more, the effect of the night's rainfall already defeated by the heat of the day. Out across the plain, water from irrigation canals caught the lowering sun, flickering and blinking. Dust rose from cartwheels and horses' hoofs.

"Suffered or not, she is dead." Jorge had obviously been teasing away at Thomas's response. "And for what? I should have been with her, not on some foolish quest with you." He paced to the edge of the drop where the land fell away beneath the trees. He kicked at a stone and it clattered away through the undergrowth. Birds flew up, screeching from the sound.

"It is no foolish quest and you know it." Thomas stared at Jorge's back where tension bunched his

shoulders. "Now there are two others to avenge. Finding the killer is the best way to honour Safya's memory."

Jorge reached out and wrapped a hand around the branch of a wild olive. His knuckles turned white, his arm quivering. "No, you're right, no foolish quest. When we find this man, I will kill him with my own hands."

"He will be a soldier."

"Then you will have to help me." Jorge would not look at Thomas.

"Yes, I will help you. But you know one man isn't the end of this."

Jorge shook his head. "I leave the theories up to you."

Thomas scowled. "You live within the palace. The answer lies there, not with me. Why are you being so stupid?"

Jorge released his grip on the olive and finally turned to Thomas. "Because to think on why brings too much grief." He pushed against Thomas's chest, sending him staggering backwards. Jorge followed. "Because everything I love remains there." He pushed again. This time Thomas was prepared and took the blow. "Because to know who lies behind this will only bring more pain and death—most likely our own. Is that what you want?"

"I want it ended."

Jorge dropped his head. His shoulders shook. "And you think I don't? Even if it ends tonight, there are too many people I love already dead." Tears flowed down his cheeks.

Thomas hesitated, then stepped forward and put his arms around Jorge. The man was two inches taller, but he leaned into Thomas like a child as sobs wracked his body. The sun had sunk behind the distant Elvira hills before Jorge recovered himself and Thomas released his hold.

For a moment, they stood toe to toe, then Jorge nodded and turned away.

"I am ready now."

"Then let's go. I want to find this man before he kills anyone else."

Helena laughed when she saw the Sultan's seal.

"What foolishness is this? In which back alley did you find such a cheap trinket?"

Thomas hadn't intended to make anything of it. In fact, he would have preferred she didn't even know it was in his possession—that no one knew. But as he and Jorge entered the house, he had tripped on a pile of washing left inside the doorway and his stumble sent the seal spinning from his pocket to the floor. For a moment, he feared it would break, then remembered it was forged of metal. Still, even metal could shatter.

When he bent to retrieve it, Helena reached it first and made her comment. She glanced at the seal, giving it little attention before looking towards Jorge standing in

the doorway. Thomas saw something change in her face. *Of course, she knows him.*

"Jorge and I have matters to discuss." Thomas turned to Jorge. "You can follow the courtyard around to my workshop."

"If you can get inside," said Helena.

Thomas hesitated a moment, then reached out for the seal, waiting.

Helena examined it again, turning it over in her hands. Her eyes narrowed, and he saw the moment she recognised its authenticity.

She wrapped slim fingers around it. "This is real, isn't it?"

"Not according to you."

She opened her palm, staring once more at the seal. "It is real. What are you doing with this? Did you steal it?"

"The Sultan gave it me. He wants me to…" Thomas hesitated, unsure if Helena knew of the events that had occurred in the palace. "Did you hear what happened today?"

"Everyone heard." That dismissive note of scorn again, and Thomas tried to remember how long since he had first heard it, or if it had always been there. "That still doesn't tell me why you have this in your possession." Helena's thumb stroked the rounded head of the seal, a slow, sensuous movement.

"A poisoned gift. The Sultan has asked me to investigate the killings."

"You? Why you? He has ... other people for that, surely? He should have asked my father."

Thomas noted the hesitation, knew Helena had been about to say *better people*. He agreed with her.

"I don't think he trusts anyone inside the palace. Not now. If someone can find their way into a Sultana's bathing chamber, nowhere is safe."

"Unless it wasn't a man who killed Safya," said Helena. "I heard it was a djinn."

Thomas started to laugh before he caught the expression on her face and knew she more than half-believed the tale.

A flash of anger at being found out tightened her lips, deepening the scar on her face.

"It was no spirit did this. It was a man—a strong man. Someone who knows his way around the palace."

"Believe what you will." Helena tossed the seal into the air and Thomas snatched it before it could fall to the stone floor again. "Does this mean you'll be in and out at all hours? What do I tell people when they come asking for treatment?"

"Take a name and tell them I'll see them when I can. If it's urgent, send them to al-Baitar."

"And if their arm is hanging off?"

"Then no doubt they'll die with or without my assistance."

Thomas knew al-Baitar was not as skilled a surgeon as he, but he was good enough, and better with potions and salves. Thomas used his friend's ointments in

preference to his own, and in turn al-Baitar sent those he couldn't help to Thomas. Neither man was growing rich.

"Is the eunuch staying for dinner? I'm not sure we have enough food."

"Give him my share. He and I need to talk."

Helena brushed past Thomas and strode into the courtyard.

Thomas followed, stood behind her a moment, her scent enveloping him. There was a tension in his body brought on by the events of the day, anger at her attitude, lust for her body. After half a year, he had grown accustomed to her easy availability, to the silk of her skin beneath his touch. It should have been enough, but Helena was difficult to like, even harder to love.

Jorge hadn't gone to the workshop. Instead he sat on a stone bench, head resting against the wall, eyes closed. Above the wall, birds swooped in pursuit of the insects of dusk, their cries filling the air.

When Helena caught sight of Jorge, she came to a sudden halt and spun around, only to find Thomas blocking her way. She shook her head, placed her arms on his and moved him aside. Thomas looked up to find Jorge, his eyes open now, watching them without expression. Thomas scowled and walked fast along the side of the courtyard to the workshop, not waiting to see if Jorge followed. He pushed a heavy table to one side, pulled two chairs out and sat in one, waiting. It took Jorge only a moment to appear. He looked around with curiosity, and Thomas studied him in turn.

Jorge was a handsome man. Even in the silk and finery a eunuch was expected to wear, he possessed an aura of solid masculinity. If Thomas hadn't turned him into what he was now, he wouldn't have known Jorge was not a man in all aspects.

Jorge pulled a chair close and sat so their knees almost touched. A fragrance crossed the space between them, a residue of perfume from the harem.

"So now you live with one of the most beautiful women in all Gharnatah, eh? Some men have more luck than they deserve."

Thomas remained unsettled after his conversation with Helena. "And what would you do with such a beautiful woman?"

Jorge chose not to take offence at the sharpness in Thomas's voice. "What do you think I would do?"

Thomas snorted a sharp laugh. "Of course, I forgot, eunuchs are all the same."

Jorge lifted a shoulder, eased back in his chair and crossed a leg. "I may lack balls, but thanks to you, I still have my cock. Anyone else would have taken that as well. Don't believe everything you hear. I can get as hard as the next man. Well, perhaps not as hard as you, I admit, but then I don't share my bed with someone as exquisite as Helena."

"You share a palace with over a hundred women. Most of them so beautiful they would make the gods hard." Jorge had recovered his usual unwavering good

humour, but if anything, it only served to fuel Thomas's unease.

"Ah, of course, how careless of me to forget." Jorge smiled, and Thomas knew this man—yes, he admitted, a man in all qualities but one—was used for more than fetching and carrying and preening. "What—do you think I lead a celibate life? Thanks to you, I have most of the equipment necessary to give a woman pleasure. In fact, also thanks to you, I have the perfect equipment for my station in life. I have this." Jorge cupped his groin, his smile flipping into a grin. "But I lack those two items that would prove dangerous to a man in my position. No surprise pregnancies. No suspicions."

Thomas's frown deepened. "If the Sultan knew you were—"

Jorge laughed. "Do you think a Sultan—especially one as old as Abu al-Hasan Ali—can service all those young and nubile women himself? He's not a stupid man. As long as there is discretion—and I am very discrete—I am able to carry out all the duties expected of me." Jorge sighed. "All of the duties. I know it is a challenging role life has placed on me, but I try to rise to the occasion."

Thomas stared back, then felt a smile crease his mouth, a smile that turned into a laugh.

"How on earth is the harem going to manage without you? Perhaps I should dismiss you from service so you can return to your arduous duties."

The amusement left Jorge's face, draining like water

from a broken pot. "We both know this task is the most difficult, possibly the most dangerous, of our lives."

Thomas nodded, sitting back, weariness pulling at his limbs; a weariness that would have to wait. He would never start operating on a man without knowing what outcome to expect. This task required the same set of skills. They needed a plan. A strategy.

Jorge leaned forward, his face expressionless. "Have you spoken with Helena about the time she was attacked?" He had obviously been sharing similar thoughts, but his mind had gone in a different direction.

Thomas shook his head. "About her injury, nothing else." He stared at Jorge's face, now serious, seeing in it the man's grief held hard in check. Jorge had loved Safya, loved her perhaps more than any other man, even her husband. This was difficult for him.

"I think a conversation would be worthwhile."

"You believe the events connected?"

Jorge reached out and rapped his knuckles on Thomas's forehead. "Come on, use that brain you're meant to have. She was attacked within the walls of the palace only six months ago. The first servant died three months later."

"Three months is a long time between attacks. And Helena lives."

"And before Helena, when was the last time you heard of anyone—anyone at all—being attacked within the palace?"

Thomas nodded. "Never."

"Right. Never. I hear all the gossip, every tittle and tattle of it, and there's never been an attack on a member of the harem that I've heard of. Do you still believe the two events are not connected?"

"We need to talk to her," Thomas said.

"Yes, we do. But carefully. Do you have such a thing as wine in your house?"

"Wine? Where does a eunuch get a taste for such forbidden fruit?"

"A man needs more pleasures than just those of the flesh. Do you have any?"

"Yes, I have wine."

Jorge smiled. "Even though its consumption is frowned on?"

"I'm *ajami*, remember. No one expects me to follow the rules. Besides, I keep it for my patients."

Jorge's smile grew. Thomas rose and filled a jug from a small barrel which rested on a side bench.

The wine was palatable, just. Thomas rarely drank, but the small cask was always available. Sometimes it helped pacify a patient. Other times a great deal was needed to act as anaesthetic, although if pain was likely to be severe, he preferred extract of poppy.

Jorge took a long draught, barely pulling a face.

"Where did you acquire a taste for alcohol?" Thomas asked.

"The life of a eunuch is not all scented pleasure and attending on our ladies. Sometimes we are allowed a little free time, and Gharnatah is awash with taverns."

"More so than ever," Thomas agreed. The second mouthful of wine tasted better than the first, and he was sure the third would improve yet again. He tried to remember the last time he had drunk wine and failed. It would have been before Helena came to live with him, certainly, and in the company of others. He would never have drunk alone.

Jorge drained his cup and placed it on the table, casting a meaningful glance towards Thomas, who said, "Help yourself."

Jorge needed no further encouragement. Thomas placed his own cup on the table, still half full.

"Your friend the cleric wouldn't welcome seeing what you're doing," Thomas said, as Jorge drank more slowly from his refilled cup.

"My friend the cleric is friend to no man, and I doubt he'd approve of anyone enjoying themselves. He knows nothing of pleasure."

"All men know something of pleasure, otherwise what is the point of life?"

"He knows the words of Allah. They are his pleasure. Little else concerns him."

"Is he a good man?" Thomas knew little of Abd al-Wahid al-Mursi, other than he was the leading cleric to the Sultan.

"He is like all men who attain great power. He has lost sight of what he wanted power for and now sees only the power itself."

"He is austere."

"I'm not sure that's a good thing in a cleric. Sometimes the fat, contented ones are easier to deal with. The hard men have little sympathy for those unlike themselves."

"Did he or the Vizier have any idea who might be behind the attacks?"

Jorge drained his glass, but didn't refill it. Thomas sipped at his own, his head already loose from the alcohol. The taste filled his mouth, tart with an undertone of cedar.

"They made it clear to me it is our job to find the killer," said Jorge. "Did the Sultan say any more to you?"

"He sees threats everywhere and is incapable of telling what is true from false. He's concerned the nobles will see him as weak if he can't stop what is happening."

"You and I know there are men in this city who love nothing better than to plot against the Sultan. Perhaps in this instance, he is right to be worried."

"Why would anyone from a wealthy family want to kill women of the harem? The Sultan, yes, even his sons. But his wives? I see no advantage in it, and too much to lose. And why the girls?"

Jorge rose and refilled his cup. "We both know it's not a fair world. The lives of servants don't carry the same value as that of a Sultan's wife. If a man is willing to kill and wants to practise his skills, what better way to start?" His voice was as bitter as the wine.

"And Helena?" Thomas said. "You're right, the

attack on her might well have been the start of everything."

"But she wasn't killed."

"No. Was that because she was his first—that he meant to kill her and failed?"

Jorge uttered a sharp laugh that contained no hint of humour. "I suspect whoever this man is, it won't be the first time he has killed."

"I agree. He has to be a soldier. The injuries inflicted on Safya and Alisha could only have been made by someone familiar with the ways of death. But a soldier would be unfamiliar with the ways of the harem." Thomas watched Jorge. He was more relaxed, the wine smoothing the lines from his face as it smoothed the pain from his heart.

"You told me you discovered something when you examined Safya," said Jorge.

"Are you ready to listen to me now?"

"If I have to."

"If you intend to work alongside me, then yes, you do. There are things you might not want to hear, but need to hear. This is one of them."

Jorge shook his head. "I still don't understand how you could do such a thing."

"I studied them, that is all. It needed to be done."

"Could you not allow them the dignity of death?"

"Not in these circumstances."

"You are too familiar with death. It has made you heartless."

"Perhaps so. That may be why the Sultan asked me to help. He recognises something within me." Thomas studied Jorge a moment longer before making a decision. "I learned nothing from Safya we didn't already know. The cuts were clean, deep, made by a sharp blade, but it could have been any blade. There was nothing special that I could see."

Jorge's face contorted, but Thomas couldn't stop now.

"Alisha was different. Her wounds were clean, too, the same blade, but there was something else. The attacker must have gripped her shoulder." Thomas rose and moved behind Jorge. He placed his left hand on Jorge's shoulder. "Like this." He dug his fingers in for a moment, not hard, but hard enough. "And he held her tight. Much tighter than I hold you. He left a mark. His mark."

Jorge continued to stare straight ahead. Thomas could feel the tension in the man's body. He waited, knowing it was important that Jorge ask. That his asking would bind him tighter to their task.

A minute passed. Two. Three. Thomas remained with his hand on Jorge's shoulder. Patient. He felt muscles tighten beneath his fingers.

"What mark?" said Jorge.

"He is missing two fingers." Thomas released his grip, returned to his seat and held out his left hand, the outer two fingers folded across his palm. "These fingers."

Jorge shook his head, emptied his cup. "Half the soldiers in the Sultan's army are missing one thing or another, some of them almost half their bodies. This is meant to help us?"

"How many palace guards have those two fingers missing on their left hand?"

Jorge threw his hands up. "How am I supposed to know that? Do you think I spend my time appraising the guards for missing digits?"

"I thought it might be the kind of thing you would notice," Thomas said.

"Well, I didn't. I'm sorry to disappoint you. Is there more wine?"

"You can have more wine with dinner."

"Then is it time for dinner?"

CHAPTER TWELVE

They ate in the courtyard with the sky holding a pale violet line in the west. Lamps set into the wall cast a glow across the tiles and attracted insects to batter against their glass bowls. The moon rose behind the ramparts of al-Hamra, which appeared to loom over them.

Helena appeared to have forgotten her annoyance at Jorge's presence, even bringing a flagon of wine when asked, then chatting about old times. It was meaningless conversation and Thomas ignored it as he examined his own thoughts, wondering how to broach the subject of the attack on her. He knew from experience how reluctant she was to relive the night her beauty had been stolen.

Staring at her now, he saw how she ensured her hair covered one side of her face. The scar was healing well, but she would never fully recover the flawless beauty she

had once possessed. To Thomas, the flaw only made her more beautiful, but he accepted he wasn't most men. He wondered if she was genuinely grateful for the repair he had managed to effect, but doubted it. All Helena saw was what had been lost, not what had been recovered. No doubt she blamed him for not being a better surgeon.

Thomas fought his impatience, the pressure to do something. He knew that now, immediately after the attack on Safya, was the time to pursue the killer. Instead, they sat in the warm evening air, eating a meal of goat stew, fig and apricot, while somewhere in Gharnatah a killer remained free to choose his next victim.

"Have you thought more on what I said?" Helena asked, and Thomas frowned, trying to remember what she meant. She caught the expression on his face and said one word, "Lubna."

"I don't need another woman in the house." Helena had picked away at the topic for over a week, seemingly unwilling to accept his answer. Her broaching the subject again on their way to the palace that morning seemed a lifetime ago.

"Don't you want to be thought of as a great man?" said Helena.

"Why would I want that?" Thomas saw the expression of amusement on Jorge's face as he watched their conversation.

"Great men have many wives. People will believe you have your own harem if Lubna comes, even if she is

no great beauty. You should think of your status in the city."

"Such things are of no importance. I thought you knew me better."

"Perhaps I do. Have you considered I might be doing this for you, not myself? You don't care enough about what people think of you. Someone has to if you won't."

Thomas tried to recall what he knew of Helena's sister. He brought to mind a slight girl who was on the pivot between youth and adulthood. Despite Helena's words, Thomas remembered her as shy and pretty. Not beautiful like her sisters, but their beauty was too perfect for him. Seven years shy of Helena's twenty-five, Lubna was the youngest of Olaf Torvaldsson's five daughters, and the only child born of the new wife he had taken following the death of Helena's mother in childbirth— Helena's birth.

Olaf's seed was more adept at producing females than males, a matter he had consulted Thomas on once, but only the once after being informed there was nothing could be done to change or even predict the sex of a child, despite what others might say.

"I have little time to think of anything other than work," Thomas said. "That and this new task given me." He was aware of both Helena and Jorge staring at him.

"She is waiting for an answer," said Helena. "I told her you would consider my suggestion."

"You had no right to do that. I will give the matter thought when I have time."

118

"She cannot stay with my father forever. He won't keep her under his roof much longer and I fear to think what will become of her then."

"When I can." A sharpness entered his voice. "There was a battle, and now this killing. How can I consider anything else at the moment?"

"She would make herself useful." Helena continued as though Thomas had said nothing.

Thomas picked up his spoon and sawed at a piece of meat, chewed the morsel he managed to work loose. It gave him an excuse to end the conversation. He caught Jorge watching. Was that a spark of amusement in the man's eyes? A lift at the corner of his mouth? Jorge would know Olaf, of course, and Thomas wondered what he thought of him. There could hardly be two more contrasting men in the entire city.

Olaf was a man of the cold, distant north, even more distant than Thomas's homeland, brought to this place along with many of his countrymen to fight for the Sultan and his predecessors. Olaf was no recent incomer, but his Arabic was spoken with such a thick accent, it often gave him trouble.

Thomas knew Helena's elder sister continued to reside as a courtesan within the harem. The others had found places in the houses of nobles or the wealthy of Gharnatah. All except Lubna, and what the reason might be for that, Thomas couldn't guess. She was the youngest, certainly, and perhaps her father had run short of favours. It was true she wasn't as beautiful as her

siblings, except for her eyes. Perhaps it was because she was half Moorish, her mother a dark-skinned Berber, so was not considered exotic enough in this dry land where every other person carried Berber blood in their veins.

On the few occasions Thomas had spoken with Lubna, she had demonstrated a keen mind, and a curiosity about his work that surprised him.

"We need to talk," said Jorge.

Thomas looked up from his meal, aware a conversation had been going on without him.

"Later." Thomas knew he was a coward for avoiding a difficult subject.

"Jorge was asking if I had any idea who might have done such an evil thing," said Helena.

Thomas glanced at her, pleased Jorge had taken the initiative and posed the question.

"And do you?" he asked.

Helena smiled, and as always when she looked at him with compassion, she touched his heart and he knew, despite her often difficult manner, he was grateful she had come into his life.

"It might be easier to suggest who might not."

Thomas frowned. "I don't understand."

"The palace is always full of rumour, with everyone trying to position themselves to advantage."

"Murder is a little more than positioning for advantage."

"You know the harem as well as any man other than

120

Jorge. It is not the place of sensual ease people believe it to be. Safya was a well-considered wife, but the coming of the child changed her position. It always does. If she has a boy, then the balance of power shifts in her favour."

"Except," Thomas said, "the Sultan has two older sons already. And it could have been a girl."

"But it wasn't."

Thomas glanced at Jorge. He knew Helena might have discovered the sex of the child in a thousand ways, not that it mattered whether she knew or not. Soon the whole city would know of a new prince. They would also know of the killing—though the spread of that news might not be passed quite so keenly.

"A son so far down the line of succession is little threat."

"Not just the child," said Helena. "Safya's change of status. A Sultan can sire a thousand children, but I hear it spoken that this one is growing old and soft in his dotage, though I find that hard to believe."

Thomas laughed. "Hardly his dotage. He returned from battle only yesterday. He's still strong, still respected."

"He is older than he was, and no one lives forever. Those who want to replace him must start manoeuvring early, because if they don't, there are others who will. It is how lands are ruled. You know this, Thomas. You, Jorge, know this better than Thomas, who doesn't understand the world as you do."

There it was again. The soft smile, the touching of his heart, the dismissive phrase.

"So it could be almost anyone." Thomas was disappointed. For a moment, he had hoped for useful information.

Helena pushed her chair back. "I see I am no use here. I will leave you men to discuss such weighty matters."

"I would have you stay a moment more." An unfamiliar nervousness touched Thomas. "There are questions I need to ask."

"Questions? Of me? I know nothing of what happens on the hill these days."

"My questions do not concern recent events. I want to ask about the night you were attacked."

Helena rose suddenly and began clashing plates together. Thomas watched her, then said, "Sit."

Something in his voice, the curtness, the command, stopped her. She returned the plates to the table and stared at him.

"Please," he said.

For a moment, he was sure she was going to turn away. The tightness in her body where her hands pressed against the table made the hair that hung across her face shimmer. Then the tension softened and she took her seat once more.

"What do you want to know? It was a long time ago."

"But you haven't forgotten, have you?" Jorge's voice was gentle.

"Do you think I ever can?"

"Anything you recall will help," said Jorge.

Thomas leaned closer, wanting to reach for Helena's hand, but something held him back. "Did you see the man who attacked you?"

"I saw nothing that would be of use to you. Everything happened so fast, and there was much pain, terrible pain, and the blood. All I saw after he cut me was the blood."

"Tell us everything you can remember. Where were you when he attacked you?"

"In the courtyard of the lions."

"Alone?"

"With Yasmina." Thomas knew her. Another concubine no longer in the Sultan's favour.

"What time of day?" Thomas was aware he should have known the answer, but had never asked. He had been sent for in the middle of the night, so Helena's response came as no surprise.

"Evening. Dark, so it must have been late."

"What were you doing in the courtyard at that hour?"

"I couldn't sleep. Yasmina was already there, listening to the water, watching the stars."

"Were there no guards?"

"Not that close to the harem. No eunuchs either." She cast a glance at Jorge as if the attack was his fault for not protecting her.

"What did you do when you sat with Yasmina?"

"Do? We did nothing."

"I'm not accusing you of anything. Did you talk? Walk? You must have done something."

"We talked, I suppose."

"And Yasmina was still there when you were attacked?"

Helena nodded, staring down at her hands.

"Tell me everything you remember, however small."

"We were talking, our heads together, whispering so we wouldn't wake anyone. I think Yasmina saw him first, possibly saw more than I did. One moment, we were giggling over some silly matter, the next a figure came rushing towards us. He was black, everything about him black, and he moved oddly, as though … I don't…" Helena closed her eyes in an attempt to gather the memory. "As though he hopped." Her eyes snapped open to stare at Thomas. "As though he had no legs." Her eyes widened. "He was the djinn! I didn't realise, not then, not even today when I heard what happened. He was the djinn, wasn't he? The same one!"

This time, Thomas did reach across the table and took her hands between his palms, her fingers cool to his touch.

"Please," said Jorge, "try to picture exactly what happened that night. Everything."

"I don't want to." Helena shook her head, hair now completely obscuring her face.

"Was it you he was attacking?" Thomas said, his

voice soft. "Are you sure it was you, or could it have been Yasmina?"

"Why her?"

"Why you?"

"Could he have mistaken you for someone else?" said Jorge.

"Such as whom?"

"Safya perhaps?"

"I look nothing like Safya. How could anyone mistake this hair of mine for hers?"

"In the dark?"

"The courtyard was lit by torches, as we are here. He would have been able to tell."

"Yasmina then? She is dark haired, dark skinned. Did he attack Yasmina in mistake for Safya?"

"Why? Because of the baby?"

"No one knew of the baby, not then," Thomas said.

Helena pulled her hands free from Thomas's, scooped her hair back over her shoulders and faced him. "Not you perhaps, but in the harem, women are always the first to know. Her bleeding hadn't come for two months and the gossip was of a new son for the Sultan. A Moorish son."

"Tell me again, everything you remember."

Helena breathed deeply, her shoulders tense. However gentle they tried to be, it was obvious she found the questioning, the memories, hard.

"One moment we were alone, the next he was there, a whirling spirit cloaked in black—"

"Cloaked?" said Jorge. "He wore a cloak?"

Helena shook her head. "No. Perhaps. I cannot recall. It was so long ago and the pain was terrible. If I told you I saw him clearly, it would be a lie."

"What would not be?" said Jorge. "Tell us what you do remember. Where did he appear from?"

"I have already told you—I didn't see!"

"What Jorge means is from which direction did he come?"

Jorge cast a glance towards Thomas as though to say *that is* not *what I meant*, but Thomas chose to ignore it.

Helena looked past Thomas's shoulder and he saw her eyes move as she searched her memory. "He came from the passageway. It was to our right as we sat, and he came from there. So fast. I remember he moved without hesitation. He—" Helena sat upright, her gaze returning to Thomas, flicking to Jorge, and then back. "He didn't even glance at me. He went directly for Yasmina. Whoever he thought she was, whether he was mistaken or not, it was her he was trying to kill. Not me. Her."

"But it was you he injured," Thomas said.

"Yasmina screamed and fell back over the bench." Helena's eyes darted from left to right, not seeing this courtyard now, but another. "His sword was raised. He brought it down, but she wasn't there anymore and he caught my face as it swung around."

"Where did he flee?"

Before Helena could answer, Jorge added, "No—*why* did he flee? He struck out only the once, yes?"

"I think so. He…" Helena cast her eyes beyond Thomas's shoulder again. "He had a sword. A scimitar—"

Jorge interrupted. "Are you sure it was a scimitar?"

"The blade was curved. I can see it now as he raised it, as he brought it down. He wanted to kill her. I saw it in his eyes. He—"

"You saw it in his eyes?" said Jorge, his voice sharp.

"Yes. He wanted to kill Yasmina."

"You saw his eyes?"

Helena huffed a sigh. "Did Thomas cut off your ears as well as your balls?"

"If you saw his eyes, then you must have seen his face," Thomas said. Helena reached for her wine and drained it. Jorge leaned across and refilled the cup.

Helena sipped at the fresh wine, gaze turned inward.

"No … he wore a hood. A deep hood. His eyes glowed like coals, but his face was in shadow."

"Afterwards," said Jorge, returning to the earlier question, "in which direction did he flee?"

Helena shook her head. "I have no idea. By then my face was split open. I was in agony. Yasmina was screaming, and then others came, wives and concubines, eunuchs woken from dreams of whatever eunuchs dream of, and finally the guards."

"Where did the guards come from?" asked Jorge, relentless, ignoring Helena's barbs.

"I assume where they always come from. The guardhouse, of course."

"Which is where?"

Helena cast a withering glance his way. "You live in the same palace as I did, don't you? You know where they came from. Stop asking stupid questions and go find this djinn before it kills again." She stood from the table so quickly, her chair toppled backwards. "I'm going to bed. Thomas, don't stay out here all night with this…" She hesitated. "This man."

Thomas watched her go, the sway of her body, the flick of pale hair, and wanted to follow. Instead, he reached for the jug and poured himself more wine. His head swam and he needed to think, but knew he had already drunk too much to stop.

Jorge held his cup out and Thomas filled it to the brim, some decision made. He had done enough thinking for today. Oblivion beckoned with its charms, while Helena's charms awaited him upstairs.

"Are you going back to the palace tonight or shall I find you somewhere to sleep here?"

"I won't return until this is over," said Jorge.

"Why not? Eyes and ears inside the palace would be useful."

Jorge held up a hand and started counting off on his fingers. "One: I am associated with you and this task, no longer trusted by my companions or my charges. They will tell me nothing now I am tainted." Jorge raised

another finger. "Two: if this killer can enter a bathing chamber without being seen, I won't be safe inside the palace walls." He held a third finger up, but said nothing.

Thomas waited, watching emotions play across Jorge's normally placid features. He had known this man for over fifteen years, but never felt closer to him than at this moment.

"You loved her, didn't you," he said, knowing Jorge didn't want the opulence of the palace to remind him of the woman who had been killed.

"Of course I loved her." Jorge's voice hitched. "I love them all."

It wasn't the first time he had said it, but Jorge's answer remained beyond Thomas's understanding. He was incapable of loving the one woman he lived with, however hard he tried. He had emptied himself of love a long time ago, the memory of it distant, something that had happened to another man.

"How can you love them all? Do you love them equally?"

Jorge glanced at Thomas, his face painted by flickering shadows from the lamps. "Sometimes yes, sometimes no."

"I don't understand."

"I know you don't. And that is why I love you too."

"You're doing it again."

"Doing what?"

"I'm trying to have a conversation and you belittle everything I say. It's as if nothing touches you."

"You're wrong." Jorge's hand wrapped around his cup. "It is because *everything* touches me."

"I still don't understand."

"It seems you understand nothing at all."

"You may be right, but explain to me how you can love everyone."

"Not everyone."

"Don't." Thomas held up his hand.

Jorge looked at him for a long time, finally nodded.

"All right. I will try to explain, on one condition."

"Which is?"

"You try to understand."

"I'll try, but I can make no promise."

Jorge stood and walked to the wall. He leant against it and stared up at the magnificence of al-Hamra before speaking.

"For me—and I believe for everyone, if only they will let it—love is boundless. Love is the ocean. Take one thimbleful from it and an infinite amount remains. All the people in the world working together couldn't empty the ocean." Jorge turned to Thomas. "But you understand this already. You have loved too, haven't you?"

Thomas turned away, the question a reminder of a pain he had wrapped tightly inside himself and hidden deep.

"You have," said Jorge, a teasing amusement in his voice.

"It was long ago, and it ended badly."

130

"How?"

"I don't think about it anymore."

"How did it end?"

"She…" Thomas sighed. He had never mentioned Eleanor to anyone in the years since, had no idea why he spoke of her now. "She married someone else."

"They do. Did it make you love her any the less?"

"No."

"So?"

"I didn't stop loving her, but she belonged to someone else."

Jorge smiled. "Nobody belongs to anybody."

"She did."

"No," said Jorge again. "You believed she did."

"As I said, it was a long time ago."

"But it still hurts."

Thomas stared at him.

"It still hurts, doesn't it?" said Jorge.

Thomas turned away, but muttered an answer under his breath. "Yes, it still hurts."

———————————

After Jorge had grudgingly accepted the cot in the workshop, Thomas left him with the remains of the barrel of wine and returned to the courtyard. The plates from their meal remained uncleared, but he left them where they were and sat on the bench beneath the balcony. Unwelcome memories flooded him, too strong

to resist. He had spent more than twenty years trying to bury them, but had failed. One short conversation and here they were, the wounds as fresh as if they had been made an hour before.

Her name had been Eleanor. He hoped it remained so, and that she continued to live—his child, too. Not a child anymore. They would be an adult of twenty-five now. Had it been a boy or girl? He had no way of knowing. Married by now almost certainly. Or dead. Knowing nothing of their true father.

It was for the best. Thomas had been someone different then, someone he had been hiding from ever since.

In his memory, Eleanor possessed an impossible beauty and grace. She was a jewel held captive inside the box of his mind, something that could never be stolen from him. Each time he opened the box, she became more perfect, more angelic. Except she had been far from such a state of grace. She had been feral and wild, as had he. It was what drew them together. But her beauty—he did not exaggerate her beauty. It was the reason he had lost her, of course. The baby growing inside her belly was a surprise to them both, though it should not have been. No doubt it was also a surprise to the nobleman who took her from him.

Drifting aimlessly through the southern lands of France, lost and alone after the death of his father, he had found Eleanor by accident. Thomas's father had died on a battlefield, of course. Perhaps that was why he felt the

need to revisit such places, to help the wounded, to ease the pain of the dying. As he had eased that of his father when he finally accepted it was a kindness to end his suffering. It had not been the first time he had offered such mercy. There had been others on that scorched field at Castillon, but his father had been the last that day— and for a long time afterwards.

Thomas closed his eyes and leaned against the wall. A residual warmth seeped into the tense muscles of his back as he tried to remember the year of the battle. He knew how long ago, knew his age at the time—but his mind no longer thought in the same measure of years it once had. In al-Andalus, the year was 885. That was the one familiar to him. He knew how to perform the conversion, but his mind was tired and the wine sang in his blood. He should let it go and sleep, but for some reason it felt important to remember. It was the day he had been left an orphan, cast adrift in a foreign land. Of course, that was how. He had been thirteen years old— born in the year of Our Lord 1440 outside the town of Lemster, which lay in the English Marches—son of John Berrington, who was squire to the Earl of Shrewsbury. Thomas had been alone since the year 1453, abandoned by man and God close by the town of Castillon in France.

Thirteen years of age was too young to go to battle, but there had been no other choice. The great pestilence had taken both his mother and brother—the one who was meant to go to war, who wanted to go to war—leaving

behind the three of them. He hadn't thought of his sister in many long years, and it took a moment to conjure up her name. Angnes. Her name had been Angnes, but however hard he tried to recall it, her face refused to come, eroded by the years between. He wondered if she still lived. If he believed in any god, he would pray she still lived.

He knew Eleanor believed him dead. That was how he had been left, discarded at the side of the roadway from Ancizen to Guchen while the Count d'Arreau's men stole away the woman he loved. Could love truly be infinite as Jorge claimed? It had always felt to Thomas to be something a man held close in case it trickled away like dry sand from a closed fist. What if Jorge was right? All the years he had wasted while he held the pain inside, shunning others.

Thomas rose, the movement sudden and sharp. He shook his head, scattering pointless memories into the night. No more wine, no more conversation of love. There was work to do. Hard work. Dangerous work.

Helena was asleep when he entered their bedchamber and he stood for a moment watching her breathe. The linen sheet was cast aside and her body lay bathed in moonlight, her perfection almost frightening. She was far more beautiful than Eleanor had been, but standing at the foot of the bed, Thomas felt nothing. Nothing at all.

CHAPTER THIRTEEN

"I don't see why I can't just stay at your house," said Jorge the next morning as they followed a narrow alley that wound down the steep hillside into town.

"Are you sure you can't go back to the palace?"

"The women will make demands of me. They won't understand there are other calls on my time. But you can bring in another bed. That cot in your workroom isn't big enough to hold someone my size. And it smells strange in there."

"Herbs, that is all. You didn't touch anything, did you?"

Jorge cast him a glance.

"The inn will suit you better," Thomas said.

"I have no money."

"Money isn't a problem. You'll need better clothes, too."

So far they had seen only one other person, and that

man had been too polite to stare at Jorge for long, but once in the town, Thomas knew how it would be. Jorge stood out. Which no doubt pleased him.

"I have other clothes. I wear them when I come to drink and enjoy male conversation."

They reached a set of steps, steep and twisting, and Thomas led the way down.

"They're at the palace, I take it?"

"They are."

The steps deposited them on a street running alongside the Hadarro and Thomas turned right. The day was still young, and fortunately for them, not many of Gharnatah's citizens were out and about. It was a different matter when they entered the square. They passed stalls piled high with almonds, fruit, vegetables, pots, local silks and imported cloth. The odours of a dozen lands drifted through the air and the sound of a score of languages babbled.

"Am I dressed so strangely?" Jorge drew attention even among the brightly attired stallholders.

"Not for the harem, I expect, but here? Yes. You do know you're dressed strangely, don't you? But the inn is on the other side of the square. We'll find you a room, and then find something for you to wear."

"Nothing too coarse," said Jorge, and Thomas smiled.

Khadar the innkeeper was more than happy to take Thomas's money. The room he showed them was adequate, with a small glazed window offering a view across the square. They didn't stay long before making their way through winding streets, and then quieter, more opulent ones to where the workshop of Carlos Rodriguez sat three doors down from the house he lived in with his family.

Carlos was an acquaintance of Thomas's, one he occasionally beat at Mancala while they sipped sweet coffee or tea at Khadar's inn. He was not in the workshop, but the door was opened by a wide Spanish woman who conveyed a message, and within a short time, Carlos entered through a rear door, trying to make his appearance casual.

"Thomas—have you finally come to let me dress you more appropriately?"

"I am not here for myself. I need clothes for my friend."

Distaste showed on Carlos's face, but both Thomas and Jorge chose to ignore it.

"Are you sure I cannot tempt you with something more matching to your status, Thomas?"

"He does look like some desert Bedouin, doesn't he?" said Jorge, and Thomas scowled at him.

"I am surprised anyone recognises him as a physician." Carlos warmed to the subject. It was an old and tired topic for Thomas, one he was determined not to be swayed over, even if Helena had now joined the

chorus of those wishing to attire him like some cosseted parakeet.

"Can you do something for him, or must we look elsewhere? We want nothing fancy, he only needs to pass as an ordinary man."

"I would prefer the material to be less coarse than you wear," said Jorge.

"I believe I can promise you that," said Carlos. He approached Jorge, moving around him, measuring with his eyes. "I could have something suitable made by tomorrow evening."

"We need something now," Thomas said.

"I..." Carlos again surveyed Jorge, who was now wandering the shelves stacked with bolts of material from all over Spain, others imported from Africa, Italia and beyond. "He is tall, isn't he?"

"He is," Thomas agreed.

"And broad across the shoulder."

"And belly, a little."

"I am not fat," said Jorge, running some cloth between his fingers.

"I didn't imply you were. Well fed, I would say, no more than that."

"I may have something to fit him, but it won't be fashionable or of fine material. If you could offer me a little more time..."

"One outfit will suffice for today, and perhaps you can make him two more for tomorrow. You did say tomorrow evening, didn't you?"

"Two outfits?"

"I like this material," said Jorge, lifting a bolt of black silk run through with fine gold thread. "This would make a wonderful pair of trousers."

"It is a special order, not for sale," Carlos said. "Besides, it is too good for trousers—and you would not wish to pay the cost if I was to use it."

"Something similar, perhaps?"

"I will see what I can do." Carlos turned to the woman. "Teresa, will you measure him while I see if I can find something he can wear now?"

Thomas leaned against the edge of a large table where cloth was laid out ready to make up and watched as the woman expertly prodded and pushed Jorge, making him stand tall as she measured his chest, shoulders, waist and leg length, writing everything down on a scrap of paper. By the time Carlos returned, Jorge was back to fingering the bolts of cloth.

"I have decided," said Jorge, "that I favour silk over cotton or linen."

"It's the silk that makes you stand out," Thomas said. "Carlos, cotton is what I want for him."

"Then I have brought the right outfit. This will fit him, I believe." He laid trousers, shirt, cloak and scarf on the table. Jorge offered the garments a glance as disdainful as they deserved.

"Those are perfect," Thomas said.

"If I wear these, no one will know it's me."

"Exactly."

"We will leave you in privacy to change," said Carlos. "Come, Teresa, we'll use the other room to look at his measurements and decide what we can do."

"I'm not wearing them," said Jorge once they were alone.

"You can't wear what you have now."

"I told you, I have clothing at the palace."

"Which no doubt still makes you look like a eunuch."

"I am a eunuch!"

"But you want nobody to know you are, for our task."

"Why?" Jorge picked up the shirt, white, of good quality linen with a fine weave, and weighed it in his hand.

"It's a good shirt," Thomas said. "At least try the clothes on and see how they feel. It might only be for a few days. Carlos will make you something better tomorrow."

"I hope so. Why couldn't I have some of that exquisite silk over there?"

"No silk. And you need to cover your head."

"But it is my second best feature."

"Only until your hair grows out. A beard would be useful, too, if you can manage one."

Jorge sighed, shaking his head. "What are you trying to turn me into?" He began loosening the fine silks that draped his body.

Thomas turned aside, not from guilt or shame, merely to offer some encouragement and speed him

along, though he suspected an audience would be welcomed. Even if it was necessary, buying clothes for Jorge was wasting time.

For the second time in as many days, Thomas found himself cursing the steepness of the path from the Hadarro to the palace. It seemed irrational to him it should be separated from those it governed by a steep gorge and river. Or perhaps not. As he trudged upwards —with Jorge striding ahead, hardly even drawing breath —it occurred to him the separation of governor and governed was a wise decision, for they often made for poor neighbours.

"The clerks first?" Jorge asked, picking up on their initial plan before Safya had been slain.

"I think so. And I'd like to speak with those two girls again—they may have remembered more overnight."

They drew close to the doorway where he had entered the day before, the same guard standing beside it.

"We have urgent business within the palace," Thomas commanded.

"I heard your urgent business of yesterday is dead. What else brings you here, *qassab*?" The guard drew the word out, making it clear what he thought of the practice of medicine.

Thomas delved into the pocket of his robe and drew

141

out the Sultan's seal. "This brings me here. Now let us pass."

"Hold up, that could be anything." The guard laid his spear across the doorway to bar the way. He glanced briefly at Jorge but, with his head covered and dressed as he was, didn't appear to recognise him.

"It could be anything, certainly, but it is not." Thomas raised the seal, making the guard take a step back. "Do you want to explain to Sultan Abu al-Hasan Ali or his Vizier why you turned away men on their business?"

The guard glanced at the seal, but he was no longer seeing it. The surety in Thomas's voice was enough, although face still had to be saved.

"And how do I explain letting two strangers walk past me while a killer is on the loose? For all I know, it could be one of you."

"Foolish man," said Jorge. "Don't you know me? I belong here. And Thomas is no stranger. We've walked the palace halls longer than you've lived. Now stand aside and let us pass."

The guard wasn't bright, but bright enough to realise he had pushed his authority as far as he could. Boredom, perhaps, had gotten the better of him. He withdrew his lance and stepped aside. Thomas passed through into the dimness of the corridor, up steps rising ahead, but Jorge deliberately jostled against the guard in passing and spat quiet words in his ear.

"We need cool heads," Thomas said as Jorge caught him up. "Don't allow his stupidity to make you angry."

"I'll try to remember your words of wisdom." The sarcasm was thick in Jorge's voice. "If I allowed stupidity to get beneath my skin, I'd have been driven mad years ago. There's a surplus of it inside the walls of this place."

Thomas led the way along the same route as the day before, except yesterday Safya had been alive and the world had been a different place.

They passed through the palace and across the narrow bridge to the Vizier's offices. They were not expected, but the seal once more gave access, and they were shown to a room where four men stood at high desks. A fifth larger table sat in the middle of the space, scattered with scrolls, papers and books. There was a musty smell to the air, mixed with a bitter wooden fragrance from ink made of oak gall. If the Sultan's chambers were the heart of the palace, the harem its sex, then this was the head that controlled everything that went on.

The clerk nearest the door turned to them.

"Can I help you? We do not hear petitions until later in the day."

"We're not here to petition." Thomas felt into his pocket again, searching once more for the seal. "We come on the Sultan's business, with questions."

"Ah, you're the physician. My master told me we should expect you." He looked Thomas up and down.

"You don't look much like a doctor." He turned his attention to Jorge. "Nor you a eunuch."

"Needs must," said Jorge.

"Who would you question?"

"I assume you know what happened to the Sultana, Safya?" Thomas asked, and when the man nodded, "And the earlier attacks?" Another nod. "I would talk with whoever was tasked with investigating those. Was that you?"

The man shook his head. "I would not have been asked." He turned to look over the others, shaking his head slowly as though his memory was deficient. "Habib, you were involved with the questioning, were you not?"

A short man turned away from his work. The others continued, scribing information on to paper, each of them with fingers stained dark with ink.

"I was asked to record some of the conversation, but Bilal Abd al-Rahman was in charge."

"Can we speak with this Bilal, then?" Thomas asked.

"He no longer works on the hill," the first clerk said, as Habib returned to his work, incurious.

"Then where does he work?"

"Somewhere in the city, but not here. If that is all...?"

"I would speak with Habib first."

"He said he only noted some facts, nothing more."

"I would still speak with him. I take it you don't

144

intend to refuse my request?" Thomas's fingers closed around the seal.

"Of course I will not refuse you. Habib, go into the courtyard with these men and tell them what you know."

"I have a document to finish by noon."

"We won't take long," Thomas said, not knowing if he spoke the truth or not.

"I will explain if you are late," the man's master said.

Habib nodded, laid his pen on the desk and led the way through an archway into a small courtyard. The surroundings were not as opulent as those of the main palace, but there was water, trees for shade, and two stone benches set in the far corner. This was no doubt a place the scribes came when they took a break from their work. It was to the benches that Habib led them. He sat in the centre of one. Thomas and Jorge settled opposite.

"What do you wish to know?" He obviously wanted the matter over with so he could return to his work.

"You recorded the findings of this other man, this Bilal?"

"Some. He did much of the work himself, but at times I accompanied him to record their words when he questioned people."

"And who did he question?"

"It has been some time since those events and I am not sure I recall their names."

"What kind of people, then?"

"Oh, servants. Those who knew the girls who were

145

attacked, those who were nearby when the attacks happened."

"And you recorded this testimony?"

"Some of it. As I said, Bilal did much for himself."

"Where are those documents now?"

"I gave everything I worked on to Bilal. What he did with it I have no idea."

"Do you recall what was said in your presence?"

Habib shook his head. "I scribe—I don't usually take note of the words I write. Sometimes it is the safer course of action not to know."

"Weren't you curious?" Jorge asked before Thomas could pose another question.

"Curious?" It appeared to be an alien concept to Habib. "Why would I be curious?"

"Two girls were killed within the palace walls. I heard much rumour and gossip, many spoke of it."

"This is not the harem," said Habib.

"Do you remember anything at all?"

"I am sorry." Habib shook his head. "I am not trying to be obscure, but I spend my days transcribing and recording. It would be impossible to take notice of everything I write. If I could remember something, I would tell you, but this happened months ago. And Bilal, as far as I know, discovered nothing."

"So why did you stop?"

"Bilal reported whatever he had discovered to the Vizier. Shortly afterwards, he left his employment here."

"Left," Thomas said, "or was asked to leave?"

"All I know is he left."

"Do you know where he works now?"

"For the Jew, Hasdai ibn Shaprut. They work out of a house in the Albayzin, writing wills and contracts and land treaties."

"Was his move voluntary?" Thomas returned to the question Habib had not answered.

The scribe looked aside. He seemed to be thinking, judging his answer, perhaps wondering if Thomas held more power than his master.

"I believe he was asked to leave."

"As a result of his findings leading nowhere, do you think, or for some other reason?"

"As I told you before, I do not think anything. But in this instance, there may be truth in what you say."

"Because of what he discovered?" said Jorge.

"I don't know." Habib rose from the bench. "Now I must return to my work."

"Should you recall anything relating to this matter, I would ask you to contact either myself or Jorge," Thomas said.

Habib nodded briefly. "I will, but do not expect any revelations."

He returned to the room without glancing at Jorge, who said, "Do you think he doesn't like me?"

Thomas looked at him. Even in his new clothes, Jorge stood out, his whole body telegraphing an instinctive sensuality.

"You may be an acquired taste."

"All good things are. Was he telling the truth?"

"What do you think? I saw you watching him."

"I believe he was. He's not an imaginative man, and his job demands he suppress any vestige of curiosity he may possess. So yes, he was truthful, if unhelpful."

"We'll have to speak with this Bilal. I know Hasdai ibn Shaprut, I've used his services on a few occasions."

"Do we go there now?" Jorge asked.

"We should finish our work on the hill first. There's little point going all the way down only to have to climb back again. And I want to ask Habib's master about the documents Bilal made, what became of them."

"They'll be gone," said Jorge.

"What makes you say that? Documents are the life-blood of people such as these. They destroy nothing."

Jorge only smiled, and when Thomas went inside, it was to find there were indeed no documents.

"Why not?" Thomas moved to stand too close to the senior scribe. "What has become of them?"

"They will have been passed to the Vizier and Sultan."

"So they have them?"

"No." The man looked unhappy. "All palace documents are stored here. If they existed, we would have them."

"Will you look?"

"I know everything we store, and they are not here."

"I still want you to look, and send a message to me

one way or the other. If you find anything, keep it safe. I want to read what is written there."

———————————

"So who do we talk to next?" said Jorge as they stood outside the clerk's offices.

"You're enjoying this, aren't you?"

Jorge lifted a shoulder. "Sometimes luxury and the company of beautiful women grows dull."

"I want to speak with Zoraya while we are on this side of the hill. I saw Helena crossing the bridge when I was here before and wondered if that was where she had been. Zoraya has rooms here, doesn't she?"

"The Sultan keeps her apart from the harem, for good reason."

"She is disliked?"

"Indeed she is."

"Because she is Greek, or are there other reasons?"

"How many do you have time to hear?" said Jorge.

CHAPTER FOURTEEN

Zoraya's chambers were in the north wing of the smaller palace and owed nothing to the harem which housed the Sultan's other wives. This place had been fashioned in an image of the homes of Spanish royalty. Tables and chairs were set throughout the rooms, rugs covered the tiled floor, and tapestries hid the religious messages on the walls. The hangings showed hunting scenes and court gatherings. Many faces and figures were depicted, alien to Moorish decoration, which shunned the human figure in preference for scripts celebrating the all-consuming power of Allah.

Zoraya possessed her own guards, her own clerks and minders. Thomas and Jorge were made to wait in an outer chamber while one was sent to enquire if they might be admitted. Two others remained to ensure they made no attempt to wander.

Jorge went to the nearest man. "You are aware we are here on the Sultan's business, aren't you?"

"Your companion showed us his seal," the guard said, unimpressed.

"So why are we kept waiting?"

"It's not his fault, Jorge," Thomas said. "We won't be here long, I'm sure."

Jorge turned, offering Thomas a look which expressed his doubt, before crossing the room to stare through a small window which afforded a view across the plain. From the rooms within came the sound of conversation, occasional laughter, the clattering of pans and plates, the scent of roasted meats. Thomas realised it was almost noon, but there would be no interruption for prayers here.

Minutes passed, and then some more.

Jorge left the window and sat on a chair, testing it with his weight, rocking from side to side.

"I could get used to sitting this way," he said. "I saw you have such furniture in your house."

"I'm *ajami*, remember. And the older I get, the more my bones protest at sitting on the floor, however many cushions there are beneath me."

"The Sultan is almost twice your age but he keeps the tradition."

"The Sultan is a stronger man than me." Thomas lowered his voice. "Do you think she will send us away?"

"She may. Zoraya knows her own power, and

151

believes she possesses even more than she truly does. We will see. Take a seat, Thomas, rest those ancient bones of yours."

"I would prefer—" He broke off as there came the sound of footsteps from the corridor, booted feet as befitted the style of this place. The third man returned, shaking his head, but in confusion rather than negation.

"My lady is about to take her noon meal, but she says you are welcome to join her and the children."

Jorge raised an eyebrow in surprise, and Thomas smiled at him.

"She must want to meet me," Jorge whispered as they followed the man along a wide corridor lined with more wall hangings. In rooms to right and left lay rich furnishings. "I expect she has heard of my reputation."

"She knows she can't refuse us," Thomas whispered back.

"Believe what you will. I'm not sure I like the idea of her children being with her, though."

"You concentrate on them while I speak to Zoraya. Bear in mind she prefers the Spanish form of address, so use that if you can still recall it."

"I don't think I ever met much with Spanish royalty, but I'll try."

Their destination was a high-ceilinged chamber with many windows. It offered views east to the Sholayr Mountains, their peaks now almost denuded of snow, and west across the plain.

Zoraya sat at the head of a long table laid with fine

plates, crystal glasses and silver cutlery. She didn't rise when they entered and neither did her children, two boys and a girl, the elder boy of an age with Abu Abdullah, who was eighteen, the other a little younger than Yusuf, the girl somewhere between the two. All at the table were attired as though they held court in Qurtuba rather than a Moorish palace.

"I'll not ask you to sit, it would not be seemly, but welcome, Thomas Berrington, you also, Jorge al-Andalus." She spoke in fluent Spanish and Thomas had to make a rapid re-adjustment to understand her words.

"We thank you for seeing us, My Lady. You are most gracious." Thomas switched to the alien language, aware his words sounded coarse.

"You don't mind if we eat? Good food should not be allowed to grow cold. Do you know my children?"

"By name and reputation only, My Lady. They are fine children indeed."

"And healthy. They have no need of the services of one such as you."

"I can see that. Healthy indeed. Are we free to talk in their company?" Thomas noted that Jorge had moved to stand to one side of the girl, who sat opposite her brothers. He leaned down and spoke with her, his voice too soft for Thomas to make out, but her brothers heard, leaning forward to listen.

"Talk of what, surgeon?"

Although the children were eating, they had also started to converse with Jorge as though he was an old

and valued companion, and Thomas envied him his ease with people. Zoraya left her cutlery untouched, the meat on her plate cooling. Instead, she lifted a crystal goblet holding what appeared to be wine and took a long drink.

"Have you heard of the task set us, My Lady?"

"We are isolated on this side of the hill, but yes, I have heard something, and I wish you well in your endeavours. Safya had become a good friend to me. I can scarce believe she has gone. You must forgive me if I appear abrupt with you as we talk, but I still mourn her loss."

"I understand." Thomas felt as though he was walking across hot coals, the next footstep likely to lead to disaster. He had not been aware Zoraya and Safya were close and wondered if it placed this woman in danger as well. "I was asked to look into the deaths that occurred in the palace, and now matters have taken a more serious turn."

"Indeed they have." Zoraya lowered her voice as she glanced at her children. "Perhaps it would be wise to speak of this away from the table. Your companion appears to be making a fine job of amusing my little ones. Shall we leave them to it?"

Thomas nodded and waited as Zoraya rose, a slow, complex operation involving much adjustment of silk skirts. When she was finally satisfied, she led the way towards the windows. Thomas had expected them to move to another chamber, but Zoraya obviously thought this short distance enough.

"What is it you want of me?" A flirtatious look entered her eyes, which made Thomas uncomfortable. It sat uneasily with her claim of being upset. Perhaps he and Jorge should have exchanged roles.

"A few questions, nothing more."

"Then ask so I can return to my meal." She glanced at the table. "Although I expect it will be cold by now."

"You already know the mission Jorge and I are on. I need to question everyone who has information that might shed light on the deaths."

"Does the Sultan know you place me under suspicion?"

"You are under no suspicion, My Lady. I merely ask if you have heard any rumour that might assist us, that might explain why Safya was attacked. As you were her friend, she may have mentioned something to you the importance of which was not obvious at the time. The palace is always alive with secrets."

"I keep my place on this side of the hill, sir, and other than Safya and Helena, I rarely mix with the other wives or concubines."

"I understand it was not always so, that you lived within the harem for several years. You must have made other friends there?"

"A few, perhaps." Zoraya stared through the window. "But now they keep to themselves. It is as difficult for them to cross the bridge as it is for me to travel in the other direction."

"It must make for a lonely life," Thomas said.

She turned from the view and her eyes traced his face. "I have my children. And I am not a complete hermit. Friends visit me now and again."

"But none from the harem."

The fascination with his face could last only so long and she turned aside. "I thought I had already made myself clear."

"In which case, do you have any suspicions of your own? Any trace of an idea why someone would want to kill women of the harem? Would want to kill a Sultana?"

"There are always plots. Or do you not live enough in this world to know of such things? I have heard it said you are often distracted from the commonplace things in life." Zoraya's voice was cold, her gaze now locked on a distant spiral of smoke rising from a field.

"I am learning to live in the real world, My Lady. You have no theories, then, on why they died?"

"The girls, certainly not. Safya? She was a Sultana, and women of power always attract enemies. If I were you, I would be concentrating my questions within the harem. That is where the real intrigue lies. Ask your friend, for he must know this better than anyone. Are you finished with me?"

"Not quite." He saw annoyance cross her face. "One more question. Helena says Yasmina works for you now. Would you allow me to speak with her?"

"Why?"

"She was with Helena when she was attacked, and I believe it was the same man who killed Safya."

Zoraya made a dismissive sound between her teeth. "Yasmina is no longer in my employ. She was ... unsuitable."

"Do you know where she is now?"

Zoraya waved a hand. "Gone elsewhere. Malaka, I believe. Yes, I am sure she was sent to Malaka."

Thomas decided not to press her further for the moment. He could always return if he needed to. Something about the woman didn't sit right, her switch from flirtatiousness to impatience too contrived, her answers too vague.

He watched her return to the table. It was obvious she had already dismissed him from her mind. She was, he had to admit, a striking woman. Her hair was finely cut and braided, darker than Helena's but lighter than most women's in al-Andalus. It was clear from the way she moved that beneath the voluminous skirts lay a sensuous body. Her features were finely sculpted, her skin clear, but something cold sat in her eyes, marring the effect of her beauty. She reminded him of Helena.

Jorge rose from his conversation with the elder boy and Thomas joined him as they made their way towards the doorway. He glanced back as Zoraya clapped her hands and saw a servant hustle to the table to remove her plate; cold now, as she had said. She raised her eyes and shot him a glance of such malevolence, he almost stumbled. There was raw hatred in it, and he wondered what had triggered such venom. Not his questions, surely, but if not them, then what?

"So," said Jorge, as they left the building and started across the narrow bridge, "did she admit to plotting to kill her rivals?"

Thomas had to look at him to make sure he was joking.

"Did you discover anything from the children?"

"Other than that they are spoiled and have ambitions to be Spanish nobility, perhaps one or two things. The girl hasn't a single thought in her head other than which Spanish prince she should marry. The younger boy enjoys hunting, but not with a bird, and the elder, I believe, is also starting to weigh his marriage options. He even grew bold enough to ask me questions regarding the bed chamber."

"You, of course, told him you could hardly know of such things."

"Not quite. I dropped a few pebbles in the still pool that is his mind to disturb the waters. I think he may want to talk with me again."

"There's no point questioning the children."

"Is that so? Sometimes knowledge comes from the strangest of places. You of all people should know that. So if Zoraya didn't confess to you on her knees, did you discover anything at all?"

They reached the far side of the bridge and entered the palace.

"Only that I believe she's hiding something, but exactly what I have no idea."

Jorge sighed. "I suppose I had better tell you of the

few things I managed to uncover, then. They may help explain Zoraya's attitude."

"What did you find out?" Thomas felt annoyance rising. This task was difficult enough without Jorge holding back information.

"It has nothing to do with the matter at hand."

"Tell me anyway. You obviously believe it significant enough to tease me with it."

"I overheard you asking Zoraya if she still saw anyone from the harem."

"You could hear us from across the room? The boys, too?"

"They weren't interested."

"Whereas you were."

"Would you prefer me to be uninterested?"

Thomas shook his head. "I apologise. I'm not used to intrigue, and you were right to listen. You might have heard something I missed."

"No, I heard the same as you. She was hiding something, but it's nothing to do with our task. I believe Helena accompanied you to the palace yesterday."

Thomas stopped walking and turned to Jorge. "She did. Was that only yesterday? It feels like a month."

"Zoraya spoke the truth when she said she doesn't see anyone from the harem. What she didn't say is she continues a friendship with someone who used to be part of the harem."

"It was Helena who came to visit, wasn't it? She mentioned they remain close."

159

"I think her eldest, Nasir, is more than a little besotted. And who can blame him? He mentioned her name twice. And then, a little later, he asked me what tips I might have to make a man a stallion in the bedchamber."

"I hope you told him he needs first to grow a pair of stallion balls."

Jorge only smiled and started along the corridor, shaking his head. "How many times do I have to tell you, physician, a man's balls are not always as essential as most believe."

"You told Nasir that?"

"Of course not. I told him nothing. It was hardly appropriate for me to offer such advice to a young prince. I do have one other discovery that might interest you, though."

Thomas waited, refusing to ask.

Jorge maintained his silence.

"What?" Thomas said when he could stand it no longer.

"Helena isn't the only member of her family to visit. Olaf is teaching the boys how to use a sword. It was obvious they don't like him, but he's not a man you can refuse."

"Whose idea was that, do you think?"

"All princes must know how to fight. Zoraya would have asked, or more likely the Sultan. The whole world knows he favours her and the children."

"But does it mean anything? I can't see how, unless

Olaf is her lover and the training is no more than an excuse."

Jorge raised a shoulder. "Are we going to speak with Aixa now?"

"Do you believe we should, so soon?"

"We've spoken with the Sultan's current favourite wife. It would be impolite not to speak to the mother of his children. After all, she may be in danger herself."

Thomas walked alongside Jorge for a while. His mind pulled at the tangled threads of information he had acquired that day, but all he did was to tangle them even further.

Eventually, he said, "I'm not sure I want to talk to another feted Sultana of the harem. I should go to see Olaf Torvaldsson and sound him out. Will you speak to Aixa for me?"

Jorge stopped, turning to face Thomas. "If you think she'll speak with me, you are deluded."

"Why not? She must know you well enough, doesn't she?"

"As a eunuch. Not as a man who is allowed to ask her questions. We must both go. She's more likely to accept them from you. You can speak to Olaf later while I talk to the serving girls—they all like me."

CHAPTER FIFTEEN

"That interview was a complete waste of time," said Jorge as they made their way from Aixa's chambers. Thomas doubted whether interview was the right word for what had occurred. He was beginning to hate what he had been asked to take on. His previous dealings with these women had been as their physician. Now he was an interrogator, their attitude changed completely, their hostility clear, and he wondered if it was possible to ever return to the relationship with them he had once enjoyed.

Even so, he thought Jorge was wrong.

"Not a total waste of time. She didn't like us questioning her, and she's obviously afraid she might be the next victim, which tells us she has nothing to do with the deaths. I believed she, at least, was being honest with us."

"Is there anyone you don't suspect?"

Thomas smiled. "Should there be? Other than you, me, and the Sultan?"

Jorge nodded. "Of course. And you're not sure about me, are you?"

"Are you going to speak to some of the girls now?"

"If you can manage Olaf alone."

"I intend to ask him about Zoraya's sons. He's not a subtle man and may let something slip if his relationship with her is more than the one she claims. After that, I need to report to the Sultan—although report what, I don't know."

They had reached a corridor which led to the bathing chamber where Safya had died and were about to split up when a figure stepped from a side door, blocking their way. Not a soldier. Worse than a soldier. Thomas recognised his face, but not his name. The man had been with Faris al-Rashid's group on their return to Gharnatah, and was no doubt one of the hangers-on who sought power.

"We would speak with you, surgeon." Thomas noted his use of *we* even though he was alone.

"And we are on the Sultan's business." Thomas closed his hand around the seal in his pocket, but left it hidden, knowing it would hold little power over this man.

"Which is what we wish to speak of. Come, join us." The man turned into a side chamber, used to giving orders, certain they would be obeyed.

There were four men and two women in the room. The women—servants—stood to one side, invisible, eyes downcast. The men reclined on couches and cushions. The scent of strong coffee perfumed the air, but so far it remained unpoured.

The man who had invited them in sat, but it was another at the head of the table who spoke. "We will be leaving soon to hunt with the Sultan, but I thought we should talk to you before we do, Thomas Berrington. I assume you know everyone, or should I make introductions?"

The last time Thomas had seen Faris al-Rashid had been outside the city walls in the company of the Sultan. Thomas looked the small group over. Valentin al-Kamul had been there, too, a long-time companion of Faris—half-Spanish, half-Moor, a man whose loyalties could never be completely pinned down. The man who had confronted them in the corridor was a stranger. The fourth was a surprise to Thomas. He considered Don Domingo Alkhabaz closer to a friend than acquaintance and his presence was puzzling.

Thomas glanced at Jorge, who stood to one side, as though in the presence of these men, he had reverted to being a servant. Except these were not men of this city, or Thomas would have known them all. He knew for certain two lived beyond the walls, and he wondered what they were all doing gathered here in the palace. Had

they really been invited to hunt with Abu al-Hasan Ali? If so, they were highly honoured. Thomas also wondered what their interest was in him. He would prefer to be ignored by men such as these.

"Sit, physician." Faris's voice was thick with command. He reclined on a stack of cushions from where he clapped his hands. The serving girls began to arrange five fine glasses encased in silver cages on the low table before pouring dark coffee.

There was no invitation offered to Jorge. Knowing his place among these men, he moved away until his back was against the wall. Thomas noticed that, unlike the women, Jorge's eyes did not look down, but took in each of the men in turn.

While Faris was the only member of the group of pure Moorish descent, able to trace his lineage back centuries, it was not unusual for those of Spanish extraction—if such still existed after 700 years of Moorish rule—to hold high office in al-Andalus. The Sultan and, perhaps more importantly, those who carried out his wishes appointed the most politically advantageous person. Often money changed hands, or if not money, then favours of one kind or another.

Thomas nodded to each of the men as he took a cushion, then reached for his coffee. It was too hot to drink, but he allowed the aroma to rise around his face, breathing it in.

"I don't know this man," Thomas said, indicating the

well-dressed individual who had invited them in, now sitting between Valentin al-Kamul and Faris.

"Don Antonio Galbretti," said Faris. "He has suffered greatly during the conflict between our nations. His lands, although extensive, span the border between our own and those of the Castilian King and Queen."

"And to which side does his loyalty lie?" Thomas was unwilling to give any quarter, aware there was meaning in every word and turn of phrase uttered here. He hoped Jorge was taking note and not really studying the serving girls as he appeared to be doing.

"A man's loyalties lie, of course, with his master," said Don Antonio.

"At any particular time?"

Don Antonio gave a slow nod. "That is a taken, of course."

"Your surname, it sounds more Neapolitan or Sicilian than Spanish."

"My ancestors can be traced to most of the noble families of Europe. Naples, certainly, could be called home at one time, a century ago."

Faris interrupted, a strain in his voice hinting at impatience. "I am sure Don Antonio would love nothing better than to talk of his lineage all day long, but there are other matters to discuss. You know Valentin and Don Domingo, of course." Faris indicated the fourth companion, seated at the end of the table.

"You do not usually mix in such exalted circles, Don Domingo," Thomas said.

"These are troubling times. A man does what he must to survive." Don Domingo's eyes avoided meeting Faris's stare, and Thomas wondered if his position at the far end of the table was deliberate, an attempt to separate himself at least a little from the others. Except his mere presence in this room meant he was involved.

"Have you started your enquiries yet, Thomas Berrington?" Faris's question was asked in a throwaway manner, as though the answer mattered neither one way or the other to him.

"Barely. We are on our way now to question more people and would have started but for your kind invitation." There was no chance Thomas intended to mention anything he already knew.

"I want you to know we support you fully in this matter."

"And the Sultan, too, I am sure."

"Of course. Except..." Faris hesitated, took a moment to sip his coffee. Thomas mirrored him, the dark, sweet flavour coating the inside of his mouth. "It would make little sense to trouble the Sultan with every tiny thing you might discover."

"Surely that is for him to decide."

"I believe you an intelligent man." The others nodded, agreeing with their master, even Don Antonio, the new member of the group. "I am sure you will know what is relevant in this matter and what is not. That is why I invited you here, to offer any assistance we can."

"Do you have men I can call on?"

Faris smiled. "I believe we all have men, but as you know, they will be far from the city on our estates. No, I was thinking that five heads would be better than one in deciphering this riddle. I have no plans to return to my fields for some time. I am not sure if I speak for my companions, but believe me when I say I am at your disposal."

"You do me much honour offering me the gift of your time." Thomas glanced around. "All of you. But—"

"I would suggest we meet here at the end of each day, just after evening prayers, and you can update us on your progress."

"That will not be possible," Thomas said. "There are times when I may be away from the city, and a regular meeting, coming all the way to the palace every evening, will be inconvenient." He made no mention of the Sultan asking him to do exactly that.

"Then somewhere else. In the town, if you wish. Don Antonio has a fine house on the banks of the Hadarro. I am sure he would make it available to us."

"Of course," Don Antonio said.

"I thank you," Thomas said, "but I regret I find myself unable to accept your invitation. Who knows what might happen, or where I may be? And my time is better spent on investigation than discussion."

"I wish to be informed of any findings," Faris said, steel entering his voice even as he made an effort to appear relaxed.

"After I have informed the Sultan, perhaps, and with his permission."

"If that is your wish," said Faris. "But the Sultan has no need to worry himself over our arrangements. He has matters of greater importance to consider."

"I will not go behind his back," Thomas said.

"Nor I." Jorge spoke for the first time.

Faris raised his eyes, distaste on his features. "We were not speaking to you, eunuch."

"I have been set this task alongside Thomas," said Jorge. "I take those orders seriously. I would never offend the Sultan."

"No one said anything—" Valentin al-Kamul spoke for the first time, his outburst cut dead as Faris raised a hand, master in this small domain.

"I see you have set your minds on the matter, both of you. Very well—but remember my offer—help is at hand should you need it. All you have to do is ask. There are no secrets here, only honest men offering honest advice and assistance."

"I won't forget your words," Thomas said, starting to rise.

"We are likely to remain in this chamber for a little while longer," said Faris. "Should you wish to return, you will be made most welcome." His eyes didn't take in Jorge.

"Physician," Don Antonio spoke, stopping Thomas in the act of turning away, "do not think you can act independently in this matter. Faris has made you a

generous offer, but we make just as good enemies as we do friends."

Thomas reached out to stop Jorge moving forward. "There is no reason for us to be enemies. All we wish to do is follow the Sultan's orders."

"An old man," said Don Antonio. "Who knows how many years he has left? You would be wise to look to the next generation."

"The Sultan returned from a great victory only yester—"

"A great *skirmish*," Faris interrupted. "You forget I was alongside him."

"I saw little sign of blood on your clothing," Thomas said.

Jorge continued pulling against Thomas's hand, which remained gripping his shoulder.

Faris smiled. "Some of us fight more elegantly than others."

"And further from the chaos." Jorge couldn't hold his anger in check any longer. Faris didn't even glance in his direction.

"Don't get confused over where true power lies in this land, physician. Abu al-Hasan Ali is a figurehead, nothing more. It is land and gold that counts here, just as it does throughout the civilised world."

"Not for everyone," Thomas said.

"I've heard it said you are not like other men. If that is true, then you are an even bigger fool than I have already been led to believe."

"Enjoy what little power you have while it lasts," Thomas said, "for the Spanish are coming, just as sure as winter snow on the Sholayr."

Faris smiled. "The Spanish are the same as everyone else. They love gold as much as the next man."

"Don't expect to see either of us again." Thomas turned away from these men he despised.

Don Antonio rose to his feet, moving fast. His hand fell to a dagger tucked into his belt, but he didn't draw it.

"Expect to see me again, Thomas Berrington. Expect to see me when—" He stopped abruptly as the door opened to admit a giant of a man.

Olaf Torvaldsson, the Sultan's general, glanced at Thomas and Jorge, then to the others, a frown touching his brow. He was someone else Thomas hadn't seen since the day the soldiers returned—but he was glad to do so now.

"Thomas, I have been searching for you everywhere. The Sultan wants to see you before he goes to hunt. You are to come with me now."

Thomas saw Don Antonio's hand fall from the hilt of the dagger.

"We were about to leave." He made a bow, as though these men meant something to him. "It has been a pleasure I look forward to not repeating any time soon. Good day, gentlemen."

CHAPTER SIXTEEN

The Sultan waited in the throne room, an austere place designed to impress rather than offer comfort. Unusually for Moorish accommodation, there was a physical throne, an ornate object carved of dark wood imported from Africa. It was positioned in an alcove where light entered behind so that whoever sat there was bathed in illumination, but their face remained obscured. At the moment, the throne was empty. Instead, the Sultan lounged on cushions against one wall, a jug of sweet tea scenting the air. He looked at ease, as though he had no worries, and Thomas wondered at the man's powers of recovery. The Sultan was closer to his sixtieth year than fiftieth, his eyesight failing, but he appeared to have shrugged off the events of the past week—a battle, murder, plots—as though such things happened every day. Perhaps for someone such as him, they did.

"What have you found out?" he asked, his voice curt.

It was his way. The man made a score of decisions each day and had no time for the niceties of conversation.

Thomas stood at a respectful distance. "We have made a little progress, Malik. I have spoken with Aixa, some servants, and Zoraya. Tomorrow, we—"

"You spoke to Zoraya?"

"Yes, Malik."

"Who gave you permission to do so?"

"I told you I needed to speak with everyone, Malik, and you said I could do so. I didn't know I had to provide a list for approval. I cannot judge who possesses information or not until I have spoken to as many people as possible."

The Sultan made a noise. "I expect she was not pleased."

Thomas tried not to smile, gauging the Sultan's mood. "You are correct, Malik."

"Will you be visiting her again?"

"I don't know." It wasn't a complete lie. Thomas didn't want to air his suspicions of Zoraya yet, not to the man, it was claimed, who loved her above all other wives. Later, if need be. "We have a new line of enquiry."

"Tell me." The Sultan clicked his fingers, and the girl standing against one wall padded across and poured tea into a silvered glass before resuming her position. None was offered to anyone else.

"In the morning, we go to speak with the clerk who carried out the first investigation."

The Sultan made a noise again and Thomas recognised the dismissive nature of it, wondering if this was how the man conducted all his business, through hints and subtle body signals. This was a new side to the man, and Thomas realised he had stepped across an invisible boundary. Before, he had been the respected physician, the man who had saved the Sultan's son, who birthed his children. Now he was one more instrument to be directed and used.

"I remember the investigation. He discovered nothing. I had him stop and return to more fruitful work."

"I still believe speaking with him will be of use, if only to rule out certain lines of enquiry."

Abu al-Hasan Ali nodded, sipped at his tea. "Return tomorrow, then, after evening prayer. If I am not here, then speak to no one else."

"Are you expecting not to be here, Malik?"

The Sultan waved a hand. "There are reports the Spanish gather on our northern border. It seems my victory at Tajar has stirred up a hornets' nest. I may have to leave without warning. If I do, you are to continue your work, and remember—report only to me."

Thomas decided to keep his meeting with Faris al-Rashid to himself for the moment.

"What about your son, Malik?"

"Which one? I have a surfeit of sons at the moment, yet one more thanks to you."

"I meant Abu Abdullah," Thomas said. "Should I not

speak with him in your absence?"

"No. Particularly not that son. I will most likely be here tomorrow in any case and you can report to me directly. But if not, then tell no one, understand?"

Thomas nodded. "As you wish, Malik."

The Sultan's curt nod was a dismissal and Thomas backed from the room, head bowed. Before, he would have turned and stridden out, but now something had changed in their relationship and he felt his old position slipping away from him.

Olaf and Jorge stood outside the throne room where Thomas had left them. "We need to talk to those two girls to see if they've remembered anything else."

"It's Bazzu again, then," said Jorge.

"Olaf, I would speak with you later if I can?"

"You know where to find me." The tall northman turned away in the direction of the barracks.

"Is he under suspicion?" Jorge asked as he led the way through the courtyard of lions.

"At the moment, everyone and no one is under suspicion. But yes, after what Zoraya's children told you, he is. And don't forget, Olaf sold his services to the Sultan many years ago. A man willing to do so might sell himself again to a higher bidder. He sees the way this war is going—who would blame him for wanting to protect himself?"

"Then be careful when you see him. Olaf thinks nothing of killing men, even you."

The smell of spices and cooking grew stronger as they moved deeper into the working rooms surrounding the palace. Eventually they entered a large, busy kitchen. As they passed through, Jorge stole fresh bread from a girl who swatted him and laughed when he swatted back. This was his world, Thomas knew, one Jorge felt comfortable in. Unlike Thomas himself, who could work in the palace, but was glad to live on the other side of the river.

In Bazzu's room, the same wide table lay scattered with scrolls and papers which looked identical to those of the day before.

"Kitma and Mahja," Thomas said, raising the subject of the two servants who had witnessed Safya's murder, too impatient to respect the niceties. "I want to speak with them." The girls had been little use the day before, but perhaps by now, with some distance from their fear, they would remember more.

Bazzu looked up from the document she was reading. "Did Alisha suffer? Her wounds were fearful when I helped prepare her." She had obviously been giving thought to the attack on the girl.

"She wouldn't have known she had been struck before her heart stopped. It was swift."

"That is good, I suppose. But I have bad news for you. The other two are no longer here."

"We were with them yesterday," said Jorge.

"I know you were, my sweet. And I spoke with them afterwards and they had only kind words for the pair of you. But they have been sent from the city."

"Where? By whom?"

"Tahir sent them early this morning, before dawn. A caravan was travelling south to Malaka carrying silks and salted meat. It seems a message came a few days ago requesting additional servants be sent south. Tahir came and asked me himself if he could send those two."

Malaka again, Thomas thought. How convenient. "Why both of them?"

"I don't usually question the commands of the Vizier, but this time I did. It seemed strange after what had happened. He said he was worried about them, that staying within the harem would remind them of what happened, and if the killer returned, they would be in danger. It made sense so I agreed. Did they really see who he was?"

"You've heard the rumours?" said Jorge.

Bazzu snorted. "A djinn? Of course it was a djinn. A far more serious suspect than any man, I am sure."

"Did you believe the Vizier?" Thomas asked.

"What reason would I have to doubt him? He appeared concerned for their welfare. I am sorry—had I known you wanted to question them again, I would have held them back. I suppose you could always catch them up. A caravan moves slowly, and two men on fast horses would reach them before morning."

"I'm no horseman," Thomas said. His days of fast riding were long in the past.

"Nor I," said Jorge. "Besides, I doubt they'd be any more help than they were yesterday."

"If they've gone, so be it," Thomas said. "We also wanted to speak with Yasmina, but it seems she's in Malaka too."

"Yasmina?"

"She was with Helena on the night she was attacked. Nothing was made of it at the time, but I believe the two events are linked."

"You suspect it is the same man? After all this time?"

"That's what I intend to find out. It's some time ago now, but Yasmina might have recalled something that she missed in the shock of what happened."

"I believed her still in the employ of Zoraya."

"No longer," Thomas said. "We have spoken with Zoraya and I doubt we would be welcome again so soon."

Bazzu rose, the interview at an end. She came around the table and hugged Jorge, released him and turned to Thomas. She hugged him too. Her succulent body pressed against his in a way that made him uneasy, and when she finally released him, it was with a sultry laugh.

"Ah, my two beautiful men. Such memories, such bliss. Look after yourselves and each other. Catch this killer and perhaps I will reward you in ways you have never been rewarded before."

"I look forward to the moment," said Jorge, kissing her once more.

They had reached the doorway when Bazzu called after them.

"Thomas—how is Helena now? I was sad to see her leave the palace. She was such an asset to the harem. Such an enthusiast."

Thomas turned and Bazzu stared into his eyes, knowledge within her own.

"She is well. I will tell her you were asking after her."

"She is an agreeable companion for you?"

Thomas tried to interpret the smile on Bazzu's lips as anything other than knowing, and failed.

"I am not sure whether she's happy, but I don't believe her unhappy." It was not the question Bazzu had asked, but it was the only answer Thomas was willing to give.

"I am curious—do you enjoy living with her? She is a skilled woman in many ways. I hope she makes those ways known to you."

Thomas felt his face warm. "I prefer to keep that side of my life private. I'm sorry if I offend you."

"Offend me?" Bazzu glanced at Jorge as she laughed. "Tell him, my beautiful man, is it possible to offend me?"

"She cannot be offended, Thomas. God knows, I've tried often enough."

CHAPTER SEVENTEEN

"We are blocked at every turn," said Jorge as they passed back through the kitchen. Only a few workers remained, and Thomas realised it was close to *Asr*, the time of afternoon prayer.

"If I was a suspicious man, I might wonder what is happening here."

"You are a suspicious man."

"I didn't used to be, but I'm learning."

"Do you wonder about the manoeuvring behind these events?" asked Jorge.

"Or is there nothing more than coincidence here?"

"Certainly one should never underestimate the subtlety of coincidence. Still, it would have been good to talk to the girls again. They will have slept since the attack and perhaps recalled something new."

"Yasmina might have known something too, if we had been able to talk to her."

"If," said Jorge as they reached a junction. "The attack on her and Helena was half a year ago. She would have forgotten much by now."

Coming from the kitchens, they could have turned back towards the palace, or made their way out through the Alkazaba. The small township to the east of Al-Hamra housed workers and businesses servicing the palace with goods, furniture, fruit and vegetables, as well as livestock. It was a whole town above a town, one raised both physically and, if one were to believe the inhabitants, socially and spiritually as well. It was where the Sultan had asked Thomas to live when he made him the gift of Helena. Somewhere there lay a house he had been gifted, but never seen.

"I believe we have no one else to question today," said Jorge. "Perhaps we should return to the city and see if my new clothes are ready."

"I have more questions."

"Of whom?"

"I want to speak with Olaf Torvaldsson. If he's been training Zoraya's children, he might have seen or heard something."

"You can't believe she is behind these deaths, can you?" Jorge slowed, stopped.

"I don't know what I believe other than I need more information and Olaf might provide it. For all I know, it's he who is behind everything, or the pair of them together. Zoraya's a beautiful woman—enough to tempt any man."

"Even if they were lovers, why would he want to kill Safya? Or anyone else within the palace?"

Jorge turned towards the barracks lying beyond the township and Thomas fell into step beside him, thoughts tumbling together in his head, each one demanding attention.

"Because he was asked?" he said.

"By Zoraya?"

"Men have done worse than kill for a woman. Olaf's a soldier—killing means less to him than other men."

"Even the killing of a Sultana?" said Jorge.

"I believe Olaf regards his adopted land as home now, but can we be sure?" Thomas worked through ideas as his feet carried him down the slope, thoughts coming to him in a rush he barely filtered. "The war goes badly. What if he believes he can change its course?"

"Make himself Sultan?"

Thomas shook his head. "Not Sultan, he knows he wouldn't be accepted, but King, perhaps?"

"King Olaf?" Jorge barely suppressed a laugh.

"He knows the Sultan is making mistakes. He sees it every time there is a battle. Abu al-Hasan Ali isn't the man he was. Everyone sees it, not just Olaf. Zoraya wants to protect her children, to give them a future in a unified Spain. A long war puts that outcome in danger."

"You just said Olaf believes he can win the war."

"He's cleverer than that. It's not the war that needs to be won, but the peace. Peace with honour."

"Abu al-Hasan Ali doesn't believe we can make any kind of peace, honourable or otherwise," said Jorge.

"Exactly."

They stepped to one side as a cart pulled by two mules came trundling down the dirt roadway. Empty barrels bounced and knocked against each other on the back, the sound a rattling cacophony, dust rising from its wheels.

Jorge squinted against the sun and rubbed at his head where stubble was starting to show. "Did you know Olaf's first wife?" It seemed he was as weary of the intrigue as Thomas, seeking a little gossip to lighten their mood.

"Hardly. I was fifteen years old when she died and a long way from Gharnatah. I had enough troubles of my own to deal with."

They reached the edge of the township and stopped. A roadway led down through trees to where the barracks housing almost a thousand soldiers lay.

"Could you have saved her if you had been here?" said Jorge.

"Not at fifteen, I couldn't. I don't even know what caused her death, but birthing is a dangerous business."

"What if it was now? You've saved others, I know you have."

"And had others die."

"It is said if a birth is difficult, Thomas Berrington is the man to call."

"Don't believe everything you hear. I'm human, the same as every other physician."

"But better than most."

Thomas preferred his work to be appreciated rather than acknowledged. "It's ancient history anyway. We should be talking about Zoraya—she has light hair and fine features—"

"A fine body, too," Jorge interrupted.

"You would notice that more than me."

Jorge only smiled.

"She resembles the northern women," Thomas said, "and we know Olaf still misses his first wife. I'll keep a watch on him, but I want to talk to his men, too. One of them might have seen something, heard something, suspected something. I need you to go back and talk to any servants you can find. Soldiers and servants, those are the eyes and ears of the palace even if they don't speak of what they see. Meet me at the eastern entrance when they call *Maghrib*."

"You know, I considered my selection for this task as some kind of cruel joke," said Jorge. "*What can I bring?* I wondered. And then as I lay unable to sleep last night, I made a decision. Perhaps choosing me was deliberate and meant to cause us to fail. But if so, they have underestimated this eunuch. I'm more of a man than all of them put together. I will catch this killer, with your aid, and when we do, I may just strangle him with my bare hands."

Thomas nodded and slapped Jorge on the shoulder.

He left his hand there a moment, feeling the play of muscle beneath his palm. Before this was finished, they might have need of that strength.

Thomas found Olaf in his rooms adjoining the barracks and practice yard. The accommodation was spartan, with no decoration or finery. From beyond Olaf's workroom came the sound of female voices, too low to make out what was being said.

Olaf rose and embraced Thomas, almost squeezing the breath from him. Thomas had known the general a long time—stood beside him in battle, witnessed the ferocity of the man—but this was the first time he had ever felt uneasy in his presence.

Fortunately, Olaf appeared not to notice Thomas's discomfort.

"So, what do you want with me—am I a suspect too?"

Thomas gave the big man a glance, but Olaf's face was unreadable.

"Why weren't you asked to look into this matter after the first killings?"

"I understand the reasons. I am not a subtle man. Give me a sword and a battle to fight and I am content, but do not expect me to think."

"You miss little, though. What have you seen or

heard? Where should I be looking?" Perhaps a direct question would provide some answers.

Olaf took a seat, a straight-backed chair which he dwarfed. It seemed he too preferred wood over cushions.

"Have you eaten today?"

"I had something at the inn with Jorge this morning."

Olaf nodded at the mention of the name. "He might have made a good soldier had they not made him soft. Have the two of you made any progress?"

"We are asking a lot of questions, but I'm not sure that counts as progress."

Thomas was concentrating so hard on Olaf's body language, he almost jumped out of his chair when the man raised his voice and called out. A moment later, a slim figure entered the room. She caught sight of Thomas and hurriedly drew her veil across her face.

"Bring us water, and some of that lamb left over from midday. A little of the bread you made, too."

"I don't—" Thomas started, but Olaf raised a hand.

"Eat. You've met Lubna, haven't you?" Olaf nodded at the disappearing figure. "Helena tells me you are going to offer her a place in your household."

"She tells me the same, but I have made no decision as yet." Thomas wanted to get the conversation back on track, but Olaf had seized its direction for now.

"I would consider it a personal favour if you took her in. She cooks better than Helena, and she's a willing worker. Not a beauty like my other daughters, but not displeasing to look at, either, is she?"

Thomas wondered exactly what was being offered. A blunt man, with few social graces, Olaf no doubt considered his offer generous.

"No, she is not displeasing to look at." Thomas knew it was the wrong thing to say, but didn't want to risk antagonising the man.

"Think on it, my friend. But perhaps we should discuss the matter later," said Olaf as Lubna returned with plates and cups. She laid them on a side table and withdrew, but not before her eyes had met Thomas's and he'd read a hope there that troubled him.

Olaf took bread and meat and chewed. After a moment, Thomas did the same, only recognising his hunger as he put the food in his mouth.

"Did your wife make this?" he asked.

"She and Lubna. The girl bakes well, don't you think? And she has other skills, too."

"I will give it consideration," Thomas said. Were the entire family this persistent? "Why has she no place already?"

"She did have, but Lubna is a girl of strong principle and would not comply with all the duties expected of her by her master."

"I see."

Olaf only nodded. "So what do you need from me in return for this favour you intend to do my family?"

Thomas pulled more meat from the chunk on his plate and wrapped it inside the still-warm bread. And Olaf claimed he lacked subtlety?

"I want permission to talk to your men. I need to discover if someone could steal into a Sultana's bathing chamber and take a life, then escape without anyone seeing them. The man who did this would have been covered in blood." Thomas stared at Olaf's face, seeking any clue to what was going on in the man's mind.

"The same with the other killings, too. These attacks were not subtle."

"You saw the first bodies?"

"I am the Sultan's General. He called for me, just not for the clever stuff."

"Were they the same?"

"Swift and clean. Fine executions." Olaf stopped when he saw the look on Thomas's face. "Forgive me, but I am what I am. Death is what I deal in and these deaths were done with much grace and strength."

"A soldier, then?" Olaf was either the cleverest man in Gharnatah or Thomas's suspicions, vague as they were, were misplaced.

"Only a trained soldier could have done it so well."

Thomas leaned forward. "But why wasn't he seen? That is something I don't understand. A man covered in blood, fleeing through the palace? Someone must have seen him."

Olaf nodded. "However skilled the man, it would be impossible to get close enough to kill in the way he did and not get caught in the spray of blood, not when a blade cuts that deep. But he wasn't seen, and I don't

know why not. There are people throughout the palace who should have seen him and didn't."

Thomas chewed his food a moment, watching Olaf keenly as he started to look for the answers he really sought.

"We visited Zoraya this morning."

Olaf nodded.

"A strange woman."

No reaction.

"I believe you are teaching her sons to use the sword?"

Olaf laughed. "Teaching them badly. They are poor students. I only hope they never have to use my lessons in anger for both are poor swordsmen. I wager even you could beat them in a fight."

Thomas smiled. "Was it the Sultan who asked you to train them? I would have thought a man as important as you would not bother with such lessons."

"Zoraya came to me," said Olaf. "I tried to persuade her to use one of my arms-men, but she insisted she wanted me."

"You have a reputation," Thomas said. He licked his fingers clean and stood. "Can I talk with your men, ask if they have heard anything?"

"You will need to be careful, but ask away. There may be some rumour that hasn't reached my ears yet, though your friend Jorge is better suited to that kind of work. The girls of the harem will have been closer than my guards, who are not allowed in all places."

"We will speak with them, too, but I want to talk with your men first."

"As you will. Say it is with my permission." Olaf rose. He had agreed readily enough to the questioning of his men—but if he had carried out the attacks himself, then he knew Thomas would discover nothing. And it seemed there was a price to pay for his agreement.

"I'll tell Lubna to come to your house this evening, shall I?"

CHAPTER EIGHTEEN

It was dark by the time Thomas and Jorge made their way down the lesser slope from the Alkazaba. *Maghrib* was being called as they met at the gate, the faithful within the palace moving away to say prayers, and it formed a natural punctuation to their questions. By the time they reached the inn on al-Hattabin square, the devout were returning to the streets to find and eat their evening meal.

Thomas slowed, looking for a spare table. He saw Carlos Rodriguez deep in conversation, but hoped the man hadn't seen him in turn. Unfortunately, Jorge had caught sight of the merchant too.

"Do you think my new clothes are ready yet?"

"The ones you're wearing will last a day or two more. I'm too tired for conversation, and if he sees us, he'll want to play Mancala. The way I feel, he might even win."

"I can't wear the same clothes again tomorrow." A look of horror showed on Jorge's face.

Thomas turned away. "Let's find a quiet corner and get something to eat, then I might feel more in the mood to pander to your sense of fashion."

Thomas saw a table set against the far wall and started towards it. He supposed he should be grateful to Rodriguez for providing Jorge's clothing, but the day had already been long and his mind seethed with possibilities, the constant worrying at details sapping his energy.

Jorge remained on the edge of the tables and Thomas noticed he didn't stand out as he had the evening before. He continued to draw attention, but now it was because of his height and beauty. If anything, he was more handsome without the clothes of the harem.

All around him, people ate, talked and drank. Some, like Thomas, were dressed in plain robes and headdress, though few with the full tagelmust. Others were attired more ornately in an attempt to advertise their wealth. And then there was the detritus to be found in any city. The waifs and strays in rags, boys and girls in equal number, but cleaner than in many places thanks to the washing fountains and basins scattered throughout the streets and squares. There were fewer women, but more than might be expected. Some covered themselves completely, but those were the minority. Most wore a simple headdress to cloak their hair, others even going

bare-headed. The city of Gharnatah was a melting pot for the cultures of the south and west. It drew in the peoples of Africa, Arabia, Turkey, Italy, France, and Spain beyond the borders of al-Andalus. In spite of over three centuries of warfare, trade continued to thrive, both inward and out. The fertile plain around the city provided much needed food for the rest of Hispania. Almond and olive groves climbed the foothills of the Sholayr, together with mulberry, fig, olives, pomegranates, lemon, lime and orange. Al-Andalus was still the larder of Spain. In return, other goods made their way inward. Wine, of course, in spite of it being against the law of Islam, and other darker trades: weapons, armour, raw metal, and slaves. War was war, but trade was trade, and Thomas knew that in the end, trade always won.

"Thomas!" Khadar al-Abidah came weaving through the tables, still lithe despite his age and size. "You want something to drink, to eat? Where is your... your friend?" There was only the slightest of hesitations, but after a day listening with suspicion to a hundred answers, Thomas's ears were finely tuned to such subtleties.

"Yes to everything. And my friend is over there trying to decide whether fashion or hunger is more important to him." Thomas saw Jorge turn towards him and waved for him to come and sit.

"Does he like his room? I have others now if he wants to change."

"You were full this morning," Thomas said, "and

claiming extra payment as I recall for the room you did manage to find. What happened in between?"

Khadar moved aside to allow Jorge to seat himself. "They fear the djinn! It's the talk of the city—a demon stalks our streets, hungry for blood."

"There is no djinn," Thomas said, but Khadar had already stopped listening as he called to a serving girl who was snaking between tables to clear them of bowls.

Unfortunately, Jorge's passage had not gone unnoticed.

"Do you have time for a game tonight, Thomas?" Carlos Rodriguez approached their table as Khadar moved away to organise the food.

"Not tonight, I'm sorry."

"Are my new clothes ready?" asked Jorge.

"You may call for them in the morning."

"Tonight would be better," said Jorge.

"My storerooms is closed for the night."

"But you have a key," Thomas said.

"You ask a lot of a simple merchant."

Thomas smiled. "If you were a simple merchant, then perhaps I would be, but everyone knows you are more than that. And no, don't pretend false modesty. I would be grateful if you could help Jorge tonight, we have much to do tomorrow."

"Perhaps the promise of a game of Mancala will loosen my resolve before we have to leave at this ungodly hour to do *trade*." He spat the final word as though tainted.

"Fetch the board in a while, then, after we have eaten."

The serving girl arrived, tiny, dark haired, sullen faced, but her expression changed when she laid eyes on Jorge. She stopped dead in her tracks, eyes wide, the tray containing two bowls of stew and a jug of wine starting to tip forward. Thomas reached out and retrieved the tray before their supper landed on the floor.

"Boo!" said Jorge, his voice quiet so as to attract no further attention, loud enough to make the girl jump. She stepped back, staggered across an uneven paving stone, turned and ran.

"I thought I was meant to be passing unnoticed," said Jorge, looking down at his clothing.

"It's because your head is shaved," Thomas said. "And there's a softness about you she recognises. I thought women were meant to like you."

"Some do. Some don't. I've ceased worrying about the latter as there is always a surfeit of the former." Jorge helped himself to the larger bowl of stew and drained half his flagon in one draught. "What am I to do? I can't woo them all, however much I might wish it. And she was a little young and skinny for my taste. Pretty, though, if she would only stop scowling."

"Khadar only employs the pretty ones, boys and girls both. He says it's good for trade."

"I suspect he's right. This stew is good."

"Better than that made by my ... by Helena."
Recently, Thomas had to stop himself calling her his

195

wife. He had no idea how the notion of marriage kept popping into his head. It wasn't one he welcomed. Even so, he knew most men would be jealous of his position. A courtesan, even one with a damaged face, would be highly prized. Thomas wondered if it was Helena's beauty he was afraid of—a reminder of what he had lost, the pain carried across the years in memories he kept hidden even from himself.

"I thought you must have a maid," said Jorge.

"No, Helena cooked the stew."

"I would offer her congratulations, but she would be upset I knew she cooked."

Jorge fell silent as he filled his belly, tearing off hunks of dark bread and dipping them into the fragrant stew. Either mutton or goat, no matter which, it tasted good. Thomas spooned the mixture into his mouth, hungry again. When he was finished, he wiped his bowl with the last of his bread while Jorge looked on with an expression of mild disgust. *He must have known hunger*, Thomas thought, *but perhaps not for some time*. He knew from his own experience it wasn't something you forgot.

"What did you find out from Olaf today?" Jorge asked. "Anything to help us?"

"In a moment. I want to hear what you discovered first." Thomas had important news, but a lassitude filled him almost too deep to ignore. He lifted his cup of wine and sipped, determined to make it last.

"Nothing. I spoke to everyone I could within the harem. The courtesans, the wives, the servants, even the other eunuchs. Nobody admits to knowing a single piece of useful information."

"You pressed them?"

"As hard as I dared. Remember I have to return there when our task is finished."

"If it ever is."

"You talked with Olaf—is he under suspicion or not?"

"I am undecided. He's not the kind of man you accuse to his face, not if you want to walk away alive. He appears innocent enough, though if I had pushed him harder … I don't know."

"It might come to that. How would we handle the situation if it did?"

"We'd need men of our own."

Jorge learned forward. "That noble who threatened us —he did threaten us, didn't he?"

Thomas nodded. "I believe so. What of him?"

"I don't like him. Don't trust him. Another one for our list?"

"Another one for the list," Thomas agreed. "Together with Zoraya, her sons, and Olaf. And…" Thomas recalled the Sultan's order to report only to himself. "Abu Abdullah too, perhaps." He watched Jorge closely, interested in his reaction at mention of Abu al-Hasan Ali's heir.

Jorge was unsurprised, which told Thomas much. "He has eighteen years now. He's a man full grown and believes he can run this city better than his father."

"Except Abu al-Hasan Ali isn't ready to step aside yet," Thomas said.

"And in truth, I believe Abu Abdullah a weak man compared to his father. You know him well enough, what do you think?"

"He's strong in body, certainly, but he lacks the inner confidence needed to rule, to get men to follow him without question."

"Olaf wouldn't take his orders," said Jorge.

"Could they be in this together?"

"All three of them?" Jorge sat back and looked around. "Against his own father?"

"Maybe not all three. I don't know. Abu Abdullah and Olaf, say?"

Jorge shook his head. "I can't see it. Nor Abu Abdullah and Zoraya either. No—we are wrong, Abu Abdullah might be weak, but he wouldn't plot to kill his father's wife."

"There are other sons." Thomas saw his words bring a smile to Jorge's lips. "You spoke with Zoraya's boys. They're close in age to Abu Abdullah. Are they ambitious?"

"Ambitious enough to plot murder?" said Jorge. "Perhaps. And they will no doubt be afraid of what happens to them if Abu al-Hasan Ali is deposed."

"Retaliate before you're attacked. A good strategy," Thomas said, and something in his tone made Jorge frown. "Zoraya is raising them as Spanish nobility. You know why, don't you?"

"Of course. She sees the way the war goes. When the Spanish fought amongst themselves, we were left alone. Since Fernando married Isabel, they have a common purpose and powerful allies. I don't know how long we have until we are defeated. A year, ten years, twenty? But defeat is our ultimate destination, there is no doubt of it. What better way to maintain power than to become Spanish yourself?"

"And what better way to gain power than to kill your rivals?"

"Abu Abdullah is their rival, not Safya or Aixa."

"Both are powerful in their own right. The mothers of princes always are. And they would want to make the Sultan and his sons appear weak. If he can't even protect the women in his own harem, how can he protect a city and a land?"

"How do we prove any of this?" said Jorge. "Prove it well enough to make an accusation against the woman the Sultan loves more than any other? Even if we had her confession, he might choose to ignore it."

Thomas felt what little energy their conversation had sparked drain from him. Jorge was right. They were dealing with far more than a simple crime here. This was politics, and he hated politics.

"We have to ignore the possibility and continue as if we can make a difference. That or give up."

"We can't give up. We wouldn't be allowed to, and I wouldn't want to." Jorge dragged his thumb and forefinger across his cheeks, tiredness there, too. "So tell me, if you didn't confront Olaf—and I don't blame you for not doing so—what did you find out?"

Thomas knew Jorge was right. They had to go on. He took a breath, trying to summon his energy.

"I talked to the guards. I went to the barracks and spoke with those on duty yesterday. It took me longer than it should because I found myself checking their hands."

Jorge smiled. "And did you find our three-fingered culprit?"

Thomas shook his head. "I found a score of them. Have you any idea how many soldiers are missing those two fingers? It's a hazard of their profession, it seems. Most hold a shield in their left hand, which makes it vulnerable."

"Even so, the killer does have those fingers missing. It is one of our few clues."

"I don't dismiss it," Thomas said. "But as with you, everyone claims to have seen nothing at all. The consensus is it truly was a djinn that carried out the attack. The guards all claim it would be impossible for someone to find their way into the harem without being seen. Particularly a man dressed head to toe in black, as our killer was."

"So we are no further forward?" Jorge drained his cup and refilled it. He held the jug out to Thomas, who nodded.

I am a weak man, he thought, *I allow myself to be seduced by Helena, and now I'm getting drunk again for the second night in a row. What next?*

"Not quite," he said. "As I was returning, I stopped to speak with a guard I hadn't seen before. I had to show the seal to gain re-entrance to the palace. I almost neglected to ask him, thinking only of finding you and getting away, but something made me turn back. This one seemed more intelligent, more obliging than the others. He claims it is possible for someone to find their way into the harem unseen, if they have the right knowledge and a little assistance."

"Assistance? So are we looking for more than one man?"

"Or man and woman. The assistance required does not demand strength. The guard's name is Galib ibn-Ubaid. Do you know him?"

Jorge shook his head, smiling. "Guards don't talk to me. I think they believe I might contaminate them. In truth, I make them uneasy. So no, I might recognise the man if you pointed him out, but the name means nothing. Is he a Moor?"

"Arab, I think. Tall. Strong."

"Sounds interesting."

Thomas gave Jorge an irritated glance, never sure how seriously to take his words when he spoke this way.

"He told me there are ways a man can pass through the palace undiscovered, secret ways to move from place to place unseen. They are there for a purpose. For a concubine to find her way to a room for a secret assignation. For a man to gain access to the harem when he shouldn't."

"I have heard tales, but as far as I know, no such places exist."

"Oh, they exist. Galib says he will show me tomorrow how it can be done."

"Not today?"

"There wasn't time. He had duties to return to, and he said he wanted to consult with others to work out how a man could find his way to where Safya was killed. I plan to return first thing in the morning and have him show me. Our killer may have left some sign of his passing."

"This Galib ibn-Ubaid, can he be trusted?"

"I don't know the man, but he seemed loyal and honest. I'll talk with him more tomorrow. Perhaps Olaf can assign him to assist us."

"Stranger things have happened on the hill. By the way, that merchant has been staring at you for the past five minutes. If we are to get me more suitable clothing, I think you owe him his game. Are you going to let him win?"

"I never have yet."

"But tonight you will?"

"Why would I do that?"

"Because you are a kind and generous soul who would not wish to see me garbed in rags."

Thomas sighed. "You realise my reputation will be lost?"

Jorge shrugged. "You sound as if you expect me to care."

CHAPTER NINETEEN

In the darkness of the night, Helena shook Thomas's shoulder. He came awake slowly, exhaustion clouding his mind. He saw nothing, sensing only a shape as she sat up and leaned over him.

"I'm tired," he groaned.

"My face hurts. The scar—it burns."

He sat, the last trace of sleep departing. There had been a dream of being chased through corridors, but it faded at once as he turned to Helena, feeling out for her in the dark. She wasn't where he expected and his hand grasped at air. He moved left, bumped into something soft and curved, her right breast, and jerked away. When he returned, he found her shoulder and traced her neck to the jawline. Delicately, he touched her cheek. The scar felt warm beneath his fingers and Helena gasped.

"I need light." He turned and found his way by touch to the door. Outside in the hallway an oil lamp burned

low, always lit in the event he was called out during the night. When he returned, Helena was sitting up in bed, the covers pooled at her waist. Thomas tried not to stare, but concern overrode any sense of shame and he moved the lamp closer to her face.

"Is it bad?" she said.

"A little inflamed, nothing more. I'll make up a fresh cream to soothe the ache."

"Some poppy would make me feel better." Helena reclined now his examination was finished, making no effort to cover herself.

Thomas sighed. "It's not wise to overuse some medicines."

"But it aches. It aches deep inside my face." In the lamplight, her eyes glittered and Thomas knew he could refuse her nothing.

"Perhaps a little."

"Thank you." She smiled, relaxing against the pillows. "The Sultan showed great kindness in sending me to you."

Thomas drew a robe around himself and descended the stairs, the lamp held high. Outside, the courtyard was starlit, pale cloud streaking the sky. On the hillside, lights burned in al-Hamra's many windows. The night wasn't quite silent, it never was, but at this hour, it was as quiet as the city ever became. Occasionally a dog barked, a man shouted. Here in the Albayzin, life was good and bad in equal measure. The people too.

Thomas pushed open the workshop door and went

inside, lighting more lamps. The poppy first, he thought, a weak mixture, just enough to take the edge from Helena's pain. He turned to his workbench, almost dropping the lamp in shock as a slim figure moved beneath a blanket on the narrow cot where he had slept himself on so many nights.

"Thomas, is that you? What are you doing here?" Lubna tried to sit up. Unlike her sister, she held the blanket against her body, covering herself to the neck.

"I could ask the same of you."

"I..." Lubna wiped a hand across her face, more asleep than awake. "My sister came for me. You told my father I could come, didn't you?"

Thomas tried to remember one conversation among the many he had had over the past two days and suspected she was right, as he recalled the way Olaf had tricked him. Not a stupid man, despite his protests. Thomas knew it would be difficult if his suspicions proved correct—how would he deal with accusing a man whose daughter shared his bed? And now there was a second one in his house.

"So you came. Why are you sleeping in the workshop?"

"Helena told me this is my place. Is there somewhere else I should be?"

Thomas shook his head. "No. Not at the moment. Do you plan on staying?"

"I have nowhere else to go." Lubna cast her eyes down. When she raised them, they contained a

question. "Did you not mean what you said to my father?"

"I'm a man of my word," Thomas said, uncomfortable.

"Then I will stay."

"I will find you somewhere better to sleep."

"This cot suits me fine. I am small, and I like the smell in here. What brings you downstairs in the middle of the night?"

"Helena's scar pains her. I need to make up some cream and mix a little poppy." As Lubna swung her legs to the flagstone floor, he turned away, conscious of the delicacy of her feet and an unwelcome emotion their sight raised in him.

He listened to the sounds she made as she rose, a rustle of clothing.

"You can turn around now." There was a murmur of amusement beneath the words. "Can I watch you work, or will I disturb you?"

"You won't disturb me. I'm only mixing herbs and oils. Heating some poppy heads to extract a tincture. It's not exciting."

"I am interested. I was looking around earlier, you have so many different things here. I recognised a few, but most are a mystery."

"Did you touch anything? Some of these bottles contain poisons." For a moment, he scanned the shelves, searching for anything out of place. So many bottles, pots and phials, each labelled in his own hand, so many

of them lethal if used in the wrong way: sensel, meterre, gemoro, burbira. He stopped looking, afraid.

Lubna smiled. "I touched nothing. But I am interested."

"Truly?" Thomas turned away, reaching for a bundle of poppy heads that hung from a hook. He pulled three loose and examined them for signs of the white putty being exuded. He found none, so reached for more. If he couldn't find any, it would take an hour to steep the seeds in water. He knew he should make time to prepare a supply of the liquor—both for Helena and his other patients. But time was a commodity he had in short supply.

"What are you looking for?" Lubna came to stand beside him, her slight body leaning inward as far as she could without brushing against him.

"The heads of the poppy, if they are mature enough, exude a white milk. This is the opium that eases pain. I am looking for signs."

Lubna reached for some more poppy heads hanging from a hook to the left, barely able to reach. Her fingertips knocked them loose and she caught the tied bunch before it landed on the bench. She bent close, examining each in turn, and Thomas smiled at her concentration.

"You really are interested in all of this, aren't you?"

"Shh…" said Lubna, focusing on her task.

Thomas's bunch of heads yielded nothing and he pulled three more free and broke them up, allowing the

small, dark seeds to drop into a mortar. He turned and retrieved dry straw and twigs and started making a small fire in a depression set into the stone wall. He let the fire catch and returned to the bench, began adding water to the seeds.

"Is this what you are looking for?" Lubna held two heads out to him. Each exhibited a sticky substance oozing from cracks in their sides.

"It is." Thomas took the poppies from her.

"Can I watch how it is done?"

"If you want." He used a small knife to open the sides of the poppy head and scraped the milk, now partially dried, into a small bowl. By the time he had removed the sticky milk from the outside, the head was oozing more and he teased this out and added it to the first.

"Get me that bottle over there, it's raw alcohol."

Thomas watched, making sure she retrieved the right one, pleased when she showed only a little hesitation. She turned and held the bottle out to him, a question on her face, and he nodded. He poured a little of the alcohol into the bowl and swirled it around. Lubna, back at his side, stared in fascination.

Thomas glanced down, amused at how she leaned forward, her eyes keen. He recalled someone else, even younger than her, doing the same beside an old man in a stone hut high in the mountain range that separated France from Spain, and how that fascination had sparked

an interest that brought that boy to where he now stood mixing the same liquor.

"Do you think you can do this?"

"Me?"

"Swirl the alcohol around in the bowl, let it dissolve all the milk until only liquid remains." He demonstrated.

When Thomas placed the bowl on the bench, Lubna reached for it, hesitant.

"You can do no harm."

Her slim brown fingers closed around the bowl and she lifted it. Her first attempt almost sent liquid spilling over the rim, but she quickly adjusted until soon her movements mirrored Thomas's almost exactly.

"Good." He was pleased to see the smile that fleetingly touched her lips before she suppressed it. He turned away, picking out the herbs and mixtures for the salve. A little remained in a jar, but it was always more effective when freshly mixed.

Thomas set small brass scales on the bench and weighed the ingredients, adding some to one stone bowl, the remainder to a second. He caught Lubna trying to watch him at the same time as mixing the opium tincture.

"How is that coming along?" he asked, and her eyes darted back to the bowl. She brought it across to show him and he nodded. "Yes, it's ready. Pour a little over half into a cup, then add wine from the barrel over there. Mix it well and take it up to Helena."

"Me?"

"Yes, you."

Lubna tipped the contents out. Thomas watched to ensure she didn't add too much, pleased to see she took her time, pouring only a little more than required. She took the cup to the barrel and opened the tap gently, allowing dark wine to dribble in.

"Enough?" she asked, her back turned but knowing he was watching.

"A little more … yes, good."

Lubna straightened and left the workshop without looking back. Thomas returned to the salve. It was already half finished when she returned several minutes later.

"She drank it?"

Lubna nodded.

"All of it?"

She nodded again, something taut in her face, as though she held some emotion in check.

"She can be rude when she is in pain," Thomas said. "I've learned to ignore her."

Lubna made a soft snorting noise. "Then she must have been in pain much of her life." She came and stood beside him again, her left arm touching his side. Thomas was conscious of her closeness, the pressure of their contact rising and falling as he mixed first one bowl, then the other.

"I can help with one of those if you want."

"I expect you could. But this is no job for a woman."

Lubna let her breath loose. "Are there no women physicians?"

"There are. What I meant was…" Thomas hesitated, his hands still working, then he pushed the bowl along the bench. "It needs to be done hard. Everything must be ground to a soft paste."

The tendons in Lubna's arms stood out as she put effort into the mixing, and slowly her breath came harder. Thomas returned to the other bowl, a mix of seeds and berries, and started to grind them to a fine powder. When it was done, he took down two jars, one containing a white cream extracted from the grease which coated a sheep's wool, the other a pale golden oil. He put a little of each into a third bowl, poured in the fine powder from his own, then went to see how Lubna was getting on.

She glanced at him, her mouth compressed from the effort, then asked, "Is it finished yet?"

"Stop a moment." Thomas dipped the tip of his finger into the mixture, ran it along the side of the bowl, feeling for any residual coarseness before nodding. "It's ready." He took the bowl and scraped the contents into the one he had already completed, using a wooden spill to stir the mixture.

Lubna came to stand beside him, once more close enough to press into his side, her eyes locked on his work.

"How do you know all these things?" she asked.

"Books, good teachers, a great deal of practice. I was given a note of introduction to the school in Malaka. I spent three years watching and learning, and then they

allowed me to practise a little, and then to practise some more. But you never stop learning."

"Not all physicians are as you," said Lubna.

"No, not all. Some have lost their way. When we ruled this entire land, we knew more than we do now."

A smile touched Lubna's lips. "We, Thomas? Are you a Moor now, like me?"

He smiled and patted his chest with his palm. "In here I am. And you? You are not like your sister, are you?" Even as he spoke, he knew his words might be interpreted the wrong way, but Lubna seemed to accept what he said.

"After Helena's mother died, my father lived alone for some years before he took a Berber wife. I think he believed she might bear him sons, but she did not. I am the only child they have, and I am sure when I was born, Father lost heart and gave up the pleasures of the flesh for fear of bringing even more women into the world."

"You're not bitter?"

"Why would I be bitter?"

He shook his head. "I don't know. It sounds a sad tale, somehow."

"Not sad. My father is incapable of being sad. Pain and loss and anger, all those emotions he has in plenty. But sadness he does not recognise. I think he simply moved on."

"And your mother?"

"She lives in his house still. Cooks his meals when he

is at home, which is rarely. He lives to fight, revels in battle."

"I like your father," Thomas said, because it was the truth—he had liked Olaf a great deal, and found himself conflicted now the man was under suspicion.

"So do I. I love him. But I know him for what he is—a hard man."

Thomas shook his head. "You do him a disservice."

"Then perhaps you know him better than I do." Lubna turned away. "Have you finished your salve? I am tired now and would like to go back to bed."

"Yes, I'm finished." Thomas took the bowl and carried it to the doorway. He stopped, meaning to apologise, but Lubna had her back to him, already drawing her robe over her head, and he turned away quickly.

As he started to close the door, she said, "You and the eunuch are the talk of the hill with this fruitless task you have been set."

Thomas hesitated. Lubna sat on the cot, the rough blanket pulled to her chin.

"Why pointless?"

"No one expects you to succeed. How can you when you seek a spirit?"

"So you believe in the djinn?"

Lubna shook her head. "No. But most do."

"You think we are wasting our time."

"You have better things to do."

He hesitated, wanting to tell her she was wrong, but all that came was, "I made a promise to the Sultan."

Lubna released an arm from beneath the blanket and waved it at the shelves, the books, the instruments. "You know all of this. I have heard it said you are the best surgeon in al-Andalus, perhaps the best in the whole of Spain. You are wasting your talents on this stupid investigation."

"I made a promise," Thomas said again. "And people have died."

"And if someone dies because you do not do your job?"

It was the same accusation Helena had made, but from this slip of a woman, it cut deeper. Thomas wondered why he felt such an obligation to complete the task, to find the killer and whoever guided him, and all he could come up with was duty. The same sense of duty that made him a good surgeon. The same sense of duty that would not let him turn away from the quest, however ill-equipped he might be. He believed they had made some progress. There were threads to untangle and trace, one more to follow when dawn came, which wasn't far away. He turned from the room without giving Lubna an answer.

The sky was lightening in the courtyard as he passed alongside the wall. From the mosque beneath the hill, the muezzin began calling the faithful to prayer.

When he entered the bedchamber, Helena was asleep, the opium bringing her relief. She sprawled on the bed

and Thomas stared at her for a moment, awed as always by her beauty, but feeling no other emotion. Her effect on him was purely physical, and it was no longer enough. Perhaps it never had been.

He knelt on the bed and applied the salve to the red line across her face. She stirred in her sleep, but didn't wake, and when he was done, Thomas dressed and walked into town.

CHAPTER TWENTY

Jorge was snoring softly when Thomas entered the room. Instead of waking him, he turned to the small table and took a seat. *Let the man enjoy his dreams a little longer.* It was too early for the palace to be awake, and Thomas was still tired himself. He had slept barely three hours before Helena woke him.

As he stared at the sleeping man, a smile softened Thomas's normally stern expression. Even in repose, Jorge was distinct from other men. He lay half turned on his side, chest uncovered, one arm beneath his head, the other draped over the side of the bed. A leg had crept clear of the rough blanket and Thomas watched the foot twitch. Thomas turned his attention to Jorge's face and saw his eyes roll beneath closed lids. He had observed the same in other men, women, and some animals. Dogs dreamed this way, their legs running as they chased imaginary hares. He wondered what Jorge dreamt of. The

women of the harem, or something darker? His face looked at ease, so perhaps it was the women.

Jorge's skin was soft, smooth—partly a result, Thomas knew, of the mutilation done against him. Lying revealed as he was, the changes were even more dramatic. Dressed in the rough clothing Carlos Rodriguez had supplied, Jorge might pass for an ordinary man, but even then people noticed him. Thomas had seen them stare, men and women alike, seen them look and turn away, unsure what it was about the man that attracted them; perhaps feeling guilt at their attraction. Thomas knew Jorge was aware of it, but never seemed concerned. He wondered if it was the same way within the harem, or whether Jorge resented being a pretty plaything to the women there. It was all conjecture, fantasy, and Thomas laid his head on the table and closed his eyes. For a moment only, he promised himself.

Thomas jerked so hard, he kicked out and sent a chair tumbling to the floor with a loud clatter. He had been unaware of the moment he slipped from consciousness into slumber, but his waking came in an instant. A deep noise sounded from below, barrels rolling into a cellar. It must have been that which roused him.

He stood, unsteady a moment, then took four paces and shook Jorge's shoulder, the skin smooth beneath his hand. Jorge rolled over, burrowing beneath the covers.

"No sleep for either of us until this is over," Thomas said.

"I have an urge to kill someone," Jorge muttered into the bedclothes.

"Then make use of those urges and get up. Khadar has put out bread, cheese and olives for us." Thomas returned to the small table. "We have much to do today."

"Turn your back on me at your peril," Jorge grunted, swinging his legs from the bed.

"I hear that said often in regard to eunuchs, but I dismiss such rumour."

Jorge dressed in the clothes they had bought from Carlos Rodriguez the night before, the merchant holding out for a high price even after winning his first ever game of Mancala against Thomas. Dressed, Jorge looked less conspicuous than on the day he'd arrived, but still there was an other-worldly aura around him that made him stand out. There was nothing that could be done about that—it was part of the man himself.

He started to wrap a length of dyed cloth around his head.

"Wait," Thomas said, rising.

"What, you want to study my head now?"

Thomas reached out and ran a hand over Jorge's skull, feeling the roughness of stubble. He ran the back of a finger along Jorge's cheek.

"And I love you, too, my friend, but later, perhaps," said Jorge.

"You hair is growing out fast."

"Of course it is. I've had little enough time to remove it. I have been busy, or did you fail to notice?"

"Let it grow. On your cheeks too. It will make for a good disguise. No one believes a eunuch can grow hair."

Jorge rolled his eyes. "Show me this poor excuse for a meal, surgeon, and let us get this day begun, the sooner it will be finished."

———————————

They went first to the garrison quarters beside the palace, a large stone building with a red-tiled roof. Thomas wanted to find the guard he had spoken with the day before, eager to discover more of the secret ways he claimed ran through the palace.

They asked for the duty officer of the day and were directed to a small office at the rear of a long building. Thomas expected to have to introduce himself and their purpose, but as they entered, a stocky man looked up and said, "So you're the two, are you? I'm told I must do whatever you ask, by order of the Sultan and Vizier both." His face showed what he thought of such orders. "So what is it you want?"

Thomas made no effort at drawing the meeting out. "I spoke with one of your guards yesterday, Galib ibn-Ubaid. I would speak with him again."

The officer uttered a short bark that could be interpreted as laughter. "So you speak with the dead, do you, surgeon?"

220

"I spoke with the man only yesterday."

"As well you might. But today he is dead, and the one who slew him has fled the city."

Thomas looked around, pulled a stool from beside the wall and sat.

"Explain."

For a moment, he thought the officer was about to refuse and he reached inside his robe and closed his hand around the Sultan's seal. Something in his eyes must have shown his resolve because the officer lost all bluster and breathed out, sitting back in his chair.

"It was a falling out over, of all things, a game of dice. Galib threw three sixes in a row. Darras accused him. Galib grew angry. Darras angrier still. Knives were drawn. Someone tried to stop them and was cut. Darras stabbed Galib through the heart. He died at once." The brusque repeating of the facts appalled Thomas, but he knew death was a constant presence among these men—something they believed might lie around the next corner for any of them. The less attention they gave it, the less power death held over them.

"This Darras, is he being searched for?"

"He will be long gone by now. Stole a horse, and in the confusion, nobody saw in which direction he rode. He'll be thirty miles away or more by now."

"Was it truly a stupid argument or did something else lie behind it? Had there been friction between the men before?"

The officer lifted his hands in a gesture of

hopelessness. "As I said, one is dead, the other gone, that is all I know. All I need to know."

Thomas sighed. "And nobody here knows anything, I suppose?"

The officer smiled. "They told me you were a clever man."

Thomas stood, his blood quickening with anger. "Who gives you your orders?" His voice was louder than he intended. "Who are you really working for?"

The officer also rose to his feet, facing up to Thomas. "Working for? I work for the Sultan, and below him the Vizier, and below him Olaf Torvaldsson."

"You know what I mean!"

"Thomas, leave it." Jorge pulled at his robe. "Anger won't help us. Let us seek answers elsewhere while the day is still young."

"This man knows something." Thomas raised his hand, pointing. "And he is keeping it from us."

"Am I? Is it treachery you accuse me of?" The officer started around his desk, a hand dropping to the hilt of his sword.

Jorge tugged harder at Thomas's robe. "Come away. There are other means. Come away now while you still can."

"I won't forget this," Thomas said, allowing himself to be led away through the barracks.

Once outside, he turned to Jorge, still angry. "That man is part of this. There's something more behind this

222

than a simple killing, can't you see that? And he admits he takes orders from Olaf."

"Of course I see it," said Jorge, surprising Thomas. "Do you think me stupid? But antagonising men like him won't help your cause. He's a cog in a pulley, nothing more. Someone else pulls the strings. Let's go, you already know who can help us."

———

Dawn was breaking as they passed through the barracks, which seemed unexpectedly busy, but when they reached the kitchens, only a few bleary-eyed girls were preparing pots and carrying in boxes of oranges, limes and pomegranates. Thomas more than half expected Bazzu to still be in her bed, but she was in the same place they had left her the day before, as though she had not moved since. She looked rested, eyes bright, skin clear, and he studied her a moment with a professional eye and knew she was in robust health.

"Jorge! I knew you couldn't resist my charms for long. Come in, send this *ajami* away and give an old woman something to remember."

"You forget I am *ajami,* too," said Jorge.

"You are a good Spaniard, as I am a good servant of Allah. This physician is from far off." She cast an amused glance at Thomas. "Unless he would like to join us? Ah, those were good days, were they not?"

Thomas glanced at Jorge and raised an eyebrow. Jorge lifted a shoulder.

"I am afraid we come seeking your help once more," said Jorge.

Bazzu sighed. "Not even a quick coupling before we break the palace's fast? You know I'm more than enough woman for both of you. The surgeon's a little skinny for my taste, but he may be hiding a treasure beneath his robe."

"We must disappoint you for now, sweet dumpling. We are on the Sultan's business."

"I never forget a debt, you know that. And your debt is increasing day by day."

"I will repay it three-fold, I promise."

"What is it you want of me now?" There was more amusement in Bazzu's voice than anything else, and Thomas wondered how much reality lay behind her teasing.

"Thomas spoke with a guard yesterday and was told of a means for someone to find their way secretly through the palace. You may not know of such ways, but—"

"I know of what you speak."

"Good. We went to find the guard this morning, but it appears he has been remiss overnight and gotten himself killed."

Bazzu's face showed concern. "How? Were you involved?"

"A game of dice turned bad, nothing more."

"Such things happen. Usually it is no more than fists and a broken nose, but sometimes … these men are trained to kill, they find it hard to hold back when anger takes them."

"So I believe. But we would know more of these secret ways. If anyone can help us, I know you can."

"As I said, at one time I would have happily taken you along any secret passage you wished to explore, but regrettably these hips no longer allow me to assist you."

"But there will be someone you know who can, I am sure."

Bazzu sat back, staring up at the low ceiling. From beyond the ever-open doorway, the sound grew louder as others started to arrive in the kitchen. Clashing pots, running water, a myriad of scents and sounds drifted in. Thomas and Jorge waited, patience forced on them.

Bazzu leaned forward. "Prea!" Her voice, so soft, so sultry a moment before, became commanding. "Prea—come in here, girl, now!"

There was the sound of a pot banging down, then bare feet running. A waif of barely sixteen years darted into the room and bowed her head.

"Yes, Bazzu, how can I serve?"

"I have a task for you, girl, one that is highly important. You are to help these men. Do whatever they ask. Understood?"

Prea looked up, dark eyes taking in Thomas and, apparently, finding nothing to fear, she checked Jorge and looked less sure. A frown touched her brow.

"You already know Jorge. This other is Thomas Berrington, surgeon to the Sultan and the harem."

"Welcome, sirs." Prea's voice caught, the girl unused to serving such dignitaries. Thomas looked at her with sympathy. They were not such dignitaries as Bazzu was trying to make out, but he saw the point. This girl would better serve those she feared.

Bazzu signalled the girl close and whispered in her ear. She grinned, her eyes flashing as they took the two of them in. *Bazzu is a marvel*, Thomas thought. One brief whisper and the girl had gone from uncertainty to excitement in a heartbeat.

"Go with them," said Bazzu. "Do as they ask."

The girl bowed and accompanied Jorge from the room. Thomas was about to turn away when Bazzu's voice stopped him.

"Thomas, take care of Jorge, won't you? He is dear to me. And take care of yourself too, even though I know little of you other than by reputation. Jorge seems to like you, so I have decided I like you, too. And when you know something, I want you to come back and tell me." She steepled her short, plump fingers and gazed at him. "Know this—I can be of assistance to you in whatever manner you desire. I served as a concubine for many years, and I have served the Sultan's household faithfully ever since. I know everyone and every place in this palace. These killings have disturbed our peace and I would have it returned for whatever small time we may have before the infidel Spanish rape our fertile land."

226

Thomas felt a tightness in his throat. This still beautiful woman held within her a love of this kingdom as deep as his own.

"Of course we will return."

"But most of all, keep him safe. I place on you that responsibility and will hold you to it."

Thomas nodded and rushed after Jorge and the girl. He found them in the corridor beyond the kitchen. Jorge had gone on to one knee so his face was level with the girl's. He glanced up as Thomas approached.

"I have explained our purpose and Prea says she knows these secret ways well. One of her jobs is to take small favours to those inside the harem and elsewhere without others knowing. She also tells me she has, on occasion, been asked to spy on certain individuals and report their actions to Bazzu."

Thomas smiled. "And I wonder what she does with such information?"

"Only what is best for the palace, I am sure. Now, where would you have this waif lead us?"

Thomas turned to the girl. Despite her slimness, her short-clipped hair shone and her skin was clear and smooth, her eyes bright. She might be a servant at the bottom of a long chain of command within the palace, but she was well cared for.

"How much do you know of the harem, Prea?" Thomas deliberately used her name, wanting her at ease.

"I know all of the palace, sir."

"You heard of what happened two days past? To Safya and the others?"

Prea lowered her eyes, her face losing some colour. "I heard, sir. It was terrible."

"You know where the killings occurred?"

She nodded.

"Are there ways a man could find his way through the palace unobserved if he wanted to reach them?"

She nodded again, but her dark skin grew paler still.

"I want you to show me how someone could get close to that place without being seen."

"There are many ways, sir, but they are narrow and twisting." She looked Thomas up and down, appraising him. "I think you might pass, but this one?" She cast a glance at Jorge, her face making her meaning clear.

"I am not built for tight spaces," said Jorge. "But I have a few ideas of my own I can follow up. Go with the girl, Thomas. I'll go into town and make enquiries there. We'll meet at the inn this evening."

For a moment, neither man knew how to part, then Jorge stepped forward and hugged Thomas, a strange gesture in the palace corridor. When Jorge was gone, Thomas found Prea staring at him, and his face flushed for some reason he couldn't fathom.

"Show me, then. I want to see all of these ways, and hear everything you know of them."

"A day may not be long enough, sir," said Prea as she turned away.

"Then show me what is important. And you don't need to call me sir."

"How am I to know what is important, sir? I am a serving girl. I do what I am told, nothing more."

"You are more than a serving girl, I see it in your eyes. You have intelligence and wit. And call me Thomas."

"Of course, sir, this way, there is an entrance nearby."

CHAPTER TWENTY-ONE

Prea turned into a narrow corridor before stopping opposite an arched window which presented a view over the Alkazaba. Thomas expected her to lead him to a side corridor, but instead she turned away from the sunlight towards the far wall. Her nimble fingers searched below the writing which ran throughout the palace, almost all of it stating the same stark message: *There is no victor but Allah.*

Her fingers found a depression. There was a soft click, and a small section of wall opened. Prea pushed her arm in almost to the shoulder, straining. Her face showed satisfaction when a louder clunk caused the panel to hinge outward. Thomas looked at the opening with growing wonder, and not a little uncertainty. He had been expecting quiet corridors, hidden alcoves, not this.

Prea turned to him, a grin flashing small white teeth against her dark face.

"You have done well," Thomas said, hesitation colouring his voice.

She nodded as though praise was her due and turned to slip into the darkness. Thomas approached the opening and breathed in. He angled himself sideways and pushed, his robe catching on stone. He knew he had done the wrong thing and released the air from his lungs. As his chest deflated, it gave him enough room to squeeze into the passage. He was glad to discover the tunnel itself was wider than the opening, but not by much. Prea pressed against his side as she reached behind him. The panel closed, shutting them in total darkness.

"How do we find our way through this?" Thomas blinked, but the darkness remained as dense as before.

"Stay here and don't move." Prea moved away and Thomas was left on his own, trapped inside the walls of the palace. The air was damp, cold against his skin. He rubbed his sandal across the floor and found it covered in a fine grit. He touched the wall to one side, then the other, a hand on each, his arms barely parted. He tried to turn so he was facing directly along the passage, but couldn't. The only way to progress was by shuffling sideways. Panic tightened his chest and he found it difficult to breathe, as if the walls were already crushing him. Then Thomas made out movement, a shape ahead of him that resolved into Prea. Light filtered in from somewhere, brighter ahead than where he stood.

Prea spoke quietly, her voice barely a whisper. "There are channels and spy holes cut throughout the

passages. They admit a little light, enough to find your way if you know where you are going." Prea stood directly across the tunnel, slim enough to make it appear roomy. Thomas couldn't make out her features, but a sudden flash revealed her teeth as she grinned. "Is it a little snug for you, Thomas?" She used his name now, an equal here in her domain.

Thomas tried to match Prea's tone, aware of peopled rooms just beyond the walls. He wondered what would happen if they were discovered spying on the occupants. "How close are we to the bathing chamber where the attack took place?"

"It is a little way yet. We need to pass beneath the courtyard of lions and then climb to the level of the harem. Come, I will show you. And keep up. If you lose me, you will never find your way out on your own."

"I won't lose you," Thomas said, starting after the slight figure.

Progress was hard, and Thomas knew Prea had to keep stopping for him. She would dart ahead, almost disappearing from sight, and panic would start up, then she would wait for him to catch up, his heart slowing only for her to rush off again.

At intervals, the light grew brighter. They would pass a small niche, a shelf, some marker, and there would be a narrow aperture in the wall. At first, Thomas stopped at each to peer through. Most rooms he gazed on were empty, but in one he glimpsed a woman dressed in a long silk robe.

"How many people know of these passages?"

"Only a few. Those like me who are asked to deliver contraband, sometimes..." She hesitated, her voice trailing to silence. She shuffled onward, her bare feet almost silent on the coarse floor. Thomas followed, his own movements loud in his ears.

"Sometimes what?" He raised his voice a little now there was no aperture nearby.

Prea halted and he bumped into her, almost knocking her over. The passage was almost pitch black. The last illumination lay behind the last turn. Nothing showed ahead but velvet darkness.

"Sometimes I am asked to escort a concubine for the pleasure of the royal household. Sometimes a woman from outside if they are especially beautiful or skilled."

"And men? Do you lead men through these tunnels?"

"Most men don't fit. You are thinner than most men I have known."

"You have known many men, have you?" Thomas smiled, amused at her precociousness, knowing full well female servants, even those as young or younger than Prea, were often the thoughtless playthings of high-ranking nobles and officials.

"I work in the palace, sir. I perform the duties demanded of me."

Thomas felt sad for this slip of a girl, then thought of Bazzu, the mother hen at the centre of everything. Did she look out for the innocent and protect them? Thomas was sure she did.

"Is it far now?"

"Not far. Soon we climb some steps, and then we are almost there."

"It's dark here. Will it grow lighter ahead?"

"Not for a while. Would you like some light?"

"You can do that?"

"Of course." In the dimness, Prea placed a foot against each wall, extended her hands and climbed upwards as though she had been doing so all her life, which perhaps she had. She wedged herself into position and reached sideways, tugged at something and a shaft of light flooded in, the sudden brightness blinding Thomas for a moment.

"There are vantage points everywhere," she said, her voice once more barely audible. "Many are closed off. Those that show the more delicate vistas are only revealed to those who know. Would you like to see, Thomas?" She used his name again, amusement colouring her voice.

"See what?"

"Climb up and you will discover for yourself." Prea shuffled along to make room for him. He tried to emulate her, but his sandals kept slipping on the rough stone, so he kicked them off and managed to gain traction with his bare feet. His ascent was halting, and at one point he slipped all the way down and had to start again, but eventually his head came level with Prea's. She had left enough room for him to stare through a narrow vertical slit.

Thomas found himself gazing at Aixa in her chamber. She was starting to rise from sleep, her face soft. It reminded him that the day was still young, and Sultan's wives had no need to rise at dawn with the rest of the populace. Thomas had treated Aixa in the past and knew her body well, but seeing her now was different. A voyeuristic thrill ran through him as she turned aside, unaware anyone gazed on her.

Thomas's feet lost their grip and he tumbled to the ground, landing awkwardly. He had managed to wedge himself in so tightly, he feared he was trapped for good, his knees locked solid against the stone.

Prea closed the slit with a block of wood and slid down to squat beside him.

"You are too loud, Thomas." She leaned close, spice on her breath. "The passages amplify any sound you make. You must be silent as a mouse, even quieter if you can. I don't think the Sultana heard you, but you must take more care. She is beautiful, is she not?" Once more, her teeth gleamed in the dark.

"I've treated her often enough in my role as a surgeon," Thomas said, his whisper robbing the words of any note of authority he sought.

"But watching her now is different, is it not?"

"Do you spy on people often?"

"You call it spying? I call it doing my duty."

"Always duty?"

Thomas sensed movement in the dark. It was Prea shrugging. "Duty-duty-duty. Sometimes a person grows

tired of duty all the time. I like to gaze on beautiful things."

"And what else do you see?"

"You can use your imagination, can't you? Come, we are almost there." Prea moved away.

"Prea," Thomas called after her. She stopped and turned back. "I don't think I can move."

She giggled, covering her mouth with her hand to mask the sound. "Perhaps I ought to leave you where you lie. A punishment for spying on a Sultana."

"Help me. Please."

She put her hands on her hips and stared at him, eventually nodding. "All right, though I am tempted to leave you where you are, except you will start to stink up the tunnels and I wouldn't want that." Prea knelt and cocked her head to one side, judging Thomas's position. She reached in and grabbed an ankle, tugged hard.

"Ow!"

"Be quiet. This is all your own fault."

Thomas grimaced as she pulled at the other leg. His knee scraped along the wall, and then was free. He twisted, aware of how inelegant he looked, but Prea had already turned away and was moving along the passage. Thomas used his hands to pull himself upright, sore, blood seeping from one knee, and followed.

A set of steps led upwards, turning on themselves, turning again so that by the time they reached a higher level, Thomas had no idea in which direction they were facing. There was more light here, frequent gaps in the

walls casting patterns against the roughly hewn stone, and he realised they were passing between two carved arches above a doorway.

They descended stone steps, then Prea stopped at a particularly light section.

"We are here." She raised her hand and Thomas turned to gaze through several small holes bored in the wall.

The bath chamber was occupied. Two concubines who Thomas knew by sight but not name lay in the water, steam rising around them, while two servant girls washed their bodies. A third entered the room carrying a jug of oil and a blade. She slipped into the hot water and each concubine in turn raised their arms, allowing the girl to remove all trace of hair beneath. Thomas stood, stunned, both aroused and guilty. He forgot about the slip of a girl standing beside him until a movement distracted him. He glanced sideways. Prea, too, was staring into the chamber, her eyes bright in the light catching them. She also watched as in a trance, unaware of Thomas in turn observing her.

"This is the same chamber?" Thomas asked, and Prea jerked, startled. She might have flushed, but her face was too dark to show if she did.

"The same chamber," she said. "I heard no one wishes to use it now, but these two are minor concubines and have no choice. They are beautiful, are they not?"

"I live with a concubine. An ex-concubine."

"You do?"

"It's a long story."

"I like stories."

"It is not for now. Would there be an entrance into the bathing chamber?"

"I do not know of one, but I can look." Prea moved away along the passage.

"Wait. Let them finish. No one must know of what we do."

Prea padded back, a grin on her face. "A secret, Thomas? Is this our secret?"

"Not a secret. A surety. I believe someone stood where we stand now. That they entered the chamber and killed Safya, spilling her blood into the water. I seek that man, whoever he is."

"He will be as skinny as you, then. How could someone like that be strong enough to wield a sword?"

"I have wielded a sword," Thomas said.

"In anger?" Prea's tone of voice made clear her feelings about Thomas's claim as she resumed her observation of the chamber. Bright rays of light splashed against her skin to paint it with cold fire.

"I have fought in battle when I had to, when there was no other choice. But my calling is to save lives, not take them."

Thomas was unable to tell whether she believed him or not. Most likely, as everyone else did, she considered him a coward. Prea turned to look into the chamber again.

"You should watch this."

Thomas sat against the wall, hunching his knees tightly to his chest.

"I would prefer not."

"They use the blade and wax. It looks as though it should hurt, but the women appear to show no pain. Does someone grow used to such a thing?"

"Their skin is soft from the water. And the hair grows more slowly after a time, and less dense. It becomes easier the longer they perform the act."

"Perhaps one day, when I'm no longer a servant, I will do the same. It is an interesting idea."

"You have ambitions?" Thomas asked, curious.

"I have been told I am not unattractive. I might snare a man, a rich man, and have him take me as one of his wives. It would be a better life than the one I have here."

"Are you mistreated?"

"They don't beat me, but to those within the palace, I barely exist. I just am. I fetch, I carry, I do as I am told. I believe they don't even see me. I am as the air, essential but invisible."

"Were you born in Gharnatah?"

"In the desert. I was captured and carried across the narrow sea."

"I am sorry."

Prea glanced at him a moment, quickly returning her attention to the ablutions being performed in the bath. "Don't be. I recall nothing of my life from before, other than a memory of hunger and fighting. My tribe was always at war with some other. There was little food.

239

Here I am not mistreated and they fill my belly all I want, they let me wash and keep myself clean. All I lack is freedom, and freedom is overrated."

"What will you do when the Spanish come?"

"The Spanish? Why would the Spanish come?"

Thomas realised the girl knew nothing of the world beyond the palace walls.

"They are finishing now, they will be leaving soon." Prea crouched against the wall, mirroring Thomas's position, except she didn't look as though she had been wedged in place. "When they have gone, I will look for a doorway for you."

"How will you find it?"

"There are signs. You can watch and learn." Prea cocked her head to one side. "Did you hear that?"

"Hear what?"

Prea said nothing, but held a finger up. Thomas stilled his breathing and closed his eyes. After a moment, he thought he did hear something. Not close, but when it came again, he was sure it was the soft movement of feet on the gritty floor. His eyes snapped open and he stared at Prea.

"How many others use these tunnels?"

"A few. Not many." Prea's face was serious, but she showed no fear.

"Could that be one of those few?"

"I don't know." Prea rose to her feet. "Shall I run and look?"

"No!" Thomas reached out and grabbed her wrist a

moment before she could move away. "What if it's him? I have to come with you."

Prea knelt, her face almost touching Thomas's so her voice barely troubled the air between them. "If it is the same man, then he will hear you. You make too much noise, Thomas. Let me go. I am as silent as the night, and my skin is too dark to stand out like yours does."

Thomas retained his grip on her wrist, aware of how small she was, how brave ... or foolish.

"Let's listen a little longer. Perhaps he'll come to us and this will be finished today."

Prea stared at him for a long moment, then she let her breath go and sat across from him again. Thomas listened for further movement, but if someone else had been creeping through the tunnels, they were gone, or had heard them in turn and waited as still as did they.

Eventually Thomas rose to his feet. He offered a hand to help Prea. She stared at it, then smiled and let him lift her up. They both knew there was no need.

"I want to thank you for helping me."

"It is what I was asked to do, and I do as I am told."

"But you didn't have to show such willingness. I am truly grateful."

"Will you pay me, then?" Her teeth gleamed, the presence of someone else in the tunnels already dismissed.

"If you would like me to, yes." Thomas searched inside his robe for his purse.

"Not now. Afterwards. When the day is done."

"What will you do with the money?"

"I don't know. I could go into town and buy myself something pretty. I've never had money so it will be an adventure. Do you need a servant, Thomas?"

The question caught him by surprise.

"My needs are simple. And the life of a servant in my house would lack the luxury of the palace."

"It would? I thought you were an important man."

"But not rich."

"In that case you don't need to pay me much." Prea stood and gazed through the spy-hole. "They are gone. Come on, let us search for an entrance."

CHAPTER TWENTY-TWO

When Thomas found Sultan Abu al-Hasan Ali, the man was preparing to leave the city. He strode the barracks' yard, issuing orders while soldiers ran to obey. Horses clattered, carts creaked, swords and armour clashed as men armed themselves for battle. The air stank of horse dung and sweat. Thomas stood to one side, waiting his chance, uneasy because Olaf stood beside him.

"When does he go?" Thomas asked. "Tomorrow?"

"Today."

"It is gone noon already. How far will they get before dark?"

"There is a full moon and the men will ride until midnight. Word is the Spanish are a small force, but have come as far south as Aznalloz."

"That's barely a day from the city."

Olaf nodded at the bustling soldiers. "Hence the urgency."

Thomas glanced at the general. "You seem calm enough. Is someone preparing your horse?"

"Apparently I am not needed on this expedition. The Sultan said I would prove more useful here in case of insurrection."

"Insurrection? The city is peaceful, surely?"

"There are rumours," said Olaf.

"I have heard none."

"My daughter tells me you don't have an ear for rumour."

Which daughter? Thomas wondered, knowing there was only one answer. "I do at the moment."

"Of course." Olaf nodded towards the Sultan. "He is free now if you want to talk to him."

Thomas offered a final glance at Olaf, whose face showed he would rather be preparing for a skirmish than left to babysit a city.

Abu al-Hasan Ali caught sight of Thomas as he crossed the yard and finished giving hurried instructions to two men. One of them lacked two fingers on his left hand, but Thomas had seen the same disfigurement often enough now not to be suspicious.

"I have little time, Thomas, so tell me what you know." Another soldier approached and the Sultan waved him away. "Give us a moment, we will not be long. Quickly, Thomas."

He hesitated a moment, trying to work out where to start, how much to say. "We have made some progress, Malik. I've now discovered how the man gained access

to the bathing chambers." Thomas took the opportunity of urgency to neglect telling of the tunnels. For some reason, he didn't yet want the Sultan to know he had almost certainly been watched on during his visits to the harem. "I have also identified the man who conducted the first investigation and plan on talking with him in the morning."

"You have done well." The Sultan clapped Thomas on the shoulder. "I may be away several days, it depends on whether this band of infidels are alone or have company." He stared around at the men milling across the yard. "In my absence, I want you to report to Olaf. He asked if he could remain behind and I agreed. It is a good idea not to leave the city undefended. This move may be a feint to draw us away. Have you a suspect yet?"

"Not yet, Malik. Perhaps by the time you return." He considered it unwise to mention his suspects were the woman the Sultan loved and his trusted general.

"It would be good if you did. Time is passing. And..." He hesitated.

"Is there more, Malik?"

"The nobles. Faris al-Rashid, those who swarm to him. I hear they have been visiting the palace and I would like to know why. Have you investigated any of these men?"

"I have spoken with some," Thomas said, "but not questioned them. Do you think they know something?"

The Sultan looked around at the organised chaos. "They are close to my son." He had no need to mention

which one. "It might be worth your time looking into their affairs. Or I may only be seeing plots where none exist."

"I will do as you ask, Malik. I believe they were invited to hunt."

"Not by me. Abu Abdullah, perhaps. I want this matter settled before I return."

"It may not be—"

"Settled, Thomas. The others took too long—I expect better from you. Do what you have to and find me the killer." His voice was cold, and Thomas wondered what would happen if he failed in his task.

The Sultan turned away, leaving Thomas standing alone, while around him soldiers hustled to make good their preparations. The Sultan raised his arm and led them through the gate, turning east towards the rising foothills of the Sholayr.

A movement caused Thomas to turn his head to find Olaf walking to join him.

"The Sultan thinks this may be a trap to draw him away from the city."

"If he thinks that, he should have stayed and sent me instead. I can deal with a band of Spaniards as well as he."

Likely better, Thomas thought, puzzling over the discrepancy in their stories. "He said I am to report to you, not the Vizier or Abu Abdullah."

Olaf turned to stare at him. "Why me?"

"I think…" Thomas shook his head. "No, I don't know what I think."

"Unless you have something positive to say, don't bother finding me. I would rather you direct your energies towards finding this killer than talking to me. Are you making any progress at all?"

The question sounded innocent enough, but Thomas only told Olaf the same as he had the Sultan, once more missing out the revelation of the tunnels.

"Is Jorge proving any use to you? Helena has no time for him, but…" He shrugged and left the sentence unfinished.

"He is better with people than I am. They like him and I trust his judgement."

"He is no man of action, though, is he?"

Thomas smiled. "Neither am I."

"Perhaps it is not men of action we need for this task. Don't listen to me, Thomas, all I know is how to fight. I am sorry, I have to go. The young princes need my attentions." He started away towards his quarters.

"Zoraya's sons?" Thomas called after him.

Olaf stopped, his face puzzled when he turned back. "Yes, the young princes. As you know, I am teaching them swordplay, though they are enthusiastic more than skilled. A boy must know how to wield a sword, but I hope they never have to use one in anger."

"Can I join you?" Thomas asked.

"Have you not more important matters to attend to?"

"Will Zoraya be there?"

247

Olaf's frown deepened. "She comes to watch sometimes, but not always. Why?"

"I talked to her yesterday and would like to talk with her again. She might be more relaxed if I am not alone with her."

"If you think it will do any good. Come if you want, but if it was me, I would be following the Sultan's orders and looking for this killer."

Yes, Thomas thought, *that is what I am doing.*

Thomas sat on a stone bench set in the shade, his back against the wall. The small courtyard was uncluttered, the middle cleared of all planting and furniture. He saw Olaf had been right about the princes' skills. The two boys stood stripped to the waist, sweat streaking their chests while they followed the general's instructions, but enthusiasm only went so far. Thomas's professional eye studied them. Slim, but not muscled, clear-skinned, healthy. He compared them to his memory of himself at their age. He had arrived in France young, but strong, years of work on his father's farm building lean muscle. He had also been fast, and naturally gifted, as the local boys in Lemster discovered. Later, as he wandered alone through the French hinterland, it was those skills that kept him alive. He had honed them in the field until he believed himself invulnerable. That had been a long time ago, and he no longer possessed such certainty.

Nasir and Said took a break, both breathing hard. They drank water from a jug a servant brought to them. Thomas was waiting for Zoraya to appear, but already he had been here half an hour and she had not shown herself.

He rose and walked to the small group gathered in the sun, meaning to make his excuses and leave. Olaf was trying to explain a move to the boys. They listened attentively, but it was obvious they didn't understand what he was trying to teach them.

"Thomas, come here and show them what I mean."

"Me?"

"You have been on the battlefield, haven't you? Don't pretend you are innocent in the ways of war. They need to be more aware of what is happening behind them."

"How can we do that?" It was Nasir, the elder, who spoke. No doubt he considered himself the leader. "We don't have eyes in the back of our heads."

"But you have other senses," said Olaf. "Your ears most of all. And your bodies, your noses—these all tell you what is happening around you. You must learn to use them if you are to survive."

"Do you think we will ever need to fight?" Said asked. He was a little younger than Yusuf, the Sultan's younger son by Aixa, and slimmer. He had the face of a scholar, not a warrior.

"The Spanish are coming."

249

"Mother believes the Spanish will save us," Nasir said.

"People respect strength," said Olaf. "If you *can* fight, you don't *need* to fight. If you can't fight, you will be taken advantage of." Olaf reached out fast and took the sword from Nasir's hand, snatching it away before the boy could react. He swung it through the air and tossed it towards Thomas.

Without thinking, the blade turning as it came at him, he raised his right hand and snatched it from the air.

"See?" said Olaf. "Thomas has seen battle. He was prepared. Take a seat, lads, and see how men fight."

"I don't want to fight you," Thomas said.

Olaf grinned. "Then you will demonstrate how the weak are slaughtered. That is a valuable lesson they also need to learn. Take off your robe."

Thomas shook his head.

Olaf paced forward, his own sword descending quickly. Thomas raised his arm and blocked the move, instinct taking over.

"Take off your robe. I will turn my back on you. Come at me as if you mean it." Olaf stepped close and lowered his voice. "I know you can do this. Helena told me she has seen your scars. A man does not get scars like those working as a surgeon."

Thomas paced backwards. He had told Helena nothing of what he had once been. But it was true she had traced the scars on his body with her fingertips, and he had seen the curiosity in her eyes. No doubt she had

made up stories for her father, inventing some heroic past that might put her in a better light—concubine to a hero rather than a physician. Her father would have instilled in her respect for those with strength rather than knowledge.

Thomas loosened his robe and tagelmust and tossed them away, feeling Nasir's eyes on him. Unbound, his brown hair fell free to curl against his shoulders. The sun warmed his skin and he stepped softly as Olaf turned his back on him, his own badges of honour criss-crossing his skin.

The swords were deliberately blunted, but they still carried weight and could inflict damage in the right hands—and Olaf's were the right hands. Thomas moved fast and swung at his broad shoulders.

Olaf twisted, quicker than seemed possible, and their blades clashed. The general was grinning, a fierce light in his eyes. This is what he lived for, even if his opponent was a poor excuse for a challenger.

"See," he said, "I heard Thomas approach. Feet on sand. I saw his shadow from the side of my eye."

"A battlefield is a noisy place," Nasir said. "You would not hear him with the sound of battle all around you."

"Then come make some noise," Olaf ordered. "Nasir, fetch another weapon and fight me, see if Thomas can get to me then."

Nasir smiled, enjoying the game. This was far more interesting than practice. He retrieved another sword, and

he and Said ran at Olaf, shouting at the top of their voices. Olaf deflected their blows easily, used to far better opposition. Thomas watched carefully, picking his moment, then attacked, sure Olaf was distracted, but the man swung his blade behind him, not even bothering to turn, and Thomas's own was jarred and knocked aside. The boys, believing they had an advantage, came at Olaf harder, but he only yelled and forced them back until Said stumbled and fell over. Then he spun and came at Thomas, his face cold.

Thomas raised his blade, deflecting a rush of blows. When they stopped, he was breathing hard, his own chest sweat-streaked. He caught movement from the edge of his vision. Zoraya had come out and stopped, observing the scene. She called to her sons, who ran across the courtyard. Words were exchanged, too faint to carry.

"Shall we show them how men truly fight, Thomas?" said Olaf.

"It would be a poor show."

"Would it?" Olaf's gaze took in the scars on Thomas's chest, shoulders and belly. No match for his, but they were not the scars a scholar should possess. "I am curious about the tales my daughter tells. Are you really the warrior she claims?"

What had Helena told the man? "She knows nothing of me," Thomas said.

"My daughter knows men," Olaf reminded him. "She is skilled, or so I have been told. Come then, surgeon, show this family what you are made of." Without

252

hesitation, Olaf came at him again, his blade flashing in the sun, his blows a constant barrage against Thomas's sword.

Thomas fell back, deflecting strike after strike. They came faster and he darted aside and counter-attacked, almost landing what, with sharpened swords, would have proved a fatal blow, but Olaf's sword parried just in time.

"Good, this is what they need to see. Two grown men fighting for their lives." Olaf's gaze moved to one side, for a moment taking in Zoraya, and Thomas thought he saw something in the other's eyes and attacked fast.

Olaf had expected the move and parried. Thomas came again, twisting, turning, his blade sparking shards of reflected sunlight across the shadowed wall.

"Yes, Thomas—come at me, show them what real men do!" Olaf attacked again. Thomas parried. Olaf increased his blows and Thomas stumbled. The general grinned, raising his sword for what could be a killing blow. A strike to the head or neck would prove fatal, blunted blade or not.

Thomas allowed himself to fall as Olaf's blade swept through the spot where his head had been a second before. He hit the ground and rolled, coming instantly to his feet to launch into a fresh attack. Olaf parried, fell back. Now it was Thomas's turn to increase the pressure, strike after strike landing as blades clashed. Thomas felt his rational mind fade, replaced by a cold fire he had not experienced since he came to this city. He allowed it to fill him as he fought even harder. It was as though the

world stilled, awareness drawing in until there were only the two of them, moving fast in the sun.

Olaf counter-attacked and Thomas deflected the blows easily, buried muscle-memory returning to him as though it had never gone away. He had no notion of how long they fought, but gradually he knew he was gaining the ascendancy. He was younger than Olaf, and, he realised, a more instinctive fighter.

Thomas put together a rapid series of blows, a deliberate diversion. He saw it laid out, the moves, the execution, exactly as he saw the moves to the end of a game of Mancala.

Thomas's blade came down hard against Olaf's exposed neck.

Thomas almost carried through with the blow, but at the last moment he held back, laying the blunted blade against Olaf's skin. A sharp blade, fully executed, would have removed his head. Even with this one, it would have been a killing blow had he put enough power behind it.

That was when Thomas felt a pressure against his ribs and looked down to see the point of Olaf's sword pressing against his chest.

"I think we can call that a draw," said Olaf, grinning. He lowered his blade and slapped Thomas on the shoulder, drawing him against him, his sweat-slicked skin slippery. "I always thought Helena was exaggerating your past, but I think she may have underestimated you. Where did you learn to fight like that?"

Thomas stepped away, shaking his head, offering no answer. That was when Nasir and Said, sensing their chance, came at him from behind.

Thomas swung around, his body still pulsating with a remembered skill. Said's blade flew off in one direction, Nasir's in the other.

"Stop! Stop this now!" Zoraya strode out to stand between Thomas and her sons. She was breathing hard, her face flushed, and Thomas realised watching him and Olaf fight had excited her. He shook his head and tossed his own blade to the ground, disgusted with himself.

"I am sorry, My Lady, we were lost in the moment. I meant no harm to your children."

"And you, Olaf, what were you thinking?"

"We were teaching your sons a valuable lesson."

"You were showing off, that is what you were doing."

Thomas studied the interaction between them. Olaf was at ease—although Olaf was at ease in almost all situations, certain of his status and power—but Zoraya exhibited some masked emotion. Could they be lovers? Was that the hold she had over Olaf? Was that why he was involved in the plot? Thomas knew he couldn't simply throw an accusation at her, particularly not here. He wasn't even sure he could let the Sultan know of his suspicions, because the man loved this woman. He walked away and retrieved his robe.

"How did you learn to fight that way?" Nasir came to stand close by, but not too close.

"I have tried to forget," Thomas said.

"If I could fight like that I would never want to forget."

Thomas ruffled the boy's hair, even as he made the gesture recognising how inappropriate it was, but it seemed his demonstration had given him permission.

"When you are older and have seen more of the world, you will understand."

"I am old enough now," Nasir said. "And I have seen much of the world. I have travelled. And..." He hesitated, his eyes tracking Thomas's face, and a sly smile came to his mouth. "And I have known women. I am a man. Mother says I am a man, and that a man must know all there is to know."

"And books?" Thomas said, tired of this strutting cock of a prince. "Have you acquired the knowledge that comes from books?"

Nasir scowled. "Princes have others to do that for them."

"Of course." Thomas felt an urge to argue, to try to convince him there was more to life than position and prestige, but knew it was a hopeless task. Nasir was right, anyway—princes only had to surround themselves with clever men, they didn't need to be clever themselves.

"Boys, come inside and bathe, you stink like commoners." Zoraya clapped her hands and her sons ran to obey.

"I would speak with you again," Thomas said.

"On what matter?"

"The same one as before."

"I told you all I know the last time. I have nothing more to say on the matter."

"I would still speak with you. The Sultan commands me to talk with everyone."

"He does not mean me, surely you know that?"

Thomas watched Olaf dressing, gathering together the blunted weapons. The man seemed uninterested in their conversation, but it could be a pretence.

"I take his instructions seriously, My Lady, and so should you. One Sultana has been killed already. Where one is attacked, so might another be. Have you considered you might also be in danger?" He watched her carefully for a reaction, but her face remained as cold as it had through the entire conversation. If she was behind the plotting, then she would know she was safe. "I will talk with you, out here or in your quarters, but we will talk. And this time you will answer me truthfully."

"Zoraya let you question her again?" Jorge's face showed disbelief and amusement in equal measure.

"For what good it did." Thomas kicked Jorge's legs aside and dropped on to the bed. His body ached from the fight with Olaf, his mind from the verbal battle with Zoraya. The latter had been harder than the former. She had been stubborn, convinced of her own invulnerability. Thomas had refused to back down, even when she resorted to tears. It had made for an interesting meeting.

"Tell me what she told you."

"Later. I need food and wine. What did you find out?"

Jorge smiled. "I can play coy as well, and I'm also hungry and thirsty. When we first went to your house, you told me you didn't drink wine."

"I may have lied. Are we going downstairs? If that

merchant is down there, I refuse to give him a game of Mancala. Losing once was bad enough."

"But he gave me such beautiful clothes," said Jorge, holding his arms out and grimacing. "Nobody looks at me in these."

"I believe that was the point of them." Thomas pushed off the bed. "Come on, let's go downstairs and I'll tell you what I know."

The stew was indistinguishable from the previous night's, and no doubt would be tomorrow and tomorrow's tomorrow. The same girl brought them bowls and a jug of wine, today her scowl washed clean. Her pretty face reminded Thomas of Prea. The city was full of girls and boys like them, making their way as well as they could. He pressed a coin into the hand of this one, hoping she didn't misinterpret his generosity.

"Tell me what Zoraya said," asked Jorge as he reached for his cup of wine.

"You first. Did you find anything out?"

"Other than the entire city believes the foolish tale that a djinn did the killing, I know no more than I did this morning. And you—have you had more luck?"

Where to start, Thomas thought, and told Jorge of his meeting with Zoraya, because for him it felt the most significant event of his day, even above the tunnels.

Jorge listened without comment, sipping at his wine, staring out over the crowd.

"Did you ask her outright about Olaf?" he asked when Thomas had finished.

259

"I didn't want to show my suspicions openly, but she knew the implication was there, and I saw in her eyes she understood what I meant."

"They are lovers?"

"I don't think so. Although…"

Jorge waited a moment. "Although what?"

"Olaf and I fought."

Jorge laughed. He leaned across the table and gripped Thomas's chin, turned his head from one side to the other.

"No, it is still attached. For a moment there I thought you said you fought with Olaf."

"When we were done, Zoraya was excited."

Jorge grinned. "As in sexually excited?"

"I believe so."

"If only I'd been there, I would have known for sure. So she is aroused by men fighting. But does that mean she takes the general into her bed?"

"I wish I could say yes, it would make our job simpler. I pressed her, came at her from different directions, and although I discovered a little more, she remains stubborn. But her stubbornness only makes me more suspicious. Why not answer me openly, unless she has something to hide?"

"You have made an enemy of her?"

"She was already that, I believe, but yes, even more so now."

"Will she strike out?"

"At me?"

"Or someone else. Someone close to you. Helena, perhaps. If she does, it would be proof of a kind."

"I would rather Helena remain alive and have less proof."

"Tell her to be careful. Zoraya will know of others close to you as well."

"We can't protect everyone."

"We don't have to. Most will be safe. People like Yusuf are always surrounded by guards and servants. But she may try to attack us directly, so we need to bear that in mind."

Thomas took a mouthful of wine and swallowed. "When did you become so filled with suspicion?"

Jorge smiled. "Oh, there is enough plotting and intrigue in the harem to outshine even the cleverest generals. So—do we accuse them? Tell the Sultan?"

"Abu al-Hasan Ali's not in Gharnatah. He's off fighting more Spanish. He left Olaf in charge."

"This gets better and better. Not only have you upset Zoraya, our suspect is now running the city. My life was so much simpler a few days ago, not to mention safer."

Thomas looked around, thankful he couldn't see the merchant Carlos Rodriguez anywhere among the busy tables. He caught the eye of the girl who had served them earlier and pointed at the almost empty jug of wine and she nodded.

"I was thinking it through as I came down the hill, and I'm not so sure Zoraya and Olaf are behind this thing after all. Both of them have too much to lose, and what

do they gain? Olaf is already the Sultan's general—he has no ambition other than that. And if Zoraya's involvement is uncovered, the least she can expect is banishment, the worst execution."

"Don't forget Abu al-Hasan Ali loves her above all others. The entire palace knows it. She will believe herself invincible."

"Olaf already believes he is invincible." Thomas drained his cup and reached for the jug, but it was empty. "When we fought today, I think he tried to kill me."

Jorge leaned forward. "What?"

"He was training Zoraya's sons with blunted swords. He claimed he wanted to demonstrate some technique to them. I was foolish enough to accept the challenge, but I thought I might learn something. Instead, he almost took my head."

"He tried to kill you?" Jorge looked into his own cup. "Where is that little serving girl? Thomas, if Olaf tried to kill you, you would be dead. No question. I was joking before, but I am not now."

Thomas shook his head, not in disagreement, more in wonder. "I am sure he wanted to kill me."

"So why are you still here?"

Thomas didn't want to explain himself, not in this. "Luck. Ah, here's our wine."

The girl replaced the old jug with the new.

"I think you have an admirer," Thomas teased.

Jorge smiled, watching the slim girl weave through

the tables. "Too young for me." His gaze returned to Thomas. "Is wine medicinal? You're the man to ask."

"I believe there are differing opinions on the matter."

"And yours is?"

"Moderation is the key. I've seen men with distended bellies from swollen livers, their skin the colour and texture of parchment, who have drunk too well and too often over many years. And I've seen others who live beyond any expectation, partaking of a little wine on occasion."

"I believe I'll follow the practice of the latter then."

"How did you acquire the taste? Alcohol isn't allowed within the palace, is it?"

"You would be surprised what is allowed within those walls. But tell me, I've waited long enough, how did you get on with that slip of a girl today? Was she useful or did she lead you down another false path?"

"She was useful."

"So there are a few secret corridors in the palace?"

"More than that. The place is a warren of tunnels. Prea showed me only a few, but she says there are many others."

Jorge looked off into space for a moment. "Have I been spied on?"

Thomas smiled. "Almost certainly. There was much to see, and many surprises..." Thomas hesitated, remembering his unease at spying on the women of the harem. There would be men willing to pay a great deal to be awarded such a privilege.

"So Bazzu has been of use again. I didn't recognise the girl, but there are many like her, too many to take note of them all."

"Prea is different. She is sharp and observant, and she was more than helpful. There is a way a man might make his way through those hidden passages from a score of secret entrances. We found our way to the bathing chamber where the attack took place. It was in use, but once the ladies left, Prea discovered a secret doorway and we were able to enter. The opening is hidden behind the balustrade. It would be possible for someone who knew those tunnels to enter the chamber unobserved."

"Is that what happened?"

"I know it is, but we had to be quick, fearing discovery. I think we heard someone else in the tunnels as well. It might have been someone on an innocent errand, or it might have been the man we seek."

Jorge stared at Thomas, but said nothing.

"I want no one to know what I am seeking, not yet," Thomas said. "I believe Galib ibn-Ubaid was killed because of the little knowledge he imparted to me. He didn't know he was in danger, but I'm convinced the argument over a game of dice was manufactured and his killer was instructed to remove him. I wouldn't want Prea to be placed in the same danger." Thomas smiled. "She asked if I could find a position for her."

Jorge laughed. "She's too skinny for any position I can think of."

"As a servant," Thomas said, but his smile remained.

He had been enchanted by the girl's intelligence, the way she quickly grasped what he wanted. "She pretended to bathe while I used the secret entrance and crept up on her. It wasn't entirely realistic because she knew what was happening, but between us we concluded it was possible for someone to approach the bath without being seen until the very last moment."

"Someone dressed in black from head to foot?" said Jorge. He had finished his stew and pushed the bowl away, filled his flagon with more wine.

"Someone who might easily be mistaken for a supernatural being with their miraculous appearance and disappearance. Once we fathomed how the deed could be done, I examined the passageway and door. I found several signs of his presence." Thomas reached inside his robe, drew out a small hemp sack and shook out a few scraps of material.

Jorge leaned over. "Can I touch them?"

"Help yourself."

Jorge lifted a strip of cloth, one edge ragged where it had caught on something and been torn. The strip was small and seemed to have been trampled on, the material stained so badly it was impossible to tell its true colour.

"There is little we can discover from this," he said, "other than the man wore black, which we already know."

"There were more signs I couldn't bring. Marks on the stone inside the tunnel, as might be made by a sword catching against it. And the ground was disturbed more

than the passage of Prea and I would account for. Jorge, those tunnels honeycomb the palace. With enough knowledge, a man might travel anywhere he wants to, perform any act he wishes, and disappear as though into thin air."

"A djinn." Jorge stared at the trampled scrap of cloth. "He might truly appear as some djinn, might he not? But it would be a huge risk. How often are these passages used? What if someone discovered him? You said you nearly did. Was it him, do you think?"

"It's possible. We went in search of any other sign, but found none. I had to make Prea promise not to enter the tunnels on her own. I think she wants to lay a trap for him, but I told her exactly what would happen if this man found her."

"Did she agree?"

"She said she wouldn't go without me, but I still worry. She did say the tunnels may be used only once a month, at other times more often. She recalls one time she was sent through them four times in a single day, but more usually it's less often."

"Still, this man must know someone could discover him?"

"Prea showed me how it's possible to avoid discovery as well. As I said, she's a sharp little thing. She bid me move around a corner and give her a few moments, then to return swiftly and find her. I did as I was told. I tell you, I was hidden from her less than a

minute, but when I returned, she was nowhere to be found."

"Another passageway?"

Thomas laughed. "Not at all. But it would require someone with strength and agility to do as she did. As I stood there puzzling where she had gone to, I felt something rap against the top of my head. When I looked up, she was wedged against the ceiling like a spider. Had she not dropped a pebble on to me, I would never have seen her."

"Whoever did this would need to know the passages well. And how they are used, their frequency, the escape routes. They would need to know many things."

"Indeed they would."

"Someone who knows the palace well."

Thomas nodded. "As do you."

"You suspect me now?"

"Of course not. For one thing, you wouldn't fit inside the tunnels. I became wedged myself at one point and Prea had to free me." Thomas experienced an inner shiver at the memory of being trapped inside the walls.

"Who then? Not Olaf, for sure, if you said you had difficulties."

"Olaf has a thousand men under his command, any one of whom would do his bidding without question." Thomas drained his cup, refilled it. "And Zoraya's sons are slim. Either would be comfortable in the tunnels."

"But?"

Thomas knew Jorge had caught the hesitancy in his voice.

"The wounds I saw on Safya's body were made by a strong man who knows how to wield a sword." Thomas didn't like the reminder of how the life had been stolen from the Sultan's wife.

"And?"

"The boys are poor warriors. Even you could defeat them."

"Don't overestimate me," said Jorge. "Perhaps they were hiding their skills in front of you. Are they suspicious?"

"The boys? No. Zoraya, yes, but not her boys."

"You discovered something else, didn't you," said Jorge.

"Perhaps. Zoraya spoke of much, to distract me I think. She never answered a question with a direct answer, but there were answers hidden in what she said, even more in what she didn't. She let slip the Sultan visits her often, and I now know Helena goes there regularly."

Thomas's expression wasn't lost on Jorge.

"You already knew that."

"Not that she visits most days. Why have I not noticed before now? What have I been doing? Or not doing?"

"Who does she visit?" asked Jorge. "Zoraya, or..." He didn't need to finish.

Thomas reached for his cup and drained it. He didn't

want to think what Helena had been going to Zoraya's rooms for. There was more than friendship going on.

"Can it work to our advantage, do you think?" said Jorge.

"What—ask Helena to spy for us?"

"She's a gift to you, Thomas, she has to do whatever you demand of her."

Thomas rubbed a hand across his mouth. "It's too late for that, not after the way I've treated her."

"It's never too late with one such as her."

Thomas looked at Jorge, surprised at the coldness in his voice. "You never liked her, did you?"

Jorge shrugged and refilled their cups. "I love many, but not all."

Thomas didn't need to ask Jorge why. He had lived with Helena long enough to know that—despite her obvious charms—she lacked something of humanity.

"I see why she and Zoraya are friends."

"And the boys...?" said Jorge, not needing to say more.

"Yes, the boys. And then she—" Thomas couldn't go on, the sense of betrayal too painful. The thought of Helena's perfect body lying next to one, or both, of those spoiled brats was more than he could bear. He didn't want the woman under his roof a moment longer, but saw no easy way to evict her. She was a gift from the Sultan, not someone to be easily tossed aside. It seemed to him all the Sultan's gifts were tainted in some way.

Jorge leaned forward. "So did you discover anything we can use against her?"

Thomas saw what his friend was doing and was grateful. "Yes and no. Zoraya told me little that was new, but it was her attitude I found more interesting. She believes herself above the law. I pressed her hard, far harder than on our first visit. I let her know I suspect her involvement. She was angry, defensive, even aggressive, but not once did I sense fear."

"The Sultan favours her. The children, too."

"It was more than that. She has a certainty about her, a sense of invulnerability. I believe she has connections with Spain. She plays Moor off against Spaniard, Spaniard against Moor. Whichever side wins, she knows she is secure."

"Why kill Safya? That I don't understand. What gain does it bring?"

"It clears the ground for her ascendancy. Without the other wives, the Sultan is free to make her sons his heirs. She rises with them. Most mothers work for their children, not themselves. I think Zoraya does both. I have never met a colder, more calculating being."

"You said other wives, Thomas. Do you believe Aixa the next victim?"

"If I am right, then yes, there will be more killings, and Aixa is certainly in danger."

"And is it Olaf who does Zoraya's bidding? You said the boys are not skilled enough, but that man has access to the best warriors in the kingdom. We have to unmask

270

the pair of them." Jorge banged his fist on the table, setting the jug rattling. "I will have no more deaths in my harem. None."

"We need proof. Solid proof. Tomorrow we visit this Bilal who was first given the investigation. I believe someone stopped him before he could find out who was behind it. Knowing who did that would tell us who carries some of the guilt."

"Then call for me early," said Jorge, "for you scare me with this kind of talk."

It was late before Thomas arrived home. Despite the ache in his limbs, he was energised. At last it felt as if progress was being made. He was tired, but knew sleep would elude him. The fight with Olaf had sparked old feelings. A coldness still filled him, and if Helena was at home, he knew he might not be able to stop himself taking her by force. He didn't want such an act on his conscience.

The house was quiet as he entered and he went into the kitchen to get a cup of water. Lubna was sitting at the table, a book open in front of her. She glanced up as Thomas entered, started to stand.

"Are you hungry? I can make you something to eat."

"Sit. I ate with Jorge. Go on with what you were doing." His thoughts of Helena turned to instant guilt.

Lubna continued standing, and Thomas hesitated as

he passed the table, glancing at the book. She had placed a knife to mark her place and the cover had closed itself.

"Is that one of my books?" Thomas leaned closer to examine the title.

"I only borrowed it."

Thomas picked it up, allowing the knife to fall free but retaining her place with his thumb. "This is al-Sahwari, isn't it?" He glanced towards Lubna, who stood with hands clasped in front of her, eyes downcast. "Look at me, girl, I'm not angry. Do you read well enough to understand any of this?"

"I read as well as anyone," said Lubna, but she didn't raise her eyes. "And I understand the words well enough."

Thomas turned the book in his hands. He reached for the knife and used it to mark Lubna's place once more, replaced the book on the table.

"You are curious?"

Lubna nodded, and he felt an enormous gratitude. Her interest had distracted him from memories of his past, reminding him of the man he had become.

"About the art of medicine, or the world in general?"

"Both."

"Does your father encourage you in this curiosity?"

"My father has many great traits, but admiration of a woman's curiosity is not among them. He doesn't discourage me, he merely fails to understand."

"You wish to know more?"

Once more, Lubna nodded. Perhaps the lack of any

edge to Thomas's voice offered encouragement and she raised her gaze to meet his.

"I could help you with your work if I gained a little knowledge."

"Do you think I need an assistant?"

"Would it help you to have one? Was it water you wanted or wine?" Lubna turned away.

"Water. I've had enough wine to last me the rest of the year. What would your sister say to you helping me?"

Lubna poured cold water from a jug and brought it back, handed the cup to Thomas.

"She would consider it a waste of both our time. She would say it is not suitable work for a woman. But I know I can do the work she asks of me and help you as well."

"What work is she asking you to do? I understood you were a guest in this house."

"A guest who must pay her keep. I have washed her clothes, and yours too. I cooked a meal and tidied the rooms. I would have tidied in your workshop, but I was unsure what I could touch and what I could not."

"You've only been here a day," Thomas said. "And what has Helena been doing with all this free time you have gifted her?"

"She visits friends."

"Friends on the hill?" Once more, a sense of betrayal washed through him.

"I don't know. She didn't tell me where."

Thomas sat and reached for the book, seeking

273

distraction. "If you truly want to learn, I will find you something better to start with than this. And you can assist me if you wish, or offer your services to some other physician. I wouldn't mind if—"

"I wouldn't want to work for anyone else."

"And I wouldn't make you do so." Thomas stood. "Come into the workshop, I'll find some texts more suitable for you to start on. Do you have any area you are particularly interested in? Herbs? Medicines?" He smiled. "Surgery?"

"I would know everything there is to know," said Lubna.

Thomas smiled again. "You are indeed a strange one." As he moved towards the door, Lubna followed close behind. So different to her sister, she reminded him of himself a long time ago.

CHAPTER TWENTY-FOUR

If what the Vizier's clerk had told them three days before was true, the man who conducted the first investigation now worked for Hasdai ibn Shaprut. He maintained offices on the edge of the Jewish quarter to the south of the city, knowing his clients would not want to venture to his household in the Albayzin. Jorge rapped on a sturdy door, and a few moments later it was opened by a boy little more than a child.

"We have business with your master," Thomas said, and the boy ducked his head and led them inside. Within was a single room ten paces deep by five across. To either side, men worked at tables, fingers stained with ink, heads bent over papers.

Hasdai ibn Shaprut presided over this industry from his own larger table set at the far end of the room. Thomas saw him raise his eyes from his work and watch them approach.

He rose, nodding to Thomas, surveying Jorge with curiosity. "You have business with me, Thomas Berrington? I have not seen you in more than a year. Do you have some new contract you wish me to draw up? Some payment you need chasing?"

"You know I don't chase for payment," Thomas said. "I am here on the Sultan's business."

"The Sultan has his own scribes, does he not?"

"This is business of a different kind."

"I heard a rumour you were set a task," said Hasdai. "So it is true?"

"That depends on what the rumour is," said Jorge.

Hasdai afforded him a brief glance. "We are intelligent men, there is no need to play games. I do not believe I am likely to be involved in anything that might help you."

"We seek someone who works for you. His name is Bilal Abd al-Rahman."

Hasdai's eyes flicked away from Thomas to find something beyond his right shoulder. "Yes, he came to me four months ago. A good worker." He raised his voice. "Bilal, these men would speak with you."

Thomas turned to see a slim man seated half way along the room start to rise. There was little space and he had to come from behind the table, moving faster than necessary. A second clerk blocked his way, preventing Bilal from reaching the central walkway, and all at once he pushed against the table, tipping it over. Papers

276

scattered, an inkwell and oil lamp broke against the tile, and then Bilal was running towards the door.

Thomas remained where he was, rooted to the spot in surprise. It was Jorge who reacted first, launching himself after the man. He would have caught Bilal, but one of the other clerks came from behind his own desk and Jorge careered into him, both of them crashing to the floor. The tumbled clerk cried out in pain. Jorge skidded beneath a desk, scrabbling to recover.

Bilal crashed through the door and was gone.

The room erupted into chaos. Two clerks stamped at papers set alight by the shattered lamp. Another picked up those not being trodden into the tiles, while yet another attempted to right the overturned desk. Clerks milled along the central aisle.

"Back to your desks!" Hasdai shouted. "Back to your desks now! Ibraham—stop destroying those documents, the fire is out." Hasdai clapped his hands, walking through the centre of the chaos as men ducked behind their desks and made some pretence at a return to work.

Jorge climbed to his feet, rubbing at his side.

"Are you hurt?" Thomas asked.

"Nothing that needs your skills, my friend. I would have caught him if that fool hadn't tripped me."

Thomas turned to the other man, only now sitting up. He had a cut on his forehead which bled profusely. Thomas pinched it with his fingers, satisfied it needed no stitching or bandage. Instead, he reached into his satchel

and held some linen against the wound and told the man to press hard.

"What just happened here?" Hasdai asked.

"You told me he was a good worker."

"He is skilled, needing no instruction for any task he is set."

"Did you know he worked for the Vizier?"

"He didn't say, but it was obvious he knew what he was doing. I had no doubts about his work, none at all. Nor, until this moment, about the man himself. I liked him."

"Where does he live?"

"In the Albayzin, of course. Where does anyone who does the real work of this city live? But exactly where, I could not say."

"Would anyone else know?"

Hasdai lifted a shoulder as he looked around. "Is anyone here a friend to Bilal?"

The men kept working, their heads down.

"Tell them you don't blame them," said Jorge quietly. "They worry you will taint them with his deeds. Better still, is there somewhere you can go for a moment while we ask our questions? They'll answer more honestly if you are not here."

Hasdai looked as if he was about to object, then nodded and walked to the end of the long room. A small door set into the wall admitted him to another chamber. He closed the door behind him.

"It is important we speak with Bilal," Thomas said,

raising his voice so all could hear. They had stopped working now their master had left the room, the excitement of the moment still fresh. "We are here on the Sultan's business."

"Is Bilal wanted?" the man three places down from where Bilal worked asked.

"He is wanted to ask questions of, nothing more. He is not under suspicion of anything." Though Thomas knew that was no longer the case. Why would an innocent man flee?

"I would not call him a friend, but we have walked together once or twice after work on our way home. He lives close to me, a little further up the hill."

"You know his lodgings?" asked Jorge, and Thomas stepped backwards, allowing him to continue the questioning.

"Not his doorway, no. He continues on when I pass through my own. But he must live nearby for he said so one evening when we parted."

"Can you show us?" asked Jorge.

The man's gaze flickered to the end of the room. "I have work to finish."

"We will ask your master," said Jorge. "If need be, we will pay for your time. How far is your room?"

"Half a mile, no more."

"How far up the slope of the Albayzin?"

"Near the top, close to the city wall."

Jorge nodded as though that was the answer he'd expected. "Thomas, go speak with Hasdai, offer him coin

if you have to. I will speak with some of these others and see if there is anything else they know."

Hasdai had been happy to accept fair payment in exchange for the man's time, and Thomas was content to pay, knowing there was no uplift in the expected fee. Jorge chatted with the man as they climbed the slopes of the hill across from the palace. The higher they climbed, the narrower the alleyways became, doors letting out directly on to the street. The steepness of the hillside meant the houses lacked any courtyard or gardens. The buildings were barely deep enough to accommodate a family, let alone the luxury of outside space.

Thomas picked up a little information about the man as they climbed, enough to know he lived alone and shared rooms with other workers, but mostly he tried to puzzle through why Bilal had fled. It made little sense, unless he was guilty of something. Or feared something. It had been a long time since Thomas had been feared, and he believed that the life he once led was left far behind when he came to this land.

"What did you and Bilal speak of on your journey home?"

The clerk turned his head as he strode forward, walking fast, used to the climb. "What do single men talk of when they're alone? You know how it is."

Thomas caught Jorge's smile.

"He didn't speak of his life before he came to work for Hasdai?"

"I never asked and he never offered. We walked together once or twice a week and always spoke of insignificant matters. I don't know why he ran."

"He'll likely be caught by now," said Jorge.

Thomas slowed. "Caught? How?"

"One of the clerks near the door went outside after Bilal. He said he was gone already, but that two soldiers were in pursuit."

"When were you going to tell me this?"

"I'm telling you now so you needn't wear yourself out on the climb. I expect we'll see him coming back down any moment. Under arrest."

"Perhaps the soldiers weren't chasing Bilal," Thomas said.

"And perhaps I'm a full man."

They reached the city wall and passed through an unguarded gate into an area beyond its protection. The ground finally levelled off, rough-built houses pressing close on either side, some using the city wall as their own. The clerk stopped in front of a doorway.

"My rooms lie within. When we part, Bilal continues to the end of the alley and turns right."

"That's all you know?"

"It is all I know. May I return to my work now?"

Thomas pressed a small coin into the man's hand and watched as he trotted back down the slope.

"He seems keen to return to his labours," said Jorge.

"Some men are made that way."

"You realise we are no closer to Bilal than we were in the workshop?"

"Of course we are. The man said he lives nearby, that he turns right at the end of the alley."

"We'll go and see, then, shall we?"

Thomas shook his head at Jorge's intransigence and led the way. At the end of the alley, they turned right along one even narrower, lined on one side with accommodation no different to that they had already passed, but on the other the buildings were more scattered and rough scrub rose along the hillside.

"We've left civilisation behind," said Jorge.

"You think civilisation ends at the palace walls."

"I'm here, aren't I?"

Thomas wondered if Jorge was finding his change of circumstance difficult to adjust to. The first few days had provided a distraction from his usual life, but now his interest might be waning.

"Leave if you want," Thomas said, his tone sharper than he intended. Bilal could be a genuine lead to something, but he was aware he was ignoring his suspicions of Olaf, the only other lead they had, in pursuit of a man who didn't want to be found.

"I didn't mean I wanted to go," said Jorge. "But how do you plan to find this man? He could be in any one of these rooms. Or even beyond." Jorge waved a hand towards an alley which dipped away from them, barely wide enough to accommodate a man's shoulders. It

wasn't the first one they'd passed. "Do we knock on every door?"

"If we have to."

Jorge looked around. "This isn't the kind of place that welcomes strangers."

"Whether they like it or not, we have little choice, so we'd better get on with it." Thomas approached the nearest door and hammered against it.

There was no response.

"These are the homes of working men," said Jorge. "Their inhabitants won't return until evening."

"I lived in a place like this when I first came to the city," Thomas said, moving the few paces required to knock at the next door.

"Then I feel sorry for you."

"It was an improvement on my life until then. I thought I had discovered the most wonderful place on earth."

Jorge laughed and patted Thomas on the shoulder. "And what do you think of life now? Living with two beautiful sisters in a large house, friend to the most powerful man in the land?"

Thomas scowled. "Sometimes I miss the simplicity of those days." He hammered on another door. "Is there no one home anywhere?"

"As I said—" Jorge stopped as there came a commotion from the end of the alley. A woman ran shouting from a doorway, waving her arms. Her words were Spanish, spoken too rapidly for Thomas to make

out more than one or two, but he only needed to understand one, derived from Arabic. *Asesinato* —murder.

The woman was distressed and Jorge took her to one side, his voice calm, one hand on her shoulder, the other holding her hand. Thomas watched, impressed and jealous of the man's ability to put people at ease. While Jorge extracted her tale, Thomas entered the doorway she had rushed from.

Within lay a narrow hallway with more doors leading off to left and right. At the end, a small window lacking glass looked out across the city, the minarets of the many mosques rising above the ochre roof tiles. In any other house it would have been a view to appreciate; here it was no more than a means of admitting a little light.

A doorway three rooms down stood ajar and Thomas went there to discover what had frightened the woman. He knew from the smell what he would find even before he saw Bilal's body tumbled across a narrow cot. Papers lay strewn across the floor, some torn, others stained with the blood that pooled on the bedclothes and tiles. Bilal lay on his side, a slash across his neck so deep his head lolled at an unnatural angle. Even so, Thomas knelt, careful to avoid the blood, and felt for a pulse, unsurprised when he found none. The body was still as warm as that of a living man, but all life had fled.

Thomas stood and surveyed the space.

The room was tiny, a narrow cot taking up half the floor, with a small desk jammed hard against the opposite wall. There was no chair, and Thomas imagined the man sitting on the bed to work, writing contracts in his own time. It was one explanation for the papers scattered about. Thomas knelt and retrieved a few, turning them over. Most were written in Arabic, but here and there he found a few in Latin, Greek, Spanish too. Bilal had been a skilled clerk, one who clearly took private work outside that given him by Hasdai. Had the old Jew discovered this, Bilal would have been dismissed immediately.

Thomas turned as Jorge came into the room.

"She collects laundry from these rooms and others along the alleyway. She says she doesn't enter the rooms themselves. Each man leaves a sack outside the door. Bilal's is still there. She said the door was open when she came to it and she glanced inside, saw him as he is now." Jorge studied the body a moment with a cool gaze before he shook his head. "We are seeing too much death lately."

"Did she see anyone else?"

"Not a soul when she arrived. She tells me this building is empty during the day. Filled with single men at night." Jorge glanced around. "It's a depressing life, isn't it?"

"I never found it so," Thomas said.

Jorge smiled. "Why does that not surprise me?

You're unlike other men, that's for sure. Anyway, she said she saw no one here, but on her approach, two men almost knocked her over, they were running so fast."

"In which direction?"

"She came from the far end of the alley, the opposite direction to us or we'd have seen them as well."

"Could she describe them?"

"It happened too fast, but she said she thought they were soldiers of some kind."

"In what colours?"

Jorge shook his head. "That she couldn't say. I pressed her a little on the matter, as hard as I dared without putting a scare into her. She's had enough scares already today, but she knew no more, I'm sure."

"You said a clerk saw two soldiers running after Bilal when he fled the workshop."

"It's too much of a coincidence that someone else came to kill the man at the same time, don't you think?"

"Too great a coincidence they were there at exactly the same time as us," Thomas said, shaking his head. He knelt again and began to collect together the scattered papers. "Help me gather these. Is the woman still outside?"

"I sent her to find a guard. Someone will need to know of the death."

"I would prefer we are no longer here when they arrive," Thomas said. "Is his laundry sack still outside?"

"It was when I came in."

"Fetch it, I need something to put these papers in."

286

Jorge straightened. "You've no need to tidy the room, he's too dead to care."

"I think the papers are important. They could be the reason he was killed."

"Wouldn't they have taken anything of importance already?"

"Soldiers? How many soldiers do you know can read? They may have taken something, but they wouldn't know what was important or not. Go fetch the sack."

Jorge sighed and ducked through the doorway, returned with a small linen sack. He emptied the contents on the floor and held the neck wide while Thomas stuffed documents inside.

He hesitated, taking a last look around the room, searching for a place Bilal might have hidden anything else. These papers had been in plain view, but if the man possessed something secret, it would be elsewhere. Thomas lifted the bed. Nothing beneath. He pulled the small desk away from the wall and upended it, examined it for a hidden compartment. Again nothing. He started tapping on the walls.

"Are you looking for more tunnels?" Jorge asked.

Thomas gave up. The room was too small, the walls too thin for a hiding place. He nodded and pushed Jorge towards the door.

"We're done, there's nothing here for us anymore."

Outside in the alleyway, it was as quiet as when they'd arrived. This high on the Albayzin, the streets were deserted during daylight, the hubbub of the city

lying far below. Thomas led the way he considered the fastest route to his house, although he didn't know the area well and found their passage blocked on several occasions. Eventually he came to a place he recognised and their progress grew faster.

"That woman will tell the guards we were there," said Jorge.

"It doesn't matter. I have the Sultan's seal, and it seems the entire city knows of our quest. I'm more worried about the soldiers that chased Bilal. I don't believe they were waiting for him."

"Do you think they were following us?" said Jorge, and once more Thomas knew he had underestimated the man.

"I was hard on Zoraya yesterday. I wouldn't be surprised if she told Olaf about it and he sent someone to follow us. It means we're getting closer."

"It means we're in more danger," said Jorge. "What if they were following us until we came to a quiet spot, and then attacked?"

"If that was the plan, they wouldn't have gone after Bilal. Whoever is behind this is a step ahead of us. They know where the threats are and are shutting them down, one by one. The soldiers followed Bilal and killed him because they knew he was a danger to whoever gave them orders. And who better to give soldiers an order than the Sultan's general?"

"It's a dangerous game they play," said Jorge. "If word gets back to Abu al-Hasan Ali, Olaf will find

himself without a head. His daughters will be in danger too. Plotting against a Sultan is no small matter. You have seen how he treats those who displease him."

"What about Faris al-Rashid? He accosted us in the palace itself, as good as threatened us, and he knows his way around. Could he be Olaf's master? I wonder. When Olaf found us in that chamber with him, did he already know we were there?"

"He would know Zoraya, too. I didn't take to the Neapolitan, but he's just the kind of man who would appeal to Zoraya. Naples and Greece are close in spirit as well as geography. Would Faris order a man killed?"

Thomas didn't bother replying to the question, the answer self-evident. "Faris is fond of his head, though, and even more aware of the dangers than Olaf."

"He is used to plot and intrigue, and a far more credible suspect than Olaf, now I think on it. He is also more useful to the Sultan. His money, and that of his friends, props up the Sultan's rule. And he has men of his own. Strangers to the city, which would be an advantage."

"We have too many suspects," Thomas said as they turned into the alley leading to his house. "Why did Faris invite us to join him? There's more going on here than we know. Have there been rumours of insurrection?"

Jorge laughed as they entered Thomas's house. "Rumours of insurrection? You overestimate me. I'm a mere eunuch who doesn't trouble himself with such things."

"Your entire life is plot and intrigue."

"Ah, but of a different kind, and all in the pursuit of love, not death. As for Faris wanting us to join him, don't they say you should keep your enemies close?"

Jorge stopped as Lubna came from the workshop.

"You are early," she said. "My sister is not at home, and I have not started the evening meal yet. If you are hungry, I can probably find something."

"We're not hungry, but I need your help. Jorge isn't staying."

"Am I not?"

Thomas lifted the sack of papers. It rustled. "Do you read Arabic? Latin? Spanish even?"

"You know I read nothing."

"Then I have more useful work for you. Go to the barracks, find Olaf and tell him of Bilal's death. See if you can slip something into the conversation and ask him if he sent anyone to follow us. You can say for our protection if it sounds better."

"And of course he will tell me all of this."

"Thank him for the lesson he gave me yesterday. His answer, one way or the other, will prove enlightening."

Jorge nodded, accepting his task. Once he was gone, Thomas took the sack into the courtyard and emptied its contents on to the table where he, Jorge and Helena had eaten.

Lubna came to stand at his side.

"I want you to help me read these, as fast as we can."

"Some of the pages have blood on them," said Lubna.

Thomas glanced at her, but saw no sign of revulsion. She was merely stating the obvious.

"I'll take those," he said. "Do you read Latin or Greek?"

"Arabic only."

"Then start on those. I'll read the rest."

"What are we looking for?"

Thomas drew a seat to the table and reached for a document, glancing at it before passing it to Lubna.

"I don't know until we find it, or even if there's anything to find. But the man who possessed these documents is dead, and the reason why will be hidden somewhere here. If you find anything significant, tell me at once."

Lubna gave him a look that contained an entire conversation, then chose to sit cross-legged on the stone slabs before starting to read.

CHAPTER TWENTY-FIVE

Thomas finished with the last of the documents written in Spanish and broke off, twisting to ease the pain in his back. He rose stiffly while Lubna turned from those she held in her hand and looked up at him. For a moment, he caught some fleeting emotion in her eyes, something he couldn't decipher, and wondered how the world might change if he threw Helena out.

A breeze had started up, plucking at the loose papers. Thomas went to the edge of the courtyard and retrieved four round stones used as decoration, carried them back and laid them on the pages.

"I need to walk around for a moment. You should take a break too."

Lubna put down the paper she was holding immediately and rose as though she hadn't been sitting on the tiles for over an hour.

"Do you want water?"

"I can get it," Thomas said.

Lubna glanced at the sky, studied the shadows in the courtyard before turning away.

"What time did Helena leave?" Thomas asked, following her into the kitchen.

"Early, for Helena at least. She didn't say where she was going."

"Friends on the hill."

"She misses her old life."

"Hmm."

Lubna poured cold water for them both and drained half her cup in three quick gulps. "The life she led wasn't real, was it? What you do is real. What my father does, even what the Sultan does, is real." She stopped with an expression on her face as though she may have said too much.

Thomas detected no hint of jealousy in her voice, only a note of disapproval. He ignored whatever might be there.

"Have you found anything?"

Lubna drank again and, when she had drained the glass, shook her head. Water had spilled from her chin and marked her shift.

"Nothing that makes any sense to kill a man over. Bills of sale, contracts for land, a request to fund an expedition of exploration. Any of it might mean something, but without more to go on, I cannot tell."

"Is there anything with the name of Faris al-Rashid on it? Or Valentin al-Kamul, Antonio Galbretti, Domingo

Alkhabaz?" Thomas reeled off the names of the men who had been in the palace chamber two days earlier. He no longer suspected them of direct involvement, but their interest still puzzled him.

Lubna held a hand up, shaking her head. "Stop, stop, too many names. Say them again more slowly."

Thomas repeated the list. When he was done, Lubna shook her head again.

"Perhaps. I don't know. I was not looking for any name in particular. You should have told me this before we started. Now I have to go through those papers again."

"You're right, I was too impatient. You continue with the others and I'll check the pages you've already read."

"No—keep working on those I cannot read, it will not take long to skim them for names." She glanced beyond him to the courtyard. "I should prepare a meal. Helena will want to eat on her return."

"Don't bother on my account," Thomas said, "I can eat with Jorge later."

"And drink, no doubt." A smile tugged at her lips.

"You're right, he's not a good Muslim, but then neither am I."

"I mean no criticism." Lubna cast her gaze from his, busying herself refilling their cups. "I only meant I found him amusing in his enthusiasm for wine."

"Yes, I believe women find him amusing. We'd better get back to work if time's short." Thomas took the cup from her and turned away.

It was Lubna who found the first document. It was signed by Valentin al-Kamul, the name printed neatly, which was fortunate because his signature was made with such a flourish, it was indecipherable. *Like the man himself,* Thomas thought.

He leaned towards Lubna as they both read the document.

She placed a finger on the paper. "Why would he buy a share in a mine?"

"Why would any man? For profit, I suspect. I doubt very much he even knows where it is."

Lubna turned the sheet over and Thomas tried not to show his annoyance. He knew the questions should have occurred to him.

"Qasada," she said. "The mine is outside Qasada." She frowned. "Where is that?"

"A day's ride east. It's a small town in the foothills of the Sholayr."

"A day east? Is it our territory or Spanish?"

"The last I heard, it was ours, just. It passes from side to side time and again, but at the moment it's Moorish."

"A dangerous spot to go into business," said Lubna.

"Commerce is commerce, and this man is no more a Moor than I am. He'll be able to deal with whoever claims title to the territory. How large is his share in this mine?" Thomas tried to take the paper from Lubna, but she kept hold, bending close to study the words.

"A quarter share, it says here." She glanced up. "He paid a great deal of money for it."

"How much?"

When she told him, Thomas shook his head. "Valentin is a rich man, that isn't a large sum for someone like him."

"I could live my whole life in luxury on such an amount."

"He already lives in luxury, and his investment will only bring him more. Do we know who the other shareholders are? Does the document say?" Once more, he reached for the paper. Once more, Lubna retained her hold.

Thomas waited—half amused, half annoyed.

Lubna shook her head. "It does not. There is another signature, but I can't make it out, and the corner of the paper where the name is printed is stained with blood and the seal indistinct."

"Put it aside, we can return to it later. It may be significant. You did well."

Lubna found three more documents containing names she was searching for, Thomas only one. He started on the balance of Arabic documents and came across something that intrigued him, even though it wasn't connected to the task in hand. A bill of trade for a roll of cloth made out in the name of the Sultan's son, Abu Abdullah. He would have missed it altogether except the trader's name was Carlos Rodriguez.

Thomas read the bill of goods, then tossed the paper into the stack already read. Interesting, but irrelevant.

The shadow cast by the courtyard wall touched them. The breeze picked up, snatching at the papers, which would have scattered had they not been trapped beneath stones. Lubna looked up and stretched.

"I ought to prepare the meal for Helena's return."

"You weren't brought here to be a servant."

"Say that to Helena, not me. I don't mind. I am not like her, I need to be kept busy." Lubna stood, as lithe as before, and padded into the house on bare feet.

Thomas watched her go, continuing to stare at the empty doorway long after she had disappeared.

Eventually, he returned to the small pile of documents they had set aside, picked them up and went into his workshop. He spread the five documents across the table and leaned in to study each in turn, searching for something he was unsure he would recognise even if he found it.

"Olaf swore he sent none of his men to follow us," said Jorge in response to Thomas's question. They were in the room above the inn, day turning to night outside the window.

"Did you believe him? Those men were soldiers."

"Not all soldiers belong to Olaf. When I talked to

him, I got a different impression to you. I no longer believe he's involved."

"The soldiers in this city are under his command. Whoever they were knew to follow us, and they knew who Bilal was. Or do you think Bilal was their quarry all along? And why did Olaf try to kill me?"

Jorge laughed. "Olaf doesn't know his own strength or speed. You surprised him, you were a little more skilled than expected, he said. I think he just reacted, nothing more."

Thomas shook his head, reluctant to let go of Olaf as a suspect yet. "Whoever is behind this, why wait until now to kill Bilal?"

"Because he wasn't a threat until we came looking. Safer to leave him be and not raise suspicion. Bilal was a clerk to Tahir—secrecy and confidentiality will be seared into his bones. I doubt he would have told us anything."

"I'm not so sure." Thomas paced the room while Jorge sat on the bed. Lamps burned across the square and the scent of food and murmur of conversation drifted through the open window. "Imagine how he must feel, dismissed from his position, forced to work in a back-street sweatshop. You saw how many clerks were crammed into that space. How would you feel if they tossed you out of the harem and you had to exist as some front of house in a brothel?"

"A man makes what he can of life, the highs and lows both. But you're right, perhaps he would have spoken to us."

Thomas picked up the small pile of documents he and Lubna had identified as of interest. "I don't understand why we didn't find anything else."

"Such as?"

"You know what. Bilal undertook the first investigation. I don't believe he would have destroyed his findings. If he has these papers, he would have kept the notes he made as well. But they're missing."

"Is that what they were after?" said Jorge. "Soldiers who can read after all—what is the world coming to?"

"And these?" Thomas waved the papers in his hand. "Does someone else know of their existence? Surely these are a threat too."

"Perhaps, perhaps not. But they're all we have. Tell me what they contain and see if I see the same pattern as you."

Thomas pulled out a chair and sat at the small table. He spread the papers across its surface.

"That's my point, there is no pattern that I can see. The only things linking them are the names of the men we saw with Faris."

"Is Faris himself named on any of them?" Jorge made no attempt to rise and come across.

"Not directly. But look, Valentin al-Kamul is on this one, and this." Thomas pushed two pages to one side. "Galbretti on these three. All of them linked."

"But in what?" said Jorge. "Tell me the matters listed there."

Thomas shook his head. "It makes no sense to me.

Here Valentin has bought a quarter share in a mine—iron ore, it seems. The other with his name on is for farmland. Poor farmland at that. It makes no sense."

"Is the land close to the mine?"

Thomas examined the papers again, though he knew the answer, had pored over the pages long after they had stopped making any sense.

"Perhaps half a day's ride apart. Both in the foothills of the Sholayr."

"Could it be there's more iron beneath the farmland?"

"It would make sense, but there's no mention of it here."

"Which there wouldn't be, otherwise the price paid would be considerably higher. Valentin may know more than is shown on these pages. Is there benefit in playing along with them so we get a chance to question them without drawing suspicion on ourselves?"

"These others," Thomas said, ignoring the question as he pushed the papers around randomly. "Another tract of farmland, this one a day from the mine in the other direction, alongside al-wādi al-kabīr. That land might be in Spanish hands by now. And here, Galbretti has sold estates in Sicily and is having the proceeds sent here."

"And Don Domingo?"

"Title to a house in Qurtuba—what link lies there? Nothing that I can see."

"Don Domingo is no fool, despite mixing with those men. He sees the way the war is going, and his blood is

Spanish, not Moor. When this war ends—and it can end only one way—he will have his place secured." Jorge leaned forward, his face in shadow but eyes bright. "Are you thinking the same thing as me, Thomas?"

"I don't know. What are you thinking?"

Jorge sat back, smiling. "There are two possibilities here." He held up a closed fist before raising a finger. "First—these papers mean nothing. They are the random dealings of wealthy men and we should dismiss them as no more than that." He allowed a second finger to pop loose. "Or second, these men are planning something and are connected with the killings. Whether they're behind them directly or not, I haven't made up my mind about yet, but they are plotting some mischief, I am sure. They are involved in some way."

Thomas stared at Jorge a long time before nodding. "And Zoraya? Is she involved or not?"

"What is to say they are not all in it together?"

"We need to know more about these land acquisitions. Is there anything here we don't see yet? They are all border land. It will be the first to go when the war finally comes. But if they are involved together, why was Bilal killed?"

"For something he knew that was not written down? He was a man of letters, as aware as you of the power of words. He would never commit something so important to ink and paper."

Thomas looked away through the window. "So whatever knowledge he might have possessed is gone."

301

He turned back towards Jorge. "You think he had worked it out? The answer we seek?"

"He was a learned man, and no fool. Yes, I think he knew who is behind this. Likely not the killer himself, for that man is merely the sacrificial pawn. It is his master we seek, the one guiding this assassin's rage."

Thomas said nothing, his mind as exhausted as his body. This task was as hard as anything he had ever experienced. Too many suspects, not enough evidence.

"But you're no fool, either, Thomas," said Jorge. "If Bilal was able to discover who lies behind the killings, then so can you."

Thomas shook his head. "Your faith in my abilities is sadly misjudged. I think I have less idea now than when we started."

Jorge smiled. "If we assume for the moment Olaf and Zoraya are not behind the plot—and we can always come back to them—then who? You must have had suspicions when we started."

Thomas returned the smile. "I thought Faris behind it, of course. And you?"

"Too simple, too obvious," said Jorge.

"As I quickly realised. So who do you think?"

"What about Abu Abdullah?"

Thomas nodded. "I considered him, too. Because we are looking for those who have something to gain. Not from the deaths, but from who will be damaged by them."

"That would be the Sultan," said Jorge. "Abu Abdullah wants his father's position."

Thomas nodded again. "It's the only conclusion I am able to come to as well. Not who gains, but who loses. But it's not Abu Abdullah, either. He would suffer as much as the Sultan."

"Explain the loss to me," said Jorge, leaning forward.

"I don't need to, you understand it better than me. You live among these people, know their ways more intimately than anyone. The only thing keeping the Sultan in power is strength, real or imagined. He is regarded as a strong leader, a warrior, and this land needs a warrior at the moment more than it needs a ruler. If he goes, his son is tainted the same way as him, and will never gain power."

"If the Sultan can't stop people dying within the walls of his own palace, he is no longer seen as strong, but weak. The wolves start creeping closer, sensing that weakness."

"Are we back to Faris then?" Thomas said.

"Faris wouldn't be accepted by the people."

"Then Faris plotting on someone else's behalf?"

"Which brings us once more to who gains most from the Sultan's removal."

"His sons."

"Which sons—Aixa's or Zoraya's?"

Thomas groaned and put his head in his hands. "I can't think on this anymore tonight. My thoughts are as

shattered as broken glass. I need sleep, I need to forget plotting until the morning."

Jorge rose from the bed. "Then let's go and eat, then walk the streets for a while. Even visit the bathhouse and seek some relaxation." He crossed the room and laid a hand on Thomas's shoulders, lifted his chin so he could look into his eyes. It was an uncomfortably intimate gesture. "Sometimes such matters are best left to mature in darkness. Turn off your mind and think of good food, good wine and, if you wish, a good woman."

"I have a woman."

"Then eat and drink and go home and make love to her. But turn this off." He rapped the top of Thomas's skull with his knuckles.

Thomas made for the door. "I'll try, but it's not easy. All I want is some idea of where to look. I never thought we would end up with too many suspects."

"Forget it," said Jorge. "By morning, an idea may come fully formed to you."

"By morning we might both be dead."

"In that case, let us enjoy living for as long as we can."

CHAPTER TWENTY-SIX

As he ascended the dark alleys of the Albayzin, Thomas realised he wasn't thinking of Helena, but her sister. An image of Lubna at the start of the day came to him. Bright eyed, fascinated as she mixed herbs and powders and oils. Her difference from Helena was obvious and intriguing. Each time he made an effort to expel the thought, a moment later it was there in his mind again. A longing for something he couldn't express. Thomas considered himself weak-willed for not expelling the jumble of images, but at least the wine had loosened his thoughts and allowed something else to briefly occupy them. Jorge had been right about that.

Narrow steps brought him to a level roadway paved with smooth stones. Thomas stopped to catch his breath, looking towards the palace of al-Hamra which dominated the entire city. As it was meant to.

He was missing something and had finally worked

out what it was. The documents recovered from Bilal's room were noise, nothing more. There had to be others.

Something sounded below, down among the twisting steps he had just ascended. A foot kicking a stone. In the still of the night, it clattered away. Thomas walked back to the head of the steps and looked down. Only darkness. A hundred men could be hidden there, and he thought of the footsteps he and Prea had heard in the tunnels. He waited, alert, but nothing more came. Some creature—a dog, a cat, a rat? It could have been anything. He hurried on, the night not finished yet.

The house was quiet and he moved carefully, not wanting to wake Helena, knowing he would disturb Lubna unless she had found somewhere else to sleep.

She was curled on the cot, a weak candle guttering on the floor beside her. Thomas moved carefully across the dim room, knowing his way precisely. He touched the wooden bench and pulled on a drawer, easing it open. His hand searched inside, found what it sought.

"Thomas?"

"Go back to sleep. I am going out again."

She sat up, clutching at the blanket as it threatened to reveal her.

"It is the middle of the night."

"Not yet. Go to sleep." He stepped away from the bench, slipping the object he had retrieved beneath his robe.

"What are you hiding?"

"Nothing."

Lubna gave a laugh that contained no humour. "I saw you hide something. Or was it no more than a pretence to wake me? Do you lust for my body as well as my sister's?"

Thomas glanced down at her. So slight. So sure of herself.

"I felt the need of some protection." He drew out the knife he had taken.

Lubna swung her legs to the flagstones and rose.

"What are you planning?"

Thomas sighed. He admired Lubna's sharp mind, but for once would have preferred her not to ask so many questions.

"Those documents we read aren't the ones I seek. Bilal must have others I didn't find."

"You said the soldiers took them."

"I don't think so, not anymore. I believe they're still in his room. We searched, but not hard or long enough. I'm going there now and not coming away until I find them."

"If they exist."

"If they exist, I will find them."

Lubna shook her head. "Wait then, I will come with you."

"Stay here."

Lubna frowned at the roughness in his voice.

Thomas closed the space between them and put his hands on her shoulders, only realising he still held the knife after he had done so, but Lubna didn't flinch.

307

"Why do you think I came back for the blade?" he said.

"I can keep watch while you search."

"If I wanted help, I would have asked Jorge." Lubna was not to know the idea had only just occurred to him. "There will be no one about at this time of night. Go back to sleep, I'll see you in the morning."

He turned and strode away fast before she could say anything.

The Albayzin looked different in the dark and Thomas found himself lost more than once. At one point, he feared he would never find Bilal's room again, then he stumbled on to the city wall and followed it, knowing the accommodation lay just outside its gate.

When at last he found the place, he discovered it had taken no time to let the room again. The outer entrance to the street was open and he counted down five doors. He expected his push to open it, but instead he found it locked. He knocked, then again, louder. There was no response from within, but voices came from behind other doors. Thomas knocked again, eventually rewarded by the throwing of a bolt.

A short man peered out, his eyes barely open. "What do you want at this time of night?"

"I need to search your room."

"I am a stonemason, sir, I possess nothing of value."

Thomas reached into his robe, withdrew a gold maravedi and pressed it into the man's hand.

"You do now." The coin was more than the man could earn in three months. "I need an hour alone in your room."

The man shook his head and peered out, looking for a woman.

"I only moved in this evening, I don't understand what—"

"Do you want the coin or not?"

The man looked down at his hand and nodded.

"Find somewhere else then. Go sit on the hillside and enjoy the stars."

The man backed into the room and started to dress in rough clothing. Thomas stepped in after him, already looking around. The small window let in some moonlight, but not enough for his task. On a stone shelf lay an oil lamp and flint, and Thomas lit it. After climbing the hill through the night, he found the little light it gave dazzling.

"An hour?" the man asked, standing in the doorway.

"No more. I will call you when I finish." For a moment, Thomas thought a second coin would be needed, but the man nodded and disappeared.

Thomas held the lamp high and looked around. A stain still marked the floor where Bilal had died. Only the bedclothes had been changed, everything else remained the same. Next week it would be this new occupant placing his soiled clothing in a linen sack

outside the door. Life goes on, measured by such small events. For a moment, Thomas wondered if the man had thrown out anything of Bilal's, but he doubted it. Whatever remained behind would be considered good fortune rather than bad luck: new clothes, perhaps even some money.

He had already searched the small desk, but did so again, placing the lamp as high as he could so its glow filled the room. Already its brilliance was fading as his eyes grew accustomed to the light.

There were three drawers in the desk, shallow but deep. Thomas pulled them all the way out and laid them on the bed. They contained unmarked paper, some quills, and a small bottle of ink as well as the makings for more. A few small coins lay scattered in the bottom of one. Thomas tipped the contents on to the bed and turned each drawer over, but they were nothing more than what they seemed. He turned his attention to the desk itself, upending it and going to his knees, feeling underneath, tugging at the joints. Nothing there, either.

He stood and surveyed the room. The only other piece of furniture was the bed.

Thomas replaced the items in the drawers and slid them back into the desk. He pulled the thin mattress from the bed and leaned it against the wall. He overturned the bed as he had the desk and worked his way along every inch of it, with the same result. He tried the mattress, probing its paltry comfort with his fingers, even taking his knife to ease loose some stitching so he could feel

inside. He kicked the bed in frustration. Only the walls remained, and he thought of the tunnels running through the palace. Perhaps.

He began next to the door. The room wasn't high, and Thomas could reach the ceiling without stretching. He pushed against each stone, used the knife between courses, but everything remained firm. He cursed the builders because the structure was sound, not a single loose stone that might be used to conceal secret documents. Thomas pulled the bed into the room and searched the wall by the window. He took special care around the narrow opening, but once more, the masons had done a good job.

He muttered under his breath and stepped back, defeated.

Something moved under his heel and he almost lost his balance.

He stepped to one side and went to his knees. His fingers splayed across a rough slab and he pushed, rocking it slightly. Thomas took the knife and forced it into a crack. The mortar joint was loose and he levered the slab to lift it a little. He pushed his fingertips beneath one edge, used the knife again and the slab came clear. Thomas laid it to one side.

A small chamber had been hollowed out beneath. It must have taken Bilal a week to make this hiding place, unless it was already here and he had only discovered it as Thomas had. Within lay something wrapped in oiled cloth.

Thomas lifted the parcel out and unwrapped it enough to see what lay within. Documents. He laid them to one side and worked the stone slab back into place, dragged the bed back and re-made it. He looked around one last time. There was nothing else here for him. He had uncovered the secret he came looking for.

Another hundred paces and Thomas would be at his door. Helena would be asleep in his bed, but he was aware he didn't want to share it. He shook his head. What other man would turn their back on such a woman, even if she had betrayed them? Helena had been raised to give pleasure. Other men would use—and abuse—her, but Thomas knew he was not one of those men. His head spun with fatigue, but he knew he couldn't sleep until he had examined the documents tucked beneath his robe.

He turned aside, stopping at a sound from behind, coming from the steps he had recently descended. Thomas stood, listening for the second time that night. For a time, nothing, and then, on the edge of hearing, came a scrape, a second following close behind. Someone was coming down the steps in near silence.

Thomas walked on a dozen paces before slipping into a narrow doorway, just deep enough to hide him from the street. He drew his dark cloak around himself, loosened his headscarf and covered his face, waiting.

He was beginning to think he had been overly

cautious when a figure moved across the doorway's entrance, robe flowing behind. Thomas listened as the steps moved away ... slowed ... stopped. There was a scuffling sound, and then they started to return, slower now.

Thomas felt beneath his robe, his hand seeking and closing around the handle of the knife. He drew the blade, readying himself, fearing he was a poor soldier in comparison to whoever came after him. Then his body chilled as voices sounded. There were two of them.

One must have been waiting further along, close to his house in case the follower lost him. Two men. Two men pursuing him. As two men had pursued Bilal. There was no other reason for them to be here, to be acting in this way. Thomas pressed himself hard into the small protection of the doorway, trying to calculate if he was safer there or in the open where he would have more freedom of movement.

As the footsteps came closer, the whispered voices grew louder. He tried to make out what they were saying, but nothing made sense, and Thomas realised they were speaking a language he didn't understand. The odd word caught in his memory and he tried to place them.

A chill ran through him.

They were speaking the language Helena used with her father, Olaf still uncomfortable with that of his adopted homeland, grateful for anyone who could ease his mind with words he readily understood.

Two northmen.

Was there significance in that? There had to be. Coincidence could stretch only so far. But if there was significance, what was its nature?

Then they were on him, Thomas still trapped in indecision. He closed his eyes, not wishing to see his own death coming. The voices grew louder, peaked and faded. They had walked right past his hiding place. Thomas let out the breath he had been holding, opened his eyes and peered around the edge of the doorway, not believing they could have walked by without seeing him.

The men moved along the alleyway, approaching the foot of the steps Thomas had descended only a few moments before. They were dressed in black robes, black leggings, but their heads were bare. The hair of one looked dark in the starlight, the other's almost white. Thomas considered slipping from his hiding place and making a dash for home. The door would be unlocked, and once inside, he could bar it from within. There was a second entrance at the side which opened directly into his workshop, but that was always kept locked.

The men stopped and spoke. One turned and Thomas ducked into the shelter of the doorway, but he was too late. A muffled shout sounded, followed by running feet, and he dashed into the alleyway, running as fast as he could for home, not even knowing for sure if these men meant him harm, but convinced in his heart they did.

He knew they had caught him ten paces short of safety when something tugged at his billowing robe. The loss of momentum sent his sandalled feet skidding. He

stumbled, caught his footing and turned, the knife held in front of him.

The men stopped, grins lighting their faces in the gloom.

"What are you running from, surgeon?"

"Why are you following me?"

"We are two soldiers on our way home from the brothel. Why would we want to follow you? Or do you have women we could share? Perhaps a beautiful concubine with skin as pale as milk and hair like snow?"

"Who sent you—was it Olaf?"

"Olaf?" The dark-haired man laughed. "Olaf is the Sultan's man." The soldier's accent was broad, his companion yet to speak, but Thomas knew from past battles always to watch the silent ones. As the man spoke, both moved slowly apart, giving themselves space for an attack. Thomas's stupid knife felt tiny in his hand. Even tinier as the blond man drew a scimitar.

Thomas heard the whisper of steel from the other, but didn't turn his head, eyes locked on to those of the silent attacker.

"Come on, then, kill me if you can." Thomas feinted forward, pleased and surprised to see the man take a step back. That had been the time to attack in turn, to move swift and sure, to finish him. Thomas had seen it often enough in battle. Some men blustered, putting on a good show, but when it came to the job of killing, they were reluctant. He had also seen those who walked away alive, and they were the ones who showed no hesitation. They

were not evil men, but he had seen something turn off in their eyes a moment before they flung themselves into battle. The same thing he felt drain from himself when he followed their example. He kept his momentum going and slashed out at the blond man, his blade flashing in the starlight, the world dark and cloaked in confusion.

Thomas sensed rather than saw the second man move in, too slowly, too cautiously, and Thomas was filled with a rage of exultation, of blood lust. He struck out, spun, knife darting. It caught on something and the dark-haired man staggered back, swearing in his own language, calling out to his companion.

The man made too much noise. The other at least had the sense to keep his silence.

"Help!" Thomas yelled at the top of his voice. "Murder! Help me!"

He turned again, dismissing the loud attacker, lunging fast against the silent one. The man had recovered his wits and didn't fall back this time. He jerked to one side, narrowly avoiding Thomas's blade, then slashed back, his sword coming in from the side. Thomas darted away and the blade hissed through the air, its passing catching a fold of his scarf and slicing clean through. Thomas didn't flinch, but stepped forward again, inside the attack, and the second blow held far less force than the first. He lifted his left arm and took the blade against his robe, the thick folds cushioning the strike. He thrust his knife forward, satisfied when it met resistance. He twisted and the blade caught, tugged from

his hand. The man gasped, fell back, his sword sliding along the fold of Thomas's robe. The movement of razor-sharp steel did what the blow had failed to, slicing through linen, slicing through flesh until it met bone. Hot agony flared in Thomas's arm and he stumbled away, the sword catching for a moment before slipping free. He staggered, clutching at his arm, already blood pulsing from the wound.

He was finished.

CHAPTER TWENTY-SEVEN

"Thomas!" It was a female voice. Not Helena, but her sister. A wave of nausea and dizziness swept through him, the world swimming away.

Something jarred against his side. *So this is how it ends. After all this time, all the miles I have travelled, all the things I have seen and done, it ends here in an alley in the dark.*

He looked up, wanting to see the stars one last time, waiting for the thrust that would end his life. But his attackers were falling back. One of them clutched his chest on the left side. The other held a hand to his waist. They moved faster as windows were thrown open, doorways flung wide.

All at once, there were people around him, hands assisting, and Thomas found Lubna at his side, her tiny frame trying to take his weight and half succeeding

before other hands came to her aid to lead Thomas inside the house.

"Take him through the courtyard to the workshop. I will bring a light."

Men half carried him to the cluttered space he loved more than any other in the world. *A fitting place to die*, he thought, the world tilting once more as he looked at his arm. Blood continued to pulse from the wound, a dark stain spreading across his robe.

Something caught the back of his knees and he sat hard, finding himself on the narrow cot, its mattress still warm from Lubna's slumber. Three men stood around him, dressed in a ragged mix of shirts and robes, one with a rough hank of cloth wrapped at his waist.

"Thank you, gentlemen."

"Thank your servant. It was she who saved you."

He knew each of these men, considered them friends to one degree or another.

"Where did she go?"

"She is fetching a lamp." The speaker looked at Thomas's arm, turning away quickly.

"Get me a blade. They're on the bench. Quickly."

For a moment, none of them moved, then the slap of footsteps approached, a wavering light, and as Lubna entered the room holding a lantern high, a man moved to search, returning with a sharp knife. Thomas took it and slit the remains of his robe on one side, letting it fall away to reveal a deep gash along the outer edge of his arm, half

way between elbow and wrist. Thomas let his breath go, relieved. The cut lay on the outer side and bone had stopped the blade. Blood continued to flow, but Thomas knew it wouldn't kill him unless it went untreated, and who better to treat it than the best surgeon in Gharnatah?

"I can look after him now, sirs. You have my thanks for your help." Lubna started to herd them out. The confusion of the attack and swift flight indoors was leaving Thomas now, a deeper nausea replacing it as he recognised how close he had come to death.

Lubna returned a moment later and knelt in front of the cot, staring at the hand covering the wound on his arm. No fear or revulsion showed on her face. Even through his pain, Thomas noticed she wore only a thin cotton shift that revealed the shape of her body beneath.

"Tell me what I need to do."

"Silk and a needle. You'll find both in the middle drawer of the bench. And there's an instrument. It looks like scissors, but has blunt edges. Fetch that too."

Lubna ran across the room. She rummaged inside the drawer, returned with the items in her hand.

"Are these what you want?"

"Thread the silk, then fetch a candle and light it. Hold the needle with the instrument and thrust the head into the flame until it glows. Then pass it to me."

Lubna brought a candle, lit it from the lamp and did as he asked. Thomas saw her mouth draw into a tight line as the tip of the needle glowed red and then, briefly, white. She grasped the silk and released the needle so it

hung loose. Thomas took it, burning his fingers. He gritted his teeth and thrust the needle into his flesh. His eyes watered, the pain exquisite, but he worked on, pushing the needle through and out the other side.

"I'm sorry, I can't do the next part with one hand. Pull the silk through until there are two inches either side of the wound. Then cut it off and tie it tight to draw the edges of the wound together."

Lubna nodded, drew on the thread, its passage through his flesh a tiny agony. She cut it, looked around for somewhere to lay the needle.

"Don't put it down. Here, give it back to me."

She handed the needle to Thomas, returned to his arm and tightened the thread, drawing on it. The flesh pulled together and she raised her eyes to his.

"Tighter. As tight as it will go, but careful it doesn't tear the skin."

She complied, twisting as though she too felt his pain.

"Enough?"

"Good."

"Give me the needle," she said, "I can finish the rest."

"You don't know how." His head started to swim again. Shock more than loss of blood, he knew, but there had been some of that, too.

"I am a good seamstress. It seems to me far simpler than stitching a buttonhole in a lady's dress." She took the needle from his limp fingers and Thomas slumped

321

against the cot, barely feeling anything as Lubna pushed the needle into his arm and out the other side of the wound.

"If I pass out, pour raw alcohol into the wound when you are done. And clean it with a cloth soaked in the same. There are fresh bandages in one of the drawers in … I'm not sure where, but in one of them. Bind my arm tight. Then make a draught of poppy, I may need it when I wake for the pain."

Thomas closed his eyes and drifted. He felt the tug on his flesh as Lubna added more stitches, but the pain was distant, no more than someone pinching his skin.

When he next opened his eyes, she was standing across the room unrolling bandage, and Thomas wondered how much time had passed.

"Where's Helena?"

Lubna gave a short laugh. "She is sleeping, of course."

"I expect she knew she could be of no assistance."

"She did not even wake." Lubna turned and came to the cot, the bandage in her hand. "She asked me for poppy again."

"You shouldn't have given her any. She is developing too much of a liking."

"I refused her."

"You did?" Thomas lifted his arm, looking down at Lubna's handiwork. The stitching was exceedingly fine and he smiled, wondering if it would be possible to fit a button through the raw gaps between and doubted it. She

had tied at least three times more stitches than he would have. It would be painful removing them, but he had to admit the scar would be smaller.

"I know full well what opium does to people," she said. "I have seen it in the houses I worked in. I would not do that to my sister, but she went out, and when she came back, she had acquired a little from someone else."

"One of my so-called colleagues, I expect."

Lubna glanced at Thomas. "My sister has always been able to twist men to her will."

"I won't need the poppy after all. You did a good job on my arm. I'll be able to sleep unaided." He started to sit up and Lubna placed a hand against his chest and pushed him down.

"I will make a little for you anyway. I know you are not the kind of man to grow dependent. You are going nowhere. Stay here. Sleep. I will watch over you."

Thomas let her push him back on to the cot. He lay half-awake, only the throbbing in his arm preventing sleep from taking him. He watched as Lubna took poppy heads and drew the sticky milk from them. Dark hair tumbled over her shoulders, but viewed from the side, she might be mistaken for a boy: slim-hipped, slight, steady on her feet. Thomas couldn't ignore the reaction she was starting to trigger in him. She was not beautiful in the way of her sister, but her elfin grace, her infectious smile, hinted at something genuine which Helena lacked. Even as he recognised his infatuation, Thomas suppressed it, acknowledging some kind of loyalty to the

woman sleeping upstairs, even if she had shown little to him. Whatever he felt towards Lubna, he swore, even as watching her, he would never act on it.

Lubna returned and knelt at his side while the poppy steeped in a little wine. She stared at him a long time, a frown creasing her brow.

"There is something I do not understand," she said.

Thomas smiled. "There are many things I don't understand."

"Why are you still alive?"

"Because you came to my aid."

Lubna shook her head. "No. The two attacking you were soldiers. You are a physician. They should have killed you in an instant. Instead, you fought back, you wounded them. I did nothing. Neither did your neighbours. It was you who fought them off." Her frown deepened. "Where did you learn to fight like that?"

"I was lucky, or they were careless."

"No." She shook her head harder, making her hair fly. "I saw you. You fought like..." She sat back on her heels and let her breath go. "You fought like someone who has done so before."

"That poppy will be ready by now."

"I heard them as they ran," said Lubna. "They spoke the language of the north. The language of my father."

"I know. I didn't understand the words, but I recognised the sounds. They were northmen."

Lubna continued to stare at him. "My father would not send men after you."

Thomas closed his eyes, waiting for her to grow tired of questioning him.

"I heard a name," said Lubna. "Sven."

Thomas sat up. "Which one was it?"

"I know not. All I heard was the name, and what they were saying to each other."

Lubna brought the poppy and helped him sit up.

Thomas patted his robe, searching for the document that he suspected was the cause of the attack. Panic flashed through him when he couldn't find it. Lubna tried to make him drink the poppy liquor, but he pushed the cup away.

"I had something in my robe. An oilskin package."

"It is yours? No one was sure. It was lying outside on the roadway. One of your neighbours picked it up. It is on your bench, over there."

Thomas sank back, saw Lubna's muscles tense along her arm as she tried to hold him upright.

"Keep it safe. I must read it, but not tonight. Don't let me sleep late."

The draught of poppy eased the pain in his arm, sleep engulfing him like a sudden thunderstorm, dark and heavy and loud with dreams, and he tossed his head and muttered unintelligible words.

CHAPTER TWENTY-EIGHT

"Well—I suppose I had best move my things in here so you two can share the marital bed!"

Thomas woke to bright sunshine filling one corner of the workshop. Helena stood in the doorway, the light beyond casting her perfect body in clear profile. Lubna's head lay on his chest, her legs tucked beneath her. As she dozed, her arm had snaked across his belly. The sound of her sister's harsh voice stirred her and she sat up, rubbing at her eyes.

"When do you want me to move out?" asked Helena.

"This isn't what it seems." He tried to sit, his head still spinning, but he gripped the edge of the cot and breathed deeply until the world steadied.

"There's little room for mistake, short of me catching you in the act." Then Helena's eyes caught sight of the bandage on Thomas's arm and she put her hand out to steady herself against the side of the door.

Thomas glanced down. Blood had seeped through the linen, staining it dark. It needed changing, and the wound would have to be cleaned again. He tried to sense the level of pain emanating from his arm, but was unable to judge if it was better or worse than during the night.

"What happened here?" And this time, Helena wasn't referring to Lubna and himself.

"I was attacked on my way home. Your sister and our neighbours came to my help."

"Are you hurt? Do you need a surgeon?" Helena was unaware of what she had said.

"Lubna sealed the wound for me. There is nothing untoward going on here, I promise. She is a fine seamstress." Thomas smiled, directing his gaze at Lubna, who stood to one side, arms clasped around her slim body. "I couldn't climb the stairs. I was barely able to sit. Lubna dressed my wound and watched over me. You should be thanking her."

Helena's eyes darted across the room. She offered a brief nod. "Thank you, sister." She looked back to Thomas. "You are well?"

"I ache, but I will survive, yes."

"Good. Now, I am hungry. Lubna, prepare some food." Helena turned away without waiting for an answer.

"She needs to dress my wound first," Thomas said, allowing a little steel to enter his voice.

Helena stopped, turned back. Her body flared in the sunlight and Thomas felt himself tugged in directions he

327

didn't want to even consider. His life had been easier before women came into it, his needs more easily slaked by the girls of the bathhouse.

"Of course, forgive me," said Helena, though there was little of forgiveness in her tone. "I will dress and go into town to break my fast." She turned once more, feet delicate against the warm tile of the courtyard, and Thomas sighed, wondering where she might really be going. Two days ago, he had been sure she was sharing the bed of Zoraya's son. Now the whole idea seemed preposterous.

Lubna approached, tentative.

"You have done nothing wrong," Thomas said, grateful for the distraction from his thoughts. "The opposite, in fact. Were it not for you, those men would have killed me last night."

"You were doing well enough on your own."

"What brought you out?"

"You were shouting so I came immediately." The dusky skin of her cheeks showed darker as she flushed. "I should have taken time to dress properly, but you scared me. You were clearly in danger. Shall I look at your arm?"

"Once you are dressed."

Lubna glanced down at herself, the linen slip falling only half way down her thighs. "It is a little late for that, don't you think? Besides, you are the master in this house and it is allowed for you to look on me. Allowed

for you to use me for your pleasure, if you wish. I am nothing and you are everything."

Thomas turned his head away. "Get dressed, Lubna. This house is different to others you might have been in. You are no slave here, not even a servant. After last night, you are an equal." He waited, listening to movement, the rustle of clothing, and wished he felt less uncomfortable. "I hardly know anything about you. We had met on only a handful of occasions before you came here. You have lived beneath this roof only a few days, but in that time I have seen something in you."

"What have you seen?" She was smiling when he turned back.

"You show interest in my work, or am I wrong?"

Lubna returned to the side of the cot, clothed more appropriately in a cotton robe that fell to her ankles, but her head remained uncovered. It was the attire of a servant, and Thomas disliked seeing her dressed that way. He realised it was probably all she possessed, and felt determined to do something about it. He saw the need for another conversation with Carlos Rodriguez once events settled.

Lubna went to the bench and picked up a bottle of raw alcohol, some cloth, and a roll of linen bandage.

"What you do fascinates me," she said.

"Since you came here, or before?"

"Since I was a little girl. Helena joined the harem when she was very young, her beauty recognised early, but I was dragged around after my father, cleaning his

armour, preparing his food. I saw the work of surgeons on the battlefield. I met you first when I was twelve years old, but you won't remember."

"I think I do. It was at al-Munekhar? The Spanish were attacking from the east. Your father killed a score of men that day. You were a tiny thing, all wiry strength and attitude, as I recall. We met in his tent at sunset."

Lubna appeared pleased at his recollection. "Father likes nothing better than to kill Spaniards."

"Even though he's no Moor?" Thomas thought back to the two northmen who'd attacked him. Would Olaf Torvaldsson know who they were? Or was Olaf the one who had sent them?

"He's loyal to the Sultan. More loyal than any man in al-Andalus." Her words, even if true, did little to resolve the questions in his head. "Do I cut the old bandage loose?"

"On the bench you will find a small instrument. It looks like a very small knife with a sharp blade. Use it to cut the outer layer, and then unwind the rest. And bring me that package."

Lubna brought the blade, but left the oilskin wrapped papers where they were. She started work on the bandage, pulling the sticky blood-soaked linen away. When she came close to the skin, it stuck, and as she pulled, it ripped the hairs along his arm free and Thomas winced.

"That hurts almost more than the wound itself. I want to read those papers of Bilal's. Get them for me."

Lubna laughed. "You wouldn't last a second in the harem." She eased the last of the stained bandage away and gazed at the wound, her head to one side. "And you can read the papers when I've finished. I tried, but they're in that old writing I can't read."

"Fetch them."

"Later. You are more important."

Thomas saw she wasn't to be deflected and leaned back against the table, forcing himself to be a good patient. It was a role unfamiliar to him.

"Tell me how you see the wound this morning."

She glanced at him. "Are you training me, Thomas?"

"If you wish to learn, and show ability, I will help you."

"I'm not clever enough to be a surgeon, and besides, I'm a woman. But I can nurse for you, give assistance, if you will let me."

Thomas wanted to berate her, but knew it would be the wrong thing. Too many women, too many demands. Her presence beside him carried a strong pull of attraction, not just because she was pretty, but for the assistance she could bring.

"There are female surgeons," Thomas said. "Our civilisation doesn't put shackles on women as others do. There has been enlightenment here for seven centuries."

"Then I am not clever enough. But I can be of help."

"We'll see how far you progress. But yes, if you wish, I will train you in all you can learn. It would be a boon to have someone who can make up medicines and

331

salves, to apply bandages and treat wounds. Speaking of which, you have not yet made your diagnosis."

Lubna returned her attention to his arm. She leaned close. Her fingertips touched his skin, close to the angry wound, but not too near. Her touch was soft, soothing. She leaned closer still and sniffed, and Thomas was pleased.

"Well?"

"There's no infection, but it will need cleaning again. I have better light now and more time. But I fear I will cause you pain."

"Pain is soon forgotten. Use the cloth and water to begin with. Then the alcohol, for I believe it cleans a wound better than water alone."

Lubna rose and filled a bowl with water. She stroked a wet cloth across his arm, teasing loose the flakes of dried blood, working harder against the clots that had formed. Thomas bit down hard and tried not to cry out, watching the back of her head as she bent in concentration, not wanting her to know how much she was hurting him.

Finally, she was finished and Thomas inspected the wound.

"It's good work. You have a talent."

Lubna smiled.

"Now the alcohol. Pour it liberally into the wound, into any open sections, then apply more on a cloth and rebind the arm."

"Your friend will be wondering where you are," said

Lubna as she poured clear alcohol into the wound, taking care to treat every part.

"He'll still be asleep," Thomas said, and the strain in his voice stilled Lubna's hand and she sat on her heels and looked at him.

"This is hurting you."

"It's doing me good. The pain will pass. Finish the work. If you really mean to do this, you have to learn there are times to ignore your patient's pain. We are still too ignorant of a reliable means to stop it. It must be possible, because opium dulls a pain. There will be other medicines too if we search long enough. Finish it. Work fast and hard, and ignore me."

Lubna did as he told her. "Is this the reason you are called by that name?"

"What name is that?" Although he knew the one she meant.

"Butcher," she said. "*Qassab*."

"Ignorance."

"So there is no truth in it? I have heard my father call you the name."

"Ignorance," he said again. "There are physicians in this city who would have their patients love them. I would rather my patients live."

"Many do not," said Lubna. There was no accusation in her voice. She continued to rebind the dressing on his arm.

"You know what I am," Thomas said. "You said

yourself we first met on a battlefield. There is no time for softness when lives are at stake."

"Why do you do it?" She checked the tightness of the bandage, stood and returned the instruments to the bench, standing with her back to him.

"It's my job."

"There are those who refuse."

"All the more reason for me to do it. This land is at war. To pretend otherwise is foolish. Turning away doesn't make the danger less. And without me, many soldiers would have died. We need all the soldiers we can get."

"*Ajami* soldiers," said Lubna, "like my father."

Thomas was about to say 'He's a good man', then recalled his suspicions of Olaf. Instead, he said, "It's how things work here."

"The Moors need to fight for themselves."

"Some do."

"Not many."

"The Sultan does, his sons, too."

"Few others. I despair at my countrymen. Don't they realise what is being lost?" Her shoulders hunched as she washed the instruments. "This is our land. We have as much right to it as the Spanish."

Thomas said nothing, knowing what she said was true, but he was a stranger here, too.

He left Lubna tidying the workshop while he ascended to his bedchamber. He tossed the bundle of papers on to the unmade covers, then removed his torn and stained robes. The room was thick with the scent of Helena's body and perfume and he felt his manhood thicken, despising his own reaction even as it sent a thrill through his belly. He wished he could be as other men, those who never experienced guilt over their lusts, wished he didn't have to debate with himself about such things.

He washed as well as he could and dressed in fresh clothes. Then he sat on the bed and opened the papers. There were only eight sheets, written on both sides in a small, neat hand; the unmistakeable hand of a scribe. Bilal had tried to hide their content by using Greek, and Thomas's was rusty.

He sat and started to read. When he was finished, he went back to the first page and read the words again.

———————

"I cleaned your instruments," said Lubna over her shoulder. "I placed them in boiling water and wiped them with alcohol. Is that sufficient?"

Thomas tossed the bundle of papers on to the bench. "Did you say you didn't read these?"

Lubna glanced at them. "Couldn't, not didn't."

"He accuses the Sultan's son."

"Which one, and by which mother?"

"Abu Abdullah, of course. Yusuf would never betray

335

his father."

"Was this Bilal a clever man?"

"I think so, yes."

"As clever as you?"

Thomas shrugged. He didn't believe in false modesty. Why pretend the lack of something when it was self-evident?

"Not as clever as me perhaps, but clever enough. I'm not sure what you're saying. Do you believe his claim or not?"

"He worked in the palace, didn't he?"

"For the Vizier, yes, and I know where you are going with this. Bilal would indeed have possessed a greater political sensitivity than do I."

"Take them to Jorge and ask him what he thinks."

"Jorge can't read Arabic, let alone Greek."

"But he can listen, can't he?"

"Are you going to tell me what you think?"

Lubna shook her head. "Not yet. Now—did I do right cleaning your instruments?"

Thomas pushed his fingers back through his hair. Why did he only gather awkward women around him?

"When did you learn to do that?"

"I have been watching you, and reading the books you gave me." Her vibrant mismatched eyes sparked. "You have so many books."

Thomas looked at the shelves lining one wall of the workshop. He had grown so used to the pages they held, he had forgotten how they might look to someone else.

"They contain the knowledge of centuries. Some can be traced to the time of the Greeks, others are Arabian, some from further East, and from this land too; many from this land." He walked to the shelves, studying the parchments and bindings, their scent as always reminding him of his calling. He reached out. "This one is good when you finish the others. It's old, but we've forgotten a great deal since it was written and discovered little that's new. Study this, but make up your own mind. Don't close yourself to new experiences or learning, and I will turn you into a surgeon yet."

"I will clean the house as well. And there is washing to be done. You might want to impart knowledge to me, but my sister regards me as her servant."

"Don't let her bully you."

"She isn't you, Thomas. She doesn't consider me other than what I can do for her. And truly, I don't mind. There are many hours between dawn and dusk, and I don't sleep away the afternoons like many others."

"I need to find Jorge, and then return to the palace. I want to speak with your father if I can. The men who attacked me—"

"They were northmen, I know. I saw the hair of one, heard their speech, and one of their names."

"I know, you told me, but did you hear anything else? Did you hear what was said?"

"All I heard was as they ran, and most of it concerned your lack of parentage. They hadn't expected

you to fight as you did. Certainly hadn't expected you to be so skilled."

"Exactly how much did you witness?"

"Enough. As they made their escape, I overhead one say, 'He will be displeased we have failed', and the other replied, 'He is only a surgeon, no threat to anyone. The eunuch is the danger'. And then they were gone, still talking, but I could make out no more."

"That was enough. Thank you. But you should have told me this last night."

"You needed rest."

Thomas felt an upwelling of gratitude, an urge to pull her slim body inside his arms and hug her. He bore down hard on his emotions and turned away.

"You've been of assistance in more ways than you can know. I hope to return before dark, but who knows?"

As he left the house, the alleyway outside showed no sign of the disturbance of the night. Thomas felt a momentum building. His attackers had fled, but he had the name of one of them and their nationality. Olaf might know more, and if he didn't, if he showed reluctance ... well, that would be progress too. The documents Thomas clutched in his hand appeared to prove Lubna's father innocent. Thomas wanted Jorge's opinion, but hoped he agreed with the findings—Olaf would make a far better friend than enemy.

Thomas increased his pace, eager to talk with Jorge, concerned about Lubna's comments, which meant his friend might now be in danger.

"Abu Abdullah?" said Jorge. He had lain on the bed while Thomas sat at the small table and read the document to him. He only needed to hear it the once. "I can understand him wanting to oust his father, but why kill Safya? What benefit does that bring?"

"Safya is new information that Bilal didn't have, remember. He couldn't know what was going to happen in the future, only what happened in the past, and he undertook his investigation months ago. His logic was sound at the time. He identified the attack on Helena and Yasmina as a mistaken attempt on Zoraya. Helena told us it was Yasmina who was being attacked, but memory is a fragile thing and in the darkness, who knows what the killer saw? But we know why Abu Abdullah would want Zoraya dead."

"And the girls? Why kill the servants?"

"Practice, perhaps?" Thomas said.

"You can be cold sometimes," said Jorge. "They were my girls. They are all my girls."

"So you keep saying. Then avenge them."

Jorge raised his head and stared at Thomas. "Are you convinced by those papers?"

"I believe I am, and if they implicate who I think they do, it means Olaf is no longer a suspect. I would prefer that to be the case, he will be useful on our side."

"Hm." Jorge sat up and swung his legs to the floor. "I am not so sure."

"Did Bilal make a mistake then?"

"Not at the time. But events have moved on. I can't believe Abu Abdullah is behind an attack on Safya. She was not his mother, but she was part of the inner circle in the harem and close to his real mother. He wouldn't attack anyone there."

"Perhaps I'm not the only cold one," Thomas said. "Once Abu Abdullah gets rid of Zoraya, he'll have to dispose of her children too. They're the real threat to his inheritance."

"What inheritance? If the Sultan found out his son had killed Zoraya, he would be executed in an instant, prince or not. You might be cold, but a Sultan's heart is made of ice."

"Which is why Safya was killed. Zoraya will be next. Even his own mother might be in danger. You can't kill one Sultana without killing them all. Abu Abdullah wants his father's position. Abu al-Hasan Ali would have to die, possibly even before his wives. For all we know,

he is already dead. It would be a simple matter to sneak an assassin into his company."

"No," said Jorge. He stood and paced the room, clearly upset. "You might be right, but I need proof before I believe it."

"Then we will get proof."

"From where?"

"Olaf," Thomas said. "Those men who attacked me were sent by someone—most likely Abu Abdullah himself. Olaf will know who they are. I have a name, and both men were injured."

"As are you," said Jorge. "You should take a few days to recover."

"There's nothing wrong with me. Besides, we can't stop now." Thomas rose and grabbed Jorge by the shoulders, stopping his pacing.

"I should have been with you," said Jorge. "Those men wouldn't have attacked two together."

"How skilled are you in swordplay? Does a eunuch of the harem get much practice in arms?"

"You got lucky, didn't you? Besides, don't underestimate this eunuch. Sometimes more is expected of us than simply pandering to the wishes of our ladies. I decided long ago looking beautiful wasn't enough and learned how to use a sword. I considered it wise in case my charges were attacked. But at the moment when I was needed, when Safya was in danger, where was I?"

"The palace is meant to be safe, and you can't be everywhere at once."

"I wish it had been otherwise."

"I meant no criticism. Had you been there, you would likely be dead as well."

"And Safya alive. I would gladly make that sacrifice."

"Wish all you want, we have to accept what the fates send us. But now we have something to go after." Thomas had told Jorge everything he knew, including what Lubna had translated, and the still mysterious knowledge that put him in danger.

"Why am I a threat?"

"You know something, or at least they believe you know something."

Jorge shook his head. "I know nothing. Nothing at all."

"I will tease it from you when we have time." Thomas released Jorge and led the way from the room, walking fast.

"How sure are you Olaf Torvaldsson can be trusted?" said Jorge. "These men are from his land. What if they're in it together? You escaped last night, Thomas, but Olaf is another matter entirely. That man kills for pleasure, and he's good at it."

"I have seen the light in his eyes when he looks at his children, when he looks at his wife. Savage he may be, but only when he needs to, and there's a gentleness in his heart for those he loves."

"And he loves you, does he? Only yesterday you were convinced of his guilt."

"He loves his daughter who is in my care. Two daughters now."

"There are many would be jealous. Two sisters living under your roof. There'll be gossip circulating already."

They walked out into the square, which was starting to grow busy. People and animals and goods moved to and fro, the air loud with conversation, barks and brays, thick with the scent of fruit and spices. It was later than Thomas had hoped and he wished Lubna had not let him sleep so long.

"Talk. Nothing more than talk. Lubna did well stitching my arm—I am thinking of training her. She would make a fine nurse." Thomas didn't mention the confusion of emotions she raised within him, although he knew Jorge was just the man to talk of them with, and was tempted to open himself up.

"If there is talk, you are a fool not to give it substance. I would."

"I am sure you would."

"Supposing the old northman is willing to help us, supposing he knows who these men are, or recognises a name. What do we do then? Do you believe one of them is our killer?"

"No. The killer is a better warrior than either of those two. If it had been him, I would be dead. But they may know who he is. They will certainly know who their orders came from."

"They won't have come from Abu Abdullah directly, not if he is behind the plot."

"Agreed. But there may be a trail leading to him."

"Are you going to tell Olaf you suspect Abu Abdullah?"

Thomas cast a glance at Jorge. "I'm not that stupid."

Olaf Torvaldsson laughed. "Sven? Is that all you have to go on?"

"At least it's something. One of them was dark haired, the other light, like you."

"Do you know how many northmen there are in Gharnatah?"

"Not exactly, no."

"Well I do. It is my job to know. I know to the last man. There are seven hundred and forty-three. Not all within the city walls at any time, but that is the count I can call on when required. And do you know how many of those men are called Sven?"

Thomas shook his head, feeling like a child being scolded.

"At least an eighth, possibly more. I will have a roster of Svens drawn up if you ask it, but are you going to speak to all of them? And some will be on patrol, some on loan to other cities. It would be like trying to pin down a hundred cats. As fast as you finish with one, everything will have changed."

"They won't all have blond hair," Thomas said.

"But you don't know that man was Sven. You said it

was dark. You saw one light and one dark-haired man. That covers about every Sven I have. You need to bring me more than a name."

"I don't have more than a name."

Olaf shook his head. The three of them stood in what passed for his offices, though the room lacked even a desk. Olaf wasn't a man to sit when he could stand, not a man to stand when he could walk. He paced now, to the window, to the door, across to the wall where shelves held papers—likely the list of Svens, back to the window. It looked across a dirt square where soldiers drilled and practised.

He stopped with his back to the window and crossed his arms.

"Tell me more about the attack. Were you hurt?"

"A scratch, nothing more," Thomas said, making light of his injuries.

"Show me," said Olaf.

"Why?"

Olaf lowered his brow, obviously not used to being questioned. "Because I ask it. Show me this scratch."

Thomas pulled back the sleeve of his robe and extended his arm. "It's bound up. Your daughter did this for me."

"Helena? Helena bandaged your arm?" The incredulity was thick in Olaf's voice.

"Lubna."

"Of course. She always did show interest in things it wasn't her place to know."

"She could be a fine help to me."

Olaf shook his head. "She serves you now, do as you wish. No doubt you are her best employer yet, so I have no fears in that direction. I cannot see your so-called wound with all this stuff around it."

"I would prefer not to untie it."

"Eunuch, help him. I need to see the wound if I am to help."

Thomas knew he had to either untie the bandage or withdraw, and he was not ready to give in. He had no idea why Olaf needed to see his arm, but Olaf obviously had a reason.

Thomas raised his arm and tugged at the knotted linen with his teeth.

"Let me do it," said Jorge, stepping to his side.

"You do not look so much like a eunuch today," said Olaf.

"I am glad to hear it. You still look like a soldier."

"I am glad to hear that, too." Olaf directed his attention back to Thomas, watching as Jorge unwound the linen. The bandage was cleaner than the one Lubna had removed that morning, barely stained with blood, but as the arm revealed itself, the wound was red and bruised, the stitches weeping. Thomas took the opportunity to study himself dispassionately. He decided there was nothing to worry about. A dull ache filled his arm to the shoulder, but he knew that would pass in time.

Olaf leaned close without touching Thomas to take in the spectacle presented to him.

"It was a sharp blade," he said.

"A scimitar."

"Scimitar? Northmen don't fight with scimitars. Are you sure you have this right, Thomas?"

"They both carried scimitars."

"And you had what, a sword of your own?"

"A knife."

"A knife? Was it a big knife?"

"A small knife. Middle-sized at best."

Olaf straightened. "You are telling me you were attacked by two northmen in the dark and you saw them off with a middle-sized knife, receiving only this scratch in return?"

"It is hardly a scratch."

"Hm."

"And I injured them, one badly I think. My knife went into his side, about here." Thomas patted his own chest on the left, low down where the ribs ended. "Wrong side for his liver, but he'll be damaged all the same, I swear to it."

"By God, you are a mystery to me, Thomas Berrington. I have great respect for your profession, and you seem to treat my daughter well—damn it, both of my daughters now. Are you trying to create your own harem? Ignore that. What I am saying is if these were my men, either you are the best fighter I have seen in a long time, or they were not my men. If I had sent men to kill you, you would be dead by now."

Thomas was unsure how to take the outburst. Had

Olaf forgotten their fight in front of Zoraya's children already?

"Are there other northmen?"

"A few, I am sure. The Vizier employs his own troops, so there could be some in his offices. And no doubt there are others who have come because they hear of the riches of al-Andalus, its luxury, its gold, its abundance of food..." Olaf smiled. "And even when they discover the lie, they do not return home. So what I am saying is searching among my northmen is a waste of time. Look elsewhere."

"Help me," Thomas said, but he was addressing Jorge, who proceeded to re-bandage his arm. "How do I proceed? We are two against who knows how many. Where do I start?"

Olaf shook his head. "Ask, but I have no answer. I am not a clever man. I obey orders, I go where I am told, and kill who I am asked to, but I do not think beyond that. You are the one with a brain in his head instead of straw. I will leave this kind of work to you."

Thomas knew Olaf underestimated himself, knew equally well he was impossible to argue with. It was as if the man regarded stubbornness as a positive trait.

"Then we will search for these men. One of them is injured, I know that—"

"As injured as you believe?"

Thomas heard the incredulity in Olaf's voice, but he was sure of what his senses told him.

"I felt the knife go in. I twisted. The blade caught on

348

something, a rib almost certainly, and was pulled from my grasp. So we are looking for a man who would have bled greatly, in possession of a middle-sized knife that is not his own."

"I will ask around. It is possible my men may know something. They have friends, and we of the north stick together. Even you, Thomas Berrington, might have northern blood running through your veins. Try to keep it there and spill no more, for the sake of my daughters."

"Send a message if you discover anything, however small."

"I will come myself."

"And stay for dinner," Thomas said.

Olaf frowned. "Who will cook, Helena or Lubna?"

"Helena seems to have lost any small love of cooking she might once have possessed since her sister arrived."

"Then I may stay and eat. Now return to your quest and I will pass word quietly to a few of my most trusted men. News of this attack should not spread for fear the culprits flee, or return to silence you as they meant."

CHAPTER THIRTY

"What now?" asked Jorge as they walked from the barracks through hot morning sunshine. The scent of flowering bushes filled the air, the sound of running water carried on the breeze, but the glittering beauty of the palace felt distant, separated behind an invisible barrier.

"According to Olaf, the Vizier employs northmen, too. We should speak with him about them."

"Without an appointment?"

"I have the Sultan's seal, remember." Despite the attack, it remained safe in the pocket of his robe, transferred that morning to a fresh one.

"As does he. He is a cold fish—do you trust him?"

"He's odd, certainly, but he's the Sultan's man. Whoever is behind this has a deeper motive than simple murder. But I want to see someone else before we go to his offices."

"Who might that be?"

"Your friend." Thomas smiled. "Bazzu, and Prea."

Jorge laughed. "Your little friend, you mean. What else did you get up to in those tunnels? Did spying on the women get your blood so hot you had to take her there and then?"

"Don't judge all men by your own standards," Thomas said. "Besides, I have seen practically every woman of the harem naked."

"Ah, but that was work, wasn't it? It must be different when you are hidden, spying on them from a secret vantage point. Very different indeed."

He was about to press Jorge on how he knew about such things, but they were approaching the palace and almost at the kitchens. Serving girls and boys ran to and fro, and Thomas realised it was close to noon. Soon the faithful would be called to prayer, and on their return would want to eat. He increased his pace, wanting to find Bazzu before she was called away.

As they approached the kitchens, Thomas saw a familiar slim figure ahead and called out, "Prea! Stop a moment." He trotted up as the girl slowed, but when she turned, it wasn't who he'd thought.

"Can I help you, sir?"

"I am sorry, I thought you were someone else." Even close to, there was a remarkable similarity. Her height, her colouring, her hair, even her eyes and features.

"Are you looking for Prea?" the girl said.

"You know her?"

His question was greeted with a laugh, momentarily covered by a hand. "We share a room, so of course I know her. You are Thomas the surgeon. She has told me all about you." She gave a smile.

He was unsure what to make of the news, or the smile, which was too knowing.

"Do you know where she is?"

"Working. Our duties keep us apart during the day."

"Bazzu will know," said Jorge, having come to join them, and the girl, sensing their interest in her had reached an end, darted off on whatever errand Thomas had interrupted.

They found Bazzu in her usual lair, the kitchen beyond a hive of activity. She embraced Thomas, even pecked his cheek, and when he asked to speak with Prea, she called a maid and sent her to find the girl.

"She was of help to you?" she asked, slipping behind her desk, papers neatly arranged before her, lists of special requirements, recipes, notes on expected visitors and their preferences. Thomas read a few scraps upside down, noticed one that stated: Spanish Priest—bread and water, and wondered if it was the man's wish or some punishment for being an infidel.

"A great help. I trust you didn't spread word of our undertaking?"

"Not about what you told me you were doing." No wonder Jorge got along so well with this woman, they were cut of the same cloth.

"It wouldn't do for anyone—and I mean anyone

other than us here—to know of what she showed me. The man who first told me of these passages is dead. Another man was killed only yesterday. I would not have the same fate befall you or Prea."

"We are no threat to anyone, but you are right. No one will know your secret." Her eyes glittered with mischief and he gave in.

Prea arrived silently on bare feet and Thomas left Jorge and Bazzu to talk together as he led her aside. Once they were alone, she took his hand and tugged him.

"I have something to show you, Thomas. Something important."

"Whatever it is will have to wait. You haven't told anyone else about what you showed me, have you?"

"Only Bazzu. You asked me to keep my silence and I have."

"And the money I gave you?"

Prea's face turned hard. "If it was too much, sir, I have not spent a single coin. I will return it all."

"I don't want it back. If anything, I didn't pay you enough—"

"I have never seen so much money in my life. I thank you with all my heart, Thomas."

"But you can't spend any of it. Not for now at least. Can you be patient?"

"I can wait. It is many times more than I have ever possessed before. The spending will prove all the sweeter for waiting, if that is what you ask."

"I will try and come back as soon as I can."

"I am at your call day or night, you only need ask."

Thomas wondered as he walked back to Bazzu's office whether he had not indeed paid her too much, and whether she had misinterpreted his generosity. It wasn't unknown for wealthy men to buy the services of girls as young as Prea for their pleasure. He wouldn't have her entertain that he held such ideas, but had no simple way of telling her short of blurting it out, and knew she would simply deny any such suspicion were he to do so.

Jorge sat on the corner of Bazzu's desk and Thomas was sure, in the moment before he approached, her hand had rested on his thigh, both of them drawing apart as he entered the room.

"There was a man here asking for us," said Jorge, standing and coming around to his side of the desk.

"On what business?"

"You said you wanted to see the Vizier—well it seems the Vizier wants to see us. This instant."

"That saves us the trouble of making an appointment. I thank you once more, Bazzu, and remember what I said."

She waved a hand. "You doubt my memory, surgeon? Help yourself to some sweetmeats as you pass through the kitchen. You look as though you need feeding up."

Thomas and Jorge nibbled at morsels of fruit wrapped inside strips of lamb and pigeon. They returned the way

they had come before turning to follow the opposite ridge of the hill to the Vizier's palace. Less grand than al-Hamra, it was still an imposing structure and was where the real power of Gharnatah lay. The Sultan was a figurehead and general. It was the Vizier who made the city run, collected taxes, paid mercenaries, bribed enemies to stay their hand. Tahir al-Ifriqi was a teak-dark Berber who had crossed the narrow sea as a boy and risen through the ranks. He owed nothing of his position to patronage, and was perhaps sterner as a result. He ran his own parallel seat of power employing troops loyal only to him. As they made their way to his chambers, Thomas tried to decide how much he could reveal.

They were expected, a guard despatched to the gate to escort them inside. As they entered the Vizier's public room, Thomas was surprised to find company, and strange company at that.

The cleric Abd al-Wahid al-Mursi might have been half expected, dressed as always in black, but the other man was an anomaly and should never have been in the same room as the first. He too was dressed in black, but instead of a turban covering his hair, he wore a wide-brimmed hat, and hanging against his chest was a large silver cross. A Catholic priest, here in the grounds of al-Hamra?

Thomas and Jorge bowed to Tahir.

"I hear you were injured, Thomas Berrington," Abd al-Wahid said. "I trust your wounds are not serious."

"A scratch, no more," Thomas replied, sure these

355

three would not want him to remove the bandage to check his honesty. "We are making progress, Your Honour." He addressed himself to the Vizier. "I have some questions, but don't wish to bother you with trifling matters. If you permit me, I would speak with your chief guard about the men who attacked me."

"Should there be time, perhaps, but there are more pressing matters."

"More pressing than murder?" said Jorge, and Thomas sent a sharp glance his way. They should not antagonise the Vizier.

"Politics is always more pressing than murder, eunuch." The contempt the Vizier held for Jorge was clear in his voice, which softened as he shifted to address Thomas. "You know Qurtuba, I believe?"

"I have visited there. The library, when I was young, but most of the books had been destroyed by then."

"Heresy has no place in a godly city." The priest spoke in stilted Arabic, his soft voice belying the harshness of his words. Thomas glanced his way, but no one else appeared to even hear what was said, so he bit back a reply, wanting to ask what heresy there was in knowledge.

"I want you to go there on a mission for the Sultan, and also to assist this gentleman and his superiors."

"We are in the middle of a pursuit, Your Honour. I am, of course, at your command, but do I need to remind you this task was given me by the Sultan himself?"

"I have spoken with him on the matter, and he agrees

with me that this takes precedence. You can be of great service to your country. You too, eunuch."

"Thank you, sir," said Jorge, but if the Vizier recognised sarcasm, he chose to let it pass.

"Let me at least speak with your general, Vizier, if only to ask him to do something while we are away." Thomas knew refusal was impossible. He had no idea why they were being sent away now, or on what pretext, only that he felt a momentum building that could not be wasted.

"There is no time. Tell me what it is you want and I will pass a message on. Time is of the essence here and you must leave before the day ends."

"I need to return to my house and make arrangements. I have patients to care for. A household to organise. And I must send a report to the Sultan before sunset."

"Once more, a message will be sent."

"I need clothes for travelling, Your Honour, or—"

"Enough! I will stand no dissension." The Vizier stood, trembling. For a moment, Thomas feared he would strike him. Then the man breathed deeply and calmed himself. "Walk with me, Thomas, I would speak with you in private. This man will instruct you further, eunuch."

Jorge turned to face the Catholic priest, who was stony faced.

"I take no orders from an infidel priest!"

"He will give you no order," the Vizier said, his voice

cold, "only information. Thomas will carry the message I wish to pass to the powers in Qurtuba."

"Their Graces the King and Queen of Spain, Their Highnesses Fernando of Aragon and Isab—"

"Yes, yes, we know who they are. Thomas, come. Eunuch, stay there. Try not to kill our friend before I return."

Thomas glanced at a scowling Jorge and followed the Vizier into the garden.

"Why are we being sent away?" Thomas said. "I have proof of who is behind the killings." Thomas had not intended to show his hand yet, but he needed some way to prevent the Vizier sending them away.

"Is your proof the same as that the scribe brought me?"

"His name was Bilal Abd al-Rahman."

The Vizier waved a dismissive hand. "Yes, something like that. He came to me and made foolish allegations. They were false, of course. No doubt he was put up to it by someone. He couldn't remain in the palace after making up such lies."

"I believe he was an honourable man."

The Vizier stopped next to an orange tree and reached out, plucking a white flower and holding it to his nose. The scent of the flowers filled the small courtyard, rich and cloying.

"He was a dangerous man. As you will be if you continue with false accusations. Do you understand what I am saying?"

Thomas felt a heat rise through him. "Yes, I understand. But I am a surgeon, not a diplomat."

"Which is why several weeks away from the city will be good for your health."

"I am not going," Thomas said.

"Of course you are. The priest comes with a request from the Spanish royal palace, one that cannot have been made lightly."

Thomas shook his head. "Why choose me, when we are so close to—"

Once more the dismissive wave. "We have been asked to send our best surgeon to Qurtuba, where a young prince lies injured."

"The Spanish have doctors of their own."

The Vizier made a sound through his nose. "We both know the quality of Spanish doctors. There is more of superstition and hope in their treatment than science. They may not like it, but Their Majesties are not stupid."

"If this prince is injured, he is likely dead by now. How far is it to Qurtuba? A week? At least a week since they sent their priest, another for us to return. He will be dead before we even set out."

"Do you take me for a fool? I have asked all these questions. It is a matter of bones, it seems, something broken that will not set. Their own physicians have tried

and failed, so they seek our help. Privately, of course. No one can know this."

"The Sultan—"

"Do you believe the Sultan does not know? It was his idea to send you. I have to admit I had someone else in mind, but he said you are the best surgeon in the whole of Spain. He was insistent."

Thomas wondered how the Vizier had access to the Sultan while he did not. It felt as though their investigation—the closer it came to success—was being baulked.

"Why would the Sultan help the Spanish? And what of this other duty he has given me?"

"He said you were making little progress. He should not have chosen you in the first place, should not have put you in danger. He knows you are a man of peace, not war. This new duty is more suited to your skills, is it not?"

"But we are making progress." Thomas's head spun with too many conflicting suspicions.

"The same progress the scribe claimed he had made? I have already told you his suspicions had no foundation in truth. Do not make the same mistake he did. Go to Qurtuba. When you return, my men will have found the true culprit and you can return to your peaceful life. Send me all the documents you claim as proof and I will have them examined."

They had reached the far end of the courtyard and the Vizier stopped, turned and waited.

"I refuse," Thomas said.

"You spurn me? Spurn your Sultan?"

Thomas looked back along the courtyard. He could see Jorge standing beside the dark-robed priest, both men looking away from each other. Could he make the decision for Jorge, too? Was there any choice? He took a deep breath, filling his lungs with the sweet air.

"Yes. I refuse the task. I already have one that is more important. Send the man you preferred and let me finish what I have started."

"You cannot refuse." The Vizier's voice was soft. Thomas would have preferred anger.

"But I do."

"Are you aware of the consequences?"

"No, but still I refuse."

The Vizier's face reflected an inner pain. "Then you are cast out." He lowered his gaze and shook his head. "Go. Take that creature with you and leave the palace, both of you, and never return."

CHAPTER THIRTY-ONE

There was nowhere to go but home, but first they had to follow the convoluted corridors of the palace to reach the outside world.

"Did you have to make the decision on my behalf as well?" said Jorge.

"They didn't want you, only me, but they know we are working together, that is all."

"And still you included me?" Jorge's voice was tight with anger.

Anger at me, Thomas thought, and wondered if he could have done things differently. He was no diplomat. Jorge should have been with him, he might have made a better decision.

"I did not include you, they did. You are tainted by association, and for that I am truly sorry. But you know we cannot go to Qurtuba while we are this close to exposing the culprit, don't you? We would be away at

least two weeks, likely more. How many others will be dead before we return?"

"Maybe none. This might be the end of it. Did you tell him about your suspicions of Abu Abdullah?"

"He already knew. He called them foolish."

"So you have banished us for nothing." Jorge's voice rose. "You have banished me! This place is my home. I know or want no other and now I am never to return?" He shook his head, sharp tears in his eyes. "What have you done? Can you even begin to comprehend what it is you have done?"

"They will forget," Thomas said. "A week. A month. They will forget and forgive. Likely not me, but you they will forgive. They know this is my doing, not yours."

"We will end up like Bilal. Power protects itself. What have you done, Thomas? I am disgraced by you."

"We are no scribes. I am a supposed friend to the Sultan, you an honoured eunuch. Can you see your women allowing you to be banished?"

Jorge snorted. "Sometimes I wonder how you have managed to live so long. Well—that state of affairs could change soon."

"If we left now, we would be traitors. My loyalty lies with the Sultan, not his Vizier."

"The Vizier *is* the Sultan. Why else was he sent a message?" Jorge walked faster, trying to distance himself.

Thomas grabbed at him before he could move away.

Jorge turned, pushing Thomas hard, his arms strong and Thomas still weak.

"All right, go ahead." Thomas steeled himself for a blow. "Hit me if it makes you feel better, then go show my bruised face to the Vizier and say you will go to Qurtuba with this other physician. Save yourself, Jorge."

"It is not me they want. Why would they send a eunuch unless I was with you? We are bound together, and I wish you had never come to me!"

Thomas lowered his face and waited to be struck. Instead, Jorge stepped close and drew him against his chest, drew him into a tight embrace as he began to weep.

"You are a mad man, Thomas Berrington, but I love you like a brother. I will not abandon you now."

"Nor our task?" Thomas's words emerged muffled against the taller man's chest. It was curiously comforting to be held this way, even by another man. Especially by this man.

Jorge's chest hitched. "Our task is ended. We are cast into the wind. We have no access, no assistance from any quarter. The killer will go free, his master undiscovered, and we must make what we can of our lives."

Thomas waited, allowing Jorge to release his pain. When he finally loosened his hold, Thomas held his arms and looked into his friend's face.

"No—if you go back, you will be forgiven. They know this decision is all mine."

"Don't disrespect me, Thomas. Have I played no

part in any of this? It is not who I am, it is what I know that banishes me." Jorge shook his head. "They never wanted the truth, only a cover-up." He made a noise, half laugh, half sob. "What useless creatures are they to pick first the scribe, and then us, expecting both to fail?"

"They wanted us to fail, didn't they? What are you going to do?"

"What can I do? I am a eunuch. All I know is how to please my ladies, how to care for them."

"There are other harems. You could go to Malaka. To al-Munekhar."

"My place is in this palace. I will find somewhere to hide and wait for the disgrace to pass, if it ever does. I am strong enough, and I can be subtle when needs require. And you have friends. Perhaps one of them has a place for the likes of me in their household. I will do what I have to and hope one day I am able to return."

"I had friends," Thomas said. "Once word spreads, they will fade like the morning mist over the Hadarro."

Jorge looked along the corridor. "I think it wise we leave by a more subtle exit than the main entrance."

"You know of somewhere?"

Jorge smiled and wiped the back of his hand across his eyes. "Of course I know of somewhere."

"What are you doing home?" Helena's face showed a coldness it frequently exhibited when Thomas annoyed her.

"I live here. This is my house." They stood in the main room, a wide doorway looking on to the courtyard where Lubna had finished hanging the washing and now pushed a brush around, picking up fallen leaves, feathers and dust.

"You were sent for by the Vizier."

"I was, and now I am back."

"But—but—"

"I'll go and say hello to Lubna," said Jorge, stepping around Thomas.

"What is he doing here?" Helena asked.

"You know full well why he's here. We're working together on Safya's murder. What is wrong with you, Helena? I thought you'd be glad to see me."

"You are not meant to be here!"

"In my own house? Why not? And..." Something in what she had said rose to the surface. "How did you know the Vizier sent for me?"

"It is all over town." Helena waved her hand as though Thomas was an idiot. "I heard he was sending you away. Something to do with the Spanish King and Queen, although why we would be helping them, I don't know. When is it you leave, Thomas? Soon?"

"You want me gone so badly?"

Something changed in Helena's face, some realisation she might have pushed too hard. A sly look

settled in her eyes, one Thomas had noticed more of late. He believed she thought the look seductive, but he had grown to associate it purely with her needs, not his.

"I want you in my bed, Thomas, of course I do. But a summons from the Vizier cannot be ignored. He is an important man. Think what this will do for your career."

"I don't have a career. I have a calling. And I doubt I have either any longer."

"We could be living on the hill again. Not in the palace perhaps, but the Alkazaba is a hundred times better than … than this!"

"I like this."

"And I do not. I am used to refinement and luxury and servants. I cannot live this way any longer."

He stared at her. How long had she felt this way? All the time she had lived under his roof?

"Then leave!" Thomas snapped. "If I make you so unhappy, go—make your own way in the world."

Her face changed in an instant, collapsing in on itself as tears flooded her eyes.

"I am sorry. I have overstepped my place and I apologise."

"I am not staying."

Helena stepped towards him, her face tilting to the side so her hair fell across her scar.

"Oh, Thomas, I have angered you without need. Of course I will miss you. Both here, and here." She touched a hand between her breasts, over her heart, and then again low on her belly. "So you will go to Qurtuba? For

me? When do you leave? Have we time to go upstairs one last time?"

One last time? Did she really mean to say that?

"Jorge is waiting. And I am not going to Qurtuba. We are close on the trail of our killer. I can almost taste him on my tongue. Now is not the time to abandon the chase. I won't return here until I have him. Try not to overwork Lubna. I hope this matter can be concluded within days, a week at most." He leaned in to kiss her cheek, but she drew away.

From beyond the courtyard, the sound of the muezzin calling afternoon prayer floated through the air. Helena turned her head at the sound.

"I must pray," she said, moving quickly towards the door, drawing her scarf across her head and face, leaving only sharp blue eyes exposed.

"Pray?"

"Yes, the muezzin is calling the faithful. I will see you on your return. Try not to get yourself hurt any worse than you already are."

With that, she was gone. Thomas stood in the centre of the room, puzzling through the encounter. He tried to remember the last time Helena had shown the slightest interest in prayer. She must have done so with the others in the harem, but he had seen no sign since she came to his house.

He ascended the stairs. He had enough concerns without adding Helena's sudden conversion to the list. He threw clothes into a bag, then returned to the

courtyard to find Jorge and Lubna in conversation, sitting side by side on the bench beneath the balcony. Thomas felt a momentary pang of jealousy and dismissed it. He had nothing to be jealous of. Nothing at all.

"Be ready to leave," Thomas said, and Jorge nodded. Thomas went to his workshop and took down a leather satchel, began to pack herbs and potions inside, as well as a sample of instruments, not sure what might be needed, unwilling to abandon his home without at least something.

There was a textbook open on the bench and he moved it aside, sensed a presence and turned to find Lubna beside him.

"I started reading that one," she said, reaching to take the book. She marked her place with a feather and closed it, then pressed against his side as she reached across, remained pressed against him even after she had returned the book.

"Did you know Helena prayed at the mosque?" Thomas asked, her sudden departure still puzzling him.

"Helena? Pray? You mean my sister Helena? Surely you mean some other I am not familiar with. Is it *Asr* already? I did not hear the call."

"It is a little after. You were talking to Jorge."

"Excuse me, I will be in the courtyard. If I am finished before you leave, remember to say goodbye."

Jorge had come in and sat on the cot, watching the conversation without expression. Thomas scowled, making Jorge laugh.

"What?" Thomas said. "Are you going to tell me you want to pray as well?"

"I have done so at times, certainly," said Jorge, "but only because my masters expect it of me. You know I follow no gods other than the god of sensuality."

"Ah, that one." Thomas continued filling his satchel, looking around, trying to decide what else might be needed. He saw a bottle containing extract of poppy and added it, together with a sticky cube of hemp resin. He could think of nothing else, so went to sit on the cot beside Jorge.

"Are we leaving?" Jorge asked.

"In a moment. I want to say goodbye first."

"She said only if she had finished."

"We'll wait."

Thomas returned to the bench and opened a wide drawer. He stood for a long time looking at what lay inside as the soothing music of Lubna's prayers drifted in from the courtyard. Finally, he reached in and withdrew the sword he hadn't worn since arriving in the city many years before. It was fashioned in the manner of English swords, long and straight. It had once belonged to his father, and would serve far better than a medium-sized dagger. He tied the belt around his waist and covered the weapon with his robe.

When he turned, Jorge was watching. "Do you believe we have need of weapons?"

Thomas gave a curt nod. "We would be foolish not to go prepared."

"I have nothing," said Jorge.

"I considered that might be the safest option, but you're right." Thomas turned and drew a second sword from the drawer, took it across to Jorge. Both possessed the same long, straight blade, unlike those carried by the Moors.

Jorge made no move to take the weapon.

"Do you want it or not?"

"What are you doing with two swords, Thomas? Or even one? These weapons are not new, but you have kept them honed and clean."

"You're right, they are not new. It would take too long to tell you why I possess them, but they are mine, both of them."

"And have seen fighting?"

Thomas nodded. "And have seen fighting, yes."

Finally, Jorge took the offered sword and laid it across his knees.

Thomas sat beside him once more, the cot creaking as his weight settled. The two were silent, listening to the soft cadence of Lubna reciting the words of the prophet. She was just visible in the courtyard, sunk to her knees, legs splayed to one side, head covered as she faced east. Thomas watched the sway of her head, her shoulders. She had come to his house not a week since, but already her presence felt more a part of it than that of her sister who had lived there half a year.

Allāhu akbar

Allāhu akbar

Lā ilāha illallā

Lubna remained a moment longer, head bowed, then she rose in a single lithe movement and turned. Her face lit up to find the two of them still sitting inside the workshop.

"I thought you would be gone. I expected you to be gone."

"We are going now. Jorge wanted to say goodbye first."

"I—" Jorge started to object, stopped. "I did. Of course I did." He rose and went to the tiny figure and enclosed her in his arms, lifting her from her feet and swinging her around until she squealed with joyous outrage. Jorge deposited her on the tiled floor and kissed the top of her head. "Take care, little one."

"You too, big one." Lubna smiled and glanced shyly towards Thomas. He knew what he wanted to do, what she expected, but instead, he only stood and nodded, the satchel already around his shoulder.

"We will return as soon as we can. Take care of your sister for me."

"I will. Perhaps she will pray beside me this evening."

"Perhaps she will."

He had reached the door to the alley when Lubna ran after him, stopping abruptly.

"You take care too, Thomas. No more fighting. And keep a watch out for this one." She nodded at Jorge. "He might look dangerous, but I sense he is not."

372

Thomas smiled. "Oh, I know he is not. Goodbye, Lubna."

She came on to the street and waved as they made their way to the steps which would take them into town. When Thomas turned back, just before Lubna was lost from sight, she was still waving.

CHAPTER THIRTY-TWO

The hottest part of the day was yet to arrive as the city of Gharnatah slumbered the afternoon away. Even the city's cats and dogs had sought shade, where they lay comatose. Jorge too lay on the bed in his room while Thomas sat at the table, staring out through the open window on to the square. An occasional figure passed across it, but they moved slowly through waves of heat that shimmered from the flagstones.

"Why the haste?" Thomas said. "Why do they want us gone from the city so soon?"

"That thought crossed my mind, and there is only one reason I can think of. They want everything hushed up."

"They can't hide Abu Abdullah's guilt and pretend nothing has happened."

"He is a prince. He might be Sultan one day, possibly sooner than we think. Powerful men work to different rules to you or I. Abu Abdullah will have been taken

aside and told he has been found out, but if he stops now all will be forgiven." Jorge's face reflected his pain and Thomas knew this was hard on him, for he had lost people he loved.

"I can't just walk away," Thomas said.

Jorge stared at him. "You have fought before, haven't you?"

Thomas said nothing.

"You have fought against odds such as these. I see it in your eyes. See it in your lack of fear. You are not like me. I do this despite my fear. You?" Jorge shook his head. "You have none."

"You're wrong. I have plenty of fear."

"But only for others. Tell me, Thomas, for I need to understand—why do you think we can win? What makes you believe we can possibly win after this?"

"I haven't always won." Thomas smiled. "No, perhaps that is a lie. I thought I had lost, but that loss was what brought me here, through a long, circuitous route, so perhaps it was a victory as well, even if it didn't feel so at the time."

"You are talking about what brought you to al-Andalus, aren't you? You have dropped a hint here and a hint there, but never revealed the full tale. Was it a woman? Someone you loved?"

"How long have you been thinking on that?"

"What was her name?"

"Eleanor." Thomas wondered why he was talking about her at all. Perhaps some of the poppy still clung to

him, eroding his resistance. "And she wasn't a woman. She was a girl on the point of becoming a woman."

"How old were you?"

"Sixteen. We were both sixteen years old, but it felt like more."

"And you loved her." This time there was no hint of a question.

Thomas nodded, not meeting Jorge's eyes, but he knew they were on him.

"Yes, I loved her."

"And you have never loved since."

Thomas shook his head. He felt emotions well inside him and pressed them down hard.

"Let your barriers down," said Jorge, as though he could see directly into Thomas's heart. "You have nothing to lose but the pain you carry. Allow someone else in. Not Helena, not that bitch. But Lubna. I can see how you feel about her. She feels the same about you, I see that too. It would be funny if it wasn't so tragic."

"She's a—"

"Yes, yes, I know, you keep saying. She's a help to you. Does that stop you wanting her? What happened to this Eleanor?"

"I don't know. She was promised to someone else, but she chose me. We were going to have..." No, he wouldn't go there. "We were ambushed. So many men against just the two of us. I fought. She did, too." He smiled, and knew there were tears on his face. "She was a wild creature. You would have liked her."

"Are you sure? Go on."

"Too many men," Thomas said. "I was injured, then injured again. They took her, kicking and screaming and scratching. I lay on the ground, bleeding my life away, and watched them bundle her into the back of a cart and take her away to the man she was promised to. A count. Older than her by twenty years."

"But you didn't die. And I can't see you abandoning her, either."

"I didn't mean to. I woke a day later on the side of the road. People must have passed, must have seen me, but they no doubt thought me already dead. I lay there another night before I could move. A fox came sniffing at me and I scared it off. Then something larger, but I still had my sword." Thomas touched his side. "This sword. I dragged myself into the undergrowth and waited to die. Except I didn't. It was a week before I could move. Two before I could walk. By then, Eleanor was gone. The count had fled with her." Thomas raised his gaze to meet Jorge's. "I looked for her. I spent half a year looking. Then his men came for me. I must have made myself known—all the questions, all the anger. This time, they made sure. They threw me over a cliff."

Jorge sat silent. Thomas saw there were tears on his cheeks, just as there were on his own. Then Jorge smiled.

"Is it even possible to kill you?"

"I expect so."

"Why didn't you die?"

"I hit a tree growing out from the cliff face. Hit it

hard enough to break my arm and thigh. It should have been enough to finish me, stuck half way down a cliff, wedged into a birch tree, but somehow I managed to climb down, although God knows how. This time, I knew I wasn't going to make it, so I crawled away, seeking high ground, and an old man discovered me and took me in." Thomas stood and walked across the room. "Make space. I'm tired of talking and want to sleep."

Jorge shifted his legs and Thomas fell across the bed. The moment he closed his eyes, the world faded. He expected dreams, but none came.

When Thomas opened his eyes, the room was still bathed with light, but he felt refreshed. Jorge was shaking him by the shoulder.

"I have remembered," he said.

"Good." Thomas draped an arm across his eyes. "What is it you have remembered?"

"Why I am considered a danger."

Thomas sat up. "Tell me."

"I know who the killer is. Or I can identify him, at least."

"You—" Thomas banged his head against his hand. "You can identify the killer? Why didn't you wake me at once?"

"Because it won't do us any good until we find him."

"How do you know him?"

"Ever since you told me those men said I was the danger, I have been trying to work out what it is that marks me out and failing. I don't lead an exciting life, not in that way. And then I thought back, wondering if this knowledge might not be recent, and it came to me."

Thomas waited, saying nothing. Eventually, Jorge went on, staring down at his hands, speaking softly.

"It was a month, perhaps two, before Helena was attacked. There were new guards, two or three of them I think. They change the guards often enough, not wanting the same men close to the harem for long. The temptation, you know." Jorge smiled. "There was this one man, a Berber, good looking, slim, friendly. Too friendly, now I think back on it."

Thomas watched Jorge. "Too friendly? Do you mean he—"

Jorge waved a hand. "Nothing like that. He asked questions, as some men do. About life within the harem. Except this man's questions were about specific matters. How often the ladies bathed. Where they relaxed and conversed. He asked about the hierarchy of the palace, who had position, who did not."

"You said many men ask questions, it is understandable. What was different about this one?"

"I am a fool not to have seen it sooner." Jorge looked up to meet Thomas's eyes. "The day after Helena was attacked, I saw him. He was shaken, upset. And I said, 'Don't worry, they won't blame you'. He almost jumped out of his skin and asked what I meant. For a moment, I

thought he was going to strike me. That was the last time I saw him. The following day, he was gone."

"Was he punished for his mistake, do you think? If that's the case, then no doubt he is already dead."

"Perhaps. But secrets are hard to keep, and his kind of killer is even harder to find. Suppose he was withdrawn only for a short time, given more information, told who his targets were, and then sent back?"

"If you're right and he is the murderer, it still brings us no closer to the person behind it."

"He was a guard. The guards are chosen from the ranks of the Sultan's troops. Do you think Olaf will allow us to interview each man? I would recognise him again, I am sure." Jorge held up his left hand. "And he had two fingers missing." He closed the same fingers against his palm. "These two. Exactly as you described the marks on Alisha's body. I should have realised all this sooner and curse myself for not doing so."

"We can't go to Olaf, not now we are banished. How many troops are there in the city, two thousand? Four? How could we stare each of them in the face before we get ourselves killed?"

"Less live within the city walls."

"Which means less chance he is still here. But you're right, we have to try. When the light fades, we will go to Olaf and see if he is willing to help."

Thomas pushed off the bed and went to the small window, looking for some fresh air. The square remained almost deserted, still an hour remaining

before people would leave their houses. On the far side, five soldiers appeared from the roadway leading to al-Hamra. Thomas watched the certainty of their movement, their single-mindedness. They wavered neither left nor right, but came directly towards the inn.

"Off the bed now—we're leaving."

"It is too soon. We should wait an hour at least, preferably two."

"Wait if you want, but there are men coming to arrest us."

Jorge rolled from the bed and came to the window. The soldiers were half way across the square.

Thomas grabbed his satchel and ran for the door, descending the stairs with Jorge close behind. They passed Khadar al-Abidah as they ran through the kitchen where the fat innkeeper was preparing lamb and goat for his evening clients.

"There are soldiers coming," Thomas said. "When they ask, tell them we haven't been here. We have never been here."

"Everyone knows you come to my inn, it would be foolish to pretend otherwise."

"Then tell them nothing of Jorge, only that I come in the evening to play Mancala and drink tea."

Without waiting for a reply, they rushed on, appearing in a shaded alley behind the inn. Thomas looked left and right, undecided. Left would take them to the wider streets leading from the square, and from there

to the Albayzin, but they would know where his house was and were no doubt searching there as well.

"You're sure they are after us?" asked Jorge.

"No. But do you want to wait around and ask them?" Thomas went left, turning right when he came to Babole Street, then running fast along the wider avenue. The stalls and shops were still closed for the afternoon, their shutters drawn, panting dogs the only life to be seen.

From behind came a yell and the sound of running feet.

"They have us, Thomas. Run!" shouted Jorge.

Thomas skidded right, climbing steeply through a narrow alley, cut left, right, right again. They came to a dead end, a single oak door marking the entrance to a bathhouse. Thomas tried the door, but it was locked. He hammered, knowing the gesture was useless.

"Do you hear anything?" He stood still, trying to listen above the pounding of blood in his ears. There were distant sounds, shouts masked by the maze of alleys they had run through.

"They are searching for us." Jorge looked around, trying to find some means of concealment.

"I am lost," Thomas said. "Perhaps they are too and won't find us." But he gave the lie to his words as he drew his sword. The air in the alley was like an oven, close and fetid, and sweat trickled down his face. He felt it running across the skin beneath his robes.

"We're not going to fight, are we?" There was incredulity in Jorge's voice.

"If we have to."

"Soldiers?"

Thomas nodded and said again, "If we have to."

Jorge laughed. "Ah well, I have probably lived long enough anyway. It is all downhill from here on, especially after what we have done today." He drew his own sword and they faced the alley, waiting. The sounds of their pursuers grew, faded, grew again, and Jorge said, "They will not give up, will they?"

"They have their orders, the same as we do."

"Except they are obeying theirs."

"Do you want to go to Qurtuba? To the court of the Spanish King and Queen? I hear they pride themselves on never washing and have not bathed in years. They have destroyed all the baths in the city, claiming that bathing is the work of the devil and un-Christian."

"I always knew my people were stupid," said Jorge. "I am grateful I was brought here so you could remove my balls."

There was a commotion at the end of the alley and two soldiers appeared. At first, Thomas thought they were going to walk past without looking in their direction. One of the men moved beyond his sight, but the other stopped at the end of the alley and turned his head. His shout was instantaneous, his companion running back to join him. Thomas expected them to attack at once, but they only stood there. Then one spoke to the other, who sprinted off in the direction from which they had come.

It was a mistake.

Thomas grinned and ran at the remaining man, screaming. The soldier stepped back, shock on his face, then defended himself as Thomas fell on him. Swords clashed and the man crashed against the far wall from the force of Thomas's sudden attack.

"Take his legs!" Thomas shouted to Jorge, defending himself as the man countered his blows. From the corner of his eye, he saw Jorge step close and swing his blade, trying for the back of the man's knees, but leather leggings resisted Jorge's slashes. Seeing the danger, the soldier swung sideways at Jorge, who stumbled, falling in his haste to retreat. The soldier followed through on his advantage, turning from Thomas, dismissing him as little threat. He raised his sword to swing down upon Jorge.

Thomas judged his spot and slid his sword forward. As the man lunged, Jorge raised his arms uselessly, stumbling backwards. Thomas sliced cleanly through the back of the attacker's right knee and his leg buckled. He screamed, trying to drag himself to his feet, but the leg was hobbled. He turned to Thomas, swinging wildly, but unable to reach him.

"Run," Thomas said, tempted to aim a kick at the man's face and resisting. Instead, he pushed Jorge, who was simply standing there, staring.

"You didn't kill him."

Thomas pushed at Jorge again, eventually getting him to move, urging him faster. Blood pounded through

his veins and exultation filled him. He no longer saw the alleys twisting and turning around them. His mind had returned to a time he'd hoped had been put behind him, but there it still was, only waiting patiently for him to call it into life. The blood lust. The ice in his veins. The elation of battle.

"You should have killed him," said Jorge, his face a mask of shock.

"There was a time I would have without a second thought. But we are men, Jorge, not animals. We have control over ourselves."

"He would have killed you."

"Then I am not like him."

Thomas grabbed Jorge's robe and dragged him along, running as hard as he could. There had been shouts behind when they fled the alleyway, but they had lost their pursuers. Perhaps the men were nervous, their prey more dangerous than they had been told.

There were now only four men pursuing them, and Thomas ran with Jorge close behind, skidding and tripping on the cobbles as the city began to wake slowly from its afternoon slumber.

CHAPTER THIRTY-THREE

There were no names to the alleys they ran through. Anyone coming to this place did so for a reason and already knew their destination. Thomas's house stood on the eastern slope of the Albayzin where the residences were larger and looked across to the palace. Here on the western slope, the buildings were crumbling and the alleys lacked cobbles, only bare sand and soil beneath their feet. Naked children played in the dust, laughing at the strange men who ran through their midst. Some of them ran alongside as though this was all a fine game.

At the crest of the hillside, in the shadow behind the great mosque, they crouched to recover their breath.

"Do you think we have lost them?" asked Jorge. He had kept pace beside Thomas the whole time, fitter than he looked.

"They're not going to stop looking. They want us dead."

"Or captured?" said Jorge, a note of hope in his voice.

"Those men didn't come on a whim. They were following orders. Someone sent them."

"Abu Abdullah?"

"If he's the guilty one. I need to study those documents again before I make my mind up. He wasn't even under suspicion until now. I would rather draw my own conclusions than accept another man's judgement blindly."

"I can't believe he would harm us. You saved both his and his brother's life. His father trusts you. As for me, I mean nothing to him, nothing at all."

"There are bigger stakes here than you or I. And Abu Abdullah bears me no friendship or loyalty."

"Does he have men of his own?" asked Jorge. "Is it they who came after us?"

"He has access to men, I am sure, but none of his own. He will have to be working with someone who does."

"Who?"

"Isn't it obvious? All of the soldiers on the hill are under Olaf's command. I dismissed my suspicions of him too quickly."

Shouts sounded from somewhere behind and Thomas turned quickly. The alley curved down and away, but he saw no sign of their pursuers.

"We have to leave the city," said Jorge. "We're not safe as long as we remain within its walls."

"And go where? To Qurtuba, as we have been asked?"

"I suspect it's too late for that. To one of the villages in the hills, perhaps. Somewhere they won't come looking for us."

"We can't run and hide," Thomas said. "Not now we are this close to who is behind the killings. When you are under the greatest threat, that is the time to attack."

"Or a route to a slow and painful death," said Jorge. "I would prefer my death to be slow and at the end of a long life, and I would wish to avoid any hint of pain."

"Go if you wish, throw yourself on the Sultan's mercy, but I intend to finish this thing before any more die."

"How?"

"I'm going to confront Abu Abdullah and accuse him." Even as he spoke the words, Thomas wondered if Helena's betrayal coloured his suspicions of the man.

Jorge barked a laugh as he fell into step beside Thomas. "And how are you going to do that with a sword in your guts? He will kill you. You have shown courage and skill today, but Abu Abdullah is a warrior like his father, and he is never alone."

"He won't kill me, not if the Vizier and the Sultan are present. I have a plan to draw him out, to confront him in the presence of them both and lay his treachery bare."

"Then he will kill you all."

"No, he will kill nobody."

"I had better stay, then, in case you need my protection. Where are we going now?"

Thomas glanced at Jorge and smiled. "Back to my house."

"Are you a fool? They will have sent men there. They'll be waiting for us."

"Not now. They believe we are in hiding, on the run, and that the house will be empty. I need a change of clothes and another satchel of tools. Then we implement my plan."

"I can't wait to discover more. But if you don't mind, I will stay outside, in case someone wants to try to kill me."

The house was quiet, for which Thomas was grateful. There had been nobody waiting outside for them, nobody inside either. For a moment, he stood in the entrance looking into the courtyard, listening.

Silence. Complete silence.

It was as the house had been half a year earlier when he lived alone. Except now the silence was different. It echoed a lack of something, of someone. The house had grown used to the sound of voices, the scent of a woman. The lack of one left a resonance that whispered of a need to be filled. Thomas realised how sterile his life had been before the coming of Helena, and how tainted the memory of her was now he knew of her betrayal. She

had had no intention of praying when she left the house. Thomas knew she must have gone to Abu Abdullah and told him where he and Jorge would be.

His old life felt like a shadow-dream, never to be re-captured. He returned to the street and called Jorge inside.

"Shall I fetch your clothes from upstairs?" Jorge asked.

"I've changed my mind. We need to travel light, and I can buy clothes if I need them. Carlos will be glad of more trade." Thomas went into the courtyard, turned left towards the workshop.

"If he doesn't turn us in. There will be a price on our heads by now. The entire city will know we are outlaws."

"Carlos is a friend."

"Sometimes I wonder how you have managed to live so long." Jorge looked around, sat on the narrow cot that was becoming Lubna's.

Thomas started gathering more instruments, no longer his best, those now lost at the inn, irretrievable until this affair was done. Instead, he selected the best of those he had owned the longest, no longer modern, but adequate should he need them. His supply of herbs and potions was low and he took what he could.

He went in search of something to store them in. He had used his one good leather satchel, so went to his knees and pulled out boxes, sacks containing something he must have once considered important, but which had lain beneath the bench for years. Far in the back, he

found what he was looking for. A second satchel, this one also leather, stained almost black with age. It was not Thomas's, but a gift from an old man in the Pyrenees who had saved his life when he was sixteen years of age and set him on the path that brought him to this point in time.

"Thomas!"

He banged his head on the bench, backed out, aware of the undignified sight he must make. Lubna stood in the doorway, looking between him and Jorge.

"I thought you were out."

"I was upstairs making your bed, hanging clean clothes." She stood barefoot, a homespun shift falling to her knees, head uncovered because she was indoors and alone, leaving herself uncovered now because she considered herself Thomas's servant and Jorge's friend.

"Has Helena returned?"

"She was downstairs earlier while I was working. Is she no longer here?" Something showed in Lubna's eyes, a flicker of disappointment, but it passed as swiftly as it came.

"We're not staying," Thomas said, ignoring what he had seen.

"Again."

"What?"

"It is all you do these days. Come and go. Come and go."

"We are close to unmasking who is behind the killings. We have to act now before they can stop us."

391

Her expression changed. "Who is it, Abu Abdullah?"

Thomas had pondered on who could be helping the Sultan's son as they had made their way through the back streets and alleyways. There was only one man with sufficient resources to have sent men so quickly. But he couldn't make the accusation in front of Lubna, fearing it would wound this waif of a woman further.

"Abu Abdullah and others. I can't say who, but you will know soon enough."

"Do you not trust me?"

"I trust you, but I would not have this knowledge place you in danger. Jorge and I are fugitives. If anyone comes here looking for us, tell them you know nothing."

"That will not be difficult."

"You are in no danger, but if you need to, you must betray us."

Lubna shook her head. "I can never do that."

"You may have to. If it comes to it, do it. Don't even think, just do it."

"I am not my sister, Thomas. I will never betray you."

He stared at her. The intense eyes, her shadowed skin lustrous in the afternoon light.

"No, you are not. I know you are not." He saw his words pain her as she interpreted them differently to his meaning, and said, "You are far more than she could ever be." But it was too late, and he saw she didn't believe him.

"I have to finish my chores. Helena will want a meal

ready when she returns. She is as bad as you at the moment, never home."

Thomas watched her go, wanting to run after her, knowing he could not.

"You are a fool, Thomas Berrington." Jorge had sat on the cot the whole time, a silent observer.

"A fool if we stay here. Come on, we have plans to put into action."

Jorge rolled his eyes. "Whatever they might be. I wait with anticipation to hear what my clever friend has conjured up. Come then, at least the streets are cooler now. Where are we going?"

"To the baths."

"Of course, how foolish of me. I haven't bathed today and my sweat must offend your sensitive nose."

"They won't look for us there, you fool."

They passed into the courtyard and stopped.

Three armed men stood in the shaded area. One of them held Lubna tight, making no effort to be gentle. One arm gripping her across her breast, the other around her waist. She tried to break free, but only succeeded in tightening her captor's grip.

Helena stood to one side, as though trying to distance herself from what was taking place.

"You brought them," Thomas said, addressing her, satisfied when he saw her eyes shift away in guilt.

"You are under arrest, you and that creature both. Take them," the soldier in the centre ordered.

The man grasping Lubna let her drop, drew his scimitar and came forward.

Thomas leaned across to Jorge. "The back door," he whispered, drawing his sword and making as though to confront the approaching man. He feinted as he sensed Jorge backing away. Thomas intended to give him a moment, inflict a flesh wound on the man to the right, and then follow. The thought never once entered his head that he was in any real danger.

He heard Jorge run, the throw of bolts, and then the door crashed open. Thomas feinted left, twisted, brought his sword around on to the arm of the man to his right, exactly as he had seen it in his mind, except the blow caught on a leather arm-piece. Thomas turned to run, only to see more men spilling through the door Jorge had so conveniently opened for them. Thomas lowered his sword, recognising the hopelessness of the situation. When he turned back to the men in the courtyard, they made no attempt to approach, content to wait.

Beyond them, Lubna darted to one side and pushed against the captain of the guards, throwing him off balance. She snatched a knife from his belt, leapt on the back of the man who had held her and brought the knife around in a sweeping arc.

"No!" Thomas shouted, but Lubna's eyes had lost all rationality.

Another soldier threw himself against Lubna, tapping her skull with the hilt of his sword. The knife had enough momentum to strike the man her

legs were wrapped around, to scratch his flesh, but it lacked force and fell free to clatter against the tiles.

"Bitch." The soldier twisted around, grabbing Lubna as she slid from his back. He lifted her at the waist, rushed forward and slammed her into the wall. Lubna's head cracked against stone and she went limp. The man glanced over his shoulder at his captain, requesting permission.

The officer raised a shoulder: do as you wish.

Thomas yelled, but other hands came from behind to take his sword, pinning him to the spot.

"What about the whore?" said the other soldier.

The captain looked at Helena, standing apart from the group. Her earlier expression of spite and triumph had faded. Now she looked afraid.

"We have orders she is not to be harmed." The captain's face showed disdain. "Bring those two and the whore. And Ahmad, be quick with the girl."

"He always is," someone said, the words greeted by laughter.

Thomas struggled, trying to break free, but the men holding him were strong, and for all his writhing, they only gripped him more firmly.

The man grasping Lubna pawed at her shift, his intentions clear. Thomas yelled again and the other soldiers laughed, watching their companion with amusement.

"She is too skinny for you, Ahmad, she looks like a

boy. Might as well turn her around and pretend she is one."

"I heard he prefers it that way," someone else said.

Thomas lurched, one arm pulling clear only to be instantly caught. He could see Jorge also trying to break free, tears on the big man's face. Jorge's strength was greater and he managed to free his right arm. He swung it hard and smashed his fist into the side of his captor's head. He almost broke loose, but a man came behind and hit him on the back of the skull with the pommel of his sword and Jorge's knees went slack.

Thomas kicked backwards, his heel striking a shin, but the blow was only greeted with more laughter.

"The surgeon thinks himself a fighter."

"Let me loose and I'll show you who the fighter is, you coward."

Thomas felt the hands gripping him loosen, not believing these men were so stupid as to rise to such a challenge. Hope flared for a moment, before the captain said, "Keep your hold. You can fight him when he is safe inside the palace if you must, but not here."

The man turned and strode to the doorway from the courtyard. Thomas was dragged after him. Lubna, who had lain slack in Ahmad's grasp, came alive, twisting and screaming. She reached down and grasped the knife from his waist, and this time her blow was true. Instead of lifting her arm, she turned the knife, striking up into the man's stomach, grunting with the effort as she buried the blade deep.

Ahmad started to keen, his right leg jerking up and down as though he had trodden on a hornet. Lubna fell away, her stomach and thighs slicked with his blood.

"Oh, shit," the captain said, his voice tired. "Now we have to take the girl with us too. She has a lesson to learn." He strode across to grip Lubna's chin hard, staring into her face. With his other hand, he took the knife from her grasp and tossed it aside. "You do not kill one of my men and go unpunished. Tonight you will learn what it is like to be impaled on the cocks of an entire regiment."

"Safer to kill her here," someone said.

The captain drew his sword and stared at it for a moment. Thomas tried once more to break free, but his captors' arms might as well have been iron shackles.

The captain sheathed his sword. "No, bring her. But she is mine first. Afterwards, you can do what you want to her, but I go first. And bring the whore, we are to deliver her safe."

"Thomas, stop them!" Helena shouted as rough hands grabbed her, grasping her breasts, her belly, her sex. She twisted and turned, but the movement only made the men laugh more as her silk clothing ripped. "Thomas!" she cried again, but his heart had gone cold. The woman who had shared his life for half a year had betrayed them all.

"She is not to be harmed," the captain reminded his men, but his eyes took in the exquisite flesh revealed through torn silk.

The men gripping Thomas bundled him forward. His foot caught on a terracotta pot and he stumbled. The hands holding him loosened and he jerked free. He sprinted across the courtyard, hitting the captain with his shoulder, reaching for the man's sword. He spun, crouching, ready to die, but instead something hit the side of his head and the bright day turned black.

CHAPTER THIRTY-FOUR

Thomas woke to intense pain, a pounding in his temples, a throbbing in his arm, and fled back into unconsciousness. The second time he came around, the pain remained, but he ignored it, teasing out a strand of thought like a tangled thread, searching for its source. It had come to him in an instant on waking. Whether he had worked it out in a fevered dream, or his mind remained active while his body lay comatose, the truth emerged crystal clear, fully formed.

Bilal had been wrong.

He groaned. Small hands pulled at his arm. On the other side, someone stronger drew him upright to sit against a hard wall, but he immediately slumped sideways.

Thomas forced his eyes open and looked around. They were in a cell, the only illumination a flickering glow from the corridor outside, which came through a

small barred opening in the solid door. To his left, Lubna knelt, her torn shift drawn around herself. To the right, Jorge sat with his legs stretched out, blood on his face and ear.

"I was starting to wonder if they had killed you," said Jorge, "but then I thought, no, it was only his head."

"How long?"

"Some hours. Evening prayers have been called. It is likely dark outside, but we have no window to tell."

"Where?"

"Somewhere in the palace. Not a place I have seen before."

Thomas tried to sit upright, his head spinning, and again Lubna came to help. Recollection came slowly as he stared at her, not seeing this woman, but her sister. Misinterpreting his stare, she drew the torn edges of her clothing together.

"I would have had something to repair that in my bag," Thomas said.

"They took nothing," said Jorge. "Your bag is over there. Do you want it?"

"Fetch it for me if you would. My thanks." Thomas tried not to think why they had left him his bag. It was not a good sign. More than likely it meant they had no intention of releasing them.

"My, they did hit you hard, didn't they?"

Thomas accepted the battered satchel and opened the clasp, searched inside until he found the items he was looking for. He pulled out a needle and silk and

handed both to Lubna. Then he shook some dry bark into his hand and popped it into his mouth, chewing the bitter willow in hope it would ease the pounding in his head.

Lubna stood and walked to the door on the far side of the dungeon where enough light filtered in for her to see more clearly. She turned her back on Thomas and Jorge and began to pull together the separated pieces of her clothing.

"How is she?" Thomas whispered, putting his head against Jorge's, calmed by the touch against his own. He wanted to close his eyes and sleep, but fought against it.

"Subdued. She wonders why she is here, why the soldiers didn't keep her with them."

"There is only one answer. You know it and so does she. They are Olaf's men. He wants us dead, but he won't harm his daughters. You heard what they said to Helena."

"I tried to tell her," said Jorge, "but I don't think she listened. She is too calm." Jorge's voice was as soft as Thomas's, neither of them wanting Lubna to overhear.

"And Helena? What became of her?"

Jorge shook his head. "They separated us as soon as we reached the palace. She will be with him now."

"So why is Lubna here? Why not take her as well?"

"She killed one of them. Even Olaf has to be seen to punish murder. But no doubt she will be spirited out of the city to somewhere safe as soon as it can be arranged."

"It wasn't murder," Thomas said. "It was self-defence."

"That will not be how they see it."

"Zoraya and Olaf together after all," Thomas whispered. "What a pairing."

Jorge nodded, his gaze flicking across to Lubna, but she remained with her back to them. "You have worked it out as well, then. I never could understand why Abu Abdullah wanted Safya killed. She was too close to his mother, as good as a mother to him. It didn't make sense. None at all. But Zoraya wanting her dead—that makes a lot of sense."

"For what good the knowledge does us now." Thomas leaned closer, lowering his voice further. "Don't tell Lubna. She must know nothing of the truth if she is to remain safe."

"Her father will protect her."

"He will try, no doubt, but Zoraya is a different matter. She is spiteful. Olaf will have to watch his back when her son takes the throne."

"We made a good team, didn't we? Your brains and my subtlety?" Jorge smiled, and Thomas battled between his love and frustration at the man.

"At least we found those behind the killings, even if we can't do anything about them."

"Whisper all you want, I can hear you both perfectly well," said Lubna. "I will never believe my father guilty of what you accuse him."

Thomas said nothing. It was Jorge who felt a need to

fill the silence. "You, like Thomas, have a sharp mind. You will see the truth when you think it through. It is plain who is behind this. And your sister was feeding him information all the time. No wonder it felt like we were fighting our way into a sandstorm."

"Helena betrayed you, yes," Lubna spat. "You, Thomas, who took her in when no one else would, who treated her like the princess she believes herself to be instead of the lying, vicious bitch she is. But my father would never do what you believe. It must be someone else who aids Zoraya."

"Who, if not your father?" Thomas said, his voice gentle. It hurt him to see Lubna in such pain, but he had never denied the truth, and was not going to start now.

"How am I supposed to know? You are the man with all the answers. Tell me why we are locked in here instead of dead? I do not understand why we were not simply disposed of."

"You know why you are alive," Thomas said.

"They can't kill us," said Jorge. "You are the Sultan's physician."

"We will never be found, and remember this Sultan may not be long for this world either."

"We would be missed. Half the city knows what you have been doing. Your disappearance will raise questions."

"Which might last a day and then pass. There is always some new gossip in Gharnatah."

"Then the Sultan has to know. It was he who

entrusted you with this task at the outset."

"Unless it is him who is behind our capture," said Lubna. Thomas glanced at her, wondering if she was going to blame the entire population before accepting her father's involvement.

"Why would he want us captured? Why send me to find a killer, then lock us away?"

"Because he never expected you to succeed. He could not allow you to succeed. He killed the last men he set to do the task."

Thomas sighed, his headache starting up again. "It is not him we are accusing."

"Not now, no. But when your accusations against my father prove false, you will look elsewhere, and he knows the trail leads to him."

"So now you accuse the Sultan? Why not Jorge and me, too? It is the Sultan who banished your sister to my house, why would she plot with him?"

"Because you have done too good a job. She is beautiful again, and she was a favourite in the harem. You know her skills as well as any man. She cannot be resisted once she sets her mind to a thing."

Thomas didn't like the reminder of his own weakness. "Why did she betray me? Have I not been good to her?"

"She hates you. She scatters hurt like a farmer scatters wheat. It is her stock-in-trade."

"Lubna speaks the truth," said Jorge. "You know she does."

"You tell me this now?" Thomas raised his voice. "What kind of friend are you not to warn me when she came to my house?"

"The kind of friend who was pleased for you. Yes, she has her problems, but she is also beautiful and highly skilled. I thought you might enjoy the education."

Thomas shook his head. "I ache, and what brains I possess are bruised too badly to function. I can no longer think straight."

"You have to. It's what you are good at. Don't look to me for intelligence, my skills are of a different kind."

Thomas almost smiled. The willow was finally starting to work on his head, the throbbing in his arm also growing less. He wanted to remove the bandage and check the stitches, convinced they had torn loose with the strain put on them.

Lubna padded across the cell and sat beside him, her left leg touching his right. She handed him the needle and silk. She had roughly drawn the front of her shift together, but it would never be high fashion.

"Tell me what you believe, Thomas. Jorge told me some story while you slept, but he made no sense."

"Thank you," said Jorge.

"My pleasure. This cannot be the work of my father. I refuse to believe he is capable of such deception."

"As was I," Thomas said. "But the more I look, the more I see no other explanation. I saw with my own eyes how he was with Zoraya. Olaf is one of the few who could have us arrested and thrown in here."

"Why would he want Safya dead?"

"Not him—Zoraya did. He knows her well, will have acted as guard to her on many occasions. He admitted to me he visits her rooms. I have seen him train her sons with my own eyes. And she is beautiful, as Helena's mother was."

"My mother is beautiful, too."

"Of course she is." Thomas lowered his gaze, then lifted it quickly for fear Lubna would think his eyes sought her body. "Your mother is a fine woman, but these ladies of the harem are … are something different." He felt a moment's grief sear through him like a bolt of lightning. In an instant, a thousand and one memories flooded his mind. Of the night Helena came to his bed for the first time, her skin pale gold, her hands delicate and knowing as she loosened his clothing. The sounds she uttered as they made love. The skills she demonstrated, acts of sensuality Thomas had never dreamed of.

"I will not believe it of my father," said Lubna. "Olaf Torvaldsson is pure and loyal. He has fought beside the Sultan for thirty years. He could not do such a thing."

Thomas saw a brightness in her eyes, heard the quiver in her voice and knew she was trying to convince herself, doubts already settling in her mind, gnawing away at certainty.

"No doubt he believes he does what is best for Gharnatah."

"What—to have the Sultan's wives murdered?" Lubna turned her face away.

"It would not be all the wives. Without Safya or Aixa, Abu Abdullah's claim to the title is weak, Yusuf's weaker still. The city will pass to Nasir."

"I understand all this. I am not stupid, but I will never believe my father could be a part of such treachery. Never."

"What you or I believe is of little use tonight." Thomas lifted his arm. Lubna hesitated a moment, then lay against his side and he drew her close, both comforting and comforted. He stared into the gloom, only the flickering glow of the torch beyond the door casting a weak illumination on them. "I assume someone has checked the door is locked?" he said.

Jorge snorted a laugh. "Oh, of course they would throw us into an unlocked dungeon."

Lubna slipped from beneath his arm and went to the door. She rattled the lock, pushed and pulled, but it was as solid as the wall surrounding it. She came back, a wry grin on her face.

"Suppose it had been? We would look fools, would we not?" She slid down beside Thomas, curled tight against him once more, and he moved his head a little and breathed in the essence of her. None of them smelled too sweet after this day, but the scent of her soothed him. He closed his eyes. For a moment only, he promised.

He woke to a scuttling sound, at first part of his dream, then solidifying.

"Rats," said Jorge. "This far below ground, they'll be everywhere."

"It is not rats," said Lubna.

"What's not rats?" Thomas asked.

"You are awake at last." She moved away from him and his side felt cold where she had lain against him.

"I wasn't sleeping, only resting."

"You snore loudly when you rest," said Jorge.

"What rats?" Thomas said.

There came a sound from the passage, a scraping.

"Those rats," said Jorge.

Thomas rose stiffly and went to the door. He tried to lift up far enough to see through the bars, but they were too high. He pressed his ear against the wood, sprang back when something banged against the far side.

"They are coming for us!" His stomach filled with ice, his heart beating hard in his chest.

The sound of scuttling resolved into a heavy key turning in the lock and the door swung inward.

"Hello, Thomas."

"Prea!"

"You will have to pay me even more now, won't you?" Her face showed a manic glee.

"Where are the guards?"

The girl laughed. "Sleeping the sleep of angels. Or devils more like. We heard about your capture and Bazzu

sent me down with a special meal for them, a thank you for capturing the wicked palace killers."

"Is that what we are accused of?"

"Everyone within these walls believes it." She smiled. "Well, almost everyone."

"Who first spread the news?"

Prea shook her head. "How am I to know that? By the time we heard of it in the kitchen, it was rumour built on rumour. Are we going to stand here all night, or do you want to escape?"

"Yes, we want to escape." Thomas wanted to hug her, but knew she might misinterpret such a show of affection. Not to mention Lubna.

"Follow me, then."

Prea darted out into the passageway. Jorge pushed past Thomas, but Lubna waited beside him until he finally took a step, and then she stayed close as they made their way out. Torches lit the passage at intervals. Other cells led off on one side, the other solid stone. Most likely the wall formed part of the foundations of the palace.

When they turned a corner, three guards were slumped around a glowing brazier. Thomas stopped, but Prea laughed and ran forward to slap one across the face. The guard's head rocked, but his eyes remained closed.

"Bazzu made a fine meal for the likes of these. They will sleep till morning."

"Where are you taking us?" Thomas whispered, still afraid the guards might wake.

"To the kitchens. They are the closest place of safety. Bazzu knows I have come looking for you. She will hide you until the small hours, and then we will sneak you out."

"When did you know we were prisoners?"

"I told you, it is the talk of the palace. They say you are the killers, that you fooled the Sultan into asking you to investigate when it was really the two of you behind everything. You, Thomas, were driven mad by Helena's whisperings in your ear, and Jorge was the, ah, the man on the inside. They say you planned it all between you."

"I assume you did not believe what was said?"

Prea laughed, darting ahead, the passage wider, the scent of clean air coming to them.

"Bazzu refused to believe such a thing of Jorge. She has such softness in her heart for that one."

"I am right here," said Jorge.

"And I knew you were no traitor, Thomas. You spent an entire day with me in the passages. You could have killed me at any time you wanted to hide your secret, but you did not. So we knew the rumours were false, spread by whoever is truly behind this."

"And who would that be?" asked Jorge. "Who started the rumours?"

"I told you, I do not know, but who starts any rumour? They appear as if by magic from out of thin air. I truly believe they have no source, but simply are. However, Bazzu believes this one likely started in the barracks."

"Olaf Torvaldsson," Thomas muttered.

Lubna, walking beside him with her head down, made no comment, but Thomas saw her shoulders tense and wished the truth was otherwise.

Thomas manoeuvred to put Lubna into the lead, with Jorge between himself and Prea. He dropped back, touching the girl's shoulder to let her know to fall behind, and once a space had opened up, he whispered to her, "You know Lubna's sister?"

"The courtesan? Your wife?"

"Not my wife, but she is the one. She was taken at the same time we were, but to the barracks I think. Have you heard anything of her fate?"

Prea gave a sigh that was half muffled laughter. "That one has no fate. Bazzu told me all about her. She is like the cockroaches—she will survive anything. I heard she is with Zoraya."

They reached ground level and Prea led them through dark courtyards, only the occasional lamp flickering a weak illumination here and there.

"I still need to show you what I discovered, Thomas."

"We may not need it anymore, not if I'm right. But tell me anyway."

"I believe I have found the killer's clothes."

Thomas slowed, stopped and turned to look at Prea. "His clothes?"

She favoured him with a look. "He has them hidden away on a high shelf close to an entrance. I think it is

where he enters that world. I have been waiting and watching, but he has not come yet."

Thomas grabbed Prea's arm, turning her to face him. "You must not do that. This man is a killer. He will strike you down without a moment's hesitation."

"I am not stupid, Thomas Berrington. He will never discover me. I have a safe place to hide. You know how well I can hide."

"Don't go back there without me."

"Will you let me show you, then?"

"It is too dangerous, we are all three of us wanted. You cannot be seen associating with us."

Prea laughed and started along the corridor. They were close to the kitchens, and even now in the small hours, the scent of fresh bread, fruit and meat reached them.

"Now is exactly the right time, when everyone is asleep. Just you and me, Thomas. We can pass like ghosts and no one will see us."

Bazzu was awake when they arrived at her room, sitting behind her desk, as alert as if the hour was noon. She rose when they entered and went directly to Jorge, drawing him into her arms. Thomas looked away, allowing them a moment. His gaze fell on Lubna, who was watching him in turn, her face expressionless.

Prea tugged at his hand and he saw Lubna's eyes shift to the girl, back to his.

"We must go now," said Prea. "Bazzu will look after

these two, and we need to sneak you out before dawn."
She tugged at him again.

"What does she want with you?" said Lubna, her
voice as cold as her face.

"She wants to show me something."

"I expect she does. You had better go then." Lubna
turned away, leaned against a wall and slid down, her
head dropping.

Thomas wanted nothing more than to go to her, but
Prea was still pulling at his hand and he knew whatever
she had found might be important. He allowed himself to
be led away.

Once they had left the kitchen, Prea said, "Is she your
girl, too?"

"Lubna? No, of course not. You know who I live
with."

"The woman with the white hair. Do you look at her
the same way you look at that girl?"

Thomas slowed and glanced at Prea. How many
years did she have? Barely more than sixteen, yet there
was so much wisdom in such a small package.

"I know where my duty lies. Now show me this place
so I can get out of here."

Prea walked away, muttering, no doubt thinking
Thomas couldn't hear her, but his ears had always been
sharp.

"I would like someone to look at me the way you
look at her, but never mind about me, I am just the girl
who showed you the tunnels."

CHAPTER THIRTY-FIVE

The entrance Prea led Thomas to was not one he had seen before. It lay close to the outer wall of the palace, near the barracks. For a soldier, it made a perfect place from which to gain access—a little-used corridor which would be deserted for much of the time.

Prea reached into the wall, her face a rictus of concentration. A moment later, she grinned and Thomas helped her swing a wooden panel open.

"How do we see inside?" The palace slumbered around them, only small lamps or candles burning, not enough to illuminate inside the tunnels.

"There is a lamp already here. He must come at night, and the man is well prepared." Prea disappeared into the darkness. A moment later, Thomas heard the strike of flint and a faint illumination showed him the way. He drew the panel closed behind him, but didn't let it latch shut.

"Are his clothes here?" He surveyed the space. This spot appeared no different to any other. Grey stone enclosed a narrow passage leading into darkness and grit scraped beneath his feet. It was claustrophobic.

"It is not far."

Prea went ahead and Thomas felt a chill of fear as he once more imagined being alone in these tunnels, lost in the dark. What else used these passages other than men and women? But Prea made good her promise. After fewer than two minutes, she stopped and indicated a shelf cut into the wall.

"It will be easier if you reach up. I had to climb."

Thomas stretched, going on tiptoe, and still could only just reach. His searching hand found something soft and he jerked away before realising it was what he sought. He tugged and a garment fell, fine silk billowing. Prea stepped back to avoid it touching the guttering lamp.

"Is there anything else?"

"Look," said Prea.

Thomas reached again, his fingers walking across cold stone. They found nothing and he withdrew.

Prea sighed. "Here, hold this." She thrust the lamp at him and clambered up the wall until she perched on the edge of the shelf. She reached in and the light caught on something bright. Then she handed him a curved sword.

"Careful," she said, "it is sharp."

Thomas wrapped the blade inside the silk, placed the

lamp on the ground and took the hilt. Prea slid down and landed beside him.

"When did you find this?"

"Yesterday. I wanted to show you then, but you said you were too busy."

"And you have been watching for him?"

"When I could. I have duties, but I also have friends who help cover for me. There is another shelf a little way along—large enough for me to lie concealed on. I have been waiting there, but he has not come back, though I think I hear him sometimes." She smiled. "It is almost as if he is a djinn, heard but never seen."

Thomas shook his head. "He'll kill you if he catches you. It was a foolish thing to do."

"Would you rather I'd never found this? Rather I not tell you of what I did?"

"I would rather you showed me this before."

"I tried to! What was I supposed to do, ignore it? How would you feel if he struck again and I had done nothing?"

"What were you planning to do, confront him?"

"I was going to follow him and find out who he was," said Prea.

Thomas knew her discovery was important. He would have come at once if she had told him what she had found directly.

"What are you going to do with these?" asked Prea.

"We'll take them with us. I want to examine them in a better light."

"If he returns, he will know he has been discovered." Prea cocked her head to one side as they both heard a noise. Someone in the tunnels had kicked a stone.

Thomas stared at the girl as Prea's eyes widened. She put a finger to her lips, not that he was going to give them away by speaking. Thomas let the dark silk fall from the blade of the sword and held it out, pushing Prea behind him.

Another sound came, closer, that of someone breathing. When Thomas glanced back at Prea, she nodded. This was the man they sought, and he was coming their way. The breathing grew louder, a soft rasp underlying it, and Thomas took a pace towards the corner where he expected the man to appear. As he did so, his foot caught on the discarded silk and he stumbled.

Silence.

Thomas tried to still his own breathing. Prea made no sound at all. And then whoever lay behind the turn ran, making no effort to hide his flight, and Thomas set off after him.

He reached the corner, stumbled into utter darkness and stopped, unwilling to race into the unknown. He could still hear the man, but distant now, and as he stood there, the sound faded and was gone.

"We've lost him." Prea was close behind, one hand touching the small of his back.

"No, I lost him. I gave us away."

"At least we know he was coming here and hasn't

fled yet. We should go on and see if there is any sign of where he left the tunnels, it might tell us something."

Thomas shook his head. "There are a dozen exits he could have taken and no way for us to know which one." He turned and pushed Prea ahead so they could make their way back to where the man had kept his small hoard of objects. "Let's get out of here and find Jorge and Bazzu. I should confront Olaf as well. I want to see his face when I show his this sword."

Prea shrugged. "One sword is much like another, isn't it?"

In the kitchen, Thomas laid the garment across Bazzu's table and he, Bazzu and Jorge leaned over it. Prea had disappeared, and Lubna slept, or pretended to.

"This is unusually fine," said Bazzu, rubbing the silk between finger and thumb. "And the colour is like nothing I have ever seen. Almost black, but this gold thread running through it gives a wondrous shimmer. This must look wonderful when worn."

"It's the killer's disguise, if you can consider something so beautiful a disguise."

Jorge picked up the material, draping it across his arm. A frown troubled his face.

"This material is familiar. I have seen it somewhere before."

"In the palace?" Thomas said. "Have you seen someone wearing it?"

"Not the palace, somewhere else, but I can't remember where." Jorge lifted the garment and let it hang loose. It moved in the lightest draught, the colour shifting as it did so. "Can I wear it?"

"Now? Will it fit you?"

"Of course it will. We could both fit inside it. Aren't you curious to see how it looks?"

"If you must." Thomas saw Bazzu smile. Without waiting, Jorge disrobed until he stood naked, unashamed. Bazzu openly admired him. Even Thomas was impressed. Jorge's chest was broad, the muscle clearly delineated beneath smooth skin, his legs long and shapely. Not to mention that element of his manhood Thomas had not removed.

He slipped the robe over his nakedness and closed it with delicate ties before drawing the deep hood over his head where it almost completely obscured his face.

"Move around," Thomas said, and Jorge walked to the door. The robe followed his every move, accentuating the figure beneath.

Jorge returned and took the sword which lay on the table. He returned to the door, went out into the corridor. Thomas saw Bazzu frown.

Jorge rushed into the room, turning, twisting, the sword raised high. He slashed down, turned again, struck once more. Something about the sound, his movement,

woke Lubna and she screamed as she took in the whirling figure.

Thomas went to her and laid his hand on her shoulder, but Lubna's gaze was locked on Jorge.

"You are the djinn," said Bazzu, a note of awe in her voice.

"Indeed, the djinn," Thomas said, then more softly to Lubna, "It's not real."

As Jorge moved, the robe—so light, so responsive— wrapped itself around him. His legs fused into one, his shoulders flared. The minute gold threads shimmered, offering a hint of fire.

"It is easy to see how the women were deceived. This is clever. It masks the man within and makes it impossible to judge his shape or size. Someone planned this with great precision."

"And money," Bazzu said. "I have never seen a cloth so fine."

Jorge stopped showing off and returned the sword to the table.

"I want to wear it forever," he said. "It kisses the body like a thousand lips." He bent and briefly kissed Bazzu.

"You might want to wear it, but you can't," Thomas said, and Jorge nodded.

"If I must, but I will miss its kisses."

Thomas turned his back while Jorge disrobed and dressed once more in his own clothes.

"What do we do with it now?"

"Hide it," Thomas said. "Bazzu, do you have somewhere safe?"

"I have a place."

Thomas nodded. "Good. I want to make use of it again when we confront the killer. The sword, too. Tell Prea she did well."

"You should reward her," Bazzu said.

Thomas gave her a quizzical glance. "I will give her more coin, of course."

"That is not what I meant."

"Then make yourself clear." He was in no mood for subtlety.

"She talked with me about you—it seems you have an admirer."

Thomas sighed. "She is young and impressionable, and—"

Bazzu's laugh interrupted him and he scowled.

"She does not want to share your bed, though no doubt she would if you asked. She is bright, and can do better for herself than to work in the palace kitchens."

Thomas returned Bazzu's stare and waited, half an idea where she was going.

"She told me you needed a servant. An important man such as yourself without at least one servant is in danger of looking foolish."

"I do not need—"

Bazzu held up a hand and Thomas wondered if she was ever going to allow him to finish a sentence.

"You know she is sharp and eager to do whatever is asked. Do you truly not have a place for her?"

"There is no room," Thomas said.

"Then make room. She deserves more than mere payment for what she has done, do you not agree?"

"She has been a great help."

"Shall I tell her you will consider my request?"

"Your request, or hers?"

Bazzu studied his face for a moment before offering a smile.

"It comes from me of course, so it is my request. Would you turn me down?"

Thomas wiped his palm across his forehead. His head ached, his body hurt, his thoughts swooped and curled like swallows in flight, but with far less precision.

"I will consider it. Though whether I am ever going to be able to return home is in question. But yes, if I am allowed to return to my work, I will consider your request."

Bazzu smiled and he knew she had won, wondering how he would accommodate yet another female in his household. Of course, there was every likelihood Helena would not be returning, in which case... *No*, he shook his head, *too many thoughts, too many questions*.

"In a few days you will be back in your house surrounded by women." Bazzu stared at him, something in her gaze sparking discomfort inside him. "I have known you only a little time, Thomas Berrington, but

even I can see you are incapable of what you are accused."

"Events are not always so simple. There are politics involved."

"Then Jorge will take care of those." Her eyes narrowed. "You know he can deal with such matters, don't you?"

Thomas glanced at his friend. "I know he hides his abilities well in order to play the fool. I need another favour from you and Prea, if you will ask her." He turned his head to check on Lubna, who seemed to have slumped back into a doze, before lowering his voice. "I know who is behind these killings and plan to set a trap. I want both of you to play a part, if you are willing."

Bazzu nodded. She had won her small battle and could afford to be magnanimous now.

Thomas drew up a chair and told her what he wanted.

CHAPTER THIRTY-SIX

The day was just starting as they slipped from the back of a cart that had taken flour to the palace. Stallholders were erecting tables and setting out wares, the markets and side streets busy with activity, assailed by noise and smells. Dressed in the clothes Bazzu had found for them, all three looked like poor merchants, each with a tagelmust obscuring their faces.

"Where do you plan to hide us today?" asked Jorge. "We are starting to run out of places that will have us."

"We won't have to hide long. This will end soon, one way or another."

They negotiated their way through the back alleys of Gharnatah and came to the edge of al-Hattabin Square. Thomas called a halt. He stood a moment looking around, but saw nothing to raise suspicion. With luck, they hadn't been missed yet. Thomas wondered how long they would have been left in the dungeon had Prea

not come. Forever? Locked in the dark and left to starve? More likely someone would come looking for them today, if they had not done so already. Someone planning their disappearance.

Thomas, Jorge and Lubna moved along the edge of the square, unwilling to risk its open expanse. They crossed over the Hadarro at the head of the square and took the roadway along its banks until they came to Aamir's bathhouse. Here the street was busier, people coming down from the Albayzin for work, others to cleanse at the start of the day.

They avoided the busy main entrance and instead took a narrow alley, cool from never seeing the sun. Thomas rapped on a small door set deep into the wall. Steam vented from grills set in the stone to rise into the air. There was no reply so Thomas rapped a second time, harder, and eventually heard the sound of bolts being drawn. A young boy peered out, suspicious.

"You must use the front door. This one isn't allowed."

"I am a friend of Aamir's, he will let me use this way."

The boy looked unconvinced. "I need to ask." He started to push the door shut, but Jorge leaned his weight against it and the lad had no option but to give way.

"Aamir will be displeased if he hears my friend and I have been turned away. Thomas is a distinguished surgeon, and this woman is the daughter of Olaf Torvaldsson."

"You are Thomas Berrington?" The boy's eyes widened, and Thomas nodded. The boy's resistance gave way and they entered the baths, the scent of oil and soap heavy in the steamy air.

The boy darted ahead, stopped. "I will tell my master you are here. Do not move, he will want to see you."

Thomas's body relaxed, the release of tension sapping what little reserves remained to him. Jorge placed his palm flat on the wall and lowered his head, breathing as though they had run all the way. Lubna looked around, an expression on her face Thomas had never seen there before.

"I do not like this place," she said.

"The baths? Why not?"

"It is a place of sin."

Jorge chuckled, and Thomas smiled. "It can be. But it is also a place I visit often, but not for sin." He chose not to mention the times in the past when he had come here for exactly that purpose. "How then do you bathe?"

"I wash with a cloth and bowl of water as the prophet demands."

"Hot or cold?"

"Usually cold. I cannot always get hot water."

Thomas laughed. "I'll ask Aamir to provide you with your very own chamber so you can discover the ultimate pleasure of a hot bath. A massage too if you wish."

"I need neither."

Thomas leaned over and sniffed. "Are you sure?"

Lubna turned aside, punishing him with a moment's

shame at his teasing. The past day had seen the cornerstones of her life crumble. First Helena's betrayal and now her father's guilt. He put his hands on her shoulders and turned her to face him.

"I miss her, too," Thomas said. "I worry what may become of her."

"Helena?" Lubna shook her head. "She will find a new man, as she always has. You know it is not Helena I am thinking of."

"Much as I might wish it, I can't protect you from the truth."

Lubna looked as though she might strike him. Thomas wouldn't blame her if she did, happy to accept her blows if they helped.

"The things you believe are not true," she said. "You may think they are, but I know in here you are wrong." She punched herself in the centre of her chest. Once. Twice. "I know my father can be cruel, but he is not underhand. He would never betray the Sultan."

"Everything I know points to it being so," Thomas said.

"Then everything you know is wrong!" Lubna turned away once more. She hunched her shoulders and took several paces along the corridor. "I hate this place."

Thomas followed, laid his hands on her narrow shoulders, but she shrugged him off.

"Do not touch me. I am no longer your servant."

"You were never my servant."

427

"Not in your head, but everyone else saw what I was."

"I thought you wanted to learn. I can help if you allow me."

"I cannot stay in your house with this between us. You see one truth and I see another. I have nowhere left. And now I am on the run for murder! I will not go to my father and tell him of your suspicions, I owe you that much. There has been enough betrayal already."

Thomas placed his hands on her shoulders a third time, and although Lubna tensed, this time she didn't pull away.

"Go to my house. Your house. You will be safe there, and it's close to the mosque. Get something to eat. Sleep. Wash. Wear some of Helena's clothing as a disguise. Stay as long as you wish. Forever, if you want."

"And you?"

"I will return if I can."

"If you can?"

"The path I choose isn't without danger. If I survive, I will return to you."

Lubna's shoulders trembled beneath his hands and he saw a quiver in the fall of her robe. He was unsure if this waif could manage her pain alone, but asking her to stay would only make the pain worse. Thomas pushed at her and released his grip.

"Go. This place isn't for you."

Lubna walked away without looking back, wrapping a scarf around her head.

"She needs time," said Jorge. "The news of her father has come as a shock, but she will learn to accept the truth. She has a brain and knows how to use it."

"I don't know if I care anymore. I've had enough of women and their ways."

Jorge smiled and patted Thomas on the shoulder. "You, too, will change your mind."

"I heard there were three of you." Aamir came bustling towards them. "Is your companion nearby?" He ignored Jorge to stop in front of Thomas. "I prepared a private chamber if you wish to make use of it."

"She is not that kind of companion. Besides, she is no longer here."

Aamir shrugged. "Then you will have to make do with the eunuch."

"I need you to find me some items while I bathe. I can pay well."

"You know I will take no coin from you, Thomas."

"It will make me feel better to pay."

Once more, Aamir raised his shoulder, and as he led them to the promised bathing chamber, Thomas gave him his list of requirements.

They stopped a moment outside the chamber as Thomas finished talking with Aamir. By the time he entered, Jorge had already stripped out of his soiled clothing and was pouring hot water over himself, a contented smile on his face.

Thomas discarded his own robes and stepped beneath the water gushing from a spout set in the wall, its weight

beating against his head and shoulders. It was an hour before they emerged. Aamir had provided a small room with two cots, a meal, wine, and the supplies Thomas had asked for. There were no chairs or table in the room, so Thomas sat cross-legged on the floor, dipped a quill into dark ink and started to write.

"Love letters?" Jorge asked, already starting on the food.

"Of a kind. It's an invitation, anyway. Leave me some of that food."

"Don't take too long, then."

But Thomas took his time. The document had to look authentic.

He scattered fine sand on the paper and shook it, tipped the sand on to the floor, then lit the candle Aamir's boy had brought. He felt inside his robe, for a moment experiencing panic that he had lost the seal, but it was there, caught in the side of a pocket.

He melted dark wax and let it run on to the folded paper, pressed the seal, holding it there while the wax solidified. After he had eased it clear, he checked carefully. The document looked authentic. No—the document *was* authentic. It possessed the seal of the Sultan of Gharnatah. It would be unquestioned.

Thomas laid it aside and took another sheet of paper and started to write a second note. This one—less formal —required no seal.

Lubna didn't wash, nor did she visit the mosque, even though midday prayer had been called. Instead, she cleaned the blood from the courtyard tiles, forced herself to eat some fruit and nuts, then gathered up the papers she and Thomas had studied and laid them on the table in his workshop. Those written in symbols she didn't understand were reluctantly laid aside. Those in Arabic, she set apart. When there were two piles—that which she could read containing three times the quantity of the one she couldn't—she sat and began to work through them again.

She didn't believe her father guilty of the crimes Thomas accused him of. These documents were the only means she had of proving his innocence, and if proof lay somewhere within these pages, she meant to find it.

Lubna barely noticed the chatter of the swallows as they swooped above the courtyard, or the movement of the shadows on the walls as the afternoon passed. The city of Gharnatah slumbered in the heat as she continued to read, over and over again, the minutiae of commercial life within the city.

CHAPTER THIRTY-SEVEN

The market was a tumult of sound, scent and texture. Men and women shouted, great brass pots cooked food from a dozen countries, chickens, geese, goats and sheep milled about underfoot. Boys and girls in rags ran through it all on errands and mischief. The noise was overwhelming.

Thomas sat deep in the alcove of a merchant's house, hidden behind a stall selling lamps from across the narrow sea, rolls of cloth from Egypt, lengths of dark wood from the forests of Africa, and sticky balls of resin extracted from poppy, together with a score of other items. None were related other than by the fact each might turn a profit.

Thomas watched crowds that surged and ebbed like the tides of the great western ocean, and waited. He knew all he wanted to of the ocean, of its ebbing and flowing, its waves and storms. He had seen more than

enough and wanted never to see or cross its waters again. He searched the crowd for a sign. It had not come yet, but he was patient.

Jorge spent his time either standing nearby looking furtive, or wandering the stalls while he also studied the milling throng.

It was late morning before Thomas saw what he was waiting for.

Two merchants talking together were startled as a slim figure darted between them. One of the men turned and shouted, believing the girl a pickpocket, but Prea had already disappeared into the crowd. Thomas lost sight of her for a moment, then she was standing not twenty paces away, looking around. She was searching for him, but his alcove was shaded and the square bright with sunlight.

Thomas scanned the crowd both near and far, then took two paces forward so light fell on him. Prea's face showed excitement, cheeks flushed, this intrigue beyond her usual experience. She ran to him.

"He's on the way?" Thomas asked, grasping her shoulders to prevent her hugging him.

"He will be here any moment." Prea turned, lifting on tiptoes as she surveyed the crowd. "I see Bazzu, I have to go. Come and find me later if you can. And thank you for saying you will take me in." This time, he couldn't prevent the hug. Thomas knew he needed to be firmer. First Olaf had tricked him into taking Lubna, now Bazzu was making promises to this girl on his behalf, but he

couldn't be displeased. He only hoped he lived beyond tomorrow so there was a place for her to come to.

When she eventually released him, he retained his grip, preventing her from moving away.

"You haven't been back to the tunnels, have you?"

"You asked me not to," said Prea. She tugged away again, this time breaking free.

"Don't—" But she was gone.

"I think you have another admirer." Jorge appeared at his side like the djinn they were chasing.

"Just what I need. A fifteen-year-old girl. Did you know Bazzu is sending her to me as a servant? How long have you been there?"

"Long enough." Jorge looked Thomas up and down. "How do you attract all these women to you?" Jorge shook his head. "It's not even as if you're good looking. And we both know fifteen-year-old girls marry and have children." Jorge shrugged. "Or maybe not even bother with the marrying part."

"So now I am marrying her?" Thomas caught sight of Bazzu moving through the far side of the crowd. For a large woman, she was light on her feet, her body twisting through gaps that appeared too narrow for her size. Behind her trailed a line of boys, none much older than Prea, and as Bazzu chose their goods, the merchants loaded the baskets they carried. Despite the lateness of the morning, Bazzu was a familiar figure here, and the stallholders held back some of their best produce for the palace, where price was no object.

434

The last boy in line was dressed the same as the others, except for a tagelmust which obscured most of his face. His dark eyes searched as Prea's had. Thomas saw her approach the boy and lean in to speak. They drifted from the end of the line, the boy still carrying his empty basket. Bazzu, who expected the move, continued shopping as though nothing had happened.

"Time to hide you even further," said Jorge, and Thomas rose and moved without haste to the rear of a stall selling silk and linen owned by Carlos Rodriguez. The Spanish merchant no longer dirtied his own hands in the markets, but he had briefed his stallholder and informed Thomas the man could be trusted.

As he approached, the grey cotton cloth which covered the table top and fell to the ground on all sides was lifted to offer him a place of concealment. Thomas ducked beneath into warm dimness. A moment later, the side cloth was raised again and the small figure of the Sultan's son, Yusuf, crawled in. His face glowed in the filtered light.

"Thomas—this intrigue is far more exciting than battle." Yusuf clapped Thomas on the shoulder, what would be a familiar gesture from an older man incongruous in one so young, but Yusuf had been raised as a prince and didn't act as any normal child. His enthusiasm, however, was still that of a fourteen-year-old boy.

"You received my message then."

"That girl—what's her name?"

"Prea."

"She's pretty."

"She is."

"Do you think if I spoke with her, she would spend some time with me?"

"It depends what you have in mind."

Yusuf's olive skin flushed, but he said, "I tire of princesses and the ladies of the harem. They are all so proper and perfect. I want to run and play with someone my own age."

"Then ask her. Although be aware if you do, she will say yes to anything you ask."

"Tell her she can do as she wants, but if she wants to play, then she can do that, too. Will you tell her, Thomas?"

He smiled. Yusuf was such a sweet child, unlike his brother. Unfortunately, it was his brother Thomas would have to deal with.

"I will tell her." He laid a hand on Yusuf's shoulder, feeling the tremble there. "Now, I need you to take a message for me, and it must go to one person, and one person only—"

"My father is away from the city."

"This message is for your brother. I must speak with Abu Abdullah, and speak with him tonight."

"You will come to the palace?"

"Abu Abdullah must come to Aamir's bathhouse."

"He likes to visit there."

"I have heard he does. But tonight there will be no

436

women, not until he has spoken with me. I have something important to discuss."

"Can I come, too?"

"No. Our conversation might be … difficult." Thomas had been about to say dangerous, but feared the word would only attract Yusuf the more. "Do you have any notion of the task set of me and Jorge?"

"I heard you are searching for the man who killed Safya. Do you have him, Thomas? Is that what you want to speak to Abu Abdullah about? They say in the palace that you and the eunuch are the killers, but I don't believe it. I am not sure about my brother. He repeats the charges against you as though they are true."

Thomas knew he had no time to argue his case. "We know who is behind the plot. But I can't tell you who, only your brother, and hope he recognises the truth when he hears it. Will you do this for me, Yusuf? It is a dangerous task I ask of you. There will be those in the palace who wish to seek out and destroy me for what I know. Tell no one, no one at all, other than Abu Abdullah."

"I promise, Thomas." The thrum through Yusuf's body grew, his small frame barely able to contain his excitement. "This is real intrigue, isn't it? Bazzu and Prea are in on the plot, too, aren't they?"

"You can't mention either of them or they will also be in danger. Return to your place, and then to the palace. Find Abu Abdullah. He is in the palace, isn't he?"

"He was when I left. But you know Abu Abdullah, he likes to hawk and hunt. But he prefers to go out late in the afternoon when the day has cooled. He goes into the hills behind al-Hamra and chases down rabbits and pigeons."

"Then tell him tonight he can't hunt, but must come to me."

"Shall I tell him why?"

"This letter will tell him why." Thomas pressed the second letter he had written into Yusuf's warm hand. "You must tell him it is important I see him today. Now go."

Yusuf crept away, stopped and scuttled back. He half climbed on to Thomas's lap and hugged him, a small, hard body pressed against his. Thomas knew he should discourage the boy from such shows of affection, but couldn't bring himself to do so. There was still an innocence within Yusuf he wished to see last as long as possible. As the younger son of the Sultan, he had been spoiled, allowed to hold on to childhood longer than his brother. Soon enough he would have to act as a prince and learn the cunning needed to survive in the world on the hill.

Thomas pushed him away, and this time Yusuf didn't turn back.

Thomas backed out from his hiding place, face streaked with sweat, and strolled back to the shaded alcove. Jorge had remained, keeping watch in case any guards had followed the kitchen party.

They watched Yusuf retrieve his basket. Bazzu placed a few token objects into it before turning and weaving back through the crowd to return to the palace.

They reached the bathhouse just before noon prayers while the streets were still busy. As Jorge lay on a cot, Thomas used his teeth to untie the knot on the bandage covering his arm. The wound beneath itched, and he needed to know if the itch was from healing or something more sinister.

With the stained bandage removed, Thomas held his arm close and sniffed it. He detected no hint of infection.

"You should wash that," said Jorge.

Thomas smiled. "Are you the doctor now?"

"I have spent enough time around you to know you should wash it."

"I was planning on doing that next."

"How is the arm?"

"Healing," Thomas said.

"Do you want me to re-bandage it after? I know I am not as skilled as Lubna, but I will try if you ask."

Thomas studied the arm. "I think I will leave it open to the air. The stitches have knitted now and the wound is no longer weeping."

"So you will live," said Jorge.

"Allah willing."

"That girl is rubbing off on you."

"It's a saying," Thomas said. "Nothing more."

"She's a pretty thing. And bright."

Thomas gave Jorge a look and he shrugged.

"I am only saying what I see, in case you happened to miss it."

CHAPTER THIRTY-EIGHT

Abu Abdullah came a little after sunset. Smoke from the many lamps spiralled upwards to be captured by the vaulted ceiling. Thomas watched from the vantage point of the balcony which ran around the large bath in the centre of the building. He had not expected the prince to come alone—no member of the royal palace ever went anywhere alone, unless like Yusuf they sneaked away—but Abu Abdullah entered accompanied by only two guards. He swaggered. He always swaggered, the affectation becoming more pronounced the older he grew.

"You will need to separate him from his guards." Jorge stood beside Thomas, his head and cheeks rough with stubble, his clothing creased. Thomas knew he looked equally unkempt. It was almost a week since his last shave, which had been in this same bathhouse. He

would ask Aamir for a barber when their business was done. If his head still remained on his shoulders.

"Separating him won't be easy."

"Why not just ask him to send them away?"

"Ask him?"

"That's right. Tell him you will only speak with him alone and to send them away."

Thomas laughed, raising his hand to mask the sound.

"And he will agree, of course."

"He will once you are both undressed and he sees you can do him no harm. He is a vain man and wouldn't believe it possible for you to attack him on your own."

"In that he is right. Abu Abdullah, for all his arrogance, is a skilled warrior."

"I have heard him say so on many occasions."

"It is true. I have seen him fight, and he is a dervish."

"You have not done so badly yourself," Jorge pointed out. "You surprised me when you attacked those soldiers who came after us."

"I did? How?" Thomas was only half listening, watching Abu Abdullah speak with Aamir, the old man making a suggestion the prince seemed not too keen on.

"You are still alive for one thing. I didn't expect that."

Thomas turned away and moved along the balcony, heading for the set of stairs at the end. Jorge fell into step beside him and he stopped.

"Go back to the room. He won't see me if you're there."

"Does he fear me so much?"

Thomas didn't bother with any reply other than a smile.

As he made his way along the corridor, Thomas wondered if he was making a mistake. What if Bilal had been right after all and Abu Abdullah was the guilty party behind everything? But it was too late, the die had been cast, and all he could do now was watch how it fell.

The prince waited in a small bath-chamber set deep in the rear of the building, close to the one Thomas and Jorge had shared the evening before. The same damp rock formed one wall, the same girls and boys moved about carrying soaps and scented oils, each dressed at most in a strip of cloth.

Abu Abdullah turned when Thomas entered, a grin breaking out on his face.

"I have you now, Thomas Berrington. Guards, arrest this man. He is wanted for murder."

Thomas held his hands up as the men came to stand one either side of him.

"Murder now, is it?"

"And treason. You will lack your head come morning, and not before time."

"Your brother gave you my message?"

Abu Abdullah glanced away. He waved a hand and the two guards resumed their positions against the wall.

443

"He did. Some foolishness about the killer and a plot against my father. As if anyone would plot against Sultan Abu al-Hasan Ali."

"Indeed. But he told you the truth, at least as much as I passed on to him. I would speak with you if I may. I deserve to be heard after what I have done for your family."

"After what you have done? You have done nothing. My father has already been far too indulgent. I would not have been so soft."

"I know you wouldn't, but I have never asked a single thing of him. What he offers me are gifts of his own choice, not ones I sought. Dismiss your guards and let us talk, and then, if you still want to, you may take me to the palace and throw me into a dungeon again."

"Again? Why would I send my men away—so you can kill me like you did Safya?"

So, Thomas thought, *Abu Abdullah didn't know of our arrest.*

"I killed no one." Thomas pulled at his robe, loosening it, allowing it to drop to the floor. Naked, he held his arms out from his sides. "You can see I am no threat, and I am wounded." He turned his arm to show the livid scar that ran from elbow to wrist. "You are twice as strong as me and ten times the fighter. You don't need these men here to indulge me in a moment's conversation, do you?"

Abu Abdullah glanced at the guards, back at Thomas. Thomas watched the thought processes flow through

444

him.

"Leave us," said Abu Abdullah. "This *ajami* is no threat. Wait outside, but come at once if I call. Now, Thomas Berrington, talk to me about your foolish accusations."

"I would prefer they were out of earshot."

"They will be as long as you do not shout. Now, what more would you have me do, *qassab*?"

Thomas smiled. "Nothing, My Prince, and I thank you." He stepped beneath the flow of hot water falling from a sluice set in the wall. Beneath lay a stone bench and he sat, stretching his legs out, resting his arms along the ledge to either side. The water felt good, its warmth seeping into his tired limbs.

When the guards had departed, Abu Abdullah sat on the opposite bench, his eyes searching. Thomas knew he was tracing the scars on his chest and tried to act as though he was not aware of his study.

"You are not joining me, Prince?"

Abu Abdullah laughed. "You are an insolent man, are you not?"

"It was a question, not an invitation."

"Which will never happen. Unless you wish to turn around and let me bugger you. Now that would be interesting."

"I am sorry to disappoint you, Prince, but my arse is not on offer."

"I would not want it if it was." Abu Abdullah was amused, a state of affairs Thomas would prefer to

445

continue. Despite his protest, the prince began to remove his clothing: fine silk and linen, freshly washed and pressed that morning, perhaps even a new outfit to venture out in this evening. He folded nothing, letting it lie where it dropped. Naked, he stood before Thomas, deliberately displaying himself.

The man—for despite having only eighteen years, he was definitely a man—possessed broad shoulders and a flat stomach. He bore his own set of scars which traced across his chest and arms, three on one leg, two on the other. Prizes of battle proudly exhibited. Thomas took in the prince and nodded as if impressed. Only then did Abu Abdullah step beneath his own fall of water.

He stared at Thomas, an expression of open contempt on his face.

"What is it you want of me, *ajami*? Much as I enjoy your company, Aamir was telling me of two new girls recently arrived from across the narrow sea. They are fresh from Africa. He says their skin is like burnished charcoal and they have skills no Moorish woman possesses. So tell me quickly before I grow tired of this game."

Thomas told him what he wanted.

When Thomas returned to the room, Jorge was stretched on one of the beds, staring at the ceiling.

"So, did he dismiss you without listening?"

"It was confusing. When I told him I suspected Olaf of being behind the killings, he didn't appear in the least surprised. He asked me why I was telling him this, so I said I needed his help. He laughed."

"Laughed? I know there are times you can be amusing, particularly when you are unaware you are being so, but murder is a serious business."

"I think he enjoyed watching me beg. He hates me, I know he does, and loves it when I am beholden to him. He only takes Helena into his bed because she is meant to be mine."

"But you told him what you wanted, didn't you? In spite of all that?"

"I did. I expected resistance, disbelief, but he agreed with everything I said. He told me it made a great deal of sense, that Olaf Torvaldsson possesses too much power, and if anyone in this city might plot to overthrow his father, it would be him. With the palace guard behind him, who could stop him?"

"You don't think we are making a mistake?" asked Jorge, reflecting Thomas's own doubts. "If Abu Abdullah agrees this easily, does it mean he is hiding something?"

"I think not. The more I spoke with him, the more I became convinced that nothing he heard was new. That my suspicions matched his own. Was Bilal's document a deliberate misdirection, do you think? He was part of the palace. The entire investigation could have been a show, a distraction from the truth, nothing more."

"Why protect Olaf? The Sultan wouldn't hesitate to execute him."

"Are his men loyal to the Sultan, or to Olaf?"

Jorge nodded. "I suppose we will find that out, won't we? Did Abu Abdullah agree to help?"

"I'm not entirely sure help is the word I would use. He will do what is best for Abu Abdullah. In this case, what is best for him is best for us. He agreed to have my letter delivered, and to provide soldiers when we confront Olaf. We will see what happens then."

"Did you say it would be better if the Sultan was present? If it comes to a confrontation between Abu Abdullah and Olaf, I'm not sure where the loyalties of the soldiers will lie."

"I tried to say so without demeaning his authority, but he says his father is away from the city and nobody knows where, or when he intends to return."

"So we go ahead anyway?"

"I would prefer the Sultan there, but failing that, I believe Abu Abdullah has the authority. Perhaps it won't come to anyone having to decide what to do. Once Olaf knows his plot is uncovered, he may submit."

"And if he doesn't?"

"Then I am a dead man."

"No, we are both dead men," said Jorge.

Thomas shook his head. "You must stay here. If I don't return by nightfall tomorrow, find Lubna and flee the city. Take her to safety. You must leave al-Andalus, you won't be safe within its boundaries. Qurtuba is three

days ride on a fast horse. Go there first. You are a Spaniard, you will be fine."

"But Lubna is not."

"Who is Spanish these days? The Moors have lived here so long, no one possesses pure blood anymore. I wager even King Fernando and his Queen have a little Moorish blood flowing through their veins."

"I'll try to remember not to mention that fact should I ever be unlucky enough to meet them."

"Take care of her, Jorge. I have grown fond of Lubna in the short time she has lived in my house."

"And her sister?"

"Helena is nothing to me anymore. Abu Abdullah is welcome to her spite."

"You take care, too, Thomas. The path you follow is dangerous."

"Which is why I remind you—if I fail to return, you must leave. By nightfall tomorrow, either we will be together again or you will be fleeing through the western gate. There is gold at my house, hidden beneath the bed. There is more in the workshop. Take it and run."

"You state a hypothetical case. By this time tomorrow, we will all be back in your house drinking that awful wine of yours and laughing at our fears."

"I pray it is so."

"If you prayed."

"Then Lubna can pray for us."

"I am sure she will," said Jorge. "Whether we deserve it or not."

CHAPTER THIRTY-NINE

Thomas climbed the hill with Jorge close behind. There was no room to walk side by side on the narrow track, which was barely passable through dense bushes, the soft soil to their left falling away sheer to the Hadarro.

"I don't like this way," said Jorge.

"I told you to stay behind."

"And let you walk into danger alone?"

"Lubna needs you."

"No, Lubna needs you. She likes me, but she needs you. And I still don't like this path."

"Would you rather we knock on the main gate? I expect there's still a dungeon waiting for us."

"Why could we not go directly to Abu Abdullah?"

"Because I need the robe Prea found, the sword too. They are our only physical evidence and I have a plan for them."

"You and your plans. I wish I had turned you down

when you asked me for help. You should have told me there would be danger."

"You were keen enough at the time." Thomas knew Jorge wasn't serious—he wouldn't be here if he was.

The path narrowed and he turned sideways. The sheer wall of the palace to his back felt like it was trying to push him into the ravine.

"Are you sure there's a doorway?" said Jorge, following Thomas's example. "I know of no entrance on this side of the walls."

"Prea told me of it. The door is small and used to smuggle people and goods in and out."

"I can imagine the kind of people. The kind of goods, too."

"And you such a paragon of virtue."

The path opened out a little and came to an end. Thomas turned to face the wall.

"There is no doorway," said Jorge. "You have been sent on a fool's errand. That girl should be punished."

"The door will be here," Thomas snapped. "If it was easy to find, it wouldn't be secret, would it."

Thomas edged along the stained rock forming the base of the palace wall, which soared high above, seeming to lean outward, everything conspiring to push the unwary into the void. He ran his hands over the stone. At one point, he stopped and pushed his fingers into a crevice, but it was only where mortar had fallen loose.

"I still say we should continue to the meeting place."

"The door has to be—ah, I have it." Thomas reached into another crevice, his arm disappearing to the shoulder this time. "Prea tells me the door is used often, so the mechanism should work easily." Something made a metallic noise, muffled by stone. "See?"

Thomas withdrew his arm and pulled at where a section of rock had created a gap.

"Come and help me."

Jorge looked at the narrowness of their perch, at the chasm to their back, and stayed where he was.

"I will remember how helpful you were," Thomas said as he leaned out over the drop. The door swung to his touch and he retained his hold, pulling himself back upright and ducking inside. The air was cold and damp, the only light coming from behind.

"I do not—"

"Yes, I know, you don't like it. Then stay behind, or meet me at the place we agreed on, but I am going inside. I want to see Bazzu and Prea before we go on." Thomas moved forward, bent almost double in the low passage.

"How far does it go on like this?" Jorge had come to stand in the entrance.

"Prea didn't say, but it can't be forever. I see more light ahead. Are you coming or staying?"

"Coming, I suppose."

"Pull the door shut behind you, then. We don't want someone stumbling in on us."

"As if anyone else is going to take that pathway,"

said Jorge, but he did as requested before following Thomas along the dark passage.

Soon steps rose steeply upwards, turning on themselves again and again, rising through layers of rock, dungeon, chamber, until they came to a solid wall.

"Do your magic," muttered Jorge.

Thomas searched, found the niche he knew would be there, and a wooden panel opened to his command.

"You're getting too good at this," said Jorge. "When I return to the harem, I will have to be more careful in my assignations."

"Don't worry, I have no wish to enter these tunnels ever again, nor spy on your assignations, whatever they might be."

"It is your loss," said Jorge.

They found Bazzu in her usual lair, but there was no sign of Prea.

"Did you get my message?" Thomas asked.

"I did. And that boy was asking about Prea as well."

"He is a prince."

"Prince or not, he is still a boy. Perhaps he found her, for I have not seen her since yesterday. There is work to do and she decides to go missing."

"You have the robe and sword?"

"Of course, exactly as you asked." She nodded to

where a rolled blanket sat on a shelf. "Disguised, as you also asked."

Thomas knew Bazzu's shortness was caused by fear —her fear for Jorge, mostly. Having a plan didn't mean it was going to succeed, and there were a hundred ways it could go wrong.

Thomas unrolled the blanket and checked the contents.

"It is all there," said Bazzu. She reached a hand out to Jorge, who was perched on the corner of her deep table, and he took it.

"Can we go?" said Jorge. "I never thought I would say this, but I am nervous inside the palace now."

"I want to speak with Prea before we leave. Are you sure you have no idea where she is, Bazzu?"

"She returned with me from the city. The prince took your message to his brother, and she..." Bazzu frowned, trying to call up a memory. "She said she had one more task to do for you, but didn't say what it was."

"I gave her no task."

Bazzu's frown remained. "I am sure that is what she said. 'One more task for Thomas'."

His blood chilled. There was only one place she might have gone. The place he had asked her not to go. The girl thought she was too clever for the killer. Thomas bundled up the blanket once more and thrust it at Jorge.

"I have to check something before we go. Wait here."

"How long are you going to be?"

454

"Not long. Not long at all. But if I don't return within an hour, follow the plan without me."

Jorge scowled. "What plan, Thomas? Without you, there is no plan."

"Then I will return."

It should have been a matter of moments to reach the entrance to the tunnels from the kitchen, but Thomas was forced to hide in doorways and alcoves each time he heard someone coming. It was mid-morning and the palace was busy with guards, officials and servants, but eventually he reached the quiet side chamber and thrust his arm into the opening he had seen Prea use.

A panel jerked open an inch and he drew it wider, clambered through and immediately stopped, one leg inside, one still in the sunlit chamber. There was an odour in the air, one he recognised. It was the taint of the battlefield, the smell of freshly spilled blood. He ran to where Prea had shown him the cache of robe and sword, ignoring the pain in his shoulders as they scraped and banged against the walls.

Prea sprawled awkwardly in a lake of blood, and in an instant Thomas saw how it had happened. She had lain in hiding on the ledge she had shown him, so pleased with her own cleverness. But something had gone wrong. Perhaps she had moved, dislodged a pebble, or the man sensed her, smelled her. The how was

irrelevant because the what lay tumbled on the floor of the tunnel. Thomas went to his knees and moved her gently, re-arranging her tangled limbs.

Prea's face was at peace, and he hoped the attack had come too fast to cause her much pain. She had been dead some time, a day at least. The rigour had come and gone and her limbs were slack beneath his hands. Her once vibrant eyes were dull, staring at nothing, and he reached down and closed them, fatigue flooding through him as he closed his own eyes, breathing deeply, trying not to think of what he had done to this girl who had barely started to live. He stayed that way for long minutes before shaking himself. Weakness now would only make her death even more futile.

He knelt and searched her slight frame, finding wound after wound. One had pierced her heart and he prayed that had been the first blow. Others ran through her belly and thighs, another to her neck. Any of the blows would have proven fatal, and Thomas recognised most as redundant. These were strikes made in anger. The killer had returned for his robe, his sword, perhaps to continue his work, to take another victim, most likely Aixa, and Prea had been in the way. This was not over yet. Unless the man was stopped, Safya would not be the last.

Thomas lifted Prea's slight figure and carried her along the tunnel. He kicked the panel out, no longer caring who knew what lay behind it, and walked with her in his arms through the corridors. He made no effort to

456

conceal himself. Around him, people stared. There were cries of fear. Some ran. Others came towards him only to be stopped by the feral rage in his eyes.

Bazzu screamed and fell to her knees, wailing as he laid Prea on the floor. Jorge stood to one side, his face pale.

"Who remains in the palace?" Thomas said.

"No one. They are all at the hillside as you planned."

"She must be washed and prepared."

"I will care for her." Bazzu reached a trembling hand towards Prea, hesitated.

"Was she religious?"

"A little, yes."

"Then prepare her in the way of Islam and have her interred. Spare no expense, I will pay."

Bazzu looked up at him, anger replacing the grief in her eyes. "How *dare* you try to buy your way out of this guilt! This is your doing, Thomas Berrington. Did you not see the girl worshiped you? She would have done anything for you, anything at all."

"I specifically forbade her to do this."

"Do you honestly think that would make any difference? She did it for you!"

Thomas looked down at the body. "Then I will bear the guilt. I deserve it. But another man struck the blow and I intend to kill him. Jorge, are you still with me?"

Jorge didn't appear to hear. Thomas went to stand in front of him.

"Are you with me or not?"

"I ... I..."

Thomas nodded. "Of course, I understand. Stay and help Bazzu." He went to the table and lifted the blanket holding the robe and sword. He was halfway to the door when Jorge's hand swung him around. For a moment, Thomas thought he was going to strike him, but instead Jorge pulled him into a hard embrace.

"I am with you, Thomas. You know I am."

He glanced at Bazzu in the moments before Jorge released him. Her eyes continued to burn with a hatred he knew would never fade. So be it. He deserved her hatred, welcomed it. He drew it into himself where it turned his heart to ice. All emotion drained from him. Fear. Pain. Grief. He pushed Jorge away and left the room, discarding his humanity as he walked through the corridors of the palace. No one challenged him. No one dared.

CHAPTER FORTY

The sun shone from a sky dotted with bright clouds. It was one of those days when a light breeze blew softly from the mountains to cool the heat of the day. An occasional updraught swirled across the ground, lifting blades of dry grass and dust into the air. Trees rattled and shook for a moment before stillness returned.

One of the miniature storms hit as Thomas and Jorge lay side by side on a rise in the ground, looking down on Abu Abdullah's hawking group in the shallow valley below. A tent had been erected on the flat ground, horses tied behind.

Thirty or so men were arranged in two groups. Abu Abdullah and three others stood apart from the rest, their guards close by. Abu Abdullah held one arm extended, a hawk sitting on his gloved hand.

A cry came, one of the men pointing, and Abu

Abdullah launched the bird upwards. It soared into the air with rapid wing beats, hovered. A further group of men appeared from the far tree line, driving everything ahead of them. Birds flew in all directions, caught sight of the men and swooped aside. The hawk continued to hover, then its stance changed. The quiver of its wings grew taut, an arrow ready to be loosed. The hawk fell, its prey unaware of danger until talons struck. There was a burst of feathers without sound. The hawk dropped to the ground, its curved beak tearing at meat.

The sound of laughter drifted up the hillside.

"I can see Olaf," said Jorge.

"So can I. In that group set apart, and he has men with him."

"Not as many as Abu Abdullah."

"Three to one. Is that enough? Olaf's men are the best there are."

"They will do nothing. Their loyalty is to the Sultan, and after him the Sultan's sons. As is Olaf's."

"As was Olaf's," Thomas said.

The wind came again, died.

"Are we going to lie here all day?" asked Jorge.

Thomas said nothing, studying the men, their positions, trying to work out the tensions between them. Abu Abdullah was at ease. Olaf watched the young prince with what appeared to be disdain. Abu Abdullah ignored everything other than his hawks.

"Are you sure he is expecting us?" said Jorge.

"Have you ever been hunting with him?"

"Me? I am a creature of the harem. Abu Abdullah hates my kind. He recognises the need for me, but wishes it was not so."

"I have been with the hunt once or twice, at the Sultan's request."

"Because he likes you."

"I wish that were not so."

"It is better than the alternative."

"Being ignored would suit me fine."

"I think that wish is about to end." Jorge nodded down the slope. A man was observing the hawk, concerned at its behaviour. Thomas looked up. The bird hovered directly over them, hanging unmoving in a rising breeze lifting from the ridge. When he looked back, men were pointing. One swung on to a horse and started up the slope.

"Hold him up for a short while if you can." Thomas rose and moved back to a cluster of olives.

"Hold him up? Me?"

Thomas ignored Jorge as he stripped out of his clothes. He bent and retrieved the opulent silk robe from within the blanket and slipped it on, ignoring the sensuality against his skin, as he tried to ignore the raging of his emotions. He had to be cold now. He sought deeply for the memory of how he had once been. He pulled the hood over his head, allowing it to drape until it hid most of his face. Then he knelt and drew the sword.

He swung it through the air as he stood ready, memory flooding him with a cold fire.

The rider reached the ridge and reined in, sat watching as Thomas walked towards him. Unease touched his face.

"Stay here," Thomas said as he reached Jorge. "Hide. Watch. And remember, if anything happens to me, take Lubna to safety."

"I would rather be at your side."

"And I would rather you stay safe. Too many have died already. For once, can you just do as I ask?"

He started forward without waiting for a reply. The rider tried to block him using his horse.

"Who are you? What are you doing here?"

"I am death." Thomas pushed the horse aside, knowing the beast would respond to his touch.

The rider tried to get in front of him again.

"You are the surgeon. The *qassab*."

"Yes, I am he."

"The prince is expecting you." The man glanced back to the ridge, but Jorge was no longer visible.

The horse knocked against Thomas again and he fought the urge to strike out. Cold. He needed to be as cold as the snow that topped the Sholayr.

"Walk on, then," the rider said. "We have been waiting on you, and the prince waits for no man."

Thomas took his time descending the shallow slope, knowing all eyes were on him, exactly as he wanted.

From within the shadow of his hood, he observed Olaf, waiting for recognition to show.

The closer he came, the more his doubts grew. The old soldier's cohort was closest to him, but so far nothing showed on the man's face.

Thomas stopped as Olaf started towards him. So this was the moment. Would Olaf strike first or try disguising the truth? Thomas wondered if he could kill the man. He had killed men both bigger and stronger, men who considered themselves great fighters—but Olaf?

"What are you doing here? They told me you were the killer. This is a dangerous place for you." There was no hint of deception in the general's eyes, and his concern appeared genuine. Olaf looked him up and down. "And why are you dressed like this? Do you know we wait for the Sultan?"

So Abu Abdullah had delivered the message. Thomas smiled.

"The Sultan isn't coming. Don't you recognise this robe?"

Olaf shook his head. "Should I?" He took a step closer, and Thomas tightened the grip on his sword. "The cloth is extremely fine, but it is cut as a fighting man's robe, not that of a surgeon. Not that you ever dress as a surgeon."

"Today I am a fighting man."

Olaf laughed. "You?"

"Have you forgotten our lesson? I was barely trying that day."

Thomas studied the general's face. His eyes were clear, without guile, but he was a trained fighter well versed in concealing his thoughts. Except … in all the time Thomas had known Olaf, he had considered the man incapable of hiding even the slightest of feelings. Thomas had seen him cry openly in response to Helena's injuries, weep at the memory of his first wife.

Thomas looked beyond Olaf, searching for some indication of the truth. It had to be here somewhere. This gathering involved everyone other than the Sultan, and it had been he who had put Thomas on the trail in the first place. The killer would be here. Thomas had worried the man might be with Abu al-Hasan Ali, but Prea's murder told him he had to be close.

Abu Abdullah was to their left, standing in front of the tent, his heavily leathered arm now at his side. Faris al-Rashid stood close by as he always did, a whisperer in the ears of men who possessed power, a supplier of coin where coin was needed, always willing to buy favour.

The other men from Thomas's earlier encounter in the palace were scattered through the group. Men of influence. Men of ambition.

Olaf's troops watched their general, tension in their stance.

"What is my daughter doing here?" said Olaf, looking beyond Thomas.

For a moment, Thomas thought he meant Helena, but then he saw the direction of his gaze and turned. Jorge

and Lubna were coming down the hillside. Lubna ran ahead, something fluttering in her hand. She had closed half the distance when she stopped abruptly, her feet scrabbling in the dust.

Thomas turned again at a commotion, a murmur amongst the troops, a shifting of attention away from him to a group of men coming down the far slope. Their horses raised dust that masked them, but the uniform was clear, as was the dress of the man leading them. Abu al-Hasan Ali, Sultan of Gharnatah, had returned from his expedition.

Just in time, Thomas thought.

He looked back towards Abu Abdullah. The prince appeared as surprised as anyone at the new arrival.

"See," said Olaf, "the Sultan comes. He asked for me to be here—something important, he said."

Thomas walked towards Abu Abdullah. He would confront him first, then the Sultan, and finally Olaf. He hoped they would reveal something when they saw him dressed in the killer's robes. He was glad Jorge had disobeyed him and decided to join him. He had skills and knowledge that would prove invaluable. Thomas turned, seeking him, and found him standing beyond Olaf. He was in deep discussion with Lubna. Thomas raised his hand, forgetting it was the one holding the sword. His gesture was greeted with a clatter as fifty men drew their own weapons.

"Jorge, come here to me," Thomas called out.

Jorge looked at him as if he was mad.

Thomas beckoned him again and Jorge reluctantly started across the space between them. Beyond him, Thomas saw Lubna now talking animatedly with her father.

"I thought you wanted me to stay away." Jorge stopped beside him.

"I changed my mind. I need your humanity."

"You have plenty of that yourself. I think I'll try to drag Lubna back up the hillside. It felt safer up there. She says she's discovered something you need to see."

Thomas grabbed Jorge's arm. "Stay with me, I need you beside me now."

Something in his voice caused Jorge to stop pulling away.

"What can you possibly need me for in this matter?"

"I'm going to walk in front of each of these men. I want you to study them. You said you would recognise the man again, now let us find out if that is true. I want you to read the signals on the men's faces and in their bodies. Watch. Tell me who the guilty man is."

"You are a fool to trust me in this."

"Then I am a fool." Thomas started walking, not waiting to see if Jorge was with him or not. He had to do this regardless.

He focused his attention on the first group. Faris al-Rashid, Valentin al-Kamul and Don Antonio Galbretti stood together, a conclave of conspiracy. Thomas expected a reaction, but although the men stared at him

as he passed, their faces showed only amusement at his strange manner of dress.

As he approached Abu Abdullah, a movement to one side distracted him, a familiar figure within the shadow of the tent. Helena's white-blonde hair shone through the darkness, glowing brightly as she walked to the entrance and stood in sunlight. Her head was uncovered, a statement she was her own woman, beyond convention. She watched Thomas, the corner of her mouth lifting, but there was nothing of affection in her expression.

Has she hated me all this time? Has she betrayed me all this time?

"I am sorry, Thomas." Jorge spoke softly beside him. So he had seen the truth as well.

Thomas turned to Abu Abdullah, studying the young prince. His face showed its usual contempt for the world, but no recognition or fear.

Thomas strode past the Sultan's men, heading for the group of soldiers Olaf commanded.

"Stop," said Jorge.

Thomas turned. "What is it?"

"You weren't looking, but there is a man." Jorge indicated with a nod of his head. "There. Three to the right of Abu Abdullah. He recognised this robe, I am sure. And..." Jorge frowned, "...and I know him."

Thomas returned to stand in front of Abu Abdullah's troops. They were dust-streaked from hunting. The Sultan spurred his horse and placed himself between Thomas and his son.

"Why are you dressed like that? Is it the latest fashion among Gharnatah's medical men?"

"I am dressed as an assassin," Thomas said, then softly to Jorge, "The tall man, thin? He has dark skin and an oiled beard?"

"He is your man. See him now?"

Thomas stepped closer, watching tightly held emotion move beneath the man's face. He scanned his companions, saw no one else who reacted in the same way. Their faces showed a mixture of surprise, amusement, disdain and hatred, but only one man showed guilt. Thomas felt himself trembling, fought back a violent urge to attack the man immediately. Instead, he turned to the Sultan.

"Malik, I know who the killer is."

"Are you sure of this?"

There was something too relaxed in the Sultan's voice.

"I am certain."

The Sultan turned in his saddle. "Then point him out to me. Accuse the man and we will see what he has to say."

From the edge of his vision, Thomas saw the soldier shift his feet.

"There—he is the one," said Jorge, then drew away, distancing himself from the scene.

Thomas raised his sword, ready to point at the man. The soldiers in front of him, to either side, raised their weapons in turn.

"Thomas!" It was Olaf, running across the ground. "Thomas, you have to listen to Lubna."

"Not now!" Thomas almost screamed. He thrust his arm backwards, the sword flashing in the sun. "That is our man. He stands there!" He brought the sword around, pointing, the tip shaking with anger as he allowed rage to fill him, to fill his entire being, pushing out any last trace of humanity.

The Sultan smiled when he saw who Thomas was pointing at.

"And what do you say, Qasim?"

"I say this *ajami* will die soon, and in great agony, master."

"Do you deny his charge?"

"I admit I am a killer. It is who I am. But so is every other man on this field. This man…" He spat. "This man is nothing."

"Do you withdraw your false allegation, Thomas Berrington?"

"I do not." His gaze remained locked on the assassin's.

"Then how do you propose we settle this matter?"

"Combat," said the man named Qasim. "I challenge the coward to trial by combat. If he kills me, I am guilty. If I kill him, he lies."

"What do you say, Thomas? Are you convinced enough in your belief to test it in such a way?"

"He is the killer," Thomas said. "I accept his challenge."

The Sultan laughed and clapped his hands. "Trial by combat. So be it. Clear the field. Qasim, come and show yourself." The Sultan twisted, taking in the groups arrayed across the hollow. He raised his voice. "Nobody interferes. The fight is between these two men. Clear the ground!"

someone and stopped. Qasim continued coming, closing
the distance. Without looking to see who was behind
Thomas stepped to one side, but a hand grabbed at the
flowing cloth of his robe, holding him back. When he
looked down, Lubna stood there, her face angry. Her
father's mule across the ground towards her.

"You have—" he started to say, but she said,

"Not now." Olaf patted her mount. "Thomas doesn't
have to fight. Don't distract him from what he must do
now. Come away and I will see he is avenged. Here, take
this." Olaf pressed something into Thomas's hand." He
glanced down to discover a knife, its naked blade honed

Qasim stepped from the line, tearing his heavy outer robes loose, discarding the turban marking him as a member of the palace guard. He drew his sword and unbuckled the belt holding it, stripping himself for battle.

Thomas stepped back. Back again. He jerked his head, the hood of the robe sliding away to reveal his face. He stopped, ready, a long-forgotten cold rage surging through him.

Abu Abdullah ran to his father. He gripped the edge of his saddle and said something, but Thomas was no longer listening. His eyes tracked Qasim as the man stepped from the line of guards.

Qasim swung his sword loosely at his side, a steady surety in his eyes, and Thomas knew the man was convinced he was going to kill him. It was, after all, the most likely outcome.

Thomas walked backwards until he bumped against

someone and stopped. Qasim continued coming, closing the distance. Without looking to see who was behind, Thomas stepped to one side, but a hand grabbed at the flowing cloth of his robe, holding him back. When he looked down, Lubna stood there, her face angry. Her father strode across the ground towards her.

"You have to know about what I found!" she said.

"Not now." Olaf pulled her away. "Thomas doesn't have the time. Don't distract him from what he must do now. Come away and I will see he is avenged. Here, take this." Olaf pressed something into Thomas's hand. He glanced down to discover a knife, its wicked blade honed to a razor edge. He recognised it. This was Olaf's own knife, the one he carried into every battle. Thomas looked into Olaf's eyes with gratitude, recognising he had been wrong to suspect the man, still not knowing who to suspect in his place.

"I must tell Thomas I know who is behind everything..." But Lubna's voice faded as she was dragged away from the killing ground. Thomas closed his ears as he turned inward, searching for emotions long buried, those he had hoped never to need again.

If I am to die, let it be because I am not good enough, not because I refused to try.

He should have been afraid to meet his own death, but he wasn't. Perhaps what he was doing was madness, but he believed not. The grinning man pacing in front of him didn't know of Thomas's past. No one knew of Thomas's past, other than Jorge, and he didn't know

everything. Thomas had buried the evil he did deep, but not so deep it would refuse to return when called on.

Flashes of memory seared across his vision. His first battlefield strewn with dead, both French and English. His flight and attempts to banish those memories, except they were impossible to purge. He delved deeper, remembering how to fight, how he used to be invincible. A demon with a strange accent and pale skin. He had been young then, and fighting came naturally. He had not lifted a sword in anger for over twenty years, but the muscle memory remained. Olaf had reminded him of that.

He swung his sword right, left, circled it in front of him in a pointless show of bravura.

Qasim smiled, his own sword still, a dagger in his left hand gripped by only his thumb and two fingers, the others missing.

Beyond him the Sultan and Abu Abdullah were arguing over something.

Faris al-Rashid stood close to both, a smile on his face.

Helena stood to one side, between Valentin al-Kamul and Antonio Galbretti. One of them said something to her and Helena hit him, her slap louder than the murmur of conversation. Thomas looked around to see men placing bets on the outcome, and knew where the money would be going. He recalled the last time a circle such as this had formed, as the troops returned from Tajir. The memory felt years old, but had been little more than a

week before. That fight had ended badly for both parties, and he knew today's outcome might end the same.

The Sultan turned away from Abu Abdullah and rose in his saddle, waving a hand. His voice when it came was rich with authority.

"Let Allah decide!"

Even before the last word was out, Qasim came fast, his sword flashing. Thomas fell back, raising his own to deflect the blow. His arm stung from the force of it and he retreated further.

Qasim grinned. "I liked your little friend, *qassab*. Liked her so much I fucked her before I killed her. She squealed like an animal both times I stuck her."

The words were a lie, Thomas knew. He let them wash over him like water across a stone. He would remain and the water would pass, carrying his fear with it.

He stilled his mind, knowing rationality was as much an enemy as the man before him. The past flooded in to replace all thought. He stopped moving backwards and attacked, a swirling djinn in a cloak of dark fire.

It was Qasim's turn to fall back beneath the onslaught. He kicked dust at Thomas, but he came through it, blade scything down. Qasim blocked, blocked again, feinted and counter-attacked. For both of them, nothing else existed. Not the nobles wagering on the outcome. Not the soldiers watching with dispassionate professional interest. Not the woman Thomas loved. He

fought for another he had loved. Prea. His heart—too soft if he let it—had turned to ice in his chest.

They swung and ducked and growled. Qasim was fast and skilled. Thomas parried, attacked in turn, seeing the confidence leach from the man as the fight went on. For long minutes they clashed without respite. Then both stopped, breathing hard, their bodies sweat-streaked.

Thomas was gratified to see this was as hard on Qasim as it was on him, but wondered how long he could keep fighting at this pace. A thousand questions jostled in his mind and he dismissed them all. It was too late to seek answers, only revenge.

Thomas spun, his robe billowing around him. He let Qasim thrust aimlessly through the cloth, heard the whisper of silk parting against the blade. For an instant, fire burned along his side as the thrust kissed his skin, then his sword flashed down.

Qasim raised his arm, for a moment his own blade catching in the swirling folds of silk before breaking loose. He barely countered the blow in time and Thomas took the moment to punch his knife upwards into the man's side. The blow jarred his arm as the blade caught on a rib and he withdrew, his hand streaked with blood.

"You cut me." There was shock in Qasim's voice, as though such a thing had never happened to him before.

"Then we are all square." Thomas parted the tattered silk on one side to show his own wound. It wasn't serious, but Qasim wouldn't know that. He would see

only blood running down Thomas's flank, and a glint of triumph sparked in his eyes.

"I have taken worse blows than this scratch. Call yourself a surgeon? Don't you know where a man's heart lies?"

"You have no heart." Thomas struck even as he spoke. Qasim parried, came again, and Thomas deflected a storm of blows. For a moment, the sound of shouting came to him, and he realised most of those watching considered this an entertainment.

They fell back, circling, both wary now.

"Why did Aixa put you up to this?" Thomas threw the name out wildly, half-rewarded when Qasim laughed.

"You have no clue, do you?"

"Abu Abdullah has much to gain from the Sultan's dishonour. He and Olaf could rule this city. Could rule the whole of al-Andalus."

Qasim spat, but Thomas knew some of Jorge's skill with people must have rubbed off on him because, for a moment, there had been a flicker of something on Qasim's face. Anyone else not looking so hard would have missed it.

Qasim came at him again, determined to finish the fight. His sword arced down, knife slashing. Thomas scurried backwards, parried, twisted. He stumbled. His foot caught on a rock and one leg skidded from beneath him. He raised his right arm as Qasim's sword came down, stumbled again. He fell, knowing as he did so that the fight was over for him.

Except Qasim didn't strike.

He stood over Thomas, legs spread either side of him, a grin on his face. His left heel trapped Thomas's hand, which still held the sword.

"You think you know everything, don't you? Clever men like you, men of letters, you make me sick to my stomach. You know nothing, none of you. Nothing at all. There is life, there is death, and there is honour. Nothing else matters. Nothing!"

"What do you know of honour?" Beneath the folds of his cloak, Thomas straightened his left arm, praying the silk would mask the movement.

"I obey my master. There is honour enough in that for me."

"Even when al-Rashid asks you to kill the innocent?"

"There are no innocents. And my master is not that perfumed clown. I answer to a greater power in this land." Qasim shifted position, searching for the perfect spot to strike. Thomas knew the man would take pride in the final blow. It would broadcast his skill to everyone watching.

Cries filtered through his fugue, soldiers calling out for Qasim to finish it, Lubna's voice cutting through them all, calling his name, her father's deeper bark.

Thomas kicked out and Qasim laughed, easily avoiding his foot. Qasim struck in an instant, the movement too fast to follow. Thomas's fist came up. The point of Qasim's sword entered through his palm, pinning his hand to the ground.

"I give you this, you fight well for an *ajami*, but I will still kill you all the same. I will kill you slowly, like I killed your little friend." Qasim knelt, his knees on Thomas's upper arms locking him to the ground. "She called your name at the end. It was so sweet. Whose name are you going to call, *qassab*?"

Thomas struggled, but he was pinned. He tried kicking with his leg again, but the blow bounced from Qasim's back as though it was nothing.

"Stop this madness!" Olaf's voice boomed across the killing ground.

To be answered by the Sultan's. "Allah decides. Let the fight run its course. No one is to interfere. Do you hear me, Olaf Torvaldsson? *No one* is to interfere!"

Qasim laid the point of his knife on Thomas's cheek and leaned in until his face was inches away, his body as close as a lover's.

"Look at me, surgeon. Take a good long look at this face, because it will be the last thing you ever see. Carry it with you to whatever hell your people inhabit. I will take your right eye first, and then the other. Finally I will cut out your heart while it still beats."

The man ran the tip of his knife across Thomas's cheek, opening it. His chest pressed against Thomas. It was the moment he had been waiting for. Qasim's knees pinned his arms above the elbow, but Thomas believed, hoped, he was allowed enough movement. He raised his unpinned hand beneath the folds of silk. Yes, he thought, just enough to do what he needed.

"You know what? You talk too much."

Thomas slipped his knife between Qasim's ribs, making no mistake this time, his aim cold and calculated. He saw the look of surprise in the Berber's dark eyes and twisted fast to one side as the man's knife came down at his eyeball. He felt it sear across his cheek again. Then the air left Qasim's body. Blood gushed from his mouth in a final cough and he fell on top of Thomas.

———————————

It was Olaf who reached them first, tossing Qasim's body aside as though it weighed nothing. He knelt beside Thomas, patting his body in search of wounds. When Thomas opened his eyes, the old soldier sat back on his heels and made a sound that might be interpreted as relief.

Then Lubna was there, her fingers on his face.

"Is it deep?"

"You tell me." Thomas turned his head to look to where Qasim's sword pinned his hand to the ground. "Olaf, pull this blade from my hand, will you? And thank you for the loan of your knife."

Olaf offered a smile and obliged.

Thomas bit back a scream, watched as blood spilled from the wound on to the dry earth.

"My face will heal, Lubna, but my hand needs attention. Someone here will have bandages. Go find

them, then bind the wound tight." Thomas groaned as Olaf raised him to a sitting position.

"Can you walk?"

"With help."

"I will help him." It was Jorge, standing tall and strong, almost unrecognisable from the perfumed eunuch of a week before. A fuzz of dark hair now covered his head and his cheeks were shadowed with stubble.

Olaf nodded and between them they raised Thomas to his feet. He swayed, not from any injury but from the draining lust of battle. He was glad to feel it leave, glad to have held it within himself long enough to triumph.

Thomas lifted his head to find a circle of men surrounding him and his last reserve of strength left him. *Take me,* he thought, *but spare the others.*

The Sultan sat erect in his saddle, his eyes cold.

Soldiers formed a solid wall between the small group in the centre and safety.

Olaf tugged Thomas forward.

"He is the victor, Malik. Allah has decided."

"And now I must decide," Abu al-Hasan Ali said. "Was the fight fair? Did Thomas Berrington win by subterfuge? In fact, how could a lowly surgeon defeat one of my best soldiers? It is not possible." He turned in his saddle. "Did you drug him, Thomas? Or poison your blade?"

"Thomas won the fight fairly," said Olaf. He released his hold and stepped forward, seeming to double in size.

The Sultan looked around, making a judgement.

He chose wrong.

"I declare the combat void. Thomas Berrington cheated and his life is forfeit."

"No, it is not." Abu Abdullah pushed forward to stand beside his father's horse. "Thomas won. He must walk free."

"You dispute my judgement?"

"When you are wrong."

"Olaf—arrest my son. We will have two beheadings today." A tight smile crossed the Sultan's lips.

Abu Abdullah made no move. Neither did Olaf.

The Sultan rose in his stirrups. "Arrest these traitors, all of them. Take them now!"

Lubna stepped forward, waving a sheet of paper. "There is only one guilty man here, and it is him!" She pointed directly at the Sultan. Around the edges of the circle, some men drew their swords. Others moved back as though to drift away.

"Are you all cowards?" the Sultan screamed, drawing his own sword. "If you will not finish him, then I will." He spurred his horse, coming directly at Thomas. Jorge stepped between him and the oncoming dervish, but Olaf pushed him aside like a reed, only to be bowled over by the onrushing beast.

The Sultan swung down at Thomas, who stepped to one side, the sword point whistling past his ear, but he knew he couldn't avoid it for long. He was trapped inside a circle of men with no escape. Too late, he now knew who had been behind everything.

So did Abu Abdullah.

Around the circle, soldiers drew their swords to form an uncrossable barrier.

Olaf stepped close to the Sultan's horse. He grabbed the reins in one hand and lifted the other to stop the blow that came at him. A thousand battles had honed his skill to an unmatched level. He gripped the Sultan's wrist and twisted, the sword clattering from his hand to the ground.

Abu Abdullah strolled to the other side of his father's horse.

"It is over, Father," he said. "Your plot has been uncovered."

CHAPTER FORTY-TWO

"I owe you an apology for suspecting you." Thomas lay against a pile of soft cushions inside the Sultan's tent. Olaf knelt close, watching Lubna bandage Thomas's injured hand. The wound was not as bad as it had first looked, but blood still welled from both the palm and back where the sword had been thrust straight through.

Olaf shook his head. "You owe me nothing. You unmasked the killer. The whole of Gharnatah is grateful."

"He was a weapon, nothing more. The killer remains." Thomas stared at the old soldier. "I have something hard to ask of you, and you may refuse."

"Ask."

"Your loyalty is to the Sultan of Gharnatah, is it not?"

"He is my master."

"And if it was him behind everything, what then?"

Olaf sat back. Here inside the royal tent, Olaf looked out of place among the opulence.

"How sure are you? My daughter makes the same claim, but I dismissed her ravings."

"It is the truth," Lubna said, applying the last of the bandage. It was dark with blood, but she had tied it tight and soon the bleeding would slow. "I have the proof. It is what I brought you, what I was trying to show Thomas before he insisted on fighting."

"I had no choice," Thomas said.

"There is always a choice."

"Not always, my sweet," said Olaf to his daughter.

She scowled and leaned across Thomas. "I need to look at your face." Her fingers touched, gentle, but Thomas winced.

"I will have a scar, I expect," he said.

"Like my sister."

He didn't want to be reminded of Helena.

"Olaf, I want you to go to Abu Abdullah and tell him what I have told you, tell him what Lubna knows. Take Jorge. I know Abu Abdullah bears no love for him, but I believe he will accept his word as the truth. Lubna, tell me again what your proof is before we take this risk."

"Tell me what?"

Thomas turned his head. Abu Abdullah stood in the doorway. To his right was Aixa, with Faris al-Rashid a pace behind her. Helena stood on the other side, uncertainty on her face, as well it should be.

"Send the others away," Thomas said.

Abu Abdullah surveyed the small group inside the tent.

"I am not sure I will be safe here if I do."

Olaf rose to his feet. "You are safe with me, Prince, you know you are."

An expression of amusement crossed Abu Abdullah's face. "You are my father's man, are you not?"

"I am the Sultan's man," said Olaf.

"And if my father is no longer Sultan?"

"I am the Sultan's man," Olaf repeated.

Abu Abdullah came further into the tent. He waved a hand in dismissal to the others. Faris al-Rashid took Helena's arm and led her outside, but Aixa remained at her son's side.

"So tell me what proof you have. I can do nothing without proof."

"I have proof," said Lubna, getting to her feet.

Aixa looked at her with open contempt.

"You are a servant. No one will believe a servant. We are wasting our time here."

"Wait," Thomas said. "Lubna is Olaf's daughter. Does that not count for something?"

"Olaf Torvaldsson's daughters do not have a reputation for honesty at the moment."

"That is as may be," Thomas said. "But tell me this, to who did Helena go to tell her tales? Was that you or your son?"

"It was not me."

"Show him the paper," Thomas said to Lubna, hoping it was proof enough.

"Father." Lubna held out her hand and Olaf reached into his pocket, handed her a single sheet. She took it across to Abu Abdullah and he studied it.

"A bill of sale?" He tossed the page aside. Lubna bent to retrieve it.

"A bill of sale for a special roll of cloth," said Lubna. "The cloth Thomas now wears."

"Let me see it again."

Abu Abdullah read more slowly, drew the page close to study the seal affixed to the bottom.

"This bill is in my name. I ordered no such cloth from this ... this Spaniard."

"And the seal?" said Lubna. Thomas was proud of her. In the face of the second most powerful man in the kingdom, she showed no fear.

"It is my seal, but the scribes conduct all such matters on behalf of those in the palace. It is not unknown for the wrong seal to be used, everyone knows this."

"I went to Carlos Rodriguez and pressed him," said Lubna. "He didn't want to talk with a woman, but he knew who I was, knew he couldn't refuse. He spoke with me because of Thomas." She glanced at him, her face a mask. "He recalls this bill of sale because of what it concerns and how it came to him. He still has some of the silk in his workshop—"

"I knew I had seen it somewhere," said Jorge.

Lubna waved him to silence. "He says it is the finest

cloth he has ever seen, imported from the East. The bill of sale is in your name, Prince, but it was your mother who placed the order. Rodriguez remembers it well, for it is not every day a merchant plays host to a Sultana of Gharnatah."

Abu Abdullah glanced at Aixa. Her face was set, cold.

"Not that Sultana," Lubna said. "Rodriguez told me the woman who came to him spoke perfect Spanish."

It was the final piece in the puzzle, and hearing it, Thomas almost felt a movement inside his head as everything fitted together.

"When was this?" asked Abu Abdullah.

"More than half a year ago, before last year's harvest. Zoraya wanted a special outfit made. Only one at first, with more to follow. Carlos Rodriguez made the robe Thomas now wears."

"How did he come upon such a thing?"

"In the tunnels," Thomas said.

"What tunnels? I know nothing of any tunnels."

"I will show you, but for now you must believe the tale Lubna tells. A girl I was fond of died to bring me this robe. The man I have just killed recognised it at once, I saw it in his eyes. He is the one who murdered those girls, the one who murdered Safya. He would have killed all the Sultan's wives but one, and anyone else who got in his way. On Zoraya's orders."

Abu Abdullah shook his head. "Why would she do such a thing?"

Thomas stared at the prince. "You know why. The whole of the palace knows why. Do you want your place usurped by the sons of the Greek woman?"

Abu Abdullah waved the accusation away. "Talk. Nothing but talk."

"Then tell me how your father treats you. Does he speak with you as he always has, or does he cut you out from discussion? What does he say of the future? Does it include you?"

"My father is a busy man. He has no time to tell me of everything he plans in his campaigns."

Thomas tried to sit up and failed.

"Help me!"

Olaf offered a strong arm.

"Fetch Helena back in," Thomas ordered, and Jorge left the tent. Abu Abdullah read again the single sheet of paper that was the only physical evidence linking the killer's robe with Zoraya.

"That paper was in the possession of one of the palace's scribes. The same man who was first asked to investigate the killings." Thomas spoke as the ideas came to him. If this was a game of Mancala, it would be perfect. "He must have recognised the importance of what it contained, may even have written it originally himself, for that would have been his job. I don't know who he went to with his suspicions, but it wouldn't have been Zoraya herself. Whoever it was, someone wanted to protect her and the man was dismissed. I consider him

lucky not to have been killed at the time, though he was caught in the end."

Jorge returned, dragging a writhing Helena alongside. Her fists struck against his chest and shoulders, but they were no more than raindrops against a cliff.

"Who is it you have so secretly been visiting, my love?" Thomas asked, disdain dripping through his voice.

"I visit with friends, you know I do."

"Who?"

"Friends in the harem."

"Have you seen her recently, Jorge, before this task dragged you from your duties?"

Jorge shook his head.

Abu Abdullah moved suddenly and grasped Helena's arm. He pulled her close and a knife appeared in his hand. He laid the edge against Helena's cheek.

"Do you want me to open your face up again? Tell us the truth."

"You will not hurt me," said Helena. "You love me, I know you do."

"Do not confuse love with lust. I used you, that is all." Abu Abdullah flicked the tip of the blade and the scar running down Helena's face bloomed red as it opened. She screamed. Abu Abdullah turned the knife to the other side of her face.

"Let us see how many men want you by the time I have finished. Tell us now or I will peel the skin from you."

"Zoraya! I visited Zoraya."

"Why?"

"She is my friend. We are both strangers in this land and she recognises a kindred spirit. I am fond of her children, too."

Abu Abdullah grinned. "Oh, I wager you are. Young men feeling the blood flowing in their loins for the first time. I expect you have many lessons you can teach them, the same as those you taught me." It was a wild accusation, but Thomas saw a flush rise along Helena's neck and knew the truth of it. All the time she had lived with him, Helena was sharing her favours with others. *How many others?* he wondered.

Helena tugged away, breaking free. She got as far as the entrance to the tent where she ran into a figure coming in.

"Oh, my love, help me, these men throw such accusations!"

Abu al-Hasan Ali pushed her aside.

"What is going on here? What plot is being hatched?"

"I know, Father," Abu Abdullah said. "I know everything."

Abu al-Hasan Ali gave his son a dismissive glance.

"You know nothing. I have tried to teach you much and you have pissed my lessons away. Thomas—tell me what this is all about."

Thomas leaned against Olaf.

"You are found out, Malik." Thomas drew himself to

his full height as he saw the Sultan's gaze fall on the silk robe, and once more caught the same flash of recognition he had seen out on the field, the same flash that caused his blood to chill. "Your man is dead, and you are no longer Sultan of Gharnatah." Thomas glanced towards Abu Abdullah, who nodded.

"You turn against me? You, an *ajami* I raised above all others? I abandon you. I abandon you all. My son, too. Olaf, come, we have killing work to do."

"I am no longer your man," said Olaf. "My loyalties lie with the Sultan."

"I *am* the Sultan!" Abu al-Hasan Ali's voice was a scream.

"No longer, Father." Abu Abdullah straightened his shoulders. "You have betrayed this city for your own interests." He looked down at his hands, frowning. "I swear I will never love, for it weakens a man."

"Traitors, you are all traitors!" The Sultan turned and tried to leave, but Olaf was faster, darting across the tent to catch him before he could show himself to the soldiers outside.

Thomas wondered what would have happened if Abu al-Hasan Ali hadn't been stopped, if he had managed to command the soldiers beyond. Would events have turned out differently?

Thomas looked at Olaf. "Will your men follow you?"

Olaf nodded. "Enough will."

"Then Abu Abdullah, go out with Olaf at your side and tell them your father is no longer Sultan. Olaf,

make sure you back him up. They will follow you or not, Prince, but the die is cast and cannot be taken back."

Thomas stumbled to the doorway and gripped Abu al-Hasan Ali's arm as Olaf released his hold. Jorge came to join him and they pulled him inside. The man was strong, and Thomas weak, but Jorge was more than strong enough on his own for the task.

From beyond the walls of the tent came a sudden commotion, the sound of clashing swords, shouts and screams as some men remained loyal to the end.

Abu al-Hasan Ali smiled. "You will die in great pain for this betrayal, Thomas Berrington."

"I have been told that once already today, and the man who made that threat is dead himself."

"You would kill me, too?"

Thomas gave the question the consideration it deserved before shaking his head.

"You know I would not."

"I thought of you as a friend."

"The friendship of a Sultan is not as welcome a gift as you believe it to be."

"And my other gift?" Abu al-Hasan Ali gave a sly smile.

"Your other gift is tainted, as well you know. No doubt she has been sharing your bed as well as that of your sons. And how many others? I wonder."

"She is skilled, is she not? She will have shown you such sweet pleasures no one else possibly could. It would

492

be a sin for her not to share such wonder as widely as she can."

"Such is the way of all temptation," Thomas said. "Why did you have to kill them? I don't understand. You could have made Zoraya your preferred wife, even named her children as your heirs, all without murder being involved."

Abu al-Hasan Ali gave a snort of contempt. "You may be the best surgeon in Gharnatah, but you do not understand this world if you think I would be allowed to do such a thing. People believe a Sultan rules them, but that is not true. We do the will of the people or the people have us removed. A foreigner, a Greek woman, would not be accepted. Nor her children." The Sultan stared into the eyes of Thomas, who saw nothing there in return: no guilt, no shame, no sorrow. "I had no other choice."

"There is always a choice."

"Not one I was willing to accept." The Sultan took a step closer, drawing himself to his full height, but this time Thomas did not bend his knee and looked down at him.

"Your man was out of control. You should have stopped him, reined him in. Innocent girls died."

"Do you mean your little friend?"

Thomas held his anger in check, but it was hard. "And others. There was no need to kill them."

"There is always need. This is your fault. Do you know that? If you had done what was expected when I

asked you to find the killer and failed, there would have been no more death than necessary."

This time it was Thomas who took a step closer. They stood, almost touching. He could smell the Sultan's sweat—sweat like that of any other man, rank and sharp —and the scent of travel. Dust and horse and leather.

"You really don't know me at all if you expected me to fail. I trusted you. I wanted to serve."

"You speak of trust? To a Sultan? You are too innocent for this world, *ajami*."

"Oh, not so innocent," Thomas said. "That is where you made a mistake, because you don't know me. You are finished."

Abu al-Hasan Ali smiled. "Do you really think so?" He struck out, a blade appearing in his hand. Jorge tried to block the blow, but was tossed aside, the old Sultan still a mighty warrior. He followed through, his knife embedding itself into Thomas's shoulder, and Lubna's screams followed him into oblivion.

CHAPTER FORTY-THREE

Thomas woke to find himself lying on a clean bed in a cool room. He lay for a long time listening to his own breathing, smelling the scent of lemon, lime and lavender in the air, and knew he was not at home. Reluctant to make any attempt to open his eyes, he waited. His chest ached on the opposite side to his wounded hand, which now seemed nothing in comparison, and gradually memory returned. He shivered, even though it wasn't cold.

He heard a voice say, "He is awake," but it was distant. Then came the slap of sandals on a tiled floor and a damp cloth touched his brow. He knew he had no more excuses and opened his eyes.

Lubna leaned over him, concern on her face as she scanned his body. When her gaze eventually rose to meet his, she gave a shy smile that said more than any words could.

"Where am I?" Thomas's voice emerged cracked. Lubna helped him sit and offered water. He sipped, felt a little better.

"The palace. I wanted to take you home, but the Sultan insisted. The new Sultan, that is. He was here earlier and sat with you for an hour before leaving. There is much for him to do, but he has asked to be sent for as soon as you wake, as has Olaf. Yusuf is still here. He is fast asleep on a cot in the corner. He refused to leave you."

"Is he dead?" Thomas had no need to say who.

Lubna shook her head. "Banished. Together with that woman."

"And your father?"

"Is still the Sultan's general. He simply has a new Sultan to call master."

"Who treated me?" Thomas asked. "You have fine skills, but my wound was beyond what I have managed to teach you."

"We had to fight them off. Every surgeon in Gharnatah wanted the honour of repairing you."

Thomas smiled. "Then who? There are some I would not want within a league of me."

Lubna returned the smile, hers strained. "Da'ud al-Baitar."

"Then I will heal." He looked at Lubna. "I will heal, won't I?"

She nodded. "Da'ud says so, and he seems to know

496

what he is doing. He is not as good as you, but good enough."

"Yes. Good enough. You tried to tell me, didn't you?"

"It doesn't matter now," said Lubna. She laid her hand over his and he turned it to twine the fingers of his uninjured hand through hers. She leaned her slim body over his, making a show of checking his bandages. Her hair brushed his face, and Thomas breathed in its scent.

"Where is Helena?" he asked, and Lubna drew back quickly. "Is she with Abu Abdullah?"

Lubna shook her head as she busied herself with meaningless work, tidying the low table beside his bed.

"You will have to learn to call him Muhammed now. He has named himself Muhammed XII, Sultan of Gharnatah and leader of al-Andalus." The expression on her pretty face showed what her opinion of that was.

Thomas reached for her hand again and held it against his chest. Slowly she relaxed and softened against him. He wanted to kiss her, but was unsure how she might greet such a familiarity.

"Thomas!" Yusuf had woken, and whatever moment had been about to happen was dashed away as the boy ran across the room and almost knocked Lubna aside.

Thomas smiled, the young prince's excitement infectious.

"I did well, did I not? I passed your message to Abu Abdullah exactly as you asked. And he came to your summons. You have solved the killings, Thomas, you

and my brother together. He is grateful to you, he told me so. I know you have not always liked him, but perhaps that will change now. He is a good brother and I love him dearly. He is not cold like Father, nor cruel. We three can be friends, can we not? What was it like to kill that man? My brother and the Vizier are planning to seal the tunnels. They did not know of their existence. Abu Abdullah says they are a threat to the security of…"

Lubna smiled and rose. Thomas watched her cross the room to wring out the cloth in a bowl of cool water. From outside the window, the sound of swallows chattered and cried.

"…shall I do that now, Thomas?"

"I am sorry, My Prince, do what?"

"Have you not listened to a word I said? And do not call me Prince. You must always call me by my name, for we are friends."

"You are older now, it would no longer be appropriate." Thomas didn't think he needed to mention that Yusuf was now next in line should an accident befall his brother.

"It is appropriate among friends. I asked if I should fetch Abu Abdullah now? He insisted I call him as soon as you woke. And see, you are awake!" The boy grinned, stood, his body quivering. "Shall I?"

"As you wish, My Prince."

After Yusuf had gone, Thomas called across the room to Lubna.

"Where is Jorge?"

"I have not seen him since he carried you here."

"Jorge carried me?"

"All the way from the hunting field. He insisted. He is strong."

"He would be stronger if he stopped eating and drinking too much."

"But then he would not be Jorge."

"You like him, don't you," Thomas said.

"Yes, I like him." Lubna seemed on the point of adding to her statement, but held back whatever words she meant to speak, if she had ever intended any and it wasn't simply all in Thomas's imagination.

"Perhaps he has returned to his former life."

"Perhaps. But if so, it would take no time for him to walk along a few corridors to visit you. That fat cook has been here." Lubna looked at her hands. "She told me about your friend. The girl who died."

"Prea."

"Was that her name?"

Thomas smiled. "She was smart, that one. Too smart to be a kitchen girl. And now her short life has been tossed aside. If I had seen things sooner, she would still be alive. It is my fault she died."

Lubna's face changed, all humour leaving it.

"Yes, it is. And you misjudged my father. I have to think on that. At the moment, I cannot find it in my heart to forgive you."

"I…" Thomas started to defend himself, then stopped. Lubna was right. He had misjudged Olaf. And

he had been a fool not to see Helena's deceit sooner. She had no doubt been working against him ever since the Sultan gifted her to him. Any feelings he might have had for her were cast to the winds. She didn't exist to him anymore.

"You are right. I thought I was so clever. I believed too much in my own intellect and didn't see the things that were in front of me. I misjudged Abu Abdullah, too."

"He saved us all." Lubna returned to the bedside, but didn't sit, didn't try to take his hand, and Thomas wondered if she ever would again. "He was strong on the hillside. A weaker man would have been swept aside. My father tells me the nobles were planning to put one of their own in the palace. Had Abu Abdullah not been so determined, it might be Faris al-Rashid commanding now."

"What is Tahir doing, and that grim cleric? They must have been involved in some way."

"No doubt, that is what Father says as well. But they are servants and follow orders given them. They follow whoever leads, so for now, they follow Abu Abdullah. When his brother brings him, you must thank him, Thomas."

"I have words to say to him, certainly."

There came the sound of footsteps from the corridor and Yusuf scrambled in, barely able to stay upright he entered so fast. Abu Abdullah came more slowly, waving at his guards to remain outside.

"I would speak with Thomas Berrington alone," he said, an easy command in his voice. He wore the full regalia of a Sultan, his bearing that of someone used to giving orders, used to being obeyed.

"But I can stay?" Yusuf rocked from foot to foot at the side of Thomas's bed.

"Alone, my brother. I will tell you everything later, but Thomas and I have matters of state to discuss. Private matters." Abu Abdullah flicked his hand. "Fetch me a chair." He spoke to no one, to everyone.

When a guard had brought a simple wooden chair and set it beside the bed, Abu Abdullah waved everyone away, waiting until it was only Thomas and himself left in the room.

Abu Abdullah looked around. "I have not been in this room for many years until today. This is where I recovered after I was wounded at Malaka, when they came across the sea at us."

"I remember, My Prince."

Abu Abdullah smiled. "I do not forget my debt to you, Thomas Berrington, even if I rarely show it. But now it seems I owe you an even greater debt than my father did. I owe you my position as Sultan."

"It is yours by right. I did nothing."

Abu Abdullah finally sat in the chair and leaned forward, his face close to that of Thomas, who smelled the fine oils on the Prince's hair, the perfume on his skin. All false friendship departed Abu Abdullah's face, his dark eyes cold.

501

"Despite all of that, you know I do not like you, but I will pretend because it is expected of me."

"Do not do so on my behalf, Pri—Malik. I did not welcome the friendship of your father and I do not seek yours now."

"Oh, but you should. My father had many friends. Less so now he is banished, but no doubt some remain, and I intend to seek them out. To them, you are a wanted man, but with my patronage you will be protected. So tell me again you do not need a Sultan's friendship."

"I am a mere surgeon, Malik, and yours to command."

"Indeed you are. And surgeons do not question Princes, even less so Sultans. It amuses me to keep you alive, you and that fool of a eunuch."

"The Sultan is generous."

"I believe I am. It serves my purpose to keep you on a leash. Just never forget, *ajami*, that I can have you killed at any time. More to the point, I know who your friends are. Cross me and Olaf's plain daughter will be the first to die. I will make you watch as my men take her over and over, make you watch as they flay her skin to reveal the bone beneath. And then we will start on the eunuch and his friends. I know everything, Thomas Berrington, everything. You are mine and you will do as I command."

Thomas stared into Abu Abdullah's eyes, his body tight with anger.

"Are you unwell, my friend?" Abu Abdullah leaned

over, reaching out to close his hand on Thomas's shoulder. "You look unwell." He squeezed hard.

Thomas bit down on his lip, refusing to scream, though the urge to do so was almost impossible to deny.

"I will heal, Prince." He could barely get the words out. "I exist to serve."

"That is good. I see you understand." But Abu Abdullah's pressure didn't ease. If anything it grew stronger and the room began to fade to grey. "It does not please me to make these threats. Know they are made only for the good of al-Andalus. We both love this land. We both want to see it survive and prosper. My father's approach has failed. Battle after battle, each time losing ground to the infidel. Castile has grown strong, but I have a rational approach, a pragmatic approach. And I have decided you will help me." Finally he released his grip and sat back.

Sweat trickled down Thomas's face, beaded his skin beneath the sheet. He breathed rapidly, the fire in his shoulder almost all consuming.

"Tell me you agree." Abu Abdullah leaned close, his voice little more than a whisper, the scent of cloves on his breath.

"I exist to serve, Prince," Thomas said.

"Good." Abu Abdullah sat back quickly, rose equally quickly, the chair toppling backwards behind him. "And as a reward, I have decided Helena will return to your house and once more take up her duties." He smiled.

"A reward?" The sweat lay cold against Thomas's

skin. "That is no reward—the woman is no longer welcome in my house."

"But that is where she will come, and you will take her back into your bed. Next to the other sister if you want, it is your house after all. I should have Helena killed for her treachery, but this punishment is so much sweeter. Tahir will visit you soon. He has sent the Spanish priest back to his masters, but he will return in a matter of months, and when he does, Tahir will ask you to travel to Qurtuba on a mission supposedly to aid the Castilian Queen, but your real purpose will be otherwise. This time you will do as Tahir asks."

When Abu Abdullah was gone, Thomas lay on the cot and closed his eyes. The old Sultan had betrayed his trust, and now the new one was even worse. Perhaps it was time to slip away, to return to the land he had abandoned almost a lifetime ago.

A familiar sound reached him and he raised his head in time to see a section of wall pivot outwards. Jorge peered through, extending one leg, grimacing as he squeezed through a gap too narrow to accommodate him. Watching his struggle, Thomas thought he looked slimmer than a week before.

"How did you manage to pass through these places, Thomas?"

"I had assistance." He didn't want reminding of Prea. "What were you doing in there?"

"Listening. Watching. I heard everything."

"Then you know I have no choice."

504

"You will go to Qurtuba?" Jorge crossed the room. He righted the chair and sat where Abu Abdullah had. He studied Thomas, taking in the bandage to his shoulder, the second covering the wound at his waist. "Do you think you will live long enough?"

Thomas smiled. He could always rely on Jorge for a tactless comment.

"I have overstayed my welcome in this city. It is time to move on."

"You can't do that." Jorge's voice took on a serious tone. "If you run away, they have won. All of them. Gharnatah needs men of honour, men of science. You have to stay."

"With a woman I hate? At the beck and call of a man I don't respect?"

"Then stay for me, and for Lubna. For the good men and women of this city."

"The city is lost," Thomas said.

"Not yet. Not if we have something to fight for."

Thomas closed his eyes again, seeking oblivion. He felt Jorge take his hand as he started to drift. A moment later, a smaller hand closed softly around his on the other side and someone sat on the foot of the cot.

"I am beginning to think death might be less painful," Thomas murmured. When he opened his eyes, it was to see Lubna and Yusuf with Jorge, and he knew he could not abandon them, or Gharnatah.

HISTORICAL NOTE

The Red Hill is the first historical mystery featuring Thomas Berrington and the eunuch Jorge. The series will take the reader from the year 1482 to the fall of the Granada on January 1st 1492. This edition of The Red Hill is a small update to that first published in 2014, but is essentially the same storyline.

If you enjoyed this book then you can find out more about the tales of Thomas and Jorge, together with a full list of titles, on my website:

www.davidpennywriting.com

You can also sign up to my mailing list there and be the first to hear of new releases and updates, as well as exclusive offers.

If you *really* liked this book why not let others know by leaving a review on Amazon or Goodreads.

* * *

I need to make some comment regarding historic and

cultural accuracy in The Red Hill. Although I have conducted extensive historical research—a list of some references follows—this is essentially a novel: a work of fiction. As such I made the decision that complete historical accuracy should not overrule the need for development of character and plot. The dates of rulers and main battles are as accurate as my research allows, but many names and characters are fictitious. In addition to this some liberties have been taken with cultural issues. The Red Hill is written for a 21st Century audience, and many of the characters think from a 21st century perspective. Whilst this is no doubt lacking some historical accuracy, many sources indicate that the Moorish culture in Spain was one of the most enlightened and forward looking of the time, and so I would like to think that they would feel a little sympathy for modern-day sensibilities. Should you disagree, my apologies, but as I have said, the story here takes precedence over complete historical or cultural accuracy.

When I wrote this book I was not aware of any network of hidden tunnels present in the Alhambra palace, but subsequently discovered an article in a Spanish newspaper about the discovery of some unknown passageways which have been uncovered. The passages described in this book are a complete work of fiction, so please make no attempt to discover them, for they are unlikely to exist … or do they?

I would like to thank Esperanza and Richard Nother for their hospitality on my second visit to Gharnatah in

2012, the first being 40 years earlier. A special thanks goes to the nameless Arab guide to al-Hamra whose knowledge and helpfulness added immensely to our first tour of the palace.

* * *

REFERENCES

I am indebted to the John Rylands library in Manchester and to the kindness and helpfulness of their staff in finding me the resources to start my research. Only subsequent to studying the original documents did I discover that many of them are available via Amazon and other suppliers.

My main sources of research are listed below:

History of the Moorish Empire in Europe by S.P. Scott publ. 1904

The History of the Mohametan Empire in Spain by James Cavannah Murphy publ. 1816

In Fair Granada (fiction) by E. Everett-Green publ. 1902

Moorish Spain by Richard Fletcher publ. 1992

Medieval Islamic Medicine by Peter E. Portman and Emilie Savage-Smith publ. 2007

Sexuality in Islam by Abdelwahab Bouhdiba, translated from the French by Alan Sheridan, publ. 1925

The Alhambra by Robert Irwin publ. 2005

The House of Wisdom by Jonathon Lyons publ. 2009

When the Moors ruled in Europe (DVD) from Channel 4, presented by Bettany Hughes. Available through Acorn Media.